WILLY WESTALL

*She gave her heart
and her hospitality to ...*

. . . a stalwart young man whose strength she needed
and whose love they both had to deny.

. . . a defeated presidential candidate, disillusioned by
the failure of a reformer's dream.

. . . a Mexican boy who cherished her small daughters
and stole a treasure more precious than money.

. . . a gaudy young woman from the red-light house who
mourned in secret for her illicit lover.

. . . the entire frontier town of Mission, Texas, struggling to transform a valley of hardship into a lush
earthly paradise.

The Band Company

presents

SHE CAME TO THE VALLEY

starring

RONEE BLAKLEY
DEAN STOCKWELL
SCOTT GLENN
FREDDY FENDER

Executive Producer . . . . Robert S. Bremson

Producers . . . . Albert Band and
Frank Ray Perilli

Director . . . . Albert Band

Screenplay by . . . . Frank Ray Perilli
and Albert Band

She Came to
the Valley

*A Novel of the Lower Rio Grande Valley
Mission, Texas*

Cleo Dawson

BALLANTINE BOOKS • NEW YORK

Dedicated to

W. T. ELLIS
and his family

Library of Congress Catalog Card Number: 43-144-64

ISBN 0-345-27593-4

Manufactured in the United States of America

First Ballantine Books Edition: December 1978

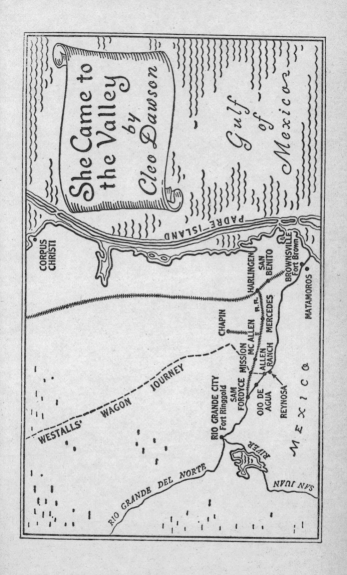

From the Author

Ralph Waldo Emerson said, "There is properly no history, only biography." With this I agree. Looking back for more than half a century through the wondrous glow of the tropic sun upon the skyline of our Lower Valley of the Rio Grande, I see only people—one by one, as they walked up and down across our strip of magic land along the River.

They came in from everywhere to match their lives with the treasured soil laid down since the dawn of history as a gift from the Mighty River. There I saw them sweat their blood to carve out the destiny of this particular spot we call "Our Land." A land of many cultures, the proud composite of the civilizations of the centuries laid down layer by layer for our advantage. First came the French; then the famed Spanish as Conquistadores who at length became the great Mexican hacendados and rancheros. And always the patient Padres of the Church journeyed in from afar to do their work. Then from the United States came the adventurers, the blockade runners, the fortune hunters, soldiers from all the wars, the big dreamers and the great visionaries. Each left his mark and made his place.

What made them do it? They loved the land! Love made them throw their very lives into the conflict. Love sustained the struggle. The land had to grow and prosper. The land must serve and keep on serving. The miracle of growth must disclose the life-secrets of land enriched by water. "Work" is the word. But more than any word is the Light behind the job well done, the deed accomplished.

SHE CAME TO THE VALLEY is a record of these people as I knew them. Only the Dawson family (Pat and Willy Westall) and Bill Lester are exact. Each of the others is made up of the parts of many others pulled apart and reassembled. But I knew them all, each component—even their telephone numbers if you were to ask me. And I wrote it all down because I loved these people and I wanted them not to be forgotten.

The many years of our great Fiesta Celebration has proved our gratitude to Nature for the extravagance of her bounties. The dedicated effort and creativity of the long line of talented producers has evolved a matchless art of Fiesta beauty that inspires all viewers with a sense of awe.

One hundred years ago a priest brought a small sack of oranges to the children of the Laguna Seca Ranch. The seeds from these oranges were planted; they were watered, and they grew. From this beginning came the magnificence of our great Valley citrus culture of today. The Centennial Fiesta producers made these hundred years come back to life so vividly that as the characters walked across the stage their breath quickened our very hearts into an outpouring of gratitude and praise.

This special Grand March of Beauty was led by King William T. Ellis, KING OF THE GRAPE-FRUIT, whose first command was: "Let us love and learn and grow!" This Ellis Edict meant that SHE CAME TO THE VALLEY must appear again as a special part of this parade. Hence this special edition.

Now these people will not be forgotten—these Special people, the people of then, the people of now, the people who will come forever after—the people who know how to "Love and learn and grow."

Cleo Dawson.

1

Willy Westall was one of the women in the world who had found her wholeness in the man she married.

She opened her eyes wide, then shut them tight. She did not want to see. She was afraid, afraid that all the preciousness might move over the edge and be gone. She squeezed her eyelids together and lay there, reveling in the close warm comfort of her covers. Then she opened her eyes, turned her head, and deliberately looked out the window. And sure enough, there everything was just as everything had been when she had gone to bed.

Oklahoma City in 1905 was a raw new town, but Willy thought it the most important city in the world. She was very young and had traveled very little. To her it encompassed all reality. Here she and Pat owned a two-storied house furnished in the ultimate that Street and Reed could produce in bird's-eye maple and golden oak. Brussels carpets covered every floor. Besides, they had a folding bed and a horse and buggy.

She and Pat had all these things together. That was what made them count. They were theirs to use and to revel in. Of course, Willy could not believe it at this minute. She never did when she first woke up. It was all too good to be really true—for other people maybe, but not for her.

Pat always laughed when she said such things. Nothing was too good for his brown-eyed little "Sweetheart."

It was Pat's habit to slip out of bed in the morning and leave her sleeping there. "The best eye opener in the world is a whiff of early coffee floating up the stairs," he said.

When she smelled the coffee, she jumped out of bed and began to brush her hair. It stood curled up in little circles all around her head. She brushed and pulled, exclaiming to herself at the hurt, "How does my hair get so tangled up!" Then she smiled and blushed very red, even to herself. "I ought to make Pat comb it out himself."

When the hair was finished, she took up wrapper-choosing. She had three wrappers, all made of the best grade of satin Lions Brothers sold. The light-pink one was made princess style, with a train; the rose tint was empire, full-skirted, with a chenille frill at the neck; the flaming cerise was almost hoop-skirted, with a tight bodice.

"I'll have to put the light-pink one aside, I guess," she thought. "But I do hope I can use the other two."

Once the thought was focused, it proved itself in fact. Suddenly she caught at her stomach and made a dash to vomit. Then she lay back on the bed, feeling very sick. If only she could shut out the coffee smell!

Pat's gay voice called up the stairs, "What's the matter, Sweetheart? The battercakes are cooking."

Willy jumped up, plunged her hand into the water pitcher, and splashed her face three times.

"I've got to get used to this," she thought. "I might as well start now."

She grabbed the cerise wrapper and started down the stairs, fastening hooks and eyes as she ran. "I'm coming, Darling. Butter my cakes for me quick!"

That breakfast was just a repetition of all their breakfasts—hugs, kisses, hot cakes, and coffee, all mixed up. Willy sat and ate, while Pat waited on her hand and foot.

"Eat lots, Sweetheart; you need food, remember," he said with every hot stack he brought in.

"You'll make me fat, Darling." Her dark eyes clouded. "You won't like me fat." She blushed very red again.

Such a challenge called for something extra. He picked her up and carried her into the parlor; then he sat down in the big rocking chair with her on his lap. Pat was not jocund when he said, "Yes, I'll like you anyway on earth. You're mine. That's what makes the difference. In my forty years of living I've met a lot of women, but the eighty pounds of you has crawled into my heart and shut the door. I love every ounce of you. You won't mind the swelling knowing that."

She hid her face on his shoulder. He rocked her like the frightened child she was.

Suddenly the clock struck nine.

"Darling, hurry; you'll be late again!" She kissed him as she spoke.

Willy stood at the front door watching when Prince wheeled the buggy around the corner of the house.

"Don't take time to kiss me," she shouted, "you're late now!"

"All right; your orders, lady-of-the-house. But tonight double portion, don't forget."

"Don't forget to call on Dr. Riley."

His answer was lost in the whirl of the buggy wheels and Prince's hoofbeats as he trotted out onto the street. When they turned the corner, Willy caught a last outline of Pat's straight body and perfectly molded head. His clean-shaven chin, lifted high. seemed to split the wind for his body to follow after.

"How beautiful he is to look at! And he is mine!" she thought.

She stood there a long time, thinking. "It's all too good to be true—just too good!"

And it was.

2

Six months later Willy was alone. Desolation cut into her heart. Maybe the cut was a deep, dull pain down in the middle of her heavy body where the burden jerked and twisted. She walked again to the box window and strained her eyes across the prairie for the glimpse of a covered wagon, a buckboard, or a horse.

All she saw was the emptiness of a Texas ranch. There was nothing to see, nothing to touch, nothing to smell, nothing to hear—just nothing—hot and bright and dry and vacant.

Tears came quickly. During the last four days she had done nothing but look out that window. Laredo lay fifty miles to the south, and travelers always came in from that direction. She took up again her pacing up and down across the floor. It was better to do something.

From somewhere deep within her very being, Willy felt the distant gripping of the demon pain; nearer it appoached, like the far-off hoofbeats of a horse coming closer, closer, until at length it caught her in the midde of one tense spasm, then trotted off into the distance.

"This is my time," she sobbed. "But I'm scared! Oh. God, I'm scared!"

Willy was young to be alone on a cattle ranch fifty miles from a railroad and fifteen miles from the nearest neighbors, the Torres Mexicans. At six that morning she had sent Benito for his mother, the curandera, but as yet she was alone. She could face childbirth without the aid of a doctor or the comfort of a human hand to hold, but what she missed was Pat.

"Where is he? Where is he?" she kept asking the question to herself.

Nine days ago she had sent Manuel and José in the wagon to Laredo to meet Pat at the train. Two days on the way, one day to stay and two to get back was the usual time. But nine days had passed! The last four had been hell. Something was wrong! She prayed that Pat was only drunk. But at worst he never got drunk enough to forget her. She could depend on that.

Or could she? Can women depend on men?

The child within her jerked. She felt the trotting of the pain as it approached her from the distance. Closer it came, until it wrenched her in the middle—harder this time. Then, she imagined, it proceeded off into space to torture some other woman. Such definite blows must be the curse put on Eve that punished women for their sins and traveled around the world to catch all females in their turn.

Again she fell down in the chair and listened as she wept.

"I believe the noise helps," she thought. Then she struggled to her feet and took up her walk across the floor. Her mind went back to the beginning.

The only verity in Willy's life was her love for Patrick Westall. She often told herself that they must have met before they were born into this world. From the moment she looked into his clear blue Irish eyes she had known that he had always been a part of her. When he reached out and touched her hand, she felt flow into her body all his warmth of living blood. In that instant it flooded out the chill of all her lonely childhood.

Her mother had died when Willy was ten. Her shiftless father gave her to a maiden aunt to rear. She eked out an education in the public schools of Franklin, Texas. College was beyond Aunt Ann's vision—they were very poor. When her best friend, Adelaide Dunbar, left for Baylor College, Willy cried a little; then she buckled up the courage and set out to find everything there was to read in Franklin. Somehow she felt her chance would come in time; she must be ready.

But Aunt Ann decided that she should go to work. They needed money. So Adelaide's father took her into his store, the Dunbar racket store, that predecessor of the five-and-ten. Willy was glad to get the job. She missed school, but more than that she missed her close friend Adelaide.

Willy was dark, vibrant, and delicious. The local dudes swarmed the racket store to gaze into her eyes and catch a glimpse of her flashing smile. She seemed to be all black curls, brown eyes, red lips, and white teeth. Her body didn't count because it was very small.

One Christmas Adelaide brought home from Baylor College the happy news that she had met a Mr. Bailey who was going to marry her in June. He was manager of the sugar mill at Sugarland, very handsome, with a big mustache. When she was married Willy must come to visit her.

When June arrived, Adelaide's plans were carried out. The wedding was beautiful, with Willy as maid of honor; and everybody cried. But somehow Willy felt grateful for the racket store in place of a marriage bed. She sensed that there was a price to pay for the glamour of the impressive wedding in the Baptist church.

In November Adelaide came home. She looked pale and worn.

"Why, Addie, are you sick?" Willy exclaimed when she kissed her.

"Yes, worse than sick. Come spend the night and I'll tell you all about it."

That night Adelaide told Willy the story of her marriage, blow by blow. She spoke of the lovely, warm, quiet, lazy days at the Retrieve Plantation, with a Negro at hand to answer every summons. But no matter how pleasant the day, night always followed; and the horrors of those nights!

"You'll never know, Willy, how terrible it is! Now I'm in the family way. But I've come home to get old Chloe to help me get rid of it."

As Adelaide talked, she punctuated the story with sobs and threats. "I'll kill myself," she said.

She stayed at home three weeks. When she went back to Sugarland, Willy went with her. The trip was not a happy one. Adelaide was disconsolate, sick, and cross. Aunt Chloe had not got "rid of it" and she was going to have to have the baby.

"Well, if you have to, Addie, just be glad about it. You'll love the baby. And maybe the other part will be easier then."

"But I have to go back and sleep with Ed every night. He kisses me all over! His breath smells like tobacco! Oh, Willy, you don't know what it's like. And besides, Pat Westall will be there."

"Who's Pat Westall?"

"He's the sugar refiner." Her eyes began to shine. "Wait till you see him, Willy. You'll love him too. He's got all his mother's Irish, and he's been everywhere on earth. Ed picked him up in Galveston, broke, last year. He had come in on a boat from Havana. But he's proved to be the best man Ed's ever had."

Ed Bailey greeted his wife with deep emotion. It was evident that he adored her as a man of over forty would cherish a young girl. Willy felt sorry for him from the start. Adelaide was mean and cross and pettish, like a child. Later in the day Willy got her off to bed for a nap. When she awoke she was in a better mood.

The girls were sitting on the gallery overlooking the Gulf when Willy first glimpsed Patrick Westall coming up the walk. He was with Ed Bailey. The sun was setting at their backs. She brushed back a curl from over one eye. That was the moment when in all her life she wanted the most to see, because she saw coming toward her, her man! She didn't know who he was or where he came from. It mattered not if it were from the moon. He looked as if he had just stepped out of a sunbeam. So straight, so briskly he walked along the boards that he seemed to split the lazy air with a braggadocio that said, "Step aside all; here I come!"

She pushed back the curl and looked again, to make sure of what she saw. "Is that Pat Westall with Mr. Bailey, Addie?"

"Yes, that's Pat. Didn't I tell you? Wait and see what he does to you!"

Then Willy knew why Adelaide resented Ed Bailey's child within her body.

The next moment the men were on the porch and Adelaide was saying, "Pat, this is Willy Gilstrap I've told you so much about."

He stepped forward to shake her hand. Willy knew that she had found her man. She knew it as certainly as she knew his eyes were the clearest, lightest blue she had ever looked into. The eyes were all that counted. Indistinctly she sensed that he was beautiful all over, but his eyes blotted out the world.

Hours later she realized that she and Pat were

walking among the oleanders in the garden. The rest was a blur of heaven that she relaxed in and never tried to analyze. In the months that followed, as she lay awake at night thinking, she realized he hadn't even kissed her.

She had left the next morning. Adelaide, plainly jealous, hurried her off on the early train.

The next six months of Willy's life tortured her. She wrote one thank-you note which Adelaide did not answer. No letter came from Pat. Willy inquired about Adelaide often from Mr. Dunbar, who always reported that she wasn't "doing very well. Things were going badly."

In July news came that Adelaide had died in childbirth. Willy went with Mr. and Mrs. Dunbar to the funeral. Pat Westall met them at the train. She just looked up at him and they both seemed to understand. She hoped God would direct her, but if not, things would have to go on just the same.

To Willy, the funeral was a joy because she and Pat did everything together. The night after it was over he led her once again down the oleander path. Beneath a fig tree he asked her to be Mrs. Patrick Westall.

No ceremony was ever necessary for that wedding, though a beautiful one was gone through in the Baptist church in Franklin, with the same local glamour that had embellished Adelaide and Ed Bailey's. The wedding actually took place on the porch in Sugarland that January afternoon when Pat's light-blue Irish eyes dissolved in the deep warm brown of Willy's.

All that Adelaide had told her of her wedding night vanished before their exultation. Pat and Willy had always been one, it seemed; one person, not two. Now the whole was made complete.

3

A little over a year it had been since Willy and Pat were married. Malaria fever forced them to quit the Retrieve Plantation and Pat took the job of selling and erecting machinery for the Murdy Cotton Gin Company of Oklahoma City.

Pat sent Aunt Ann a round-trip ticket to visit them. On the train trip the old lady took cold, fell ill with double pneumonia, and died within the week. Pat took Aunt Ann home to Franklin and buried her in the cemetery beside the Baptist church. It was Dr. Riley who said that Willy could not go.

"Do it yourself, Pat. Women're sensitive that way. And your wife's not so well, I'm afraid."

Pat did as he was told because he always listened to Dr. Riley.

"Doc Riley's the best friend I've got on earth," he said on those rare occasions when he talked about his past. The two men had met first in Silver City in 1888. Then they made "The Run" into Oklahoma City in 1889. That was the one adventure Pat enjoyed even in the telling, for in it he had found a lasting friend.

He had felt no qualms when he rode up from Texas and camped at Purcell, Indian Territory, ready for the big run the next day. He was always riding in from somewhere on his way to somewhere else. That was all he had done since his parents died in Alabama from a smallpox plague. At that time, left an only child, he sold the plantation to the highest bidder, put the money in his saddle pockets, and set out on the road. But being a young man of ultra-refined tastes in pleasure and in living habits, the money had not lasted long. When forced to work, Pat always chose a task not of the usual kind. He spurned farming. It took too long to wait for things to grow. Industry was too

9

damned crowded. A man had to get in on the ground
floor. Pat was good at anything he decided he would
do. He excelled as sugar refiner, gold miner, machin-
ist, surveyor, or cotton broker.

"No need to get stale on any job," he always said.
And he never did.

When Pat Westall had got the news of the great
opening in Indian Territory he quit his job is Texas,
saddled his horse, Snow King, and set out. Riding into
camp at Purcell, April 21, he ran into Dr. Riley,
whom he had met in Silver City. The day following
Pat made "The Run" on Snow King, and Dr. Riley
rode in over the Santa Fe. They both staked claims in
the one-hundred block of California Street. The only
difference in the claiming of the two men was that Pat
followed his usual custom of drinking to his luck to
celebrate, while Dr. Riley kept busy fighting off two
other Irishmen who insisted that they staked Pat's lot
first.

In the great confusion of that day many strange
things happened. The town plan was platted off on
the prairie by pegs and stobs, California Street running straight down through the center. The question
was, just where lots stopped and streets began. According to rule, a man had to stay on his land until
the recording could be made. That meant in many
cases all afternoon and night, because swarms of people made "The Run."

Pat was never quite clear as to what happened. But
he was later told that when the recording agents got
to him, they found him defending the very center of
California Street with a forty-five and a double-
barreled shotgun. This was his lot and any sonuvabitch who thought he could run him off would have
to smell some powder. Fortunately, Dr. Riley prevented any shooting.

The next day Pat mounted his horse and rode off
down south—he had just met a fellow who had told
him about a gold-mining deal in Yucatan. He'd take a
try at that. "One land's just like another. What difference does it make about the language people speak

just so you get in on the ground floor?" he said as he shook Dr. Riley's hand in parting.

Through the years the two men had always kept in touch. When, at Sugarland, Willy began to droop with malaria, Pat hurried off a letter to Dr. Riley.

"The best remedy is a change of climate," Dr. Riley wrote him. "Why not come on back up here? Greatest country in the world."

So when Pat and Willy moved to Oklahoma City, in 1905, Dr. Riley was the most frequent visitor at the Westall home. The week of Aunt Ann's illness he had stayed there almost day and night. During the long watches he and Pat had talked of many things. He had been one of the first to settle in the region, and in the early days he had allied himself to the wilderness by marrying an Indian girl. She had borne him one son, darker even than herself. Dr. Riley's mind was much on babies. He talked about the hard way with women, the unfairness of it all. They followed their men across the world and drew out a trail of suffering as they went.

Pat's eyes darkened in deep concern. "Is my wife in the family way for sure, Doc, or can you tell so soon?"

"I think so, though there's no way to be certain."

Then to forget the details they both got very drunk.

That's how Pat and Willy got the ranch.

Land was the subject of the hour. The West was new and wide, with expansion at its height. Everybody wanted land, quantities of land. Land was the passkey to the future. It meant money in the bank, silk dresses in the closet, rubber-tired buggies and gaited horses, fashionable Southern schools for daughters, and brokerage businesses for sons. It meant all the things men work and bleed for.

One night Pat came home hilarious, with a new half-drunk ground-floor deal. All the Murdy Gin fellows had bid on Texas school-land homesteads when they went to get their evening drink. Pat's bid had been the highest. He got four sections of land in Webb

County, Texas, provided he lived out on it three years straight.

Three months later the Westalls moved fifty miles north of Laredo to their homestead. They built a one-room box house with a lean-to kitchen, and hired three Mexican cowhands to tend the goats and cattle their savings bought. For ready cash Pat kept his job with the Murdy Gin Company, with a transfer to South Texas. Every seven weeks he got to Laredo. The Torres Mexicans met him in the wagon and drove him the fifty miles to Willy, for a week. Then he was off again to sell and erect Murdy Gins in the fast-settling Texas wasteland.

"It's a helluva way to live," he always said to Willy as he left her.

"But, Darling, think what we're getting in return. These four sections of land will be our future!" Willy had to brace him to a parting.

The whole experience proved to be a lark. Willy wore her pregnancy as a badge of faith to the future. To bear a child for Pat meant only a closer bond. She remembered Adelaide and her terror and her death. But this was all to be so different. She and Pat were finishing up a chapter that somewhere, somehow, had been interrupted in the long-forgotten past. She crowded her days with work and dreams and plans. The howling of the coyotes at night soothed rather than distressed her. She knew that longing wail. It had haunted her until she had found her Pat.

"It's the only answer. Poor Adelaide, no wonder she died. Ed Bailey was a good man, but he was not *her* man."

According to Dr. Riley's calculations, Willy's baby would arrive about the middle of January. "But I'll come on home and get you into San Antonio by the middle of December," Pat assured her on his last trip in.

On December the tenth, Manuel and Felipe drove into Laredo to meet Meester Westall at the train, but nine days later Willy woke with a strange deep pain in the middle of her body to realize that she was still alone. Now she was trapped. There was nothing she could do but pace up and down the floor and wonder why! The chaparral shut her in. Just scrub mesquite, huisache, cactus, everywhere! Nothing to come to. Nothing to go to. A vast silent brightness that beat in upon her brain.

The pain came again, harder, faster, until the past was blotted out, the present blurred. Pat did not matter any more. Nothing mattered except this cursed pain that struck her, backed off, struck again and again, with such deafening force that she failed to hear Benito's wagon when it rolled up to the gate.

In one blessed interim she heard Pearl nickering from the corral. In another, she sensed Rosita near her. Then a rattle of mesquite wood being crammed into the stove, the smell of kerosene, a flash of fire, and an anxious cry, "Por el amor de Dios, ándele con el agua, Benito!"

She never could recall the details of that next little while. Everything crystallized into pain, hard and fast and fierce. Through it all she was conscious of a warm strong hand and a soothing voice that said, "Por el amor de Dios!"

Out of somewhere the thought came clearly, "Rosita is right; it is by the love of God."

The next thing she was sure of was a great sense of peace and quiet. The battle was over. The enemy had retreated. Her one desire was to lie still and rest. Somehow she managed to raise her hand, and when it came to rest, it did so on a soft, wiggly warmth.

"Por el amor de Dios, la niñita, Madama!"

Rosita's dark hands clasped the child's plump body and raised it for her to see. Willy forced herself to concentrate.

"You're right, Rosita; it is by el amor de Dios that she is here. Let's call her Amor. Her name could be nothing else but love. We'll call her Amara, the classic of the chaparral!"

4

Two days later Manuel and Felipe drove in from Laredo bearing a letter for Señora Westall. They had
suffered no mischance in their journey. As usual, they
had been at the station when the train arrived, but the
Señor did not get off. To the post office they went as
always, but no letter awaited them. To go home and
tell the sick Madama would avail nothing! So they
kept on meeting the train for a week. On the eighth
day a letter came.

They brought the horses in at a dead gallop, changing teams at every ranch. Their eyes shone as they
looked down at the squirmy little baby and smiled at
the Madama as they handed her the letter.

The Spoll Hospital in Corpus Christi wrote that
Patrick Westall had been injured by a rolling door. It
fell from the second story of a cotton gin that he was
erecting in Kingsville and hit him on the hip. His leg
was broken, the hip socket injured. He had been
hurried to the hospital, where he was, at the moment
of writing, still unconscious. The letter was signed
"Sister Mary Holy Ghost."

Willy wept and was not ashamed for weeping.

Four weeks from that day Willy, Benito, and Amara
bumped the fifty miles into Laredo to catch the Tex-
Mex for Corpus Christi. Once settled down into the
red-plush seat of the train, Willy saw what six months
of prairie breaking had done to her. For the first time
in all those months a hat was sitting on her curly head.
Her black skirt, too little in the waist, rode precari-
ously apart on a safety pin. The gap was covered by a
broad linen belt. Her white waist stretched uncomfort-
ably across her bust; the milk she carried for Amara
doubled her in measure. Her large hands stood out
red and rough against the white of the baby's goatskin
blanket.

"Six months away from things and you're marked!" she said to herself. "I realize now that this country's meant for men and horses, not for dogs and women." Then she patted the sleeping baby and thought of Pat. The rest she resolved should be blank.

When she arrived at the hospital she found Pat lying on his back, with a heavy weight hanging from his foot. Dr. Spoll had missed the diagnosis. The hip had not been broken, but dislocated; now it refused to stay back in its place. Pat looked thin and pale and whipped. The minute she met his eyes she knew the verdict. The battle was to be hers alone. He wept softly when he looked at the new baby, wishing that she had been a boy.

For a month Willy hovered over him, fell in with his every whim, cajoled, comforted, planned. When he got no better, Dr. Spoll told her to take him home and hope that nature might complete the cure in the space and quiet of sunshine in the open, because men could do no more.

When Willy went back to the desolation of the ranch she went in her own strength alone. She had a baby girl, a defeated husband, and less than a thousand dollars to her name. But she had to go. There was no other place or no people for her to go to. "It's a challenge to ourselves and to our love," she said to Pat. They would prove up the homestead, then sell the land for a fresh start.

It was to be a solitary struggle and Willy knew it. Pat was a regular fellow when things went well. Alone he had been able to fight back when luck was against him, but the triple burden of a wife, a baby, and an injured body sapped his courage. The light faded in his clear blue eyes. He looked out dazed, surrendering to Willy's strength and zeal. And Willy squared her shoulders as in the old days when she stood before a basket of Aunt Ann's petticoats to iron. The only difference now was the heavy weight of love—"And the preciousness," she always said to herself when she touched Pat's hand, or felt his cheek against her face, or the baby reached out and clutched her finger.

Willy opened up the ranch house, knocked down the spider webs, and took a look around for snakes. Then she propped Pat up on the feather bed so he could watch Amara's crib while she set about her work. She plunged into the ranching without help. Since she didn't dare to pay the Mexicans out of her little money, she did the work herself. She corralled, herded, and rode fences some part of every day.

As she rode about she kept a sharp eye out for game to stretch the meat supply. She always brought in rabbits; occasionally a young javelina, the wild hog of the Texas prairie, or a deer. Groceries were scarce. Twice a year Benito drove the wagon to Laredo to get coffee, sugar, beans, rice, ribbon-cane molasses, flour, and meal. They counted every dollar, for not one cent was coming in.

In the mornings, as Willy rode out into the sunshine, she forgot the immediate burdens of the day. As she jogged along on Pearl, she picked up the vision of the four sections stocked to capacity, paying big dividends, the Westalls ranchers of consequence riding a buckboard into Laredo to sell the cattle and buy provisions, pointed out as they walked down the streets as the Westalls from the back country.

But when Will turned Pearl's head homeward, Pat's eyes danced crazily before her—eyes once so bright, so encompassing, bounding her universe into two circles of blue—now so faded, so drooped—glistening with tears of surrender. Those eyes had written life into her very being. Now they challenged her to conquest.

"Somehow I've got to get back to people, to a place small enough so I can reach out and touch things—where I can function for us all. Ranching takes money and manpower, and I haven't got a thing but myself. But I can run a store," she always added, as though to clasp a finite verity as defense against her fear.

She tried to pick up Pat's interest. "We'll go some place, Darling, and put in a store. I'd love to run a store." But Pat only turned over on his pillow, and she could hear him cry. Then to soothe him she would go to bed. Only in her arms could he find comfort. He couldn't sleep unless his leg rested on her hip; then she couldn't sleep herself.

She would lie there thinking, trying to make a pattern: the Dunbar racket business—Adelaide and Ed Bailey—Oklahoma City—her pink-satin wrappers—Pat's lightning movement on two legs—the joyous news of her conception—Amara's tearing into the world—the lonely fear and desolation—her tired feet and aching back—the burden of the future—their next move to what? Is this marriage? Eventually she would fall asleep, hoping unconsciously that she would never have to open her eyes again. She was very tired.

But when morning came she always felt refreshed. "I can do this easy," she said to herself every morning as she jumped out of bed, "—except milk those longhorned cows!" She had to add the cows because they scared her. They were the focus of all her terror—all the harsh wildness of expanse that shut her in boiled down to flesh and blood. She could hate the cows and curse them because they were something she could see and touch. She wore Pat's clothes to fool them, but they snorted and lunged back when she got near to tie their heads and tails. The challenge of her day was milking.

"If I can live through this milking I can do whatever else comes up," she thought every morning as she went out the door with Pat's pants on, and carrying his coat and hat.

He never failed to look at her surprised. "Are you afraid, Sweetheart?"

"Afraid, Darling? No, I'm not afraid of anything, at least not of a cow!"

The afternoon a longhorn tossed her over the corral, only one idea rang through her head—"Pat must never know!" When she hit the ground, she felt too stunned to have any idea in her head. She pulled herself up to sitting. Gradually her eyes focused. A strange man—on a horse—was looking at her!

"Well, I'll be damned!" she said. "Nobody's been here for a week. Why would you ride up now?"

The stranger didn't speak. He sat there gaping at the beauty of the woman he saw before him. For a moment he had thought she was a boy. Then she sat up, and her black curls fell about her face. He helped her to her feet, and felt almost glad when she fainted in his arms.

Willy came to under the portal. The man was rubbing whisky on her wrists and throat.

Bill Lester stayed with the Westalls a week. He had plenty of time and was glad to rest up awhile, helping Miz Westall straighten things out a bit. He was on his way up from Mexico where he had been in on a gold-mining deal. "Ridin' north," he said. "Nowhere in particular. Just movin' on."

Bill was a stocky, square-cut boy about Willy's age, with a clear, straight gaze that looked through you. He would be a hard man to lie to and one you would never want to fight with. He impressed Willy by his kindness to Pat. When he opened his mouth to speak, Pat cut him short, impolitely—with almost uncouth rudeness. Bill answered with the patience of a parent to a child. Bill was a younger man by twenty years. He could walk on his two legs and help Willy with the work. Of his own strength Pat could not put on his pants.

Bill's first night there, Willy was put to it to know how she was to bed him. They had no bunkhouse such as all Texas ranches furnish for their cowhands and passing guests. The folding bed stood in the corner awaiting the express purpose for which it had been made, but in the same room was the bird's-eye maple where she and her husband slept.

"When you live in a new country, you have to take up new ways," she told herself.

As soon as dark came on she asked Bill to go outside while she and Pat undressed. Then when she blew out the lamp, Bill came in and stretched himself on the folding bed. But he couldn't sleep. He lay there thinking.

And so did Willy. That first night Bill Lester was her guest often came back to her. To it she pinned many facts and much faith.

To begin with, God never fails. Out of the brightness of the prairie a man who could talk English had come to help her fight back coyotes, panthers, snakes, tarantulas, drought, distance—the great nothingness bristling with peril. The same force that had sent him could function further. It could liberate her from this vast isolation and surround her with things close enough to feel. She lay there holding tight to this assurance. She was trying not to see this ugly thing she had found in Pat.

"Poor darling," she told herself, "he's sick, and he's tired of pain." But her mind ran on ahead. To love is one thing; to possess is another. Love's purpose never binds. It warms and comforts. The closeness of it ties it to the one who owns it. To hold it tight for fear of loss is but to choke—at length to kill it.

Then Willy reined in her thinking. No time for fancy stuff! She had immediate fears. Her fainting was from more than the bounce over the corral. She had noticed a strange deep feeling. Could she have conceived again, with Amara only six months old? Certainly there was chance enough! She flushed hot at the thought of Pat beside her snoring softly, his leg pillowed across her hip. She thrilled again at the memory of the warm heavy burden that was Amara as the baby had grown within her body.

Then she began to reason. "But it's not the having them; it's the raising them that counts. The stranger across the room is smart. If you're going to adventure in a new country, you'd better do it by yourself. A crippled husband, one baby in your arms and another in your body saps your courage—makes you afraid. That man is fearless—and I'm scared to death!"

Bill Lester could not sleep. He heard Willy Westall's sob. And she was lying in a man's arms across the room.

5

Willy never forgot the morning Bill Lester left the ranch.

The seven days that he was there he spoke nothing of himself. He patched the barbed-wire gap in the yard fence, cut mesquite limbs to fill in holes in the corral, and grubbed out the brush for five hundred yards around the house—tarantulas and snakes avoid clear places. He rounded up the goats, cut out six cabras and their kids and brought them in to milk— "so's Miz Westhall won't have to milk them damned longhorn cows."

"Goat's milk is th' only kind to drink," he told Willy. "Never see a Mexkin foolin' with a cow. When you live in a Mexkin country, th' thing to do is take up Mexkin ways. They seem to sorta know how," he said.

On the eighth morning he saddled up and got on his horse. "Just movin' on," he said. "Adiós!" That was all. He waved his Stetson and rode off south.

It was a bright day, as all the days were bright. The sun dissolved all space into a gleaming brilliance. Willy stood at the door watching. Pat lay on his bed.

"The sun shining the way it is just blots him out— as if he suddenly disappeared before our eyes," Willy said.

"Damned good thing!" Pat snapped. "Blessing if it did!"

Willy said no more. But she stood there a long time, watching—thinking. "Love is precious but it has its burdens. Freedom is God's great gift to man. We can't seem to have them both!"

She felt more than lonely—she felt deserted, left at the post, trapped with the purpose of her female function. She was a wife, a mother, a pregnant woman, burdened down with love. She felt worse even than

20

with Amara's birth pains. The hurt, less close, was deeper. It wrenched and twisted in her heart.

"Something maybe wants to be born," she thought, "but it's not this baby in me. It's more a part of me than a man's child could be. It's me myself."

She tried to smile. "I have a lot of things to learn!" She frowned.

Then Willy looked up at the sun. Aunt Ann used to say, "Go out and look up at the sun, Willy, if you're in trouble. The sun knows a secret that man has got to learn. The moon and stars don't bump into it or make trouble of any kind. Divine order! If God can manage that, He can manage you."

Willy loved the sun. She loved its yellow radiance and the power it displayed despite the dust and sweat and thirst it gave her. Some days she blessed it; some days she cursed it. But she was glad to look straight up and see it, for it was strong, fearless, and brilliant. It gave her courage even when she woke up thirsty.

And Willy woke up thirsty every morning; so did Pat. It was one subject they never spoke of because it was the ever-present torture that they felt. The slimy, brackish water she hauled up in a barrel from the water tank quenched no thirst. It merely kept life in the human body.

What they needed was a well drilled for water, and a windmill. Pat's accident had cut short that improvement to their homestead. As a makeshift they did the best they could with a hole scooped out in the earth—called in Texas a water tank. When it rained the hole filled up; when drought came, it dried to mud.

Willy soon learned that the best relief for thirst was not to think about it—thirst, or any other hurt. Just kept on working and stay too tired to think. She worked all day, cooking, nursing, washing, ironing, hunting, hauling water, riding fences, corralling goats. At night she shut out the world and tried to absorb the human sweetness of Pat and her baby girl.

The coyotes howling in the distance made her think of many things; too often of Bill Lester. She wondered where he came from, where he went to, if they would ever meet again. She missed him—missed his help, missed his smile, missed the assurance of his blue eyes when she was scared—and she was always scared.

When they knew for sure that she was pregnant, Pat dwelt in gloom. They never spoke of the coming baby. As Willy's body thickened, Pat's eyes grew frantic.

"Thank God I'm healthy," she said every morning when she got up. She ignored her body as best she could, but her back and feet reminded her that she was tired. Lord, how tired!

One morning Pat surprised her by saying, "Saddle Pearl. I'm going out to ride."

"But, Darling, how—and where?"

"Ride, I said! Give me my clothes."

Willy did not argue. Nor did she ever forget the day she saddled Pearl for Pat's first ride.

She always felt that the little palomino was a person, not a horse. The Torres Mexicans had brought her over the first day on the ranch. Then she and Pat were gay and dream-laden with the homestead and their love.

"My God, what's that?" Pat had said when Benito led the little mustang up. She was just a shaggy yearling, with big brown liquid eyes.

"A geeft for Madama," the Mexican boy replied.

"She's got eyes like yours, Sweetheart," Pat said. He stroked the filly's stringy mane.

"And she's mine!" Willy put her arms around the shaggy neck and rubbed her nose. The filly nickered or, rather, whimpered in a human way.

From that moment they loved each other. Willy named her Pearl. "Because she's beautiful like a pearl," she said to Pat.

"My God!" he said, and laughed.

But the reason was not for beauty. Willy named her Pearl because she was precious to her, close and human, not wild and snorting like the cattle on the range. She was intimately gentle, as Mexicans raise their pets.

"If I could only hold you in my lap!" Willy often

said when Pearl hung her head in the kitchen door for a piece of bread.

In a year Pearl and Willy both made a mighty stride in growth. That's what bound them close together. By the time Amara came, Pearl's coat had slicked to shining in the sun. Her mane and tail were black. The morning Willy saddled her for Pat to ride she knew she had named her right.

"You are as beautiful as a pearl but more dear for all the comfort you have given me through this awful year," she said.

Pearl nickered. That's the way they talked.

"Be very careful with him, for he's very weak. He's making a mighty effort because he thinks I shouldn't ride in my condition, bless his heart!"

Pearl drew in her stomach instead of blowing out when Willy pulled the girth.

Pat limped up the wagon tongue, leaning on Willy's shoulder and one crutch. Pearl stood quiveringly still while Willy gently stretched his crippled leg across the mare's back, and with a little boost he was aboard. Then Pearl carefully picked her steps down the trail to the water tank.

As Willy watched them off she couldn't help but cry with joy. Once a man is astride a horse, he feels his power. Then he claims it—motion under him to direct at will. From that day on Pat's spirit leavened, his eyes lifted, his shoulders squared. Every day he found the strength to make the effort to ride out. Sometimes in the morning, sometimes in the evening, according to the dictates of the pain he suffered in his hip.

"You give him back his legs," Willy said to Pearl every day when she unsaddled her. "He's got reason now to live!"

Pearl's big eyes looked as if she understood.

Benito took great pride in his geeft to the Madama since Pearl had grown into such beauty as a horse. He rode over every week to see if he could help the pretty little Americana and the emaciated crippled man. The leetre girl he said was partly his.

"You have a right to claim Amara. You saw her first when she was born," Willy said in her best Spanish, which even so was very hard for Benito to understand.

Every week, when he came over, Benito pledged his allegiance to the Westalls in his best English; at least they thought that was what he said. Their intercourse was by gesture, guesswork, and imagination, but it was real.

The Torres Mexicans were faithful in their surveillance of the Americanos who lived so close, only fifteen miles away. Besides Benito some one or more of them came every week to visit, and they never failed to bring a gift. One time it would be a chicken and some eggs; again a basket of calabasa and some cabrito, a new goatskin rug to sit on. And once they brought a litte puppy with very shaggy ears.

They named him Popo. That was luck from Popocatepetl, or something to that effect, they understood.

When Amara pulled his ears, Popo wagged his tail and licked her hand. But one day he seemed cross, and nipped her on the leg. The next day when Willy found him slobbering at the mouth and running blindly forward, she shot him in the head.

"My God, the dog was mad!" Pat shouted. "A mad coyote bit him!" He turned pale, then began to tremble.

Willy's breath came hard. Her baby bitten by a mad dog, and no railroad for fifty miles! Where could hydrophobia be cured? Amara slobbering, frothing out her life! This was the deathblow from the desert—straight from the wolf's dark heart.

She would have fainted had Pat not done so first. She saw him reeling, and reached and grabbed him before he fell. "Don't do that, Darling," she shouted as she shook him. "This is no time to faint! Hydrophobia's desperate! We've got to think!" She shook him and slapped him; then she threw the bucket of drinking water in his face.

"If Bill Lester were only here!" she said aloud as she struggled with Pat's body. "He'd know—I know Bill would!"

"Bill Lester?" Pat opened his eyes and blinked. "Yes, by God, I wish he was," he said. "Our baby! We've got to save our baby!"

Willy's breath came short and fast. Her heart felt like a hammer beating at her chest.

"Sit down, Sweetheart, you look so pale," Pat said.

But Willy braced herself against the maguey pole of the portal and looked straight up.

She was looking at the sun.

6

Four hours later the Westalls galloped into the Torres Ranch. The horses staggered. Benito cut them out of the traces and hitched in his pet pintos. The Mexicans gathered around in sympathetic interest. In her best Spanish Willy explained the puppy's symptoms. Their eyes widened.

"Coyote con la rabia!" old Cepriano pronounced. They all shook their heads.

"The fire!" Rosita exclaimed. "Eet ees the cure!"

"Oh, no! Not fire!" Willy turned pale.

"God, yes, Sweetheart! Anything to save our baby's life! These Mexkins live in this damned country. They oughta know!" Pat cried.

The child herself was calm in her papa's arms. When Benito brought the coal of fire, Pat's face blanched as if he would faint again. Willy grabbed Amara from him. Mexicans live with coyotes. They ought to know. The picture of Amara frothing at the mouth like Popo drove her to the terrible expedient. At least a burn would heal.

"Don't look, Darling. Just turn your head," she said to Pat.

But Benito led him to the back of the jacal. When they were out of sight, Rosita put the coal of fire to the chubby leg where the puppy's teeth went in. Willy held Amara tight. The child flinched, then wimpered for just a moment, but she didn't cry out loud. Her brown eyes looked up to her mama as if she understood.

"No, Mama, no!" she begged.

The Mexican woman began to cry. Willy hugged her baby to her. She smoothed the straight black hair and wiped her sweaty face.

"That's right, Baby, you can stand it. You've got to, and you will," Willy said.

"Santos en el cielo!" Rosita murmured. Old Cepriano crossed himself.

Before the hour ended, the Westalls crawled back into the buckboard. Pat held Amara on his lap. She sat up straight and looked around, especially at her mama. Her papa kissed her leg and held it in his hand.

Willy tied her bonnet firmly beneath her chin, grabbed the reins, braced her feet against the dashboard, and raised the whip.

"Ándele!" she shouted.

The pintos broke at a gallop. They dashed out across the prairie, south, toward Laredo. There was no road to follow, just the sun.

The Mexicans stood there watching. Soon the blinding light absorbed the wagon into the mirage of water.

"Dios les guarda!" they all three said at once.

Then they crossed themselves again.

Two hours later the Westalls galloped into the Moreles Ranch. The rancheros cut out the pintos and hitched in two fresh horses. Two others replaced those at the Vela Brothers; and four mustangs from Señor Rodriques finished the fifty miles.

The tired horses galloped up to the depot in Laredo just as the train was pulling out. Willy shouted "Wait!" and the conductor stopped the train. All hands at the station helped the family aboard. The railway agent gave the Westalls all the cash he had, and prized the twenty-dollar gold piece from his watch fob as an extra gift.

"Send back the check. No time to lose! Get that baby into Austin to the Pasteur Institute!"

The Westalls were a pathetic trio when they stepped off the train in Austin the next day—sunburned, ill-clad, weary, worn, and frightened.

Pat went to the ticket window to ask about a boardinghouse. The agent spoke to him in Spanish.

"I'll have you know damned well that I'm as white as you are!" Pat shouted, swaying on his crutches. "Come out from behind that cage and I'll knock your teeth right down your throat!"

The man's eyes bugged. Pat reeled, almost lost his balance. As Willy dragged him to the cab, he kept on cursing. She felt glad to hear the old flare of temper. That was Patrick Westall!

Tired and dirty as they were, they drove straight to the Pasteur Institute. Dr. Farr was young, not yet inured to human pain. As they walked in the door, Pat shouted, "Cure my baby! A mad dog's bit her!"

The doctor looked at Willy's little body, big with child, eyes deep set and circled, face drawn—even dirty.

"Of course," he said. "It just takes time and plenty of patience. There's no hurry. We'll start tomorrow morning when she's rested. The treatment comes every other day."

"But can you cure her?" Willy's voice was a whisper.

The doctor felt her terror.

"For certain, and do you all a lot of good to boot." His voice was kind.

Willy sighed, then smiled.

Pat's eyes glared at the man before him. "We came here for hydrophobia, nothing else. You are to treat the baby, not my wife!" But his shoulders settled; his face relaxed.

When Willy and Pat were gone, Dr. Farr turned to the nurse.

"I'll be damned! She's just a girl, pretty in spite of all she's got against her. And that man—old, crippled, jealous. Maybe I shouldn't be a doctor. I see too much. What won't men drag their women into!"

"But did you see his eyes?" the nurse said. "I've never seen such light-blue eyes."

"Did you see hers? I've never seen such brown ones. God, but she could be a pretty woman with clothes and care and all that sort of thing!"

All afternoon Dr. Farr felt happy. He was glad that the treatment Pasteur had worked out for hydrophobia was a long one. He wanted to see this woman after time had relieved her body of the child inside her. He wanted to see her clean and rested, her face free from terror.

That night, after supper at the Smothers' Boarding House, Pat and Willy paired off with a Mr. and Mrs. Peterson, to talk. It was good to be back with Americans again, to talk and understand. It was better still to take a bath, to drink cool water, and to eat celery, beets, and cabbage instead of frijoles, cabrito, and molasses.

"I don't think I ever knew what comfort was before," Willy said to Mrs. Peterson when they sat down on the porch. "You don't appreciate it until you've missed it," she went on. "But it's the comfort of my heart that really counts! My baby's life is saved!"

Willy felt that comfort flow through her body. Not just the cessation of anguish but a definite elixir that warmed the bone and tissue. The weariness in her back was gone. The pain in her feet no longer bothered. The bulky heaviness within her distributed itself to a juster measure as the child kicked and moved. Her breath came evenly and with less effort because her heart had ceased to pound in protest to the death that lurked so close.

"How did you stand that trip!" Mrs. Peterson said. Leaning over close, she added: "I'm pregnant, too; and I'm doing well just to live, the way I feel. I tell Mr. Peterson every day I'll never last the nine months through. It's awful the way women have to suffer!"

"Stand the trip, Mrs. Peterson? If the Pasteur treatment is all Dr. Farr says it is, I'll be glad for this experience. It has taught me a lot of things I needed to know; for example, this peace I'm finding at the moment. It is something new, something more real than I've ever found before."

Pat and Mr. Peterson talked so loud, the women had to stop and listen. Pat was bragging about his ranch and all his cattle. They lived on it just for health. Now that he was better they would soon be moving on. Mr. Peterson was voluble in all he knew, and being a railroad man he knew many things. His enthusiasm of the evening was the new land boom down in the lower Valley of the Rio Grande, brought on by the St. Louis, Brownsville and Mexico Railroad. They were building an extension to Brownsville, where the great river flows into the Gulf. Another extension was going fifty miles up the Valley to a terminus named Sam Fordyce. Built through a barren and un-peopled land, the railroad, to sustain its existence, had to lure homesteaders to the border. And Mr. Peterson proved loyal to those who paid him wages.

"Didja ever see a copy of the *Gulf Coast Magazine,* Miz Westall? Take a look at this one. Finest country in the world. People're pourin' in there like flies in a molasses pitcher. It's just a matter of who'll get there first. Land's sellin' now from forty to seventy-five dol-lars a acre, but it's goin' up every day. It'll touch a thousand and fifteen hundred. We run three home-seekin' trains the last week I was on the job."

"But it's too close to Mexico," Pat said. "We've been livin' up in Oklahoma with th' Indians and out in Webb County with th' Mexkins. We're anxious to get back to the country where folks talk English."

"We're thinking of our family," Willy put in. "When we've proved up our land, we want to settle in a good community for education so the children can have the right opportunity for things." Then she blushed. "I wouldn't feel so safe right on the border—not for them, I mean."

"Scared to live close to Mexico!" Mr. Peterson slapped his knee in laughter. "My God, it's the safest country in the world. Old Porfirio Diaz is still presi-dent and will be till he dies. Thirty years of his rule would fix any Government on its feet. Revolution is a thing of the past down there. He hangs 'em on the roadside when they don't do to suit him. Mexico's on the gold standard just like us. Last year $800,000,000 of foreign capital went into that country. Scared? No, folks, I feel safer livin' close to Mexico. As soon as the Missus gets back on her feet we're headin' straight for the Valley. Wouldn't miss a chance like that."

"What kind of business is goin' on down there?" Pat asked. "Is it land like Oklahoma?"

"No, man; it's agriculture. You can raise anything you plant. It's like the delta of the Nile. Better not stand still too long or you'll grow yourself."

"What do they raise, cotton?"

"Hell, no. It's a truck country. They raise vegetables and get 'em on the winter market at fancy prices. They haven't even started yet at that. For years old Dick Kant and John Kender have been doin' a lot of experimentin' on their ranches. They've proved there's nothin' you can't raise down there if you water it. Saw some orange trees out at the Leguna Seca. Been there for seventy years they say, bearin' fruit every season."

"You mean yellow oranges like we buy at stores?" Pat's eyes grew eager.

"Sure, man. They say one of the Circuit Oblate Fathers took an orange to a sick kid in old Macedonia Vela's family. They planted the seed, and it's been growin' ever since. Wouldn't surprise me a bit if some day that whole country was full of orange trees."

"How about the water?" Willy ventured to interrupt again.

"Irrigation right from the river. All kinds of pumpin' plants have been installed and little towns'll be springin' up. It's the comin' country; goin' to make California look just like a dime."

"Gravity irrigation?" Pat asked.

"No, pumpin' plants—but gravity irirgation'll come in time."

As Willy helped Pat out of his clothes that night she discovered a faint hint of the old gleam in his tired eyes.

"That's the country we'll make for, Sweetheart, just as soon as we've proved up this damned land and have a little stake to start with. We'll put in a general store."

7

Three months later Dr. Farr pronounced Amara cured. Pat was improved both in body and in mind, little Serena had been born into the world, and every dollar of Willy's cache had been spent.

Willy's pregnancy had kept them in Austin until the baby's birth. Dr. Farr was careful in his attention and sound in his advice. Pat insisted that money be no consideration, but Dr. Farr arranged with Dr. Scott for a modest fee. Pat and Willy never knew what he had done. They asked no favors, wanted none.

At the first sign of labor Pat called the ambulance. "It's my wife! Move fast!" he shouted.

Dr. Scott noted the tremor in Pat's thin body as he balanced on his crutches. "Go on home and rest, Mr. Westall. I'll call you when we're ready. This is going to be long drawn out. You get some rest."

"Yes, please, Darling," Willy's eyes implored. His anguish hurt her like the labor pains.

Reluctantly, Pat obeyed. When he reached the Smothers' Boarding House, he joined Mr. Peterson. Together they went down the street to discuss the prospects of the Lower Rio Grande Valley over a few drinks of whisky while he waited.

When Dr. Scott's call came at six in the morning, Pat could not be roused from the stupor of the evening's drunk. Not until the following day did he manage to get to the hospital to see the golden-ringleted baby girl that had been born. Without a word, he fell upon Willy's bed and wept. As she stroked his hair and patted him for comfort, she tried to understand. It was not that she had wanted him to witness childbirth. She felt happy that he had been spared that revelation. It was more jealousy she felt than censure, more self-pity than condemnation. She knew that he had not

31

meant to fail her. He had wanted to stand beside her and hold her hand. But he couldn't bear the waiting, just couldn't; so he had to drink.

"If the baby had come more quickly," she kept thinking. "Yes—if she only had! That's every woman's prayer, I guess. No matter how men act, it's the women who have the babies. We watch every month out of twelve to see if we're pregnant; then wait nine months for them to come. As precious as love is, the price is high for women."

She thought a long time about the *price* of things. It's freedom, yes—but the price is lonely freedom— Bill Lester, for example. She couldn't forget that bright morning he rode off from the ranch. Did anybody else care where he went or what he did? She wondered if their paths would ever cross again.

Then she thought of Dr. Farr. He gave himself to heal the sick. The price he paid was freedom. He bound himself to people by their need of him, their suffering, and their hurt. She saw the concern in his eyes whenever he was near her.

Then she thought of Pearl and the Torres Mexicans, the chaparral, and its expanse of scrub mesquite, cactus, and huisache. "Plenty of space, no crowding," she told herself. "But the price is human comfort, not cozy and close-in like this room, where I can reach out and touch the wall. But here I've got so little sunshine!"

Then she thought of Adelaide and Ed Bailey. As her eyes closed to sleep, she was thinking, "The highest price of all is human love. Its heavy burden we want to keep. That's what binds and holds."

They named the baby Serena, for Willy's mother. Pat had thought of little Willy, or Sarah, for his mother.

"No, her name's Serena, after Mama. She'd like that if she were here."

Pat did not argue. He sat adoring the dimpled little haloed person, so different from the dark, straight-haired Amara. So enthralled he was by his new creation that he lost all interest in the world, even in talking to Mr. Peterson about the Rio Grande Valley.

Ahead of them was almost two years more of homesteading in order to prove up their land, and not one dollar had they left in money. Yet Pat could not liberate himself from the beauty of Serena to consider ways and means.

"We'll round up the cattle and sell 'em to the Torres Mexkins. The countin' will be easy. Just get in the calves and count 'em. Cows're too hard to catch. Just multiply every calf by seven. That gives you the sellin' number, with steers and bulls and all. Even with our few cattle that ought to be enough for us to live on," he said, when Willy urged him into talking. But he did not think of how or where he'd get the railroad fare to Laredo once the bills were paid.

Willy's last day in the hospital, Dr. Farr came to see her. She was rested now, relaxed, her body light and little, as pretty as he knew she could be that first day they met.

"Can I help you in any way?" he asked.

"You have already. You saved my baby's life." Willy looked up and smiled at him.

"No, I mean now. Money perhaps." He blushed a little; then he talked on fast. "You interest me, Mrs. Westall. You have from the first. Maybe it's because I know so little about why you're here, where you came from, or what had gone before that day you walked into my office—" he added slowly. "—and into my life! Whatever it is that's happened, I want to see that it never happens again. You must need money. Let me give you money, or lend it to you!"

Willy was sorry she looked into his eyes; she saw too much in them. That meant she had to refuse his help. God, how she needed money! Money she had to have!

But she held out her hand to shake his. "Thank you, Dr. Farr; thank you for all you've done—but we'll make out somehow," she said. He stared at her a moment, then walked out the door.

The day after she left the hospital, Willy went to the First State Bank in Austin and borrowed five hundred dollars. She just walked in and said to the old banker, "I must have some money." He looked at the frantic certainty in her face and knew she had to have it. He couldn't question further. "All right," he said. "How much?"

"Five hundred dollars." She wanted to say a thousand, but she was scared. "I'll pay you back the minute I get the money. The only security I have to offer is four sections of school land we haven't proved up yet."

He gave her the money, she signed a note, and that closed the deal.

"Damnedest loan I ever made," he said when Willy walked out the door. "Don't know why I did it, but wish she'd asked for more. Damned pretty woman! Wonder what she's doin' on a ranch in that godforsaken country."

Willy walked on down Congress Avenue, trying to think. Five hundred dollars was far too little for two years' living and a break for the new start, but it was something. She thanked God. Once back on the ranch she would be trapped again, away from things and people. But they had to prove up the homestead—yes, they had to now because she had to pay the banker. She thought of Dr. Farr and smiled. Health for herself and for the children. She took that for granted. For Pat she was not sure.

"The price of things!" she said, as she paused before a show window. A display of diamond rings had caught her eye. When the glanced up at the sign, she saw three balls hanging down in front.

"That's it! I'll pawn my watch and diamond ring," she said. She didn't give herself time to think or she never would have done it. She bargained quickly, took what she was offered.

When she stepped out of the pawnshop she had added four hundred dollars to her five; that made in all nine hundred. "That'll do it," she said.

As she walked on toward the boardinghouse her gait relaxed, the wrinkles in her forehead smoothed. She refused the temptations that came to taunt her. There was a deeper something she had obeyed. A

watch and a ring were but symbols. Two years of living—well, that was something she had to do.

"They filled my heart until I got launched," she
said. "Now I'm swimming—well, just so I keep above
the water."

Then she thought on through the details of han-
dling Pat. The bank loan she would confess. That was
straight business. The pawn loan would have to be a
secret. He would never understand her pawning his
engagement ring. She would tell him she had it put
away for safekeeping. The watch she had not used
since Oklahoma City days.

"He'd rather see us starve," she told herself, "or,
rather, he would think he would, than debase ourselves to pawning." Willy knew Pat could never stand
such a test.

"It's not that I want to do it myself; but I've got
to." She thought against that day when thirst or illness
might drive them back to towns and people. She had
two children now. They came without asking to be
born. She had to think of them.

Two weeks later the Westalls went back to the
ranch. Benito met them at the train, with his pintos
hitched into the wagon. His black eyes gleamed when
he saw the golden-haired new baby. The Madama
looked very pale, he thought.

When they drove into the yard, Pearl galloped to
the gate. Willy hugged her neck and rubbed her nose.
"You make up for all the cobwebs and dust," she
said.

It was a dismal place to look at. Grown up with
tumbleweed and cactus to the door; windswept, hot,
dry, deserted. The little house no longer shone bright
in new yellowness of lumber; it had sun-tanned to the
earth, gray-weathered.

Dust mantled the inside. Not a peep of bird's-eye
maple, not even the red of the oilcloth on the table;
all was gray in the sameness of prairie sand. Willy
caught her reflection in the mirror of the folding bed.
So did Pat.

"God, I hate to bring you back to this, Sweetheart,"

he said. "Look what just those few months in Austin did to you! You're too pretty to come back to this damned bleak sun that burns you up and roughs your hands and skin!"

She interrupted, to save a spell of tears. "I'm so glad we never put the carpet down. Must have had a lot of windstorm, Benito. There's an awful lot of dust."

"Sí, Madama. Cómo no?" The Mexican shrugged his shoulders.

"A damned awful place to bring such a pretty baby to!" Pat shook his head and looked off into the distance.

Willy grabbed a broom and began to sweep and knock down spiders. Benito got the hoe and started grubbing weeds.

Willy stepped to the door and looked up at the sun. It was setting.

"And I'm beginning!" Willy thought. She squared her shoulders. She tried to make them broad.

The following day Benito drove his father over to buy the cattle, as Pat had planned. He brought the niñas the leetre gift of a javelina pig. "Se llama Salita!' He beamed as he set the little pig upon the ground. She bristled her stiff hair, squealed, and darted under Willy's skirt to hide.

"What a pretty name!" Willy exclaimed. "Tell us what to feed her."

"Not like the peeg. She eet only the green theengs." Benito exuded pride in the eating habits of his gift.

The Westalls were puzzled by their pet. She looked like a pig, acted like a dog, and ate like a rabbit. But so was poor old Cepriano puzzled by the proposed sale of cattle. Pat and Willy's Spanish proved inadequate. Cepriano spoke no English. According to Mexican custom, Benito was too young to transact business for his father. The conference ended with Pat damning a country where people can't even talk your language.

"I'll write Doc Riley to send me a buyer from Oklahoma City for the whole damned outfit!" he stormed.

The Mexicans were stunned by Señor Westall's loud language and red face as he flaunted his right crutch. They got into their wagon and rode home, sadly contemplating the strange ways of the Americanos. The bright spot of their visit, however, soon became uppermost—the new babycita's hair of gold!

8

The Mexicans added "ita" to Serena's name as they do to most words expressing things they love. She was Serenita—slurred into S'rita—to them all. Her beauty was a rebuke to the desolation of the ranch. Only the brilliance of the sun rivaled her in warmth and radiance. As Willy looked down into her crib, she was always reminded of that tiny yellow center of a flower that carries the germ of life. In that small person Pat had found a new grip on living. Her pale-blue eyes were his; her yellow curls his mother's.

"I guess you're all mine, Amara." Willy smoothed the slick black hair of her first-born as the little girl's brown eyes beamed adoration to her mama.

As Amara was Willy's, so Serena was Pat's in more ways than in looks. Amara thrived; grew strong. Serena paled and sickened. As Amara ate frijole soup and goat's milk, she fattened. Serena threw up almost everything she took. Willy's milk came freely, but Serena turned her head. They tried a goat, then a cow; then various goats and cows in fast succession. Willy's breasts oozed; hurt a lot; she puzzled at the trick of nature that offered much, then would not receive its gift.

"Something's wrong, awfully wrong, when nature bucks! I wonder what it is!" she kept thinking.

"It's the water," said Pat.

She boiled every drop they drank.

Then sometimes in terror she would wonder if the cow's kick could have caused trouble. Or maybe because Serena had not been exactly planned for, like Amara, but rather slipped in of her own accord. In remorse she recalled the efforts she had made to ignore her presence, so in contrast to the ecstasy with which she sensed every quiver of Amara. The first baby had come so like a clear-spoken word in answer to her haunting plea. This second child had rather exclaimed her presence with a sassy, "Please take time to notice, folks, I've arrived!" And when they did stop to look, they saw this blinking, wiggling, smiling ball of yellow, pink and white, lighted by two blue stars for eyes.

"It serves us right for her to fade and die like a flower you pick and fail to put in water." These thoughts Willy never spoke out loud. To Pat, who seldom left the baby's cribside, she always said, "It's just getting started. I'll bet in time she'll be healthier than Amara."

But as she rode out on Pearl in the mornings, she let her thoughts loose. In time she learned she had to pin them down to earth. Such thinking oppressed her less, left less burden: Dr. Farr—the good old banker —Bill Lester—what had become of him?—the folks in Franklin—the Torres Mexicans—her money.

But when she began counting money, she always landed in the abstract. Looking out over the broad expanse of flatness, she couldn't help but think of land. They came for land. Yes, plenty of land. No crowding—fresh air—sunshine—freedom. Yes, freedom! Freedom to go and come—but to go where? Come where? And space! But space for what?

All she could ever think of was space for burial. No cramping into small lots like Aunt Ann in the Franklin cemetery. Just choose a spot. You would never be disturbed. There would be a stateliness and dignity about being put underneath the vastness of a prairie, with all the hot sunshine and distillation of clear light to mark your grave—almost like Jesus making the ascension with no designation left of body. She braced herself against the day she would have to see a little grave beneath the chaparral. "She could dissolve into clear light and we'd probably never know it. Poor baby, that's what she will do if something doesn't happen."

In moments of desperation Willy always checked her thinking. She made herself do something. Usually she looked straight up—if in daytime, at the sun; if at nighttime, at the stars.

The day Serena gagged until she choked, Pat slipped out to the corral to keep from looking. In desperation Willy carried the baby into the blazing sunshine. "Look up at the sun, S'rita, darling. The planets have an order that they keep. I don't understand it, but maybe they don't either altogether. They just keep on at their job and so must we."

The brightness blinded the baby into squinting tight; then she caught her breath. In a moment she relaxed, and looked up at her mama. She almost smiled, Willy thought. "Why, it's just like God! Just like God!" Willy bowed her head.

The next morning Willy looked out the window and saw Benito driving in. He was alone in the wagon, coming slowly, even slower than a walk.

"Wonder what's the matter," she said to Pat. "When he's alone he always rides his pinto."

"Gettin' too damn lazy to saddle up, I guess."

Willy went out to meet him. To her surprise he led a little burra behind the wagon, and following came a colt.

"My papa send for th' babycita." The boy smiled. "Th' meelk of th' burra, Madama, he ees vurry guud, more guud than meelk of goat for seek cheeldreen."

"God bless your papa," Willy said. "And what's the barrel in the wagon?"

"He ees water. Señor Gonzales seend heem for th' niñas."

Willy wanted to throw her arms around the Mexican's neck and kiss him, but Pat was watching from the window. She thought, "The best people in the world, ranch Mexkins, Bill Lester told me. Water fresh and clean, wet to touch and cool to taste, water hauled thirty miles in a wagon to thirsty children. That's the cup of cold water I studied about in Sunday school, and it took a ranch Mexkin to teach it to me!"

"What in God's world!" Pat shouted as he came out
the door.

"Look, Benito's brought a burra so S'rita can have
the milk," Willy said.

"Give my baby burra milk! It'll kill her. Just another Mexkin scheme, like fire on 'Mara's leg that
time."

"But we've got to try it, Darling. She's got to eat to
live." This time it was Willy's face that spoke command. Pat saw something in those brown eyes that
shocked him.

"Well, do it at your own risk," he screamed. "I
can't even look. Milking a goddamed mule! I'm pukin'
up my heels myself."

Willy didn't hear what he was saying. For the first
time she ignored him. She forgot that he was there, or
talking. Her baby's life came first. Pat sensed her gone.
He didn't look again. He was afraid to. He went into
the house.

Willy and Benito milked the little burra in the corral and fed the baby there. The milk was warm with
body heat, not even strained.

"We'll do this out here so Pat won't have to see,"
she said.

'Qué dice?" the boy asked.

"Nothing of importance. Benito, sing that song for
me you picked up in Laredo."

" 'La Cucaracha'? Sí!" The boy smiled. Any request from Willy was a joyous command.

The gay tune sounded a little awkward in Benito's
soft, sad tones. Willy liked it, just the same. Her heart
warmed. She rubbed the little burra's nose and stroked
the colt's long ears.

"We understand," she thought. "We mothers! That's
why we give our milk."

Serena digested her burra milk and slept soundly
that night. In a week her cheeks turned rosy; ten days
later she picked up weight, and by the end of the
month she was as well and rompy as her sister.

Willy asked Benito to bring his father to visit her so

she could thank him. On the next trip, over the old Mexican came.

"You'll let me pay you for this little burra, Señor Torres? She's saved my baby's life." She turned to Benito to translate.

Cepriano exclaimed, "No, no, Madama." He had caught the meaning of her words. Then he spoke in Spanish to his son.

"He say eet ees de geeft," Benito relayed to Willy. "You pray for all de peebles' seek cheeldreen an' for hees Martita. Hee die wheen hee ees leedre lak Amarita."

Willy's eyes blurred. She could scarcely see the wrinkled face before her.

"Indeed I'll pray for your dead child, and for you and for Señor Gonzales!" Suddenly the memory of the water he had sent her in the barrel that day made her thirsty for a clear fresh drink.

"Let's all pray for rain," she added. She was smiling the way Benito loved to see her.

The old man looked up at the clear bright blue above.

"He theenk hee rain vurry queeck," Benito said.

"What makes him think so?" Willy searched the flawless sky for the shadow of a cloud.

"Quién sabe!" Benito shrugged his shoulders. Old Cepriano touched the little saint that hung from a dirty string around his neck.

That night it rained, a long, steady downpour that fed life to plants and beasts and hope to the hearts of men.

About midnight Pat and Willy heard somebody shout "Hello!" Willy got up, lit the lantern, and went out to invite the stranger in. She saw a tall shadow of horse and man at the gate.

"I'm Jim Nelson. Meant to get here afore dark, but the rain caught me." The voice was American, deep and kind, Texas West.

"You must be soaking wet," Willy hollered. "Get off and come on in."

While Jim Nelson unsaddled, Willy built a fire. The

frijole beans still simmered on the stove. She made fresh coffee and mixed a batch of hoecake. Food was ready by the time the tall old rancher got into the house. He took off his Stetson and carefully laid it on a chair.

"Howdy, folks," he said, and sat down. "Mind if I take off my boots? Ain't useda bein' wet. Damn funny happenin' in this country, you well know, I guess."

The boots, old and run-over, had been expensive to begin with—Justin at his best. The man was a Texas rancher, old, sturdy, weathered, a product of the land he lived in.

Pat and Willy liked Jim Nelson from the start. He was the kind of neighbor they had pictured in their ranch dreams back in Oklahoma City. He filled the room, gave them assurance.

"How'd you know we were over here?" Pat asked when the conversation got along. "You're the second white man we've seen yet."

"Torres Mexkins told me. I ride over this way every year or so buyin' cattle. My home's Goliad. I've stayed with old Cepriano now for years, but thought I'd come over an' see you folks tonight. Glad to have you in the country." He crammed in frijoles and gulped coffee from his saucer as he talked.

"That was good of the Torres to tell you," Willy said. "We're glad to have you come to see us."

"Sure are," Pat said. "It's fine to see a white man. Get so damned tired of Mexkins here."

"But the Torres are good neighbors," Willy quickly added.

"Cain't beat ranch Mexkins for friends," Jim Nelson drawled. "I've lived among 'em all my life."

"That's what Bill Lester said." Willy spoke before she thought.

"Bill Lester? Say, where'd you know Bill Lester?" The old rancher pricked up his ears at once.

"He's that other white man I spoke about," Pat snapped. The he suddenly changed the subject.

Willy heard Serena fretting and went to see about her. When she got back to the table, the men were talking about cattle.

"Glad to buy your cows but don't want your ranch. I don't buy land no more; I lease it. I find it better. When you've proved up here, I'll be glad to lease your four sections and run cattle at the regular price. Wouldn't wanta sell it anyhow if I was you. Might strike oil out this way any time. You'd clean up. Big development goin' on."

Pat's eyes picked up a glimmer of their old light and shine. "Tell me about the oil." He leaned over far, to talk.

Willy poured more coffee and served the last hoe-cake. God, it was good to have this man in the kitchen. She stepped to the window and looked out. The stars were shining bright. The air felt damp and cool, delicious, good enough to eat.

Serena cried out again. Willy excused herself to lie down on the bed to quiet her into sleep. She could hear the men talking about oil, profits, futures, contracts—big business. She fell asleep and dreamed she was in Oklahoma City riding in a buggy with Bill Lester. He held Serena on one knee and Amara on the other as he drove. She wore her gray angora hat with the plume, her Eton jacket and black alpaca skirt. Nothing happened. They just rode on down the street.

Then she woke up. It was daylight. Pat lay beside her. Jim Nelson snored loudly from the folding bed. Pearl nickered at the back door for her bread.

Willy went out and watched the sun rise. Pearl nuzzled at her neck.

Jim Nelson stayed a week. From his morral he produced a goatskin of mescal, and he and Pat became the best of friends. When Nelson got drunk enough, he bought Pat's cattle on the spot but deferred payment until he could raise some cash—"and send some punchers over to round 'em up," he said.

"We've got plenty of time," Pat said; "plenty of time!" hiccuping as he spoke.

Willy thanked God for the extra four hundred dollars. Cattle or no cattle, that would tide them over in a pinch.

On the eighth morning Jim Nelson got on his horse,

waved his hat, said "Adiós," and rode off. Like Bill Lester, he rode south into the brilliance of the sunshine.

Willy stood there watching. "The sun just blots him out," she said to Pat when the horse and rider blurred into the brightness before her eyes as Bill and his horse had done.

"Not Jim Nelson!" Pat smiled broadly. "Now there's a feller we'll hear from soon. He'll be back with the money. Not like that damn Bill Lester. Jim Nelson's the reg'lar kind."

9

The sun and moon marked off days and months in the time that followed. And the Westalls lived. "How, I'll never know," Willy often told herself. "But we live."

Pat hated the ranch and everything about it. He hated the Mexicans, the food, the sun that shut them in. "Damned wilderness," he always called it. "If we'd stayed in Oklahoma this never would have happened. Me holdin' the children while you do all the work. Just look at you, Sweetheart! You're young! The prettiest woman in the world! You oughta be sittin' in a parlor all dressed up! That's where I meant to keep you! Here you wear my pants and herd up a lot of cattle, an' wash an' iron providin' there's any water! Back in Alabama niggers didn't do the work you do, by God!"

Pat's temper was a comfort to Willy. Usually he sat silent, stroking Serena's yellow curls. It was then her heart froze in terror against the day she would have to bury him beneath the chaparral. She often wished for liquor to lift his spirit when he sank so deep. She tried to get him to plan the store and talk about the future, but the immediate present was too real for Pat. He grew thinner, paler, more tired, as he waited for time to pass and Jim Nelson to come back.

"He's dying by degrees," Willy thought from day to day. "If time doesn't hurry up he'll never make it." She asked God to help her stand the torture of watching Pat wither before her eyes. She knew she had to for the children.

The little girls grew strong and sturdy, Serena healthier by the day. Except for the mad-dog bite, Amara had caused no concern since she blinked into the world. She loved to eat and play and stay close to Mama. By the time she learned to talk, her papa taught her quatrains as he plaited her straight black hair into two stiff braids and tied them tight with strings. Pat never attempted Serena's curls because pulling made her cry. He left that to her mama.

" 'Mara's not pretty like S'rita," he often said, "but she's good enough, I think."

Willy never thought of the children as pretty or as ugly. They were just her little girls to care for; different, certainly, but each occupied a separate space in her heart the other could not touch. If she ever stopped to make a contrast, Amara seemed dark and sturdy like the solid earth to stand on; Serena as light and fleeting as a sunbeam in the air.

But they were very different. Amara minded her mama's every wish; S'rita never did. When S'rita learned to crawl, she crawled at random. When she learned to walk, she walked at will. When she learned to talk, she swore like Papa.

Benito crossed himself every time he heard her. Pat smiled and said, "That's right, my pet, you tell 'em. The world won't get you down."

S'rita loved snakes; next to them tarantulas. She followed them, reached out to touch them. Willy kept the yard swept clean to keep down ambush, but every day she killed a snake or two almost beneath the arbor. Benito told her they came in pairs. She always called to the children when she killed the first one and rushed them into the house until she found the mate. Amara would say, "Yes, ma'am," and hurry on ahead. Serena always lagged and screamed and stomped. She hated indoors; she loved outside.

"Dark inside, Mama, dark," she wailed.

When Willy lost her patience and spanked S'rita, Pat sulked for days. "No understanding of human nature! It's plain stupid to hit a child!"

"But Darling, we've spoiled her. She's not easy to manage like 'Mara. She's headstrong. I have to spank her; besides, the snakes will bite her."

"The poor baby has nothing to do. She needs playthings, bright, painted toys and dolls," Pat wailed.

"But just the same, snakes bite; so do tarantulas." Willy tried to make herself forget the pretty playthings in Mr. Dunbar's racket store—tops and balls and dolls she used to sell to women for their children, wishing as she did so that she had babies of her own to buy for. Now she had the children but only nature's live things for them to play with.

"S'rita likes the color in the sunshine; snakes glitter. She has an eye for art," Pat argued.

"Of course, Darling!" That's how Willy stopped all arguments with Pat, but she never failed to take time out to kiss him on the cheek.

Benito saw Willy's plight and suggested horned toads for the little girls to play with.

"Aren't they poison?"

"No, Madama, no. Mancita like cabrito."

Then Willy tried to make the children play with the pet cabritos, the goats. Amara warmed to them as playmates, but Serena would have nothing to do with them, and what Serena did not like Amara could not love.

"Bad smell, pooh!" S'rita held her nose.

Willy had to say, "You're right, Honey, but stink beats poison any day."

Salita, the javelina, proved a better compromise. The pig took the golden-haired child as her mistress and followed S'rita everywhere. There was an order the three always took at play—S'rita out in front exploring something, the javelina close behind, sniffling at everything S'rita touched, Amara following anywhere the two went. S'rita was her god.

"That wild pig'll chase off things that'd hurt 'em," Pat always said.

"Well, I hope to change their taste to these horny

frogs, as Jim Nelson called them," Willy answered.

The yard was full of the blinking, round-eyed little creatures. They seemed to stand around and watch what happened. Lizards are sly, like snakes; they slink and slide. Horned toads walk on legs. The children poked at them, but only when they were tired of sitting on Papa's lap and there was nothing more exciting near to fool with.

Benito inaugurated the horned toad regime in style to catch the children's fancy. He brought over his pet Juliano to demonstrate. He pinched its tail a little and it ran around his hat brim. He pinched it another way and it ran up his sleeve; another jab and it ran back down again. He tapped its head and it blinked one eye, then the other.

The children clapped their hands and shrieked. At once they set about catching two toads, and penned them up in a corral Papa built from sticks. Serena named hers Chico; Amara called hers Lupe. Papa served as referee when they caught on to tricks. But when Chico lost to Lupe in a contest of running around a hat brim, Serena ran to Papa and buried her face in his lap.

"You take Lupe," Amara pleaded to her sister. "I like Chico best."

"No, Honey, you must not spoil her. She's got to learn to lose," Willy said.

"Sure, let 'em swap," Pat put in quickly. " 'Mara doesn't care and S'rita does, it seems."

"The difference is, 'Mara cares too much—we all do —for S'rita. We let her have her way and spoil her. She's got to learn to live."

"But we love her," Pat answered. "We have to see her smile."

When 'Mara forced her Lupe into S'rita's hand, the tear-wet face broke into radiance. She tossed her Chico far out into the yard, then flung Lupe after him, and threw her arms around her sister's neck and kissed her wildly. They both jumped up and down. A shiny lizard streaked across the clean-swept earth of the arbor floor. Salita looked up at her mistress and grunted shrilly. Serena's eye caught the glisten; she lit out in pursuit, the javelina and Amara keeping up as best they could.

Pat looked up at Willy. "That's why we spoil her. We're smart to do it. To see her smile and dart about like lightning is worth all the horny frogs on earth," he said.

Willy reached down and kissed Pat on the brow. He squeezed at the breast nearest him a moment.

"That's what love's for," he said. "We have to spoil the things we love; it gives us pleasure. Why do you spoil me the way you do? Just because I'm sick and worried?"

"No," Willy answered. "It's because I love you. That makes the difference."

"Then don't scold 'Mara. She worships S'rita."

"So do we all and all and all," Willy began to sing the words to a little tune she knew. She dropped down on the hammock and took Pat's head in her lap. He reached up and kissed her warmly, closely, hard.

That was the ending to every scene involving S'rita's misbehavior. That plus a lot of closeness late into the nighttime.

Willy knew that S'rita was bad, unruly, temperamental. Pat must have been the same when he was little—was yet, in fact. They both needed strong direction, a hand to hold them in bounds, but they wouldn't have it. Rein them in and they began to droop and wither. "It takes a stronger hand than mine," Willy thought. She didn't realize how much her hands were molding all their lives. She loved them and she had to see the shining blueness of their eyes when they were happy. She had to feel the warm closeness of their bodies. The trouble was that in her heart she was afraid they would die and leave her.

Pat's accident and S'rita's illness had left a lurking terror she couldn't overcome. She felt ashamed at night when S'rita crawled into her lap to go to sleep. Always Willy sensed a preciousness that was too close, uneasy almost, as the child snuggled close. She always put her hands on her mama's cheeks and patted them. She had a way of looking up clearly, straightly. It was a candid look, so deeply loving that it blotted out all misbehavior. The eyes seemed to say, "I'm sorry." The little hands always kept on patting until the eyes drooped to sleep. When Willy put her on the bed, she always roused a little, clutched 'Mara's hand, and snuggled up close to her sister.

'Mara was different even as a baby. When she got drowsy she just nodded off without thinking of anybody. She would crawl up on the bed and be asleep before anybody had noticed where she was.

Pat always said, " 'Mara makes a business of her sleepin'. With S'rita it's an art."

"That's what makes 'Mara calm and good. She's always rested. First S'rita has to quiet down," was Willy's answer.

"That's the Patrick Westall in her. Sure she has to quiet down to sleep. Don't we all?"

Such remarks never failed to bring a wicked glint to Pat's tired eyes. For that instant Willy knew he forgot the pulling pain in his hip. He always came over and held her very close to his body. In those moments Willy thanked God for the scheme of things as nature planned it.

And the children, as little things, learned love's warmth and vigor. They often kissed each other just for nothing. Every little while 'Mara would jump up from her goatskin to kiss S'rita's cheek when she somersaulted from Papa's lap or dashed out across the yard after something moving. She often stopped, forgetting what she was running after, to throw her arms around her sister's neck and hug her wildly. They usually ended up such demonstration in a game of ring-around, singing a little Spanish song Benito had taught them.

Willy learned to use 'Mara's adoration of her sister as a safety check when she was busy at her work. "When S'rita begins darting about, you run and kiss her, Honey. That'll stop her. Be especially careful to watch when Papa falls asleep."

The Westalls had to live out under the brush arbor. It was too hot inside the little house. They ate out there and lounged about the ground on the goatskins the Torres Mexicans gave them. Benito swung a cowhide hammock that Pat loved. Pat's job was to watch the children, but not often did he perform his duty. He fell asleep or lay staring blindly into space.

As Willy rode about her chores, she often talked to Pearl about it and prayed to God to keep his eye skinned for her children. Few weeks passed that a goat did not die from snakebite. Once she shot a cow whose leg had sloughed off from tarantula sting. Willy didn't worry; rather, she stayed poised on the brink of terror. She had to ride fences and haul water and look out for the cattle, to keep life in her family's bodies; yet death crawled about her yard and lurked in shadows. She couldn't find it to fight it in the open. As she jogged along on Pearl she enjoyed the glisten of rattlers' diamonds gliding through the brush. That was different. She and Pearl had a way with snakes and things. She never held Pearl in; she gave her rein. If Pearl turned quickly, cavorted, jumped sideways, she knew there was a reason for it. Resting on Pearl's horse sense was the only real peace she had.

"How I wish I could leave you at home to look after Pat and the children," she often told the little palomino as they rode along. She felt ashamed that she didn't trust God to care for them. God was probably too busy with the sun and stars to take time out to check up on a crippled man and two little girls living at the butt end of nothing on a Texas ranch.

One day Willy came in late from her morning roundup. The pet goat herd had wandered off from Chica, the lead nanny, and Willy had to bring them in, then go back to check on the gap at the water tank. A few strays had been coming in. Water was too precious to share with strange cattle. As she got into seeing distance, two deer walked down to the water's edge to drink. Silhouetted against the straight horizon of clear blue they looked painted on the skyline. Pearl stopped, and Willy, gazing at the grace of beauty, forgot everything except the rightness of the thing she saw before her, a buck and doe at water. It was December. The deer had just raised one family and soon would begin another. "Nature has its ways," she said to Pearl.

Pearl snorted. The buck raised his head and listened. In that instant Willy remembered Pat and her children. It was the deer's horns that did it to her. He was a buck. That made it lawful for her to shoot him. The groceries wre getting low. They'd had no red meat in weeks. She jerked her Winchester from the scabbard, aimed and fired before she let herself think twice. The buck fell dead; the doe turned and fled.

Pearl walked home slowly, with the deer tied to the saddle. Willy walked alongside. Her heart felt like a brickbat. Why had she done it just for stomach hunger? Thirst was different. She'd kill a man for water. But why had she killed a deer just for food? There'd be no more baby deer from this proud father. He bore eight antlers. That meant a long good life, many children; and now his hide would be a rug in the shade of her brush arbor for her little girls. But what of the pretty doe? There'd be other bucks, of course, and other babies—but she, Willy, had spoiled the picture. She had done it for her husband and her children; afraid of hunger before Benito came with groceries— afraid—always afraid—of something!

Suddenly Pearl stopped. Willy looked up, and when she did so, she froze. They were not close to the house, but in the gleaming sunlight Willy saw every detail of the brush arbor. Pat lay in the hammock sleeping. 'Mara was in his arms. S'rita sprawled on the red cowhide on the ground, the javelina's snoot mixed in her curls. Everything was sleeping—except two long sleek rattlesnakes gliding around the many goatskins on the arbor floor.

Willy reached for Pearl's mane and clutched it when the snake brushed S'rita's hair. The horse edged over close besides her. They watched the snakes glide on past all the rugs, out into the sunshine, out into the brush.

"I'll never doubt again," Willy said to Pearl. "He has His way with those who trust Him!"

That day Willy cooked venison steak for dinner, but

she didn't eat it. The children gobbled it and so did Pat.

"We've got to manage for white tablecloths and beefsteak every day," Pat said as he pushed back his plate. "Red meat in your belly gives you guts."

Willy didn't answer.

That night, in place of turning the bed halfway down to put the children in, for some reason Willy picked up the sheet and threw it back. A rattlesnake lay coiled in a neat roll at the foot. Pat fainted. Before she brought him to, she killed the snake. Pat lay back on the bed cursing the damned wilderness they lived in.

Willy turned the subject to Eve in Eden. "That just goes to show that people won't believe the truth. 'It's too strange,' they say. I myself never believed her story until tonight!"

"It goes to show this damned country was never meant to be lived in," Pat stormed. "We've got to get our children out of here. If Jim Nelson'd come back, we'd leave tomorrow. We haven't got the cash to go on as it is!"

Willy longed to tell him she had almost four hundred dollars. But knowing Pat, that would never do. His only hold on life was pride and love. To feel that she had betrayed his engagement ring would jerk away his one prop left to strength.

"Maybe we can sell the land," she said, just to keep him talking.

"But who in God's name to? The damned Torres Mexkins won't buy cattle even, and we haven't seen but two white men since we've been here. Both of them rode off and left us and we've never heard a word." He got to his feet and began to limp up and down, waving his left crutch now and then.

Suddenly Willy wondered if they had ever seen any white men. Maybe they only imagined them, as one sees water in mirage. Both men had appeared out of nowhere and both had dissolved into sunlight as they left. "Maybe it's the heat," she said. "Maybe we're getting sunstroke. Twelve months of this beating sun every year is enough to cook the brain!"

"Well, mine must be damned near scrambled now," Pat said.

They both laughed at that. The laughing broke the tension of the fear. They went to bed and let the sense of closeness occupy their heads.

Long after Pat had gone to sleep Willy lay thinking. Her mind went spinning, in a torture that to women is very real. "It's better not to think at times. You go crazy. But stop thinking for a moment and give yourself to feeling and see what happens! There's a price again!" Willy tried to quiet herself against her ever-lurking fear.

"Just now the price must be no more babies, because I've got to raise the two I have. It's not what I want or what I feel—like once; it's what I've got to do. If I could rest a second and be sure! God, I'm tired—tired of worry—tired of wondering—tired of living maybe. If I could lean just a little—something that would hold me—something strong—very strong to lean on." Her eyes grew drowsy. Sleep blurred her brain. "Bill Lester's strong!" She didn't know she thought it. It seemed so like a dream.

Benito came back from Laredo with the groceries. With them he brought a letter from Dr. Riley in Oklahoma City. Any letter was a celebration to the Westalls. There was almost nobody anywhere to write to them. Mrs. Dunbar sometimes sent a note; the Murdy Gin Company inquired about Pat's health but paid no compensation; only Dr. Riley sometimes wrote.

This time he told the Westalls he was sending down a buyer for the ranch. She would be a Mrs. Baxter, accompanied by a Mr. Thornton, an expert real-estater, who had sighted her upon collection of her late husband's insurance money. She wanted a ranch for an investment and a hunting lodge. They would be down for a Christmas hunt.

"Christmas! My God!" Pat exclaimed. He put down the letter, turning slightly pale.

Christmas was one of the many sacrifices they had made to the chaparral. Since there was no change in weather to mark it off in season, Pat and Willy practiced forgetting December as a month. Twelve months of every year the sun shone with equal zeal. During December and January a norther sometimes blew in, but the sun kept right on shining. In a day or two the cold snap always gave up in the contest. The coldest day they ever had, Willy put just one blanket on the bed. So Christmas could be erased more easily than a lot of other things they missed and longed for.

The first year on the ranch Willy made a prune pie by way of celebration, and Pat looked black all afternoon. After that she always managed to hide the calendar so she could lose all track herself.

To Pat Christmas meant eggnog, fruitcake, turkey, and plenty of whisky; trees, gifts, people, gaiety, and joy. "You can't compromise with spirit. That's what Christmas is," he said, tapping his finger against Dr. Riley's letter.

"But, Darling, we've got the spirit; in fact that's all we've got. Do you realize the woman wants to buy the ranch? That means we can leave here the minute we prove up and have plenty of money to get back to the things you love."

"But to have people find us in a place like this at Christmas!" Pat kept saying.

Gradually, however, he caught the spirit of Willy's getting ready for the guests.

She delved into her trunk and brought forth the Oklahoma City portiers as a partition between the beds. The children would sleep on pallets on the floor. Benito brought a canvas cot he borrowed from somewhere. Mr. Thornton was to sleep on that. Benito lent his two prize pintos and their flat-horned saddles for the hunting party, and herded in some extra milk goats for the food supply.

Willy got out the best dishes and scrubbed the pots and pans. The little girls were rapturous over the great preparation in the house. Even S'rita was willing to stay inside and help. Willy set them to picking weevils from the beans and rice. They dug up cactus and brought in rocks to decorate the house.

"Beautiful!" Willy said to everything they did.

"Damn pathetic," Pat said every now and then. "It's just a business proposition. We're so lonesome you'd think a king and queen were comin', the way we're goin' on."

One day the girls hid behind the bed, making something.

"S'prise for you, Mama," S'rita announced.

"To make th' house pretty for th' company people," 'Mara added.

All day they worked, laughing gayly as they did so. Salita crouched close beside them.

"S'rita's doin' all the doin'," Pat said to Willy. " 'Mara's watchin' just like S'rita is a god."

"Well, that's important. She gives S'rita inspiration. We have to have a reason for doing things—like these people coming now for Christmas. I'll bet they'll think it's fun. Remember the fun we used to have when you hurried out to see me here on the ranch, then rushed back to erect a gin? We did things for 'Mara then. She wasn't born and we had so much to live for before things got so hard." She could have cut her tongue out. The words just slipped. It was the thing she would have rather died than said. But Pat didn't seem to notice. He was thinking of Mrs. Baxter and liberation from the ranch.

"She'll build a big ranch house and bunk half the men in Oklahoma every huntin' season. I know her kind all right." When Willy looked at Pat she saw his eyes were shining with a hint of light.

"Well, we won't worry about her kind, just so she's got the money and buys the ranch."

Willy was thinking of water and clean-washed clothes—still remembering diapers not sudsed, just hung out to dry.

Just then S'rita and 'Mara came forth with their gift. It was a picture drawn with pencil. S'rita had done it and it was very good.

She handed it to her mama and looked up shyly.

"It's for the wall," 'Mara explained, jumping up and down.

"It's beautiful!" Willy said.

"What is it?" S'rita questioned quickly.

When Willy hesitated just a minute, Pat reached and took the paper from her.

"What is it, Mama?" S'rita asked again.

"That's easy," Willy said. "It's the buckboard with Sol and Pito hitched in it. Maybe that's Benito driving."

"No-o-o!" S'rita said. "It's th' wagon and Papa drivin'!" She grabbed the paper, tore it into bits and stomped the pieces. Pat stretched out his arms; she hurled her little body into them and pressed her face against his neck.

'Mara reached up her hand to Mama. Willy took it and they walked outside. They did no talking; they just walked along in step.

'Mara loved her mama's hand. It was her comfort, her haven when things went wildly wrong with S'rita, as things so often did. She never knew what was coming from her sister, slaps or kisses, hugs or tears. Papa and S'rita stomped. Mama smiled and kept on working. When she reached up to find her mama's hand, it was always there to hold to. She loved the feeling; it was rest.

"Look at the sunset," Mama was saying. "Never fail to see the sunset, 'Mara; it makes your dreams shine bright with color."

'Mara looked up quickly. "It was a pretty picture, Mama. Why did S'rita tear it and stomp it?"

Willy smiled down and said, "Well, you and I've got the sunset, Honey."

They heard Pat and S'rita talking. Pat's voice mounted clearly. He and S'rita talked in a jumble, but 'Mara and Willy understood them.

"Of course, Puddin', any fool would know you drew a wagon, not a buckboard! Any fool would know it, Baby!"

'Mara squeezed her mama's hand and set her eyes into the sunset. It was the red she would remember.

Next day when Benito drove the buckboard in with Mrs. Baxter and Mr. Thornton, everybody was surprised—probably Mrs. Baxter more than anybody else. A completely gentle woman, she spurned roughness in talking and in living habits. She did ride out with Mr. Thornton every day to hunt but she vowed she would never shoot to kill. If Mr. Thornton shot he never hit anything to eat. On Christmas Eve Willy saddled Pearl and went along with them. She killed deer and brought it home for food. Mrs. Baxter was horrified at the killing—but she enjoyed the meat.

Willy did the best she could for Christmas. Pat had ordered mescal from Laredo and some trinkets for the children. For dinner she barbecued the venison and took the eggs she had planned to set, to make chiles rellenos to go with the frijoles. For dessert she made molasses biscuits.

"My dear, how do you do it?" Mrs. Baxter said as she pushed back her chair. "All this dinner and not one servant to assist! I wonder if you realize you're married to a genius, Mr. Westall?"

"Well, I married her, I guess!" His southern pride flared hot. "We've tried to keep servants but they're hard to get. Of course we're on a lark now, but for regular livin' you'll have to do some work yourself when you spend your time out here."

"Who, me? Spend my time out here? My dear man, money couldn't hire me to live out here. All this sun and the snakes and wolves—away from human people! No, I'm too young yet for that."

Mr. Thornton reddened. "Yes, Mr. Westall, Mrs. Baxter told me yesterday that she didn't want to buy your land."

"Why, Horace!" Mrs. Baxter turned in wonder. "You know I've never had a notion of buying. You couldn't give me a place like this."

Willy was passing around the coffee. She almost dropped the pot. Mrs. Baxter looked up at her simply. "My dear, I've been wondering why you do it. You're so young and pretty yet. And these lovely children! You can't eat land, you know."

"I do it because I have to." Willy spoke too fast to think. "I just have to and I do it."

Then she realized what she had done. She turned her head so she wouldn't have to look at Pat.

When Mr. Thornton and Mrs. Baxter left, they promised to try to send a buyer for the ranch. In farewell Mr. Thornton presented Willy with his Winchester and six boxes of cartridges left over from the hunt. Mrs. Baxter gave her the divided khaki skirt she had used for riding and her Stetson hat.

"It's much more stylish than a bonnet. Now you're a ranch woman; it gives you class, makes you different."

Willy set the Stetson on her head. Mrs. Baxter clapped her hands. "You're simply lovely! You look like a curly-headed boy."

Willy gave the hat an extra yank and didn't even look in the glass. "It feels so good! Sits just right! Thanks a lot," she said.

For days Pat raved and swore at the dead beats. Willy wanted to shoot them and she would have, but they were gone. "It's for Pat," she kept thinking. "The children and I can stand it, but I'm not so sure he can. He loves crowds and lights and a host of close-up friends." To Pat she said, "We did enjoy their company. They made a break until Jim Nelson comes back. We ought not to sell but lease, just as he said we should. We might strike oil, you know. And we might make a fortune in the Rio Grande Valley."

"And we might die right here and nobody'd ever know it," Pat said back.

Often when Pat's mood was too deep to break, Willy made herself think about things to do. "At least I've got a hat. I'm all fixed up to ride." The Stetson sat squarely on her head. No wind could blow it off. The broad brim cut out the sun and glare. The divided skirt she cherished. It gave her a sense of freedom when she was astride Pearl—loose and easy, not crotch-binding like Pat's pants. The Winchester was light to carry, not heavy like her gun.

But when she did the riding she also had to think. She planned the store, recited Scripture, often prayed.

The words that came to haunt her were Mrs. Baxter's, at the table—"You can't eat land, you know."

"No, nor drink it either," she always had to add.

"I wonder why I do it!"

The answer came itself: "But what else can I do?"

10

The Westalls lived on the ranch far beyond their homesteading time. They spent all their five hundred borrowed dollars, ate up most of their food, and shot away all but a dozen cartridges. And still Jim Nelson did not come.

"Never got stuck in any damned spot before when I couldn't get aloose," Pat raged. "It's like sticking your hand in a lot of hot molasses. It's burning hell out of you but you can't let go." Pat kept on storming, but more and more he moped. Hours at a time he would sit looking straight into space ahead; then again he would peer anxiously to the south, jump up quickly and go to the gate as if to meet somebody.

"Dear God, he's seeing things!"

Willy guarded against seeing things herself. She remembered stories of people going crazy in open boats at sea. Often she found herself gazing south. The only difference in their looking was that hers was for Bill Lester. Somehow she felt more certainty in Bill Lester's coming than in Jim Nelson's. Maybe it was because he was young and strong and had helped her with the work. She knew he could perform; yet he'd promised nothing. Jim Nelson had.

Pat wrote letters to Goliad but no answers ever came. Benito inquired in Laredo every trip he made, but nobody had heard a word from the old rancher.

"He'll wander in one day. He's never reg'lar," the cattle trader said. The Kansas City broker spit and said, "Maybe he's dead. He's gettin' mighty old."

Benito brought these messages to Willy. She never

passed them on to Pat. She made up stories, invented tales. She had to keep his hope alive or he himself would die.

"Ask about Bill Lester," she told Benito.

"I do, Madama. Nobody know. About heem first I ask."

"And they call Mexicans an ignorant people," she said to Pat.

"Well, by God, they are," Pat said, never dreaming why she made the statement.

Willy said no more.

Willy slipped more of her four hundred dollars to Benito to bring groceries—just enough to keep up the race between life and time.

Then that summer came the drought. By March the mesquite grass was thwarted. April shriveled it, May parched it, and June blew it away. Cepriano and Benito looked at each other and shook their heads; Pat and Willy did not know what was coming, but the Mexicans did. The water tank dried up to a muddy bog. Benito rode over and took down the yard fence to stretch around the remaining loblolly to shut out the cattle. The little water left had to be conserved for human need. After that the stillness of space was punctured day and night by the anguished lowing of the thirsty cows.

Pat felt impelled to ride out and shoot them down. Old Cepriano said, "No, no, Señor. Eet ees de nopal! He ees vury good!" And Benito taught the Westalls the trick of singeing thorns off the cacti. Thus as the cattle ate, they drank, and fattened as they did so.

"It looks good enough to eat," Willy said one day as she stood before the mesquite fire just after sundown, holding a clump of the thorny plant on a long pitchfork above the flames. As the thorns sizzled in the fire, the thick green leaves oozed slimy juice. It did look good, and it smelled good too.

"Let me taste it, Mama," both children said at once.

"Don't say that!" Pat begged. "We may come to eatin' the damned stuff ourselves."

The wild, thirst-tortured cattle edged in from the

dark. They ventured close to the fire to bolt down the merciful food-and-drink hot from the pitchfork. The fierce longhorn pride subdued by need of body stunned Willy.

"Nature's playing a cruel trick," she said to Pat. "How different they were in the corral!"

Cows in a corral always brought back Bill Lester; Bill Lester brought back Jim Nelson; then wonder and despair clutched her heart. At such moments Willy concentrated on the work her hands were doing. The cactus itself intrigued Willy. What secret had it wrung from the desert? In the face of long drought, beating wind, and burning weather, how could it live and thrive to give not only beauty to the landscape but sustenance to the cattle? All other life the vast wasteland hated, twisted, tortured, tried to annihilate; but this one plant it cherished. It's as though the desert gives its very heart to the cactus and in turn the cactus beautifies its vastness. Nothing compares with the wonder of its design and the brilliance of its blossoms. And more than that, it proves that the desert has a heart. The love between the two won't let the cactus die. Spurning roots, it sustains itself by the power of its own being. Cut it down and pile it upside down, and it keeps on living, sending out new shoots to look up to the sun.

"It's like a love affair," Willy once said. "I'm glad I know about cactus. It proves a lot of things. It's like the sun too," she added.

Now the sun was Willy's great comfort. The set deliberation with which the huge ball of fire peeped up over the rim of the world and then, on schedule, traveled through the day, to duck down below the horizon at a precise moment, told her that there was a principle of some kind that man could follow if he could but find the rule. Methodically she watched the sunrise and sunset as a worshiper says his beads. Only from such meditation could she summon courage to fight back her growing fear. Willy hated fear in herself as most people hate sins in others. But how scared she was! In the last analysis she was afraid of death, perhaps, and all that goes before it: hunger, thirst, sickness, rot—the weakness of the spirit, the hope of human help.

"Why do I keep looking out across the prairie for Bill Lester? Because he's strong and I'm so tired," she admitted to herself.

As the drought clamped down in earnest, Pat said one afternoon, "Where'd Benito get that water he brought us in the barrel?"

"From the Gonzales' Ranch. They've an artesian well, but it's thirty miles away. In this heat I doubt if we can stand the trip." Of course she meant Pat could never stand it.

"Well, we've got to try it. I've got to have a drink. If I've got to die on this damned ranch I'm not going to die this thirsty, that's a cinch!"

"Let's stick it out a few more days." Willy thought of Hagar in the wilderness, her son dying, with a well right before her and she couldn't see it until the Lord opened her eyes.

"Wish I could open my eyes and see a windmill."

Then she gazed into the sunset, bright, extravagant in splendor.

How strong that sun was! Strong enough to perform its purpose no matter what the cost. Strong enough to kill them all. Strong enough—suddenly, she turned the thought back to herself. "That's all there is to it, after all—just strong enough! God, make me strong enough!" she said.

That night it rained.

About twelve o'clock Willy woke up choking from the heat. When she stepped out into the yard to get a breath of air, she saw a dark heavy cloud above her. A few minutes later a sharp clap of thunder, then a quick flash of lightning, and big drops of water splashing down. Suddenly a shower of hail danced before her on the ground. She had barely time to close the windows before the downpour came.

The noise woke Pat and the children. They seemed dazed.

"What's happening, Sweetheart?"

"It's raining! Look out at it! Just pouring down!" she almost shouted.

"And look, Serena's vomiting! My God!" Pat shouted too.

"She's all right. It's just electricity in the air." Willy couldn't pull herself away from the sight of water to hold Serena's head.

"Let me see, Mama!" It was Amara pulling at her skirt. Willy lifted the chubby body so that her nose could flatten against the windowpane in wonder.

"Yes, Baby, look! It's rain! Rain from heaven! Try never to forget that you have seen it."

11

The next day Jim Nelson came riding up in a buckboard. The rain brought him, he said. He offered no explanation for his long delay in coming. A deal's a deal with ranch people of Nelson's school. Time is not in the bargain. A man keeps his word, but he has to keep it when he can. Months or years don't matter. Time gets in such a mixture with the landscape that it can't be reckoned. "Patience is the price of Texas freedom," people often say.

Willy watched Pat and Jim Nelson under the portal, drinking coffee, inhaling the damp fresh morning air, transacting business.

"Last night death was stalking," she told herself. "Now life's gone into action."

"Have to take you into Laredo to sign up the papers, Pat. I know you folks want to get started down to the Rio Grande Valley, so we won't wait for no roundup. I'll give you five hundred dollars for the trip; then when we count up the cattle I'll send you the rest I owe you."

"Sure! Sure!" Pat said. "Suit yourself. No hurry. What's a cow more or less? We've got plenty of time and plenty of patience."

"Just as if nothing had ever happened," Willy said. Then she began to wonder if it really had.

"Maybe all this fear and waiting, all this thirst and hunger scare was just a dream, and I'm waking up. Well, it's the best way to think about it."

With that one statement she dismissed the past.

It was the future now that counted, the Rio Grande Valley, the general store they'd have. There was no question of where they'd go. The Rio Grande was a river; the Valley was its edge. They wanted water, plenty of water, and no distance in between. They'd go by wagon, the short cut through. They took that for granted without much talking. They owned the horses and the wagon but had little money. The trip to Laredo to catch the train to San Antonio, then down to the Valley, would make twice the distance. Jim Nelson said it would be foolish.

"Just pile your wife an' kids into the wagon an' strike out. You'll need the wagon an' the horses when you get there. Grand ride through the country this time of year," he said. The question of how to go was settled by that statement. They talked no more about it.

Willy hustled Pat and Jim Nelson off to Laredo with a list of things to buy for the trip. Cartridges, a wagon sheet and wagon bows, and an extra tarpaulin were the important items along with food.

As soon as they were alone, she hurried to the packing.

"What's wrong?" Serena asked.

"We're going on a trip."

"What trip?"

Willy stopped and thought a minute before she answered. "Couldn't do without you children to make me think. It's a journey we're taking. We're going to leave the ranch forever and go to the Valley of the Rio Grande."

"What's a Rio Grande?" Amara questioned. Mama's eyes were shining wildly. 'Mara couldn't get things straight, all this grab and snatch and hurry. Mama looked like some other person since the strange man came. Then he and Papa left.

"It's a river, Darling. There'll be plenty of water. You can make mud pies and bathe in a tub of water; you can even swim in water."

"What's swim, Mama?" S'rita's eyes began to dance. She grabbed her mama's skirt and began to swing.

Willy reached down and picked her up. "You'll love it, Honey, because it's action. You take off all your clothes and get into the water and splash and kick and sail along on top."

"But where's the water?"

"In the river, Lover! That's where we're going, to the Rio Grande and the Gulf!"

"Hurry, Mama, hurry!" S'rita said. "I wanna swim!" She grabbed her Mama's neck and kissed her cheeks and eyes. Amara jumped about and clapped her hands. Salita squealed.

"Let's get started on the trunk, then. It'll have to hold everything we take," Willy said as she set Serena on the floor.

"The trunk! The trunk!" both children shouted. Their greatest treat was for Mama to open the trunk. She seldom touched it. Today Mama seemed so different. She had never smiled at the trunk, but today she smiled and smiled.

Willy unlocked and opened the trunk. "I feel like an old Spanish pirate," she laughed. 'Mara and S'rita stood watching, wide-eyed, as she threw out in order to put in. The three satin wrappers had fallen to pieces, but the Eton jacket and the alpaca skirt retained their pristine firmness both in fabric and in line.

"Put 'em on, Mama," Amara begged, when she pulled out the crumpled angora hat bearing the mothy ostrich plume.

"Wish I could; but look, they're all too little now, especially in the waist." Willy laughed to keep back tears. The Oklahoma finery set up a train of memories that she'd practiced forgetting.

"Sure, they're too little now." She kept on talking, not to the children but to herself. "I hope I'm a nicer person than the one who used to wear those clothes."

"Who wore 'em, Mama?" Amara's eyes opened wide at her question.

"A woman who thought she held the world in the center of her hand."

"Did you like her?"

"I did then, sure. But not now. I wouldn't exchange places with her for the world."

"Did she have little girls like you, Mama?"

"No, Darling; that's what's made the difference."

Willy stopped her work to look closely at these children.

Amara hovered close, wondering at the things the trunk revealed. Serena had lost interest when all the things were out. Now she was over by the window singing a little tune to jumbled words: "Mama pretty-water swim," and a lot of others.

From the trunk-packing Willy hurried to the wagon preparation. They had a plain ranch wagon, not a prairie schooner such as we see in books. It was small but sturdy, ample for bed space, food, the trunk, and coal oil; with a wagon sheet stretched over bows on top. Benito rode over and together they nailed on a two-by-four extension to the first sideboard, thus affording a rest for bed slats to hold up springs and mattress for the feather bed. The space underneath the bed served to carry food and coal oil. Behind the wagon seat the trunk sat, and then the chuck box on behind, with two water barrels.

"Que bonito," Benito gleamed when they were finished.

"Good enough for anybody," Willy smiled. "With the wagon sheet and extra tarpaulin we'll be set to go. Not like the regular covered-wagon travelers back in the old days, but nobody can expect that since these aren't covered-wagon times."

"You go to what plaze, Madama? The train she ees not there?"

"From another angle, yes, Benito, but not from here. By making a short cut to the river we can save time and money both. Of course we would be in one place and head out somewhere else where there's no railroad! That's been our luck these past few years."

"Pero Dios les guarda, Madama."

"Of course God will protect us. I'm not complaining. I'm looking forward to the trip. For the children to pioneer in a covered wagon may someday go in a book."

Willy hurried with the getting ready, for she expected Pat home in five days. But it was fourteen before he and Jim Nelson reeled into the house, still drunk both with whisky and with dreams.

"Hell of a time gettin' things straightened out, Sweetheart." Pat held his breath and kissed Willy on the cheek.

She made black coffee to sober up the men, then went out to the buckboard to unload while they swaggered over coffee cups. She found the wagon sheet and bows, the tarpaulin, and all the groceries, but not the Winchester cartridges she had ordered.

"Dear God," she said, "how can we take the trip without ammunition!"

When the coffee had had time to take effect, she went to Pat to find out what had happened.

"Well, I'll be damned! I forgot the cartridges," he said. Then his eyes brightened, "But I brought you and the children a little gift."

He rumbled in his pockets and produced a bottle of *Mary Garden* perfume and a box of candy. Something of the old Pat was shining in his eyes. Willy took the package and the bottle and stood there gazing at her man. She wanted to laugh and cry at once. The trip and all the detailed danger of such a journey—coyotes, panthers, robbers maybe, game to kill for food. Then Pat's ridiculous abandon of all their worries; the months and years dissolved in drink! She threw her arms around his neck and kissed him on the mouth. Then she left the room. She had to get alone to memorize the moment.

"A Patrick Westall moment—the kind you don't forget! How could I help but love him? Who wouldn't, no matter what he does. Just five hundred dollars gives him back his grip. He forgets his bullets but not the perfume and the candy."

She managed to get out by the cabrito corral before she began to cry.

"Crying for joy doesn't count," she said. But she shook strangely. When she blew her nose, she felt a tugging at her skirt. It was 'Mara.

"Why are you crying, Mama?"

Willy lifted up the child. Her eyes were big and sad. "Becáuse I'm so happy today, my baby."

The next moment they heard a squeal and a yelp; then Willy, 'Mara, S'rita, all of them, sprawled out flat. It took Willy a minute to realize what had happened. Evidently S'rita had tired of whatever she was doing and decided to take a ride on the javelina. In desperation the little pig headed for Willy's skirt and knocked her down. Now they all together scrambled on the ground.

"My babies!" Willy laughed. "My beautiful little sunbeam! My comforting little sunshade! And my pretty little pig!"

"I didn't mean to," S'rita was sobbing. She flung herself into her mama's arms and hid her face.

For a moment Willy lay there on the ground, letting her body rest against the warm earth as she looked up at the sun.

It took Pat a week to rest up from his drunk, but it proved to be a happy week for Willy. Pat had money in his pocket and a ground-floor deal hatching in his heart. Willy saw dreams shining through his eyes.

"Lots of talk in Laredo, Sweetheart, about the Valley. It must be the richest country in the world. Folks're pickin' money off of trees down there, they say. Anything on earth will grow with that irrigation system. Met that feller Peterson again. He told me last year his railroad handled two hundred and fifty cars of homeseekers, from everywhere on earth! All wantin' to farm th' land. We'll put in a general store an' make a killin' sure!"

"Did you get any information on the trip?" Willy's first impulse was the necessity of getting there.

"Sure! There's two ways to go from here. One is to

hit straight down south for the river and follow it. That's what Bill Lester said to do."

"Bill Lester? Did you see him?" The question asked itself.

"Sure; met him at the bar." Pat's eyes sulked for a moment; then brightened. "The other way is to go straight through. That's closer. Nelson thinks we can make a ranch a day. There's a lot of 'em to pass."

Willy tried to say something casual to disguise her face. She felt ashamed of the pounding in her chest. "It's just that we've been so much alone here with nobody coming by," she argued to herself. Then she turned to Pat with a conscious frown upon her face. "But how about the water on the way?"

"We'll take some with us; then fill up at the ranches."

She frowned some more before she spoke. She was thinking. If Bill Lester saw Pat in Laredo and suggested the river route, he might be on the lookout and join them for the trip. Suddenly she saw Bill's muscles bulge in his arms as he chopped mesquite poles for the corral. She saw his light swing into the saddle, the pistol in the holster on his hip, the Winchester strapped tight, and his cartridge belt.

"It would be nice to have him ride along beside the wagon. He could keep a lookout far ahead and find a way for us to travel. Pat will get so tired and the children are too little," she thought.

Suddenly she felt afraid about the trip—tired, washed-out, feeble. Another lonely vigil—this time in motion. She needed human help for this next step. She turned to Pat. "I think, Darling, we'd better take the river route like Bill Lester said."

The minute she spoke she knew her plan was lost. If she had just not said Bill Lester. "Like my engagement ring," she thought. "He'd rather see us starve—or thinks he would."

Pat's eyes flashed. "Hell, no! That's damned foolish. We've got to make up all the time we can. We'll take the ranch route an' get there twice as quick."

Willy didn't argue. She had made her own defeat.

Now she had to face it. She knew Patrick Westall and she knew herself. She would make out somehow on the journey—make out, as she always had.

She set to nailing up windows and getting the last things ready for the trip. Jim Nelson was to send the furniture when they got settled. In the meantime Benito would keep watch. "Until his whiskers are long and gray, if Jim Nelson shows his usual speed in business action," Willy told Pat.

"Fine man! Fine man!" Pat said.

"Yes, when you've read a page, you've got to turn it to read on."

"What's that you said?" Pat sat up straight and asked.

Willy smiled. "Oh, nothing of importance. I'm just thinking. I've studied this ranch lesson long enough; I want to be promoted to whatever is to come next."

The "whatever" proved a man-sized challenge.

The morning the Westalls left the ranch Willy got up at four o'clock. She dressed herself in her riding skirt and Pat's old shirt. The wagon had been packed the night before, but there were a lot of little things she felt she had to do so they could be riding out the gate just at sunrise.

"It's such a pretty time to start," she said. "Serena pushed her curly head into the world just as the sun rose."

But by the time she had breakfast cooked and served, the chuck box packed, the horses hitched into the traces, Salita and the children in the wagon with Pat sitting on the seat, whip flaunting in the air to accentuate the "Ándele" he had learned to use, the departure was delayed.

Pearl refused to lead. With a rope around her neck tied to the wagon she turned bronc, reared, snorted, and broke loose.

No amount of shoulder patting and nose rubbing could quiet the wildness in the filly's eyes.

"She seems insulted. What can be the matter?" Willy said.

"It's blood. She's a Mexkin horse. Can't depend on

Mexkins. Just leave her here. Don't need her now. The Torres can have her when they come to get the burra," Pat replied.

"Not Pearl! We'll let her follow. I don't blame her for not wanting to be tied. It was my fault to begin with, to insult her so."

At that moment Benito rode up to bid adiós to the Americanos. Willy forgot her sunrise plans as she gave the Mexican his last directions about the care of things, lingering as she did so.

"Hurry up, Sweetheart," Pat shouted. "The sun's up and gettin' hot as hell."

As Willy took Benito's hand to say good-by, the boy dropped his smoldering eyes to hide the tears. Willy didn't try to hide her own.

"What a friend you've proved, Benito! You and all the Torres family!" Amara's birth came to mind, the barrel of water, the many simple gifts and humble services never once forgotten.

Then she looked up at the house, a little box unpainted one-room and lean-to, sitting out upon the eye's scope of prairie like a tiny nose upon a giant's face. Not much to look at, but it had held so much of Willy. Ecstasy with Pat in loving—Amara's entrance into the world—the mad-dog bite—Bill Lester's and Jim Nelson's coming—snakes—tarantulas—thirst—rain!

"Watch the house, Benito. Now that it's time to go, I hate to leave it." She blew her nose.

"Sí, Madama, sí," the boy gulped.

"I guess if I spent time in prison I'd cry at parting. God bless you, Benito, good-by." She put on her Stetson and pulled it down firmly on her head.

"Vaya con Dios y las santas en el cielo, Madama," he murmured.

Willy wanted to kiss him, but Pat was watching. She gave one firm squeeze to his hand. Then with her foot on the wheel hub, she hoisted herself aboard.

Pat cracked the whip and shouted "Ándele" to Sal and Pito. Pearl snorted and dashed out through the gate.

"Look, she's going to lead us instead of follow," he exclaimed.

Willy didn't look back at Benito or the house.

Never look back; look straight up instead.

12

The first day all went well. There was no road to follow, but the direction was very clear. They moved straight south to the Palito Negro ranch. Benito had told them all about old Manuel and young Carlos who was now in charge. They should get there before dark. But they didn't.

They arrived the second day. The sun was hot and glaring. By mid-morning Pat handed Willy the reins and lay back on the bed to rest his eyes and leg. The children climbed up on the seat with Mama, but soon Amara's eyes began to water.

"Never knew that brush arbor was so shady," Pat called up. "Come on back here with Papa, Sugar, and let's go to sleep. S'rita an' Mama're the horsewomen in the family."

S'rita jerked off her bonnet and slung it overboard just to show 'Mara how she spurned the sun. Her eyes didn't water. Willy had to stop and get the bonnet. For punishment she made S'rita get back on the feather bed with Pat and 'Mara. S'rita cried, and in the scramble kicked Salita on the head. Willy took the little javelina up front in the seat and kept on driving. But Pat and the children kept up an awful fuss behind.

"It's too close quarters," Pat shouted. "Let's stop and eat and rest. S'rita needs to run."

But Willy drove on until noon. When she stopped, S'rita and the javelina took off through the brush after a long-eared jack rabbit. Amara's eyes still watered. She stayed in the wagon. Willy unhitched and fed the horses. Before she started cooking, she gave Pearl a piece of bread. Pat sighed and stretched on the feather bed.

"Call me when it's ready," he called to Willy. "S'rita's tromped me; I need to rest."

Willy built a fire and let it burn to coals to heap under the Dutch oven to bake the biscuits. The chuck-box lid served as a kitchen table. Willy mixed the bread and pinched off the biscuits. That day they had plenty to go with biscuits: beans, molasses, butter even. But Willy couldn't help wondering about the days to come. She couldn't kill a rabbit even. Her cartridges were too scarce.

After they had eaten, the children went to sleep on the bed; so did Pat.

"We'll have to take out nap time every day," Willy thought. "It'll slow us up a lot, but they can't stand a day of steady riding. It's too hot and hard."

Willy sat underneath the wagon. She meant to read the Bible. She had it in her hand. It had been so long since she had had a chance to read. But instead she looked out at the chaparral—scrub mesquite, huisache, ceniza, cactus in profusion but sparsely spaced so as not to crowd. No road was necessary. The horses turned here and there to dodge a cactus and kept on going.

"Room and freedom," she said. "This wagon is the only wall we have and the only shade as well," she added. "I'm going to build myself a wall to lean on and a top to shade me, with a lot of things inside. My store will be the prettiest one in the Rio Grande Valley."

Pearl nickered, pushing her head underneath the wagon. Willy reached and patted her on the neck.

"It's been worth the ranch experience just to know you," she said. "Living in Oklahoma City I never would have known a horse close-up. Prince stomped in his stable to pull a buggy down the street. You've never even worn a shoe. You're a prairie-mustang, but your closeness to me is almost like a bare foot in my hand."

As Willy opened her mother's Bible she liked having Pearl there with her. Somehow it was as though she were a little girl again. The book was old and tattered, thumb-worn and often marked. Willy's first faint remembrance was of her mother reading verses while she stood close by to listen to the favorites. Now the old Bible seemed to remember what they were. It seemed to want to open in one special place. She read aloud:

"And I will send my angel before thee to lead thee into the place which I have prepared for thee and will cast out the enemy before thee."

"What does it mean, Mama?" Willy looked up. Amara was standing there. It seemed silly to sleep all cooped up with Papa and S'rita in the wagon if Mama didn't. When S'rita kicked and tumbled in her sleep, 'Mara woke up and crawled down to Mama.

"It means that God will take care of us, Honey."

"And will He?"

"Why, certainly. He's got to, remember that."

S'rita woke up worse than frisky.

"Let her drive," Pat said. "That'll keep her happy. The horses need no direction; they just do the best they can, ducking mesquite and cactus bushes."

S'rita took quickly to her task. She swirled the whip and shouted. The horses meandered on as best they could, but S'rita was occupied, and good.

Pat tied his handkerchief around Amara's eyes to rest them from the glare. She lay back on the bed with the javelina. Pat sat up front with Willy and S'rita.

They drove until almost dark before they stopped to camp.

"Oughta drive at night," Pat said. "It's too damn hot in daytime."

"We would maybe if there was a road to follow, but the horses couldn't find their way around the cactus in the dark. There's no shade, anyway; still or moving."

"God, no; look at me! I'm blistered; so are the children. That white wagon sheet just doesn't keep out sun."

Pat looked closely at Willy's face. "But you're not, Sweetheart. What in the hell's the difference?"

"It's riding Pearl. I'm toughened up."

Pat frowned and stopped talking.

Willy hurried on with supper. They were all tired. Soon after dark they went to bed. Pat slept on the canvas cot underneath the wagon. That spared him the pain of getting in and out. Willy and the children occupied the bed.

Before sunup the next morning they were on their way while it was cool. "We'll get to Palito Negro by noon and rest some under an arbor," Pat said.

But they didn't. They kept traveling; no ranch house came into view. They ate dinner and took naptime in the open. Pat woke up cross; so did S'rita. They started out again. "Should have known we couldn't get anywhere in this kind of a contraption. Should have gone into Laredo so we could take the train. Damn the cost! When you're headin' in a new direction you can't take time to count up the price of things."

Willy didn't answer. She set to thinking about the price of things in general, money in particular. Five hundred dollars in Pat's pocket gave him control, set up the old standard in his heart just as the dollars sewed into her petticoat gave her insurance against hydrophobia or snakebite for the children. She marveled at the power the money seemed to give, the fear it dissipated. She began to think through her plans and arrange details. For months the hopelessness of the ranch vigil had over-ridden the store idea in her head. At the last she had grown afraid to plan, superstitious almost of her hope of liberation. Now they were on their way, with dollars in their pockets. She began to build the store.

Pat sat there sulking, snorting sometimes like a horse. She tried to make him talk.

"Do you think we should buy a show case now or wait awhile for that? Since the country's new, a general store ought to be best; but of course groceries're safer. Everybody has to eat. The investment wouldn't be so big."

Pat paid no attention. "Never will get there at the rate we're goin' now! Sweetheart, why in God's name did you let us start out in a wagon?" His face wrinkled into a frown and his eyes squinted at the sun.

"We'll need the wagon when we get there, Darling. We don't know exactly where we're going yet!" Her voice was soothing, easy and relaxed. "But let's not get impatient. We're on the go now, and let's enjoy the trip. I've always loved December. 'Mara came to us in December."

"Did I, Mama?" The little black braids tickled Willy's neck as the child edged over from the back and kissed her on the chin.

Just then Pearl nickered and trotted out in front. S'rita dropped the reins and began scrambling down from the seat. Pat caught her dress and held her.

"S'rita, Sugar, what're you tryin' to do?" Pat's frown faded.

"Wanna ride Pearl, Papa."

"Well, by God, you can. We're just crawlin' as it is." He let go her dress.

"No, Darling, the heat would kill her." Willy had to interrupt. "She hates to wear her bonnet and the sun's too hot."

"Yeah, I guess so." The frown wrinkled up again. He grabbed S'rita's hand and pulled her back into the wagon. He fixed his eyes on the flat space before him.

S'rita scrambled back onto the bed, sobbing. Amara's eyes widened in concern when she looked up at her mama. Willy saw the shadow.

"See how pretty the country is, Honey." She smiled broadly when she said it and looked down so 'Mara could see the smile. "How that rain did help! The ebony is greener than I've ever seen it. And the yucca and huisache. I love the gray of the ceniza in the sunlight."

"Looks like a lot of scrub mesquite to me," Pat growled.

Amara looked up at her papa. His face was cross and ugly. She moved over very close to Mama.

S'rita cried herself to sleep back on the bed. Salita cuddled close, sniffing the air in nervous javelina jerks.

They sighted the Palito Negro just at sundown.

They saw the windmill first. It was whirling in the wind. Don Carlos himself rode out to greet them and escort them in.

The ranch was a little dreary. Since old Manuel's death the ranch house proper had fallen down. Carlos kept only the bunkhouse in repair, but all of it he presented to his guests for their entertainment. The vaqueros vanished into the monte. Only Carlos remained as host. He made excuses that his wife was in San Antonio to see her mother.

His cook served broiled cabrito for supper, frijoles, black coffee, and mescal. After three drinks Pat's mood lightened. He started asking questions about the ranches. They could make the Santa Ana by two days' travel, the Laguna by one more perhaps. Culita was next, then Vacado—he kept on naming them at random.

Willy heard water falling and splashing. She and the children went to find it. The water tank was running over as the windmill sailed around and around. The little girls stood awe-struck. They couldn't believe what they were seeing.

"Is it a river, Mama!" 'Mara asked.

"No, Honey, but just as wonderful when you come to think about it. The water comes up from a deep well in the ground."

"Can I swim?" S'rita ventured, a little bit afraid her mama would say yes. The water scared her really. It was so wet and cold, and splashed so loudly.

But when she was undressed and underneath the falling water she loved it, and whooped and screamed like 'Mara. Willy got soap and washed their hair and rinsed out their petticoats and drawers. When the children were in bed and Don Carlos had gone off for the night, she and Pat stripped off and stood underneath the tank.

"By God, I'd forgot how water felt," Pat said, soaping himself from head to foot.

Willy stepped over close to brace him to keep him from falling as he washed his hair.

"An' how pretty you are naked, Sweetheart. You look just like a kid." He pinched her on the hip.

Pearl snorted.

Pat and Willy turned and looked. They saw two tiny fire-lights in the cactus hedge close by.

"Cigarettes," Willy whispered. "It's the vaqueros; they're sleeping out so we can have their house."

Pat and Willy grabbed and snatched at clothes and got inside the house. It was a night of sweet closeness for them both. They were bathed and fed and housed with friends. As they lay stretched out in each other's arms, they planned the store, the children's future, and their lives.

When they left, the next morning, Don Carlos presented them with seven eggs, a yellow squash, a cake of goat cheese, a chicken, a leg of cabrito, a morral of chiles, onions and garlic, and a jarra of meelk for th' cheeldreen.

"Shall we ask him for cartridges?" Willy said to Pat.

"Not after all of this, my God. We don't need cartridges. We've got enough."

Don Carlos bade them good-by with great profusion, with God's blessings and all that.

"I wonder why Mexicans are so kind," Willy said when they were out of earshot. "Can't beat ranch Mexkins when it comes to goodness." She almost added, "Just like Bill Lester said."

Pat must have caught the thought. His face flared red and hot. "Hell, it's just because he saw you naked. Any man would give a lot for that."

The Santa Ana Ranch welcome was as hearty as the Palito Negro's. The only difference was a woman as a hostess. Doña Dolores' husband had died years before. He was a Scotchman named McNeil. The ranch was hers through the Martinez family. The porcion had been granted them by Cortez. The house was adobe, rambling in a crooked L. The Doña was surrounded by her children—sons, daughters, and grandchildren.

They all stood off and gazed at S'rita's hair, then came close and touched it.

"Stay long time," the old lady urged Pat and Willy. "We love th' cheeldreen."

"But we're in a hurry," Pat said. "We're hittin' for the Rio Grande Valley and the irrigation boom. We've got to get there."

The old Mexican shook her head.

But they did stay two days to wash their clothes and rest. Pat was looking peaked, Willy noticed. The wagon cramped his leg; the heat was sapping his strength. S'rita paled a little. She missed her burra milk and her exercise, but she made up for lost time with the little Mexicans. They played all kinds of running games. S'rita bossed them. 'Mara lagged along as best she could, but with so much competition she preferred to stay with Mama.

The morning they left the Santa Ana, S'rita cried. Doña Dolores filled the chuck box full of everything, begging Willy, as she did so, to leave th' cheeldreen weeth her. Such a journey was too hot and long to take them in a wagon; and Willy really wished she could leave them; but she couldn't. She didn't know why she couldn't, but she couldn't; that was all.

"When we have children we keep them with us, good or bad, rich or poor," she said. "We couldn't leave them—could we?" She turned to Pat.

"Hell, no!" he shouted, and whipped the horses to a trot.

The Mexican stood there waving. 'Mara and S'rita shouted back.

"It's funny, I don't want to leave, myself. Doña Dolores was kind of like a mother," Willy said to Pat.

"Just a Mexkin. Don't be a fool," he said.

The Laguna Ranch they never found. Maybe they passed it. They could have if there was no windmill, for the chaparral was very flat.

"But there has to be a windmill," Pat kept on saying. "You can't have a ranch without a windmill."

Willy didn't say, "We didn't"—she just kept on looking.

They camped out four nights straight, grew hotter

and dirtier by the day—and thirstier, for they were forced to cut down on the water.

On the morning of the eighth day real trouble started. Suddenly they drove out of the chaparral into white dunes of rolling sand.

"Well, I'll be goddamned!" Pat exclaimed.

Willy jumped out to take a look around. All she could see was an expanse of whiteness north, south, east, and west.

"Did Jim Nelson mention sand?" she said to Pat.

"Hell, no!" he snapped. "Nor any of these Mexkin ranchers."

"Do you suppose there can be much of it?"

"How in God's world do I know?"

"Ought we to turn around and go back?"

"Back where?"

Pat raised the whip to hit the horses. They lunged and snorted. The wagon wheels cut down into the sand. The horses heaved forward in the traces to pull the wheels along in twenty-minute stretches; then they had to rest. Willy knew she had to lessen weight. She saddled Pearl and put the children on her; then she bogged along herself. Pat cursed and lashed the whip. S'rita laughed and shouted. At last Mama had let her ride on Pearl. But 'Mara's eyes began to water.

Willy gave her Stetson an extra yank to hide her face so she could think. Pat and the children must never know the pounding in her chest.

"I'm plainly scared," she admitted quietly; then went on to think what to do about it. How could this happen! Didn't Jim Nelson know the country? Bill Lester had said to take the river route. He knew about the sand. But no old rancher would mislead any man, to say nothing of a woman and little children in the deal. They'd missed the way, no doubt. But the question was, could they make it through? Without ranches and without water they'd never reach the Rio Grande; they'd starve right in the desert. There would be nothing to kill to eat, nothing to drink. This rate of speed would never get them to the end. Pat would die first. He couldn't stand the torture; then Serena, most likely.

"I hope Amara next; I'd hate to go first and leave her!"

The sound of her voice checked her back to reason. If it would only rain. Willy did not look up at the sun lest she see a face leering, laughing at her like the sirens luring men to death.

"And I've loved the sun," she said, then frowned and gritted her teeth a bit. She began saying the multiplication tables. She added and subtracted, divided and multiplied, to mark off hours and miles.

The day wore on.

The sun beat down in fury as she struggled through the sand. The light blazed through her brain. She could hear the horses breathing and she could hear herself. Pat looked like a wild man as he cursed and lashed the team.

"Don't do that, Darling," she spoke before she thought. "You've got to let them rest."

"Well, by God, I do!" His voice was full of tears.

"Yes, Darling," was all she said. There was nothing else she could say or think of. She knew he didn't mean to hurt the horses or to urge them beyond their strength. It was just that he was frantic and knew nothing else to do.

And she didn't either, except perhaps to cry.

"I'll have to do something in a minute," she thought, every step she took. "Then maybe I can think of something else."

Her face burned; sand sifted in her shoe tops; her eyes scorched holes straight through her head. Hagar in the Wilderness came back from Sunday-school days.

"And I thought I understood! Understood?"

Her shoulders drooped, but she lifted up her head. When she raised it, she saw a man rise on the sky line just as if he'd come from air.

"A mirage," she thought. "Or am I going crazy?"

She jerked off her hat and held it out in front to shade her eyes to look. The man was riding on a horse. She shut her eyes tight to clear her vision. When she opened them, he was riding toward them.

"Look, Darling," she called up to Pat.

"My God, it's a man," he cried, pointing straight ahead.

Willy's mind did a lot of funny things before the man got up close enough to see. Could it be Bill Lester? He knew they were on their way. Pat had told him in Laredo. Could he be riding out to help them? He surely knew about the sand. Why he would come she did not reason. She just expected him because she was in need.

But it was Señor Longoria from the Rancho Seco. He sighted them from a distance and knew they needed help to get through the sand.

"The wheel," he said as he rode up close. "Eet ees too theen."

"Well, somethin's awful goddamned wrong!" Pat's face was tense and grim. "Jim Nelson never said a word about this sand and neither did the Mexkin ranchers we have seen."

"Oh, Señor Jeem Nelson?" The Mexican smiled and shrugged his shoulders. "He never come theese way. He always say he weel to veset me. He go by the reever to see Señor Hall."

"The sonuvabitch!" Pat scowled and cracked the whip he held. The horses paid no attention. They stood heaving. Their sweat dripped on the sand, making little balls roll up and bounce again.

The Mexican hitched his horse in, as a lead, to the wagon tongue. He and Willy walked behind to push.

Just at sundown they limped into the Rancho Seco.

Willy never forgot the welcome of that jacal. There were four jacales, made of adobe, thatch-roofed, grouped around a patio, cool and fresh and green with jasmine bushes and a lemon tree with a parrot perched up on a limb. Towering high above waved a windmill pumping water.

The Señora and her seven children came out to greet them in.

"Mí familia," the Mexican proudly smiled.

The Americanos were given a whole house for sleeping quarters: one room, dirt-floored, pink-plastered, showing the hand pats of its makers. It was furnished with an iron bed that bore a coverlet of hand drawnwork in the Mexican style.

At supper they all drew up around a table under the cool thatch of the patio. Two servants padded back and forth from the open-fire brasero to serve beef ribs broiled, tortillas with frijoles, and boiled milk for all the children. It was the kind of occasion that writes itself into the heart.

"This is like church," Willy kept thinking as she ate. "Food for our stomachs, oil for our feet, pillows for all our heads, in Bible language; in ours, just Texas ranch-welcome."

Before supper ended Willy liked the whole Longoria family, but it was the wife who picked up her interest most: young, pretty, contented, the mother of seven children, with another on its way.

She sat in the cool of the patio, adored by all the family, waited on by two criadas, pillowing a baby at her bosom, another close to her knee. "That's motherhood in principle; Eve with the blessing of God," Willy kept thinking. But there was an addition to the sentence that she could never put into words. Was it worth the price it cost the Señora? She couldn't answer.

Willy fell into the starched bed that night prepared to cry—she had wanted to cry all day. But she didn't. All she could do was think of the Mexican woman. What did the woman have that she, Willy, envied? Really nothing more than she herself possessed. The only advantage was that her husband owned a windmill and walked on both his legs. But she dwelt in the same desolation, the same encompassing space. The torture that she had suffered seemed to bless this dark pretty creature. Her very home and household sprouted from the hot white sand as the bright cactus flower from the heart of its juicy plant. It fitted; it belonged to the landscape; while her little ranch house had stuck like a scab on a sore. This woman was happy, contented to live always in the midst of the desert. Did she ignore it? Or did she know she lived just in sand?

"Does she think?" Willy wondered. "I wish I didn't. Why do I fight the things that this woman loves."

Were the children the consideration? Was it a better place for them? But as she kept on thinking, she began to wonder what she was seeking? What more could she wish for her daughters than she saw in the Mexican's eyes? Was it blood?

Then she thought of Benito and the Torres family and their years of kindness and care; so alike in essentials but so far removed in approach.

"Yes, it's a Mexkin country—Bill Lester is always right. But our children? What crossbreeds in thinking! What can we expect from them?"

13

The Westalls stayed two days with the Longorias, to rest up and wash their clothes. The Señor exchanged the wagon wheels for broad heavy tires to pull them through the sand. All rancheros carried two sets when they'd have to hit the sand, he told them. He stocked them with food and water, but he had no cartridges to lend. This time Willy asked for them herself.

"Can we make it?" Pat questioned. "I wanna know before we start."

"Sí Señor, cómo no?" The Mexican shrugged his shoulders.

So they headed out again.

The journey was slow and wearing. The wind and sand and sun took heavy toll. The wagon went along, but there was still no road to follow, just the direction south across sand dunes in the distance. Once off their course, they couldn't hope to hit many ranches until they got back on again; but they kept a sharp lookout for windmills.

Every day they said, "If it would only rain!"

But it didn't. Days passed. They kept on camping out.

They cut down on food and water rations. Pat fell into silence; Serena fussed and cried. She hated the stinky wagon. She wanted to run and play. Her hair smelled funny; her dress was dirty; her stomach hurt inside.

Willy saw Serena drooping. She didn't want to drive; she wouldn't eat; she crawled off into a corner of the wagon by herself. Willy knew they had to hurry.

"If there were just a road so we could be sure we're going in the right direction," she kept saying to herself. "Some outline, some designation, something more to follow than the sun. Maybe we're just wandering. Maybe there is no place to go to. Maybe we're in hell going round and round in circles."

The sun shone on, quiet, hot, blinding in the sky. Sometimes it went into that phenomenon know as drawing water, but it never rained. Willy found herself wondering if the Great Power behind such glory had any knowledge of individual people and their needs. By force of will she made herself think back to shelves and counters, grocery bills and money drawers; but day by day the store-picture faded into dimness and moved very far away.

It was Pat who first sickened and began to vomit. He did it every day at noon.

"It's the sowbelly that's got my stomach. I need beefsteak, somethin' different from these goddamned beans." Then he added, "S'rita and I can't take it like you and 'Mara. Haven't got the guts."

That day Willy shot one cartridge at a rabbit. She almost missed it, but it ran a little way, then fell. S'rita scampered off to get it and ran back with it by the ears.

"Looks like a mule," Pat said. "Never saw a jack rabbit with such long ears."

"They are lovely," Willy answered. "They're thin like paper; look at the pretty veins."

She took the rabbit from Serena and walked a long way off to skin it so Pat wouldn't have to see the blood. It made her sick herself. Jack rabbit is not good for eating. The meat is tough and coarse. But she was glad to get it. It was the first live thing they'd seen for days.

"Maybe it's a good sign," she said to 'Mara, who held the feet while Willy skinned. "We must be getting close now to the chaparral."

"And the river, Mama?"

"Of course, the river."

"When will it be?"

"Maybe tomorrow." She always said tomorrow. The children asked her every day.

She broiled the rabbit for their supper. Pat and S'rita ate a little. Amara gobbled. Willy ate none of it herself. She couldn't somehow. She saw the buck and doe at water; she felt vicious, murderous.

"It needs more salt," Pat grumbled.

"Yes, I put just a little. Salt makes us thirsty."

Pearl edged up very close. S'rita handed her a piece of hoe-cake. The mare nickered softly.

"I know you want water," Willy said. "So do poor Sal and Pito. We've had to be so stingy." She reached up and stroked Pearl's mane. "Maybe tomorrow we'll hit a ranch."

"Or die from sunstroke," Pat corrected.

Willy frowned a little. "The children, Darling."

Pat looked down quickly.

She scraped the dishes. She never washed them. The campfire flickered. She saw Pat's face. He clutched S'rita in his arms. Her little hands patted his cheeks very fast. Willy saw her reach up and kiss his eyes.

"God! God!" she whispered.

A coyote howled. Another answered. Pat shivered. She knew they scared him. They scared her too. Always coyotes had been a chorus in the distance. Now they came in close, to bark.

"They know we're down and out," she thought.

That night she heard a scream. Half waking, she thought for a moment it was a woman. Then she sat up and listened. It was a panther. Quickly Pat scrambled into the wagon from his cot. 'Mara and S'rita squirmed over close to Mama. Even the javelina cringed and cried.

"I saw his eyes." Pat was trembling. "He was close enough to touch." Then he shouted, "You can't fight a lion! You got to shoot him."

"Yes, yes, of course; if you can, Darling." Willy kissed Pat's cheek and settled the children back in bed.

They moved over to make room for Papa. Willy put Salita on the seat and tucked Pat into her place at the foot.

Willy didn't sleep that night. They were all too crowded in the bed and it was hot. She got up on the seat with the javelina. The pig snuggled close. Willy picked up the shotgun. She hesitated before she broke it down.

"Must I count the cartridges? We're scared enough already," she thought flatly.

But she broke it. Both barrels showed empty. She took the Winchester and worked the lever. Two shells fell out—just two; that was all they had between them and the Rio Grande Valley. Two cartridges swam crazily before her eyes. They were mixed up with the dollars in her skirt.

"And I wished for money," hammered at her head. "What I need is ammunition!"

Ammunition! Ammunition! Ammunition! The whole wagon began to whirl. The word began to sing.

"I'm getting fainty!" She crawled outside to get a breath of air.

Pearl lay near the wagon. At Willy's moving she got up and nickered softly.

"Thanks," Willy said as she touched the strong, warm shoulder.

She began to remember stories of fighting tactics of hard-hoofed animals stomping things to death.

"You'd do it for me in a pinch."

The mare's shoulder was just high enough for her to lean on. Pictures came and went. Sugarland—empty shotguns—satin wrappers—Serena sick—greenish water—Pat's tired eyes—Amara's birth—groceries gone —Benito Torres—little Pope—Adelaide—Aunt Ann and Mr. Dunbar—Dr. Riley—two cartridges—coffins —death! Bill Lester!

When she was finished crying, she felt better. When she looked up, day was breaking.

Light brought sanity and facts. She tired to smile. But S'rita woke up sick.

"I wanna throw up," she cried.

"It's that damned rabbit and all the sand that's in it," Pat bellowed, holding S'rita's head to vomit.

Willy didn't answer. Instead she looked up at the sun. It was rising hot and bright. The white sand gleamed in radiance; not a shadow was in sight. She hurried on to hitching up the horses to the wagon. When she took off Sal and Pito's hobbles, they didn't even snort.

"Are they thirsty?" 'Mara asked. She was doing her best to hitch the trace chains. She tried always to help Mama at anything she did. Low things like trace chains were such a comfort, for she could reach them. She was sorry she'd asked the question, for Mama's eyes began to shine almost as if she were crying; but of course Mama never cried. She asked about the horses because she herself was thirsty. She felt sorry for Sal and Pito. They pulled the wagon. Papa shouted. They breathed so loud. Pearl was different. She just followed or went ahead. Pearl was fat yet; no bones were showing. She could see Sal and Pito's ribs.

"Not very thirsty," Willy answered quickly. She stooped down and drew 'Mara to her.

"Are you? Tell me!"

"What, Mama?" She cringed a little. Mama looked so funny.

"Are you very thirsty, Honey?"

"No, Mama, honest I'm not thirsty." She wanted to cry, but she knew she mustn't. Something in her mama's face wouldn't let her.

"Do your eyes hurt much?"

"No, ma'm; honest they don't hurt." 'Mara bit her lip and reached for Mama's hand.

Willy put her arms around her and squeezed her very tight.

"Thank you," was all she said.

They got going very quickly.

"S'rita's too sick to travel," Pat argued.

"We must keep moving, Darling. Every time the wagon wheels turn over we're that much nearer the Rio Grande Valley and milk for her to drink. I've seen her drooping. She can't stand the roughness like Amara."

"No, by God, she's too fine bred. She's born for silk petticoats and diamonds, not goat stink and brain-baking, her skin all roughened up and blistered."

Willy's hand was on the dashboard; she was getting in the wagon. Pat looked down and saw it—brown, calloused, horny almost like a cowboy's, and it wore his wedding ring. How it gripped that dashboard and swung her body to the seat!

She picked up the lines and, clucking to the horses, shouted: "Ándele, boys; ándele if you can."

Sal and Pito lurched. The wagon moved out forward.

"Thank God for these broad-tired wheels. Maybe we'll get there tomorrow," Willy said.

Pat said nothing. He clutched S'rita in his arms. She heaved and fretted, but he didn't notice. He watched Willy. She held the lines slack but firmly; she leaned forward in the seat, her hat pulled forward, black curls peeping on her forehead in the sweat; her eyes searching the blank brilliance of the sand before her.

"Maybe we'll see a windmill."

Pat seized her hand and kissed it, pressed its hard palm with his lips. "Sweetheart! Sweetheart!" he murmured. His head fell on her neck.

S'rita gulped. Papa was so funny. Her stomach hurt so and he didn't notice. Things went whirling. Something was coming up. She couldn't help it. She pulled back a little. Frothy vomit gushed forth on Pat's shirt.

Willy stopped the horses and got Pat and S'rita on the bed.

"You two just lie still. Maybe you can go to sleep. 'Mara and Salita will ride up here with me on the seat."

'Mara moved up gladly. She wished so to hold

hands with Mama. But Mama's hands drove the horses. She clasped the javelina. It helped to hold something. She was scared. S'rita looked so white and funny, and so did Papa. She felt thirsty and her eyes were burning.

"Are you all right, Honey?" Willy looked down at 'Mara. Yes, thank God 'Mara could take the burning. Her eyes were bloodshot, but they would heal—not like S'rita's stomach bucking.

"Ándele," she said to Sal and Pito, and they started out again.

By noon S'rita's stomach settled, but she lay listless. She wouldn't talk or move. She didn't want to. She felt so queer inside. Things were moving in there. She wanted to lie still. Papa and Mama gave her water, bathed her head. Pat and Willy forgot they had to stint on water. Their baby's face was blazing.

But that night Willy looked at the last barrel of water and asked God's blessing.

"You've got to! You've simply got to!" She looked straight up at God himself.

She asked Pat to go on to bed with 'Mara in the wagon. She put S'rita on his cot outside and sat on the ground beside it. She fanned, soothed, and patted. S'rita fretted.

S'rita was glad to have Mama with her. She felt so hot. She hurt all over. Mama's hand felt cool to touch. She liked the humming. It sounded pretty. Her insides stopped moving. She saw a lizard and started running. She stumbled but kept on running.

Willy knew S'rita had gone to sleep, but she groaned and tumbled; her breath came vile and hot.

"Her poor little stomach just won't take it. Our smell alone would make her sick. We're all so dirty."

She smoothed back curls sticky with sweat and dust. Even at nighttime the sand was blowing. It never rested. Nothing rested—elements, beasts, or people— all struggling toward something—only God knew what!

"But can S'rita stand it? That's the question!"

She started humming "Onward Christian Soldiers," "Rock of Ages," "La Cucaracha," "La Poloma."

Pearl lay down very near the wagon. Willy moved over close beside her.

"You realize when I need you," Willy said. "I hope you never have to know the meaning of this torture—a sick baby and nothing you can do about it, no food to give her but fat bacon and frijoles. They'll kill her; in fact, they have."

Pearl's eyes looked big like saucers. The starlight caught them. Willy sat there staring at them.

"Pearl, for God's sake never breed and have a colt," she said.

Just before daylight Willy made her decision. She'd kill the javelina and make hot broth. It would nourish S'rita and make friends with her stomach. They'd find a ranch if they kept traveling, but she had to keep up S'rita's strength. She'd kill Salita before they woke. She'd bury the skin and never tell the children. She'd say the javelina ran away to join her pack.

Day was breaking. Willy sneaked to the chick box and slipped out the butcher knife. Salita slept at Amara's feet. She'd grab her mouth and hold it shut to keep her from squealing and get her out of hearing distance before she stabbed her.

She stood there looking at the pig, born to wild freedom, she'd tamed so gently to a pet. Her devotion was like a dog's, her habits clean like a rabbit's. She had meant so much to the children—but S'rita needed broth. Salita had to give it.

Willy stepped up closer. She felt the brickbat in her chest. But she had to do it. There was no choice. Daylight quickened. She had to hurry. S'rita and 'Mara would raise a fuss. She took one step nearer and reached out to grab the javelina. But before her hand touched her, the pig jumped up, bristled, glared her tusks, stood at bay to bite. She gave one squeal, but that was sharp. Pat and 'Mara wakened.

S'rita cried out, "Mama, I dreamed!"

"What in God's world!" Pat shouted. "Sweetheart, you've got the butcher knife!"

"Just to cut this rope," Willy answered, but the javelina kept snarling, backing away.

S'rita was up now, pulling at her skirt.

"I want in the wagon, Mama, with Papa an' 'Mara." She was shaking. Her eyes were bloodshot.

Willy lifted S'rita into the wagon. Not until she put the knife back into the chuck box and went to feed the horses did the javelina calm. She crouched near S'rita and sniffed the air in nervous jerks.

"Why does it have to be so hard?" Willy said to Sal and Pito as she put on their morrals of corn.

She was tired; oh Lord, how tired! She felt a little dizzy. The sun was rising bright and hot. Sand kept blowing. If she could just lie down a minute. But she couldn't. No, there was no lying for her—now or ever, not even leaning. She had to stand right up and take it. She couldn't even kill a javelina for her sick baby without a brainstorm—nerves and tension for everybody.

"If there were just some one thing that I could blame;" she said. "Like S'rita, I'd kick and stomp."

S'rita and Pat ate no breakfast. 'Mara ate her biscuits and molasses a bit too glibly.

"She's trying to make up for the others, bless her little heart," Willy thought.

All through the morning S'rita groaned and fretted. Willy planned how to trap the javelina that night while the family slept. The plan grew fiendish as the day wore on. To Willy it mounted into life and death. Just once she looked back into the wagon at the bed. Pat held S'rita's head; her arm flung out around the javelina's neck. The two wild-hog eyes seemed fixed on Willy.

"She's savage! She'll eat my baby!" Willy thought.

"Mama, you look so funny." It was 'Mara pulling at her arm.

"It's nothing, Honey. I merely strained my neck."

At noon 'Mara scratched her leg on a cactus and it bled. The sight of blood made Willy sick. She grabbed Pearl's mane and held.

"What's wrong, Sweetheart?" Pat questioned.

"Nothing; I just stumbled."

"Tonight I'll stab Salita in the dark so I won't have to see the blood," she said to herself.

That afternoon the wind picked up a gale. The sand

whirled around in circles and went straight up. Pearl trailed close behind the wagon to make a windbreaker for herself. Amara's eyes began to water. Willy had to tie a rag around her head.

Pat and Serena were very quiet, until Serena began to vomit.

"I wanna throw up, Mama." But just green liquid foamed and oozed.

"She's got nothin' in her," Pat said. "What in God's name! What in God's name, Sweetheart!"

Willy handed 'Mara the reins. "Honey, you don't need to see. Just hold 'em. Sal and Pito'll do the going." She crawled back.

Willy took S'rita in her arms and held her while Pat bathed her head and throat. The javelina kept close to her mistress, sniffing in the dirty yellow curls. Willy saw a tear splash on S'rita's grimy hand. It was hers.

In S'rita's suffering, Pat and Willy forgot the storm.

"Good God, she's choking," Pat shouted.

"Give her water! Pound her back!"

"If we only had some whisky!"

"It's the dust." All at once Willy felt the sand around her. It was thick enough to cut. She herself began to cough. Pearl nickered; Sal and Pito stopped.

"They won't go," 'Mara hollered.

Willy looked out of the wagon. She saw a wall of sand around them. Nothing else.

"What in God's name!" Pat whispered. "This means the end, Sweetheart." He threw his arms around her and drew her to him. She felt his kisses in her hair.

Then she heard 'Mara shouting, "Mama, I see a windmill! It's right out here in front!"

"A what?" Pat murmured.

"How can you see it, Darling? You must be dreaming."

"I took off the bandage. I saw the windmill flash once. I know I saw it."

Willy put S'rita in Pat's arms and crawled out to take a look. She held to the wagon, then to the horses, to keep from blowing down. She was completely blinded. The sand cut like needles, and now and then a rock hit her. But she kept edging forward, reaching

out in front. All at once she touched something. It was
a fence.

"Hello!" she shouted.

"Quíen viene?" echoed back.

A man came out to meet them. They stood at the
gate of Rancho Solitas, he told them. They had looped
in a circle.

"The sun, he crook," was his explanation.

Pat and Willy didn't bother to ask further questions.
They were there. They needed water, food, and shel-
ter.

The Mexicans gave hearty welcome. "Out in a
sandstorm with thirsty horses and sick children is not
good." To their guest they offered all they could.

The house was a three-roomed box structure, not
even stripped, but to Pat and Willy if was life's answer back to death. They hurried the horses out to
water and hustled the children into the house.

Once on the bed, S'rita quieted. The woman
brought hot goat's milk, but the child couldn't take it.

"Bathe her," Pat said. "It's the stink that makes her
sick."

Evidently he was right, for after a bath she fell
asleep.

For supper they sat down to beef. Just before the
windstorm the vaqueros had killed a steer. The meat
was gritty, but very good. Pat ate four servings;
Amara, three. Willy drank a lot of milk.

She told about the burra on the ranch.

"Like María" the woman said; then she and her
husband talked a lot in Spanish.

The wind blew on, but not so hard. Willy wished
Pearl could come inside. That's the trouble with a
horse, she thought.

Salita crouched at S'rita's bed. Willy brought a bowl
of milk and knelt down to stroke her bristly back. The
hog backed off a little, then came out to eat.

Willy looked up. "Thank God it didn't have to be
that hard!"

In the night the storm blew out. When morning
dawned, it was clear and bright. The Mexicans brought

in burra milk. S'rita took it and kept it down. A week later she was well. Pat was talking glibly. 'Mara's eyes weren't even pink. The horses' sides began to swell. The ranchero gave the wagon a greasing up. Then one night it rained a little.

The next morning, when Willy asked, how far it was to the Rio Grande, Pat's hand began to shake. His eyes besought her.

"How many days in the wagon?"

"One, two, no more than three," the Mexican answered.

"Then let's get started," Willy said, and went out to hitch up.

When Pat got into the wagon he smelled strongly of mescal.

"Rotgut," he said, "but it's a drink."

Willy picked up the reins. "Ándele, boys; let's get going."

"When will we see the river, Mama?" S'rita asked.

"If we hurry, tomorrow maybe."

The Mexicans waved. The Westalls started out again.

14

Next day at noon the sand ended sharply, just as it had begun. Pat and Willy looked and saw before them mesquite, huisache, ceniza—just like the ranch.

"My God, look, Sweetheart! Am I drunk or seein' things?"

She grabbed his neck and kissed him. "Darling, we're here!" she shouted. "We're here! S'rita! 'Mara! Look at the brush and the cactus. We're nearly to the river."

Amara bobbed her head up from behind the seat. She saw her mama's face. She had to cry. She could now. S'rita came climbing over. Amara clutched her waist and held. She pulled loose and kept climbing to the seat.

"Where's the windmill, Mama? I wanna swim!"

"That's the idea, Sugar. Water's meant to bathe in. We'll get ourselves a bathtub and fill it to the top."

"Hurry, Papa. Hit Sal and Pito." S'rita reached down to get the whip. He caught her hand.

"No, Puddin', they're too tired. They've been too faithful to put a whip to. We'll let 'em jog us in."

"Let's sing!" Willy said. "This is a celebration. We're ear-marked a little maybe, but we've come on through all right!"

"Hell, yes," Pat said. "We were bound to get here because we've been headin' south." His eyes shot sparks. He grabbed the gun.

"Darling!" Willy cried.

"Well, by God, this is a celebration." He fired straight up.

"But the cartridge We've just got two. We may need it."

"That's what they're for!" He fired again.

That was the last one. Now they had no ammunition. All there was to do was sing.

"Do you know 'Joy to the World'?" she asked.

"No; too damned high in pitch. Never learned it."

" 'Onward, Christian Soldiers'?"

"No; too damned military. I like slow, sweet music like 'Rock of Ages'."

"Then let's sing 'Rock of Ages'! Mama used to sing it when I was a kid."

Pat pitched the tune and began to sing. Willy was surprised, and felt ashamed of her own voice, but she joined in; so did the children, humming.

They all sang

Rock of Ages cleft for me, let me hide myself in
*   Thee.*
Let the water and the blood from Thy side a
*   healing flood.*

After that Willy forgot time and place. The "water and the blood" she understood. She was the song.

When the wheels rolled into the chaparral there was yet no road to follow. The horses turned and twisted here and there to dodge the scrub mesquite, sometimes an ebony, often a tall yucca plant in blossom, nothing taller than a man's head in measure.

"Just like the ranch," Pat said. "You can drive straight through and never hit a tree. Hell of a lot of cactus. Don't see how the horses stand it."

"They know how to dodge it, Darling. It's green and growing. The river can't be far."

Next day they struck a sendero. They came in upon it at right angles in the brush. The horses stopped.

Willy shouted. "Look!"—and held her breath.

It was brush beaten down by two wheels passing over it several times. The ruts were just perceptible to the human eye, but it was the mark of man upon the largeness of the space. Somebody had started somewhere and gone to somewhere else. It was a designation, a pattern, left by man. People must be somewhere near at hand.

"I believe we're here!" Willy caught her breath.

"Where's the river, Mama?" S'rita asked.

"Not yet," Pat said. "The damn road runs east and west; the river lies straight south."

"Let's take a try at left and see what we can find. That's the direction of the Gulf, and the Rio Grande empties into that."

"It's damn good to hit a road, no matter where it goes." Pat headed Sal and Pito east. Pearl had trotted off ahead.

"Good sign," Pat said. "She's got more sense than we have, anyway. She ought to; she's a horse."

They drove east down the sendero for several hours; then they saw something moving.

"It's a cow," Pat said.

"No, I believe it's a man on horseback." Willy shaded her eyes to see for sure.

"Too big for a horse. Never saw a mustang the size of that."

"But it's not a mustang, maybe. Yes, Darling, look! It is a man! I saw a flash of red. It must be his bandana."

"Maybe it's a bull just comin' from a fight." Pat loved his little joke and laughed before Willy had a chance—the first time he had laughed in a long time.

Willy thanked God—just thanked God in general for air and light and space, especially for laughter. She wanted to pull down a sunbeam and eat it—reach out and hug the air—catch up the wind by handfuls and fling it to the birds.

"Damned if 't's not a man! Hello," he shouted. Pat's voice was loud and firm.

"Hello," came back twice, once in a faint echo and once from the rider down the road.

Pearl galloped forward; so the man met her first. Pat drew up Sal and Pito to a stop.

It was hard to believe what they were seeing coming toward them. A big man riding a fat bay horse. All they were sure of was a red face and a Stetson hat. For one brief second Willy thought "Bill Lester"! Then she perceived the redness and the size.

"And he's American!" Pat's voice was now not steady.

Willy couldn't keep the tears back. Amara grabbed her mama's hand.

The man rode on up and took off his hat. "Howdy, folks! Howdy! My name's Asa Hall."

That sentence placed him Texas, the old-brand Texan who extends the heart in greeting.

"Where're you goin' on Christmas Eve?"

"Christmas?" S'rita bobbed her head out in the sunshine. The word meant something. One time when she had heard it she got a red thing that spun round. She and Salita had torn it up.

Amara looked up at her mama. Mama's face looked so happy. Everything seemed grand.

"Our name's Westall. We're on our way to the Rio Grande Valley," Pat announced. "Couldn't be Christmas, though, at that?" He looked at Willy.

She smiled wanly. This was one Christmas they had not tried to overlook. In their travail it just forgot itself.

"We skipped a week somehow, I guess," she said.

Then she smiled outright and the Texan smiled right back.

"Yeah," he said, "tomorrer's Christmas. Don' pay no 'tenshun to the weather. Down here we always have the sunshine. That's how we sell the land."

"The land! Is this the Rio Grande Valley? Where's the river, then?"

"Not far south. The sendero turns a piece down here. You head on east to Chapin, the county seat. Turn south to Madero and Hidalgo. There's a fork to them two places down the road."

"Yeah, but where's the river?"

"A-settin' right there by Madero an' Hidalgo. They're a couple of little Mexkin settlements. You cain't miss it headin' south."

"Wanna see the river, Papa." S'rita jumped up and down.

"Yeah, got to get to that river since it's Christmas now."

"Naw, now folks!" The Texan spit twice at a cactus. "Come on over to Chapin. The Judge'd like to have you. We're ropin' all the whites in t'night for a little celebration. It's his new town an' we wanta make it welcome. I'm headin' over now for some mescal."

Willy spoke up quickly. "No, not this time. But thank you just the same. We want to spend Christmas right on the riverbank."

She looked at Pat. He seemed disappointed, like a child.

The Texan spit again. "Wal, then, head on down to Phil Allen's. His place is so close to the river it damn near falls right in. I'll be seein' you afore tomorrow's done," he said, and put his spur to the bay's fat side.

In a moment he was gone.

Pat sat there glum.

"Did you want to go, Darling?" Willy felt as if she'd hit him.

"No," he said. "But it would be good to talk English and have a drink with people." His eyes were like Serena's when she didn't get her way.

"But look at us," she said. "We've got to clean up

first and put on our best clothes. We smell too bad."

"Just like you damned women." He fell into a sulk.

She talked on, but he paid no attention. They drove on down the sendero and turned south.

Willy tried to sing, but nobody joined her. 'Mara had gone to sleep. Soon S'rita followed. They rode on in silence.

When they came to the fork, Willy said, "I wish we had listened better to Mr. Hall. I'm not certain what he said."

"Matters a damn, I guess," Pat grunted. "Both places're on the river."

The horses had the rein and they turned right. Neither Willy nor Pat spoke after that.

Just before sundown a strange noise broke the hot stillness of the afternoon. It was a rhythmic pounding that came across the air.

"What's that?" Willy said. The silence had grown oppressive for Christmas Eve. She felt a little sorry for herself.

"What's that?" she asked again, anxious to start the conversation.

"What's what?" Pat said at last.

"That noise? Listen!"

"Damned if I know. Ghosts, maybe."

"There it is again. It's getting louder."

Then he listened with her. They were traveling toward whatever pounded.

They came upon it soon after the sendero ran into the railroad and turned west.

In the middle of a cleared-out space cut in two by the railroad track three Mexicans hammered and nailed boxing planks to two-by-fours, standing up in scaffold pattern in the sky.

"What's that" Willy said to Pat.

"A house, no doubt," he said.

"But what kind of house sitting here all by itself? What's it to be, I wonder. Let's stop and find out, and ask about the distance to the river."

Pat didn't answer, but he pulled the horses to a stop. Willy got out and walked up to talking distance.

All three Mexicans quit work, took off their sombreros and smiled broadly. One stepped forward as spokesman, but he and Willy found it hard to talk. Their pattern of English-Spanish just wouldn't match. The English words Willy had to use he did not know; the same with his Spanish ones to her. But Willy got the general impression that the house they were building had something to do with the railroad.

"A section-gang house, no doubt. Where're the towns aquí?" she asked; but he shook his head.

When she asked about the river, he pointed south. The sendero crossed the railroad track and headed in that direction.

As she turned to leave, she said, "Merry Christmas!"

The Mexican burst into a smile and answered, "Feliz Navidad!"

Something about the flash of blue eyes and smile made Willy's spirit lift. It was Christmas! She wished now she had gone on to Chapin as the Texan had suggested. Pat would be ashamed to meet people the way they looked; but no matter what happened when they got there, she wished they'd gone, for it was Christmas! Somehow the Christmas of all Christmases in the world!

When the Mexican smiled again she forgot about herself. The Mexican's face was freckled; his eyes were blue.

"Your nombre?" she asked.

"Pablo."

"Pablo what?"

"Pablo." He kept on smiling, and his fellow-workers laughed. Willy said "Merry Christmas" again, and inhaled a deep breath of fresh-lumber smell before she got back into the wagon.

They crossed the railroad track and headed south. Willy tried to talk about the Mexican with freckles and blue eyes. Why did they work so late on Christmas Eve? What could the house be they were building? Many things. But Pat refused to show any interest in any subject she could mention. Finally she quit trying and thought of Scripture passages in the spirit of a private Christmas celebration.

"Aunt Ann would like that—and Mama."

Suddenly the sendero ended. The wagon rolled out of the chaparral into a straight road splitting two fields of cabbage into twin prairies of gray green.

Pat drew up the horses. His eyes flashed fire again.

"It's the damnedest sight I ever saw," he said.

"It's Paradise."

"I knew it'd be like this if we ever got down here." He smiled broadly and lashed the horses' lines, to go.

They moved on.

"Wake up, children, and look," Willy called back into the wagon. They were passing through a Brobdingnagian summer garden in December—cabbage, onions, beets, celery, tomatoes, alfalfa, cucumbers—acres, miles—a universe of living freshness to rebuke the strong, hot wind and burning sun.

In a minute 'Mara and S'rita's heads stuck out, squinting in the sunshine. Maybe they had dreamed it. They felt almost frightened, except that Papa and Mama looked so happy. Everything was green. There wasn't any cactus. Things looked square, like pictures, flat and pretty. Dirt wasn't even blowing. S'rita clutched Amara's hand. They clung close together.

"What's that, Mama?"

"Onions, I think, Honey."

"What's that, Papa?"

"Beans, Sugar. You oughta know beans even if you've never seen things growing."

"Where's the river?"

"There it is. Look, Darling, look! The river!" Willy jumped up and pointed at a straight narrow strip of water by a cabbage field.

"No, Sweetheart," Pat shouted, "that's irrigation—canals. Look, there's another one on the other side."

"An' over yonder!" Amara hollered.

"Papa! I wanna swim," Serena cried.

"So do I, by God," Pat answered.

"Everything's so square and well laid off," Willy

said. "Look, they're planting palms. Look at the Mex-kins working!"

"Yeah, that must be a scraper gang. Buildin' canals fast, they told me in Laredo. Labor's awful cheap down here. That's why these snow-diggers're crowdin' in. Can't blame 'em. They bring peons across the river by the hundreds. They clear the brush and tend the crops. They work for almost nothin'. Damned if I don't get myself a valet!"

Even Pearl snorted, galloped past the wagon, and kicked back at Pito. She hoisted her black tail and sped down the road ahead.

"Damned smart horse," Pat said. "She smells the water in the river. Wouldn't trade a house and lot for her. She's been a damned good friend."

Pat's blue eyes deepened; his chin came up. Willy reached over and kissed him on the mouth.

They camped that night near a canal, and after dark they all got in the water to bathe. The children were plainly frightened. Even Pat and Willy felt a lit-tle strange.

"This'll be our Christmas," Willy said.

"No, gotta see that Rio Grande River yet."

So they went straight to bed, slick and clean from bathing, to get an early start.

"Wish we could see the river at sunrise." Willy opened the trunk and got out their clothes. Amara and Serena were to wear their pink and blue piqués made from two of her old dresses. Pat was to put on his gray suit. But for all her excuses for the Chapin party, she changed only to a clean waist.

The next morning she swung aboard the wagon in her khaki riding skirt and Stetson. She had nothing else to wear.

15

The river was not beautiful to look at, but it was good to see—broad, muddy, crooked, forbidding with quicksand and eddies. Like a wide, angry cut in dark, dry flesh, it marked off the edge of the nation in a sinister kind of way. No trees softened the parting; it was definite, hard-outlined—just running water; across it Mexico, this side the United States.

But it was the Rio Grande, the river the Westalls sought; hence a sight to rejoice at. It was to be their home.

On its bank sat the Allen hacienda that the Texan had told about. Pat and Willy knew what they were seeing the minute their eyes caught sight of it. It was like the Rancho Seco but for the river at the edge. Adobe-thatched jacales semicircled a patio of green, where orange trees, palms, some jasmines, poinsettias, and a castor bean grew. Since it faced the river, they saw it from the back, held in relief against the water by the brightness of the sun. A windmill waved in triumph over the river at its foot.

Phil Allen walked out to meet them when he saw them driving up.

Pat stopped the team. "Our name's Westall," was his greeting to the man.

"Howdy, folks." The rancher smiled. "Merry Christmas! So glad you come. Here all by myself except for Fanny. She's cookin' dinner for some land seekers Conlay's bringin' down. Folks're all up at Chapin's for the last-night celebration. Couldn't go myself. So glad you come. Get out."

The man's speech bespoke his candor. The Texas welcome spoke itself. Phil Allen was like Jim Nelson, except that he was younger, his boots were newer, his shirt was buttoned at the neck. He was one of the men

104

who came to the Valley first, learned about the people, didn't try to change the land. He took to the Mexican way of living, fitting himself into the pattern.

The Westalls got out and went in, even Salita at Willy's feet. Pat looked proud, dressed up clean, in his gray suit. The children's heads were lovely, but pink and blue dresses ill-suited their weathered skin and hair. Willy fitted the setting like a picture in a book. She took off her Stetson and held it in her hand.

They sat down in the patio and looked out across the muddy river into Mexico. It was a repetition of their well-known chaparral. The sun's brilliance on the water bridged the lands together into one.

"Great moment!" Pat said. "We've been hittin' for this river it's a helluva long time now. Hot an' tired an' plumb worn out; but we got here just the same."

"Yeah, worried some last night. Asa Hall sent word you was comin'. Thought maybe somethin' mighta happened."

"Who? That fellow on the road?"

"Yeah, he seen you; but Pablo brought the word. You passed him at his carpenterin' job back a ways."

"That blue-eyed Mexkin?" Willy asked the question quick, on impulse.

Phil Allen didn't answer.

She talked on. "He was working on a house on the railroad where the sendero cut down south." She knew she had broken into the conversation.

Pat leaned back and frowned. She squirmed, moved, and tried to look at ease.

Their host laughed. He slapped his knee. "Callin' Conlay's depot a house! Why, that's to be the newest town in the Valley, the last one on the line."

"A town?" Pat said. "My God, it's nothing! Just a cleared-out space there in the brush."

"Yeah, but wait 'til a month from now. That's the way they all began. Conlay bought three porciones from the Oblate Fathers. He named it Mission. The Old Oblate Mission's not far from here, you know. A land-seekin' party gets in here today. He'll sell 'em every one. Just wait an' see. He's as smart as hell, a Yankee from Ioway but as good a' Irishman as ever puked his sins up to a priest."

"What other towns? Where are they?"

"Startin' in from Brownsville on the Gulf up the river here for fifty miles. There's Harlingen, San Benito, Donna, McAllen, Mercedes, an' a lot of others comin' on."

"Towns? How old're they? The railroad's just come down!" Pat's voice lifted.

"Sure, just two or three years old." Then his wrinkled face skewed up into a frown. "Damned shame, too," he said, "these Yankees comin' in buyin' land off the Mexkins. Pore fools ain't got no more sense than to let it go, land that was left 'em as grants straight from the King of Spain."

"How big're these towns now?"

"Ain't nobody livin' in 'em yet. 'Bout the size of Mission. You seen that." He laughed at his own joke.

So did Pat and Willy, to be polite.

"Whose doin' all the developin'?" Pat was not to be nonplussed.

"Yankees, nearly every one. Us folks down here don't want nothin' like this to happen, plowin' up the ground an' ruinin' all the range. We're ranchers back since Cortina's time."

"Who's Cortina?"

"Bandit feller back after the Civil War, but McNelly's Rangers beat him down."

"Safe now, I guess?"

"Safest place on earth. Cain't beat the Mexkin people. Folks that don't know 'em mess 'em up sometimes. But they're fine inside. Hope you new fellers'll treat 'em right."

Willy noted that Phil Allen talking turned old and sad. His eyes peered out in front.

The children and Salita ran about inspecting the garden. They couldn't get over the wonder of it. Pat and Mr. Allen talked.

Willy was glad to sit and rest. She was so tired. It was a Mexkin country, as Bill Lester said; lazy, slow, warm, and dreamy. It made you want to sit and think. Just a river in between didn't change a people. Gov-

ernment didn't change them either, even for a
hundred years. Men like Phil Allen and Bill Lester
understood. Yes, they understood a lot of things.

Bill Lester and the longhorn cows! Bill Lester and
his advice to take the river route! Bill Lester's fearless
eyes! Bill Lester! Yes, Bill Lester! The name began
to whirl. She felt impelled to ask her host if he knew
Bill Lester. It would be a part of Christmas just to ask.
But for Pat she would.

A tall, good-looking mulatto woman stepped into
the patio with a tray hearing glasses and bottles.

The rancher looked up at her and smiled. "Folks,
this is Fanny. She an' Henry're the only colored folks
in the Valley. They come down with the railroad
buildin' an' ain't went back."

Fanny stood poised for the introduction she knew
she was to get.

"She's come down here today to give me a hand,"
he went on. "Our Mexkins don't work on Christmas
—not for Fanny, anyway."

He laughed again. "She's cookin' dinner for a whole
trainload of snow-diggers. They're gittin' here for
Christmas and wanta see how us folks live. So I told
Conlay to bring 'em down. That's why I'm here an' all
the family's gone. But with Fanny we'll make out."

The Negro broke into a smile and set down the
tray to begin to serve the liquor.

Serena walked up to her and held out a crushed
jasmine in her hand.

"S'rita, Honey, what made you pull the flower?"
Willy turned to Mr. Allen. "I hope you don't mind.
The children have never seen flowers growing."

"Let 'em pick all they want," he said. "That's what
they're for. We always have a plenty. I got five children of my own."

He got up and snatched oranges off the navel tree
and passed them around to everybody.

"Christmas, Mama!" Amara held up her golden
orange in wonder and ran and put it in her mama's
lap.

"Flower," S'rita called up to Fanny. The Negro
reached down and took the jasmine. As she looked

into those light-blue eyes and touched the little hand,
Willy saw her lose her heart.

"Come on, folks, let's drink up now to Cristmas!
I've been waitin' for you to get here."

"Make mine straight whisky."

"An' you, Miz Westall?" Phil Allen turned to Willy
as he motioned Fanny to make his the same. They
all smiled at each other.

"Clear water and plenty of it," Willy said. "I see
you've got a windmill and we're awfully dry—thirsty
from living on a ranch."

"Yeah, Miz Westall, you're right at that. Them
windmill highballs is mighty hard to beat. We sorta
base this country on liquid for the dry. If the Lord
don't send us water, we take it from the ground. That's
how we make things grow in spite of hell."

He turned to Fanny. "Say, how's Henry's cabbage
crop?"

"Not much, Mister Allen; he keeps too busy bossin'
that scraper gang to take his irrigation when it's due."

Willy was surprised at the Negro's English pattern,
her speech and voice—no more Negro than her
face.

"Well, where's Bill Lester? He's supposed to do the
bossin'? The gang belongs to him," the rancher said.

"Now, Mister Allen, you know where Bill stays
most of his time these days."

"You mean three miles north of Oblate? Why, I
thought she left?"

Just then the dogs let out a volley of announcement.
The land party approached the gate. They all jumped
up to see. Nothing is ever so welcome as visitors on a
ranch.

But in the scurry of moving Willy was unconscious
of what her body did. She was too stunned by what
she'd heard. Certainly the mention of Bill Lester
should come as no surprise. This was his country and
there were few Americans to know each other. She
was ashamed of her confusion. Pat didn't seem to
notice. But to her, every word came clear and full of
meaning: "A scraper crew—three miles north of

Oblate—I thought she'd left"—just as if one wrong note had been struck in a chord.

Bill Lester had ridden out of nowhere when she was in great need. Maybe she expected him to be a knight riding around on horseback helping women in trouble. Cetainly she'd never thought of him as working. Now to hear of him running a scraper gang and living with a woman shocked her. He was young and good-looking; he had a right to women—yes, a right to women! Then she tried to laugh. Such fancy thinking comes from living too much by yourself. She went to the kitchen to talk to Fanny.

She loved the kitchen with Fanny in it. It brought back the Dunbars in Franklin, and Adelaide, Aunt Ann, her own mama. The floor was of dirt, the stove was coals burning in a brasero. Turkeys hung on a spit. The whitewashed walls were adorned with pots and pans, pottery jugs, blue glass, and chilies in long strings—not like home, but cozy, warm, and human. She was glad to find a Negro in it, a woman who could talk. Suddenly she realized how lonely she had been for female company. She walked to the window to watch the crowd at the gate. She wanted to remember everything she saw.

Four horses pulled a large hay wagon to a stop; then another wagon came up behind, and two buckboards, drawn by mules. People scrambled off, men and women. There was a flutter of linen dusters and heavy veils in the wind; shrieks of laughter, and a medley of "Merry Christmas!" "Look, the river!" What funny little houses!" "Those're orange trees!"— all kinds of talk.

Phil Allen walked out slowly to greet the visitors. He walked that way so Pat could keep in step.

"That's Mr. Conlay shakin' hands," Fanny said. "He's the land man. Bill and Henry work for him."

"And the man with the mustache?"

"That's Mr. Fogg. They're partners. He's a Yankee too."

"And that tall fellow wearing boots?"

"Oh, that's Hal Eubank. Next to him is Rome. That little fellow is Jesse Parnell, a Texas Ranger. They just come along to help out sellin' land. Hal and Rome're engineers."

Sugar burned. Fanny hurried to the stove.

"Tryin' to make custard for the children and the vanilla's out! Nothin' but this damned Mexkin cinnamon."

Willy kept peering out the window. Among the people she looked to see a stocky fellow wearing boots and, of course, a Stetson hat.

The people were milling around, talking, shaking hands, looking at the flowers and the trees.

"Who's that fat fellow, Fanny?" Willy asked.

The Negro came to the window and looked out. "That's Ed Nickel. He come down last year and got rich on onions. That fellow in the soldier's clothes is John Sanders. He got home from the Philippines in time to get in a tomato crop and made a pile of money. Look yonder! See those big, red-faced people? That's the Weisschmidts. They're German. They live down the river. Can't talk much, but fine folks just the same. Why don't you go on out, Honey, and meet everybody? There's not many of us yet but we stick together tight."

Willy gazed up wanly at the Negro. "No, Fanny, I guess I'm scared. Let me get used to people. It's been so long—" She reached out and clutched the woman's hand. "I'm glad, Fanny, it was you I met first. I'm glad Mrs. Allen's not at home."

They looked at each other squarely. Tears filled their eyes. Fanny turned and stared out the window again before she spoke. "Miz Allen won't be home 'til next week. Miz Hall's expectin' every day. She'll stay in Chapin 'til it's over and a while." Then she paused. "I know how 'tis, honey, livin' away from people. I'm from California, but Henry's dragged me around this world and back. I live in a tent now, out with the scraper gang, but we're buildin' a house in Mission soon as Henry can find the time. I run a boardin' house for Bill and all the land men. These Mexkins can't do nothin' in a house."

Amara and S'rita dashed into the kitchen, holding a frog. "Look, Mama, I found it by the orange tree,"

'Mara said. What could it be? It wasn't a horned toad; it hopped. Their eyes spread wide.

Fanny and Willy laughed. Fanny made suggestions about some kittens out at the corral, and the children ran off to see them. After dinner she promised to take them down the river where there were a lot of frogs.

Dinner was almost ready. Willy helped thicken the gravy and lift the turkeys down. They were to serve come-and-get-it in the patio. They both hurried with the last-minute making ready.

"Mexkins're no help. I won't have 'em in my kitchen." Fanny never let work interfere with talk. "Last week when William Jennings Bryan was here, I run two off."

"William Jennings Bryan?" Willy caught her breath.

"Sure, honey. We have all the big bugs down. He bought an eighty up on the Mission tract and is comin' down to live. Bill brought him out to supper with the scraper gang. Nice man. I liked him."

Willy stirred the gravy a little faster when she said, "Fanny, tell me about Bill Lester."

"Bill Lester? Well, he was to bring me some vanilla and he ain't got here yet."

"Is he coming?"

"Why, sure; probably drunk last night is all. He was over at Chapin celebrating with the Judge." Fanny stopped her work and looked at Willy. "Say, honey, why did you ask me about Bill Lester?"

"Well, you see I know him," Willy glared down at the floor. "He came by our ranch. I landed over the corral just as he rode up."

"Oh-o-o-o!" Fanny drawled out with about four successive breaths. "So you're that woman. He tells me all about you every time he gets good and drunk. But you just had one baby—sure, that's right. I guess the golden-top hadn't come."

Willy looked up frankly then. She might as well be honest.

"Tell me about Bill, Fanny. I've thought of him a lot. He surely proved a friend to me when he helped me on that ranch."

Fanny slowed down on the salad as she talked.

"There's nothin' I know to tell except he's the best friend anybody ever had. He never talks about himself. He come in here an' started up a scraper gang to dig canals. He works for Conlay on the Mission tract. Makes money, too, for he pays Henry well. Best job we ever had. We want to make a killin' while we can."

"What about the woman north of the Oblate tract?"

Fanny looked straight at Willy before she spoke. "Say, honey, how long did Bill stay there on your ranch?"

Willy laughed. She felt foolish—giddy.

Fanny kept on talking. "Listen, Conchita's all right too; just a Mexkin girl he lives with sometimes, but she treats him right."

Mr. Allen came in to see how things were coming on. He helped carve the turkeys while Fanny and Willy dished and poured and set. When he stepped out into the patio to put something on the table, Fanny whispered loud:

"Listen, honey, Bill Lester's the whitest man on earth!"

That Christmas dinner was an occasion. Willy was afraid when she first stepped out among the people. Then she forgot herself. Pat had taken on the role of chief entertainer of the day. He introduced her to everybody present as if she'd been a queen. Several women eyed her, but on the whole they were very kind. She belonged to the place, they probably thought. Her white shirt and khaki skirt made her a ranch woman, as Mrs. Baxter said. The men were open in their admiration of so lithe a little creature with such brown eyes and such unruly curls. Pat, even on crutches, strutted in his pride. Willy knew that he was almost drunk.

The people never settled down to eating—all they did was talk. Mr. Conlay led, and everybody dreamed and planned. They would build a country in this delta valley of the Rio Grande that would top the world in the reclamation of a desert. They would pull the water from the river and give the land a drink. The land would yield its increase and make the people rich. They would be done with snow and winter, live here in the kingdom of the sun—rich, free, and easy—rid of industry's machine. They looked at the Allen patio and saw the country as it would be—oranges, lemons, jasmines, poinsettias, and castor beans.

"Why, we're talking like Isaiah," Willy told herself. "The desert shall rejoice and blossom like a rose. That prophet said it a way back there."

Mr. Conlay made a point to get over close to Pat and Willy while they ate. People who drive to a country in a covered wagon really want to come.

"Don't let this best land get away from you," he said. "Hurry and get a crop in. We give you easy terms."

"No, we're not here to farm. Wish we could, but I'm too crippled. We just left a ranch to get rid of land. We want to go in business."

"What kind of business?"

"Any kind. Most likely a general mercantile." Pat belched his whisky.

"Then Mission's your location. We're just putting up the depot. We need a store. The town will be three miles north on La Lomita up near the William Jennings Bryan place. Danger of floods down here."

"William Jennings Bryan!" Pat belched again; then he glowed. "I know you're a busy man, Mr. Conlay, so I'll just settle now for cash. I want a lot right in the middle of your town."

"That's fine." Mr. Conlay grinned. "Two Irishmen can always trade."

They shook hands and closed the deal.

Willy turned to Pat. "But, Darling, should we have bought so quickly?"

"Quick, hell!" he said. "We've been waitin' now for years. We're here; it's time to start."

He walked over to the punch table and got himself another drink. Willy went off by herself.

"Well, Fanny'll be in Mission; so will Bill," she thought. She felt uneasy, troubled, maybe just let down and tired. She meant to get back into the kitchen and talk to Fanny. The crowd confused her.

She heard Mr. Conlay talking very loud. He was making another speech. Everybody gave him attention. This time he was talking about the perfect climate of the Valley of the Rio Grande. His listeners basked in the bright heat of the sun ball overhead.

"It's never cold here! Never!" he almost shouted. "You never need a fire! Never! It never frosts! It never snows!" His face grew red; his breath came hard. He had to stop to get it back.

Amara stood listening, amazed at the noise the man was making, like Papa when he got so mad.

"Let me prove it by this child here." His voice calmed. He thought Amara was one of the Allen children and he needed time to catch up on his breathing. "Little girl, did you ever see it snow?"

Amara's brown eyes widened. She felt surprised to be addressed, but she always answered questions when people asked them. Mama said it was polite. She wished she could say yes.

"No, sir," she said.

Mr. Conlay shouted, "See, I told you."

Amara thought she'd try again. "But I saw it rain. It was so pretty coming down. Did you ever see it rain?" she asked.

Amara brought the party to an end. Soon thereafter Mr. Conlay hustled his snow-diggers back into the hay wagons to get them to their Pullmans for the night.

Late that afternoon Fanny took the children to see the frogs. Pat, Mr. Allen, Hal Eubank, and Jesse Parnell sat down to do a little extra Christmas drinking.

Willy went to her room to rest. She still felt very tired, confused, mixed up. She tried to sleep so as to blot out the picture and wake up to find it fresh and new. But she couldn't sleep. She rehearsed the happenings of the day—pulled apart and put together, analyzed. The dressed-up Yankee women brought back the train of memories she was practiced in forgetting. The Negro touched something in her heart she liked. In all Pat's dramatic haste she was glad he had happened to meet the man who sold lots in the place where Fanny was to live. She would be a great help with the children, a great comfort to herself.

Women need the comfort of other women. There are times when men or children cannot help. Some things women have to face as women. Again she had to meet the fear that never ceased to stalk. Had she conceived again? She remembered the terror before Serena came. Then she thought of the preciousness and felt ashamed, wicked, unclean almost. But for the task she faced she must have no more children. Her life must go to her little girls. She wondered what women do who take such challenge yet unmarried, like Bill Lester's woman, the Mexican girl. What degree of love could force a woman to those ends? How could a man expect it? How could any man expect the things men do of women? Why do women accept the price and never ask a question?

Finally she sat straight up. "I'm like a little girl when she finds her doll is stuffed with sawdust. I'll be grateful when I get old at last," she said.

The men were talking loud on the patio, the glasses kept on clicking. She decided she would go outside and take a look around for Pearl.

The mare was standing by the corral, nosing a big bay stud. Willy didn't interrupt. She changed her course and walked out toward the gate.

She saw two men riding in. One was the Texan of the sendero meeting; the other was Bill Lester. Dust down the road indicated a third was coming.

"Miz Westall!" Bill Lester hollered, opening his mouth so wide in smiling she caught a very vivid flash of white.

She waved. Both men jerked off their hats. They galloped in, swung off their horses, and both stuck out their hands at once. Willy reached out and grasped Bill Lester's.

"Asa told me you all was headin' down here for today, but we all got mescaled up at Judge's and got in a big argument over Madero down in Mexico. Couldn't get here any sooner."

She stood there with her hand in Bill's. It was hard

and calloused like her own, except much harder. And it was strong, strong enough to lean on—and Lord, how tired she felt! Her legs wanted to fold up and let her crumple to the ground, but somehow Bill's hand held her up.

The cloud of dust whirled up and got off. In it was a slight, dark Mexican about Bill's age, quick of eye and liquid in his grace. He undid his morral and displayed a bronze rooster crowned with a comb of brightest red.

"This is Pepe, Miz Westall. He's my compadre down this way," Bill said.

Willy squared her shoulders to strengthen her legs.

"It is good to see you all!" She expanded into the smile that was only hers. "We've had a lovely Christmas, Mr. Hall, and we owe that all to you. Mr. Lester is an old ranch friend." She let go Bill's hand at that.

"And your lovely rooster!" She turned to the Mexican standing there.

"You like heem?" Pepe gleamed, stroking the bronze feathers like a child.

"Where'd you get him, Pepe?" asked Asa Hall.

"En Torreon, Señor."

"What have you named this one?"

"Pepitón." The Mexican spoke in pride.

"Good name. Hope he wins you a lot of money."

"Sí, Señor. Cómo no?" Pepe smiled and shrugged his shoulders.

They all walked into the house.

Pat greeted Bill Lester like a friend. Phil Allen poured whisky and they all drank to Christmas and the New Year. Willy smiled back her tears.

Now Pat's legs were underneath him. His crutches held him up. Bill was young and strong; Pat was crippled and aging, but he could look out at Bill with eyes level.

16

The Westalls left early the next morning, heading straight for Mission. Bill and Pepe led the way. Fanny arranged to ride in the back end of the wagon so she could hold S'rita on her lap.

When Willy got up that morning, she found she had one thing less to worry about. The night had brought proof against her anxieties and she meant to keep them gone. No more babies; she had to raise the two she had. "Just like the ranch," she thought; "but we've got irrigation now!"

Willy climbed into the wagon. For a moment she felt conscious of herself. At every squeaky turn of the wagon wheels her heart picked up momentum.

The checkerboard landscape squared off into onions, then cabbage, beans, cucumbers—every shade of green in leaves. As they traveled north from the river, suddenly they rolled into the chaparral again. The lazy thud of axes and crack of brush rang out against the stillness of the day.

Above the brush stuck Mexican heads. They stopped to wave as the Americanos passed. Wood smoke drifted in and occasionally the pungent twang of burning cactus.

"Ornery devils," Fanny called up to Pat and Willy. "Conlay's tryin' to get his three porciones cleared to sell it all this year so's he can get the country settled."

"Where do so many Mexkins come from?" Willy turned on the wagon seat to ask.

"All from Mexico. These're pelados from the other side, not ranch Mexkins like you're used to."

"But they have to eat."

"Not much, just a little rice and beans."

At last when Pablo's hammering on the depot came into hearing, Willy insisted that she get out and

117

walk. She felt too fidgety to ride. Pearl trotted up alongside and together they swung down the sendero behind the wagon.

Mr. Conlay was to send a man in on the train to take their lumber order. In turn she would have him send a grocery salesman. She had no notion of a firm to write to, but she'd find out. She frowned when she thought of what the town was yet. Maybe nobody could sell groceries to a store sitting there in the middle of the brush. Of course she had over three hundred dollars in her skirt. Pat's five hundred would go for lumber and the lot. She heard him tell Conlay he would pay cash. She cringed to think of spending her ring-money; that was her blood-money for the children.

But it was for the children she had pawned the ring; for the children she had to have a store to make a future. And there could be no store unless she had some groceries now to sell. The man might give her credit for a month until she could turn the stock— if she could sell what she had bought!

Suddenly she felt frantic. How could she hope to sell groceries here in the middle of this nowhere! Where were the people? The snow-diggers got back on a train and rode off. They bought no groceries. Conlay said they bought land, but she didn't see them. Fanny said the Mexican grubbers bought just rice and beans. She gave her hat a yank. Well, she'd order rice and beans to start with. She had to make a start.

Bill hollered out, "Well, here we are!"

Willy looked up. There stood Pablo and his two helpers at the depot smiling greeting. When he crossed the railroad tracks, Pat pulled the horses to a stop. Fanny, the children, and Salita scrambled out.

"Where'd we better camp?" Willy walked up alongside.

"Down on your lot if we kin find it. Keep drivin' straight, Mister Westall, a little ways. You might as well mark out the main street now. In a day or two the brush'll be purty well beat down. Grows up awful quick even after clearin'. There's some stobs in the ground. We'll figger 'em out later on. Jest pick out the biggest mesquite and we'll pitch camp. Train's due in soon. Conlay's always on it an' stops while it goes down to Sam Fordyce to turn around. His camp ain't fixed up here yet. He's stayin' at McAllen. We'll get the lumber figgered out an' start buildin'. I'm roundin' up some more hombres tomorrer to get busy on the land office an' a place for Fanny."

"What's Sam Fordyce?" Pat's eyes kindled. He felt the impetus to do.

"Nothin'," Bill laughed. "Just the turn aroun' in the railroad track."

Willy felt very light and free. The weight that had been so heavy was gone. Somebody was there who could answer all the questions, make the plans. She looked up at the depot. Pablo stood there grinning, his hammer in his hand. What two days before had been scaffolding was now almost a house.

"Wonderful!" she said.

Pablo bowed politely. Pepe stepped up on the floor and smiled down at Willy. The two Mexicans made a vivid contrast. Pepe's dark eyes flashed quick and sharp like snake eyes. Pablo's blue ones were mellow. Pepe was lithe, dapper in his riding get-up—tight pants, wide leather belt and boots, a pistol in a holster at his hip. His black hair ruffled in the wind; his hat was in his hand. Pablo's hat sat on his head; his clothed bulged and dangled.

Bill saw Willy looking.

"These here're my two hombres. Not much workers I'll admit, but they're always on the job. Pepe's best at fightin' roosters an' playin' guitar music. Pablo'll take a try at anything I say. I got him carpenterin' because we gotta get some buildin's built."

"The depot's wonderful! He's finished it so fast."

"Ain't much to buildin' in this country. All we ever use is boxin' plank."

Willy looked around her. There was nothing but this one little house sitting in a space of cleared-out brush, but everybody smiled, looked pleased and proud, especially Pat.

This was a ground-floor deal all right; she thanked God for that.

They pitched camp fast, with Bill and Pepe helping. Fanny busied herself with showing the girls the
wonder of the petayah as a fruit and how to gather
it to keep the thorns from sticking in their fingers.

'Mara and S'rita loved Fanny's games. She had time
to play with them, and she knew so many things—
frogs, kittens, poinsettia flowers, and now petayahs.
She smiled so wide and looked so gay. She was like
Mama, except Mama kept so busy. She was like Papa
that way, except Papa was crippled. He couldn't move
except on crutches. They had to be careful with him.

Fanny wanted to hold their hands and lead them
places, but S'rita wouldn't let her; of course Amara
did. S'rita ran ahead and shouted, "Catch me!"

Fanny's legs were long, so she caught S'rita and
threw her high up in the air. S'rita landed in her arms.
Fanny flung her on her back. S'rita grabbed hold
around her neck and hugged.

"Ándele!" she shouted. "You're my horse."

"Better say your slave, you little yellow-headed
devil!" Then Fanny loped off, snorting like Sal and
Pito.

'Mara stood there and watched them. She felt a
little jealous; they'd gone off and left her. There was
nothing she knew how to play alone. She looked down
at the javelina. Salita seemed a little left out too. They
walked back to the wagon. There were Mama and
Bill Lester driving tent stobs. The bad feeling left her.
This was better than playing horse. To be close to
Mama was enough.

When the train whistle blew, everybody lit out for
the depot. It wasn't far—what was to be two town
blocks in time. Even Phil Allen rode up. He came in
to get his mail from off the train and to see if the
Westalls got put-up.

The train chugged to a stop. Mr. Conlay, the lumber
salesman, four Mexicans, and a Catholic priest got
off.

Mr. Conlay oozed salesmanship from every pore.

"This is Father Michael. He came down to welcome
you folks to our country. This is Oblate land. It's by
their grace we're allowed to come. They're building

the Oblate Novitiate on the river as soon as we can get some carpenters in to work. Country's growing so fast we can't keep up with it. Sunshine's fine today! Poor folks back in Iowa in all that ice and snow! Come on, let's have a little drink."

Phil Allen, Pat, Bill, and the lumber salesman followed Mr. Conlay into the depot, but Father Michael stayed behind a moment to pat Amara's head and smile at Willy.

She liked him from the start. He was big, red-faced, Irish through and through.

"Catholic?" he asked.

"No, Baptist."

"With a name like Patrick Westall?"

"It is strange! Pat's parents died when he was very young. Maybe that's the reason."

The priest stroked Amara's slick black braids a moment, then followed the men into the depot.

"That's the first time I've thought of religion," Willy said to Fanny. "I feel like a regular heathen. I've been too busy, I guess, with babies and living on a ranch. But what would Aunt Ann and Mama think? The children're growing up. I've got to start a church, especially a Sunday school."

Fanny looked away a minute. "I wouldn't worry, honey. I expect the Good Lord understands."

When the train came back an hour later, all the men's faces were red. Pat bought the lumber and paid cash. It was to come in from Brownsville the next day. Willy managed to get Mr. Conlay aside to ask him to send a grocery salesman to see her by herself.

She knew Pat's cash basis had taxed their five hundred dollars. She didn't dare ask how much was left. He seemed too set-up, too Patrick-Westall-of-Sugarland for her to tamper with. The blue eyes picking up their light were enough to make her steal the groceries if she had to. Besides, she had more than three hundred dollars in her skirt.

The train pulled out.

Bill took Fanny aside and gave her a lot of directions for Henry about the scraping. Then he and Pepe got on their horses and rode south.

"He didn't go north, and I'm surprised," Fanny said.

Willy wished she didn't know about the Mexican woman. Aunt Ann had given her strict teaching on loose women—sin, disease, degradation, hell itself. Somehow Bill's leathered face looked too fine; it could have nothing to do with all that. She felt glad that Bill had ridden south.

Phil Allen stayed awhile to talk with Pat. They sat underneath a mesquite and drank some more mescal. When he left, Pat tumbled into the bed to sleep. Fanny stayed until after supper. Henry drove a buckboard in from the scraper camp to get her.

Willy was impressed by the tall black Negro, not old, strong, with definitely a non-negroid face. Before they left, Fanny proudly displayed the sleeping Serenita.

"She looks just like an angel, but she's spunky as the very devil," Willy heard her tell him.

"Poor little 'Mara," Willy thought. "Fanny doesn't notice her at all. Nobody does. They can't see her beauty. It's a kind you have to know to see."

Willy sat a long time by the campfire. She was used to lonely camps. She had spent years at camping now, sometimes in a house, sometimes in the open. She liked the open best. It made her feel close to God and Pearl. The little mare always stayed close. When Willy went into a house, she had to shut her out. That's why houses didn't matter.

The moon was not shining but the stars were bright. She didn't let herself trouble about anything tonight.

"This is my first day and I must keep it right! But I do wish Pat had stayed awake to talk."

Pearl nickered. She was close enough to touch. Willy reached up and rubbed her shoulder.

"Thanks," Willy said.

Then she heard another nicker in the distance. Pearl answered back. Willy knew somebody was riding up the road. She punched up the coals, added a stick of wood, and set the coffee on. In a few minutes Bill rode up.

"Just come by to see how you was gettin' on," he said.

He dismounted and dropped his reins. The firelight framed him and his horse; it was a pretty sight to see.

"He's Johnny-on-the-spot all right," she thought. "Maybe he does just ride around helping people."

"Our horses are almost twins," she said.

"Yeah, I know. That's why I got this mare. I run into her in Laredo. I remembered Pearl. I named this one Chiquita."

He looked down and grubbed his boot toe against the ground a minute; then he sat down and drank a cup of coffee. They talked about the store and how long it would take to build it. He had already sent out word to all the grubbing gangs that a store was going in so they could trade close by. He called it La Tienda Caballo Blanco, the White Horse Store. Mexicans don't like people's names. He knew a fellow who would paint a picture of a horse, to hang out front. He'd corral a clerk to help her and bring in some milk goats. Tomorrow two barrels of water would be hauled in from the river.

They both laughed when he mentioned milk goats. The picture of their first meeting flashed before their eyes.

"I was sure scairt," he said, "when you keeled over dead."

"So was I!" Willy laughed. Then she remembered how tragic it had seemed when it happened.

"Mr. Lester," she started off in an entirely different tone, "I've waited these years to tell you what that visit on the ranch meant to me then, what it means to me yet. I was desperate. You came to help me. We're just as needy now and you're helping us again. I'm grateful, deeply grateful. I want you to know that."

Bill got up and stepped back out of the firelight. "Now see here, Miz Westall, I ain't done nothin' yet. You all have done for me—that's who's done the doin'. You just call me Bill, not Mister Lester, an' we'll get along."

They both laughed again.
He got on Chiquita and rode off.
Willy stood there watching.
He rode north.

Two days later they started building the store. The
same day the land office and Fanny's house were begun. Bill corralled carpenters enough to get things
going all at once. He left the scraping to Henry's su-
pervision for the week.

"You mustn't give us all your time," Willy said. She
was holding a two-by-four for him to nail.

"Scrapin' runs itself, Miz Westall. It's the mules that
does the work."

Pablo quit the depot and came over to help Meester
Beeley on his job. Pepe sat around and watched. Pat
did the bossing, giving directions with his crutch but
mostly cursing everybody.

"Take a little nap, Darling. You need some rest,"
Willy said the first afternoon.

"But we've got to build this store," he shouted.

"We can get on fine. You're lookin' awful tired."
Bill's voice was low and soothing.

"The hell I am!" Pat snapped.

Bill called Pepe aside and talked a minute; then the
Mexican rode off toward the river.

The next day things went better. Bill and Pat took
time out to do a little drinking on the side. About ten
o'clock Pat stretched out on the cot and went to sleep.
The work flew after that. Pablo did the sawing, Willy
held, and Bill nailed.

Pepe sat by on a bale of shingles, entertaining S'rita
with the wonders of his rooster. Pepitón sat on his
knee to have his feathers stroked; then he strutted up
and down and crowed. The javelina bristled up her
hair and snarled. Amara held the hog to save the
rooster's life. She felt uneasy. Poor Salita was so upset.
She showed her teeth and looked so ugly. Nobody
seemed to care.

S'rita certainly didn't. She just forgot the javelina.
She loved Pepe's rooster. He was so bright and pretty.
He made such noise. And she loved Pepe. He smiled

so, slipped her a peloncilla, rubbed her hair, and spoke such pretty words. Exquisita, que bonita—words like that she'd never heard. He'd pitch her up in the air too, like Fanny. She wanted to see a fight. He said the rooster did it. She stood by his knee and listened. She liked to hold his hand.

"Doesn't Pepe ever work?" Willy said to Bill.

"Not often, except when I need a little shootin' done. I got him out of a cuttin' scrape down at Penitas, an' ever since he follers me around. I pay him reg'lar because I like the cuss. Pablo's different. He's real good at gang bossin' all the time."

"Tell me about Pablo. He worries me. Those blue eyes—and his face is freckled."

Bill stopped hammering instantly, stepped back and looked at Willy in a way that scared her. His eyes sharpened; his face grew tense. She knew she had spoken out of turn.

"Pablo's a little mixed-bred, but he is a good hombre."

She jumped in fright. It was Bill's eyes that scared her. The boxing plank came crashing. Bill grabbed but missed it. Pat woke up.

Willy felt relieved. She wanted to escape her question. She knew now why Fanny could tell her nothing about Bill Lester. You didn't ask him questions. You just didn't; that was all.

A week later the store was finished. The sign in front read La Tienda Caballo Blanco; underneath, Westall's Store; then a picture of a white horse. It wasn't much to look at but it was beautiful to them, a boxlike, unceiled, one-roomed building, with a gallery out in front. The back they partitioned off for living quarters—just room enough for a bed, two cots for the children, a stove, a table, and the trunk.

When they moved in, they felt proud and happy. Theirs was the first house finished. Twelve tents had been pitched for the depot agent, canal riders, land salesmen, and engineers. Mr. Conlay set up his land office in a tent, awaiting a house. Even Fanny moved up to Mission to watch her building and to be close to S'rita.

"Have to brush her hair," she said to Willy, "and watch out for lice. Awful bad among the Mexkins."

Of course, the problem always was to catch S'rita first. The hair combing was the cross of S'rita's life. It wasn't fair. She hated Fanny when she pulled. Her hair always pulled. She hated hair. 'Mara's didn't pull, and 'Mara never cried. Fanny said, " 'Mara's good and you're bad," but S'rita didn't give a damn; it hurt so bad.

She always felt sorry later, but at the moment she couldn't help being bad. Things always came so fast they got her mixed up. She was too little to make people let her alone. And Mama always looked so unhappy, sad when she had to spank her, and that made things even worse. Papa got so excited and talked so loud and stamped around, himself. That made Mama look even more unhappy. If they would just let her alone these things would never happen. They never did to 'Mara, and Fanny said she was good. Someday she'd run off and leave them all and they'd be sorry too when she was gone.

Every morning S'rita tried to get away from that comb and brush. Sometimes Pepe saved her, but usually Fanny caught her and combed her curls. If she had to slap her, she comforted her by making a cake. S'rita always climbed up on the table to watch. When Fanny gave her a spoon to lick, S'rita always reached up and kissed her and patted her cheek the way she did Mama's. That made Fanny smile. S'rita loved to see Fanny smile and look happy. She wondered why they all got so mad at her. They never did at 'Mara. It really made her sad, but she'd make them think she didn't give a damn.

Willy knew the children were running wild. She thanked God that Fanny was there to watch them. She realized that it was a time when she should be very close to them to help them make the adjustment to their new home and way of living, but she was too busy. So much had to be done and done so quickly.

Things hummed to the tune of saw and hammer. It

was a staccato rhythm that fired the blood; new land, new hopes, new plans. Willy couldn't sleep; dreams swam.

The day they nailed down the last shingle Pat and Bill went down to Conlay's tent and got drunk. Willy felt ashamed that she was glad.

The grocery salesman came. She wanted to see him by herself. She seemed to sense trouble about that meeting. She had to save Pat humiliation if she could.

Mr. Dubose came in on the train and announced he would stay only the hour that it took the train to turn around at Fordyce and come back. He was an old man, little, thin, French, originally from New Orleans.

"I have awful stomach trouble," was his first announcement. "And I'm in an awful hurry," he said next. "Conlay dragged me down here against my will. It's bad enough to live in Corpus Christi. He tells me you mean to run a store."

"Yes, sir, we do." Willy smiled her best.

"Why in God's name here? The world's a big place yet!" He looked very angry and beaded his black eyes on her for an answer. She thanked God Pat and Bill were gone. Pepe was out back. Pablo worked on the shelves and counters, but he looked up. The man's voice was mad.

"Why don't you go somewhere else?" he asked again.

Willy couldn't think of anything to say because she didn't know herself. That night in Austin when Mr. Peterson told them about the new country Pat said they would come to the Valley of the Rio Grande. They had never thought of any other place. Maybe that was because they knew of no other place that went by the name of rivers. They were hot, thirsty, dry; they wanted water. But that sounded strange to say to the man before her.

"We just came here," she said. She felt stupid, ashamed, like a bad child scolded.

"Well, you'll be sorry," he growled back. "This whole Gulf Coast is Mexkin country and we oughta leave it with 'em. I'll praise the day I get back to New

Orleans again. Trouble's brewing at this minute across the border. A fellow named Madero wrote a book. *Mexico for Mexicans* he calls it. It's raising a big stir. Old Diaz has been President for thirty years and ruled the way he wished, but something's going to happen. There'll be an awful war!"

He paused and stared at her. Willy tried to smile.

"Can't downtrod the poor forever. There'll be an awful bust when they begin to ride. They'll swoop across this border and take this land for theirs. Better leave it to the ranchers and go back from where you came. This Diaz and Madero're bound to come to blows. They'll come over here and kill you in your beds." He lost his breath and coughed.

Willy interrupted. "But about the grocery order, Mr. Dubose?" She smiled with deliberation. "I don't want much to begin with: just some beans and rice; maybe a little lard and flour and some cartridges for our guns."

"How can you run a store on that?" he snarled. "You can't sell stuff you haven't got!"

"But I haven't got much money. I thought maybe you would credit us for about a month until we can get started."

His black eyes blazed. "Yeah, I was afraid of that. I told Conlay that's what you would want. Dragging me off down here on a trip for credit!"

Willy's eyes blazed too. "Well, Mr. Dubose, it's only business. People're moving in. The brush is full of Mexkins. Just give us time."

"Yeah, in time Conlay an' this whole country'll go flat broke. It's justa land scheme, hollow as a shell. None of my company's money's going down the rat hole with you!"

"But I've got to have some groceries to start in business!" Willy's voice mixed pride, anger, shame all up together.

"Then you'll pay cash!" He pounded the counter with his fist.

"Then I'll pay cash!" Willy pounded the counter back.

Pablo jumped and looked around. The loose boards

clattered. He saw Willy's face, flushed, angry; her eyes danced crazy in her head.

Just at that moment the train whistle blew. Mr. Dubose picked up his grip and started for the door.

"You take my order!" Willy commanded.

"I'll send you what you need, collect!" He was running.

"Not over a hundred dollars' worth," she shouted.

Pablo looked at Willy and started for the door.

Willy stopped him. "No, Pablo, thanks. Beggars can't be choosers. I guess it's so."

She was hurt, wounded to the core. For the first time she wanted money—lots of money, lots of dirty money—just to cram down that man's throat. Bill would cram it for her—no, she would cram it down herself. She would cry, then get busy and make that money.

She looked at Pablo. His eyes pleaded like a dog's. She couldn't cry before him—it would hurt him; so she said, "Damn it, Pablo, let's get started."

And they did. Pablo thought he'd done a lot of working but he never knew the meaning until then. The beautiful señora grabbed and snatched and pushed. "Nail here." "Saw there." "Help me lift." "Hurry, Pablo!" It was this way all the afternoon. She hurried. So did he, as best he could. They finished the counters and put in all the shelves.

Just once he stopped, to get a drink of water. He felt very hot and thirsty; so must the señora, but she didn't seem to care. They sweated, nailed, and hammered right along together.

At sundown Pepe came in to take a look. "Mira!" he murmured.

"Mira hell!" Willy shouted. "Go tell Pat and Bill we're finished, and you pass the word around."

That night Mission held a celebration in the store. Phil Allen brought his wife up from the river. She was a plain young woman, a little stretched in the middle from many children close together. Her frank good humor drew Willy to her. Willy did her best at welcoming, but she still felt too crushed by Dubose to be herself. 'Mara did the entertaining. S'rita sat on Pat's lap and smiled at her across the store. She got down once and walked over to Mrs. Allen. In her hand she held a pretty rock that she had found that day. She held it out. "Please take it," she said. Mrs. Allen took the rock and patted her on the head. Willy smiled. S'rita threw a kiss at her mama and ran back to Pepe's lap. She felt happy.

Mr. Conlay came over, Hal Eubank, Jesse Parnell, Engineer Rome, Agent Logan, Bill, Pepe, Fanny, and Henry. Everybody brought his lantern to light up the store. There was nothing but four walls and a roof overhead.

They sat on the counter and looked across at the boards in front. Moonlight could have peeped in through the cracks.

"We'll have canned goods on this side and hardware over there to begin with," Pat explained, hiccupping as he talked. "Then we'll have fancy groceries on this side and staples over there. Have to sell a few rakes and hoes to start with maybe, horse collars and stuff like that. In time I hope to put in a hardware store myself. Farm machinery oughta be big business in this country if you get in on the ground floor right."

Willy thanked God that Pablo spoke little English. On this one night she wished she could not speak a word herself.

"Miz Westall, did you order bacon?" Hal Eubank asked.

"Of course," Willy said.

"And canned apricots?" Jesse Parnell spoke up. "I love them things."

"Some pickles is what I've been hungry for," Mrs. Allen said.

"Hope you got vanilla," Bill put in.

"Canela, Madama?" Even Pepe had to ask.

"Cheese is what I want! Got plenty of cheese, didn't you, Sweetheart?"

"Well, I did the best I could," Willy answered all at once.

Bill saw her face. It was puzzled, tired. He knew she needed help.

He passed around mescal to everybody. Mr. Conlay

stood up and offered a toast to the Westalls and Mission, Texas. Everybody drank. After that the talk got off the details of Willy's order to the next land-excursion party.

Later Mr. and Mrs. Weisschmidt drove up in their buckboard. With them was Tom Jones, to see Mr. Conlay. The Weisschmidts had met Tom in Germany when he was doing research. Now he was practicing law, looking for a place to settle. His talk that followed indicated many former settlings.

After the third drink he announced, "Made the run into Oklahoma City in 1889."

"My God," Pat shouted, "we were there together!"

Then Tom and Pat mixed up bragging with drinking, in remarkable proportion. They both were very wealthy in property back in Oklahoma—just holding it as an investment. They both had come to the Valley for their health; both were down just on a lark to hunt a lot and rest up some. Tom was the better entertainer of the two. He could recite Shakespeare, and did. Everybody listened, awe-struck.

Fanny went to put 'Mara and S'rita into bed.

Willy had to slip outside. Pearl nickered and came up close. They both looked up at the stars.

17

The groceries came in C.O.D. Willy arranged with the agent not to let Pat know. If she had to pay, she had to pay. That was all. No need to sell Pat's pride into the deal. Money couldn't buy her joy. Pat was hurrying on his crutches, his eyes brightened. He met every train, welcomed every comer, planned with Father Michael, expanded the virtues of irrigation, studied the land charts, exhorted Tom Jones to hustle and build an office to start out in the swim. He was the busiest person in town, and Willy was the happiest.

The last service Sal and Pito gave the Westalls was

to haul the groceries to the store. Phil Allen bought the team and wagon for his ranch. Willy negotiated with him the day the bill came in. The bill was for three hundred dollars plus freight charge. From Corpus Christi to the Valley the desert rate almost doubled the amount. That meant all her money. Dubose padded the order just for spite. She felt desperate. That afternoon when Mr. Allen rode in, she sold him the team and wagon.

"Now we've got to stay," she said.

"Why, sure!" The rancher looked up surprised, almost hurt.

She was afraid to tell Pat. He might feel trapped, his legs jerked away again. Dubose might be right about the Mexicans across the river. They might need to get away. She felt a little worried.

When Pat and Father Michael walked in, the priest was talking. Bill and Tom Jones were just behind them.

"Why, that'll start a revolution! Old Diaz'll come right here to get than man Madero and kill us in our beds!" Tom Jones exclaimed.

"The hell he will!" Bill Lester cut him short. "Our guns're still in shootin' order and this's still the U.S.A. What'll Jesse here and the Rangers be doin' all the time? Mexkins don't wanta fight us. They wanta fight just a little on their own. Our business is to let 'em all alone."

"What's that?" Willy asked.

"Nothin'," Bill said.

"Very little," the priest added. "It's just the news. Good to have an Irishman to talk with again."

"But what's the news?" Willy asked.

"Just some from Mexico. That man Madero, who has been dreaming freedom for his people, got arrested and put in jail. President Diaz just won't have him around, it seems."

Tom Jones interrupted. "And we won't either." He turned to Willy. "And they say he got out and is hiding here in the Valley."

Father Michael looked at him and frowned.

"Well, it's not safe," Tom went on.

Bill laughed loudly. "Well, there's the railroad, friend. Why don't you leave if you're scared?"

"Sure," Pat spoke up. "That's what the railroad's for."

They all laughed.

Bill said, "Don't you worry. Nothin'll ever happen here." Soon Bill, Tom Jones, and Father Michael went out.

"Well, I just sold our horses," Willy said to Pat. "Sold them to Mr. Allen. We've got no place to keep them as it is."

"Sure," Pat said, "the very thing to do. Meant to talk to him myself about it. Oughta sell Pearl now and get rid of her."

"Pearl?" Willy's eyes and voice both fired in the instant. Not even Pat could mention selling Pearl. "I'd just as soon sell the children!" she said.

Pat said no more. Something in his wife's face displeased him; yet it was something he could not challenge.

Willy walked to the door and called Pablo. She hired him to build a corral at the back. He started in at once, with just the brush to work with. Pepe joined in the enterprise, to watch.

Willy ventured, "Why don't you build Pepitón a coop? There're plenty of shingles. He must get awfully tired riding in that morral."

Pepe's dark eyes softened like a woman's when you praise her baby. "Sí, Madama, muy cansado." He took off his pistol and went to work.

Serena was on his heels every moment. She loved doing things with Pepe; so did everybody; even Pat went out to take a look.

That afternoon Willy learned a lot about the Mexican people from Pablo and Pepe's working. She knew why Bill pledged them allegiance. She learned a lot about their art.

For the corral Pablo fitted brush between the mesquite poles as if he were setting tile in an intricate design. He was a different person from the one who hammered machine boards into place. Pepe's face was illuminated as he worked. In that watching, Willy discovered the individual charm of each jacal she'd seen. It was some one man's expression of himself in a material he understood: man and earth in the intimate relationship of touch.

From time to time Pepe stopped to stroke Serena's hair, lightly, almost as if he feared to touch it. She held the shingles while he hammered. He told her stories about his rooster. 'Mara stood and listened.

"Pepitón fight. He ween mohney lak sonomabitch," he bragged.

"Can I see him?" S'rita asked.

"No, you too leedre, S'ritita! You ride Fuego. Heem can peetch!"

Willy smiled when he laid his hand upon the yellow curls. "Como oro!" he said, "Como oro!" His voice pitched low, reverent as if he said a prayer.

'Mara came to stay with Mama. Bill was hauling groceries. They went in the store.

"How's the coop and corral comin'?" Bill stopped long enough to ask.

"S'rita's hair's the interference," Willy answered.

Bill laughed loudly. "It's the evil eye," he said. "They have to touch a thing. Somethin' evil happens if they don't. All Mexkins love yeller hair, but Pepe's gone plumb loco over S'rita. He talks about her in his sleep. Its because she's so quick and sassy."

Amara's ears pricked up. She sidled closer to Mama. She wished Bill would pat her head, but he didn't. He was like Mama; he was too busy.

It was a busy day for everybody. As Bill hauled groceries from the depot he piled them on the floor. Willy tried to assort and put them up as he brought in boxes, but he speeded up too much.

"Leave 'em there," he said. "We'll all pitch in an' shelve 'em up tonight. Tomorrow's Saturday. We'll be all ready for the rush."

"Rush!" Willy looked out at the surrounding chaparrel. "That evil old man knew we'd have to eat these groceries. That's why he sent so many."

She tried to look brave. She could do that much at least, but she was scared. Dubose had scared her. She had put her last cent into a dream. She thought of snakes, tarantulas, mad coyotes. She felt robbed, shorn, poor like a pauper.

At dark she lit the coal-oil lamps and hung them in their brackets on the wall. The regular arrangement of light gave the room an air, made it take on the role of store. "God, make them come and trade!"

"It's like seeing a baby born," she said to Pat.

"Looks like hell with all that stuff piled up on the floor. Why didn't you make those Mexkins put it up?"

Bill Lester and Hal Eubank walked in; then Mr. Conlay, Jesse Parnell, Tom Jones, and the depot agent. Later Henry and Fanny came.

"Sam here tells me you got apricots," Tom Jones began. "Let's get busy and put 'em on the shelves. Nothin' suits me better'n seein' pretty labels on a shelf. It's like Romeo said to Juliet."

"Yeah, big order," Sam Logan cut in. "Mighty proud to have some business for the railroad." Sam felt his pride in being ticket agent of the Valley's newest town.

Willy tried to smile and look undaunted.

At that moment a Mexican stepped timidly inside the door. Behind him came a woman with a baby in her arms. They were strange-looking people. Not like the Torres Mexicans on the ranch, nor like Pepe or Pablo. They were small, broad-featured Indians, a very different race. The man wore a big sombrero, tight pants, huaraches on his feet. The woman swathed herself and her baby in a shawl—head, shoulders, bust. Her feet patted bare upon the floor.

Willy rushed to meet them at the door.

"Qué quiere?" she almost sang.

"Frijoles, una libra."

The man handed her a dime. It was Mexican money—dirty, sticky. But she felt impelled to eat it just for luck. She had sold a pound of beans for cash. That broke the Dubose spell. She would sell those groceries, buy more and more and more! She would prove to that mean old man that she could run a store.

By the time she got behind the counter, Bill had the beans done up.

"Just guessed at a pound, but that'll do to start on. These Castros here are friends of mine," he said. "He's on my scrapin' gang an' she's mighty good for washin' clothes. I'll make a little deal for you all now."

Both Mexicans smiled at whatever Meester Beeley said to the Madama of the Caballa Blanco Store. This was a strange, exciting place, with lights hanging on the walls just like Meester Beeley say to all the people working in the dirt, digging cuts into the earth for what purpose they did not know—nor did they care. Sixty centavos wage a day was great fortune here. They came in herds across the river to work for these gringos who hurried so, talked in loud language, and reddened in the face.

Would she wash for the Madama? Of course. Why not?

"Tell her a dollar a week and I'll furnish soap and starch and give her a tub and washboard," Willy said to Bill.

"That's too much. She'll do it for four bits."

"No, I haven't got the heart. I want plenty of washing now that we've got irrigation." He laughed, then she laughed herself.

"Well, clothes'll be kinda dingy an' half-ironed an' smell like hell sometimes, but they'll be clean," he said.

Two more Mexicans came in. Bill and Willy rushed to serve them, filling their order from the groceries on the floor. Then two more families; then six came at once.

Hal and Jesse pitched in to help. So did Fanny. They knocked open the lard barrel and ripped open the sugar sack. Pablo brought his hammer to unnail the cases full of cans.

"No use for that," Pat said. "These Mexkins want just rice and beans." He and Tom Jones sat on onion crates watching what went on, sipping at mescal. Mr. Conlay paced up and down, exclaiming to Sam Logan. From what Willy gathered in hurried jerks, he wanted the railroad to put on extra cars for the cabbage crop. Her ears blurred in the medley of hammer knocking, tearing, ripping, paper rattling, people talking, voices

pitched—English, Spanish, children laughing—money
ringing. Bill showed her how to see if it were real—
fling it on the counter for a clear reverberation. A
dead thud meant counterfeit. Strange money came:
nickels, dimes, pesos, copper pennies big as quarters,
an odd piece called a tostón—all filthy, grimy, greasy.
But it came! Her fingers reached and got it and put
it in the drawer. Lots of money! Lots of people! She
reached and got and gave! Bill was there grabbing,
snatching, giving orders. She obeyed.

Once Pat got up in the way. He tried to find tobacco
—Tom Jones had run out of liquor and now he
wanted to chew. She stopped and found it for him.
When she got back behind the counter, a Mexican
boy was there dipping lard.

"This here's Emelio Lopez," Bill said amidst the
flurry. "He's your clerk from out here on the Lopez
ranch and knows some English."

He was slight and fair, much like the Benito she
had loved.

They worked on, all together.

About twelve o'clock the crowd cleared out. Willy
looked around. The floor was cluttered with open
boxes, sacks, barrels, cans. Mr. Conlay, Tom Jones,
and Sam Logan had gone home. Fanny had taken Pat
and S'rita back to bed. 'Mara she found underneath
the counter, sleeping on a shawl. Pablo and Pepe sat
on the gallery steps outside, smoking cigarettes.

"Let's all have a drink," Bill said.

From somewhere a José Cuervo came forth and
was uncorked. She got the glasses, and Bill, Hal, and
Jesse drank to the evening and the work. She and
Emelio stood back and watched.

"Hope you don't mind, Miz Westall." Bill suddenly
turned red. "I never thought to ask. I'm actin' like a
bull in a purty strange corral."

"No." Willy smiled. "I'm drunk myself with joy.
Where did they come from, and so fast? You said a
rush tomorrow, but I never dreamed it would be like
this before we even get things on the shelves."

"Why, they've been waitin' for a store. Word gets
'round fast in scraper-gangs an' grubbin' camps.

More're comin' every day. Goin' to clear the country an' get it sold. Tomorrow'll be better yet. Let's get this stuff put up tonight."

He stepped outside and brought Pablo and Pepe in, reluctant, but they came. They all rolled up their sleeves and went to work.

When Willy finally fell into bed she knew she was very tired; yet she never had felt so rested. Her back ached, her feet throbbed; her heels ran spikes up through her legs, but her heart's wings fluttered at her chest. Pat snored softly at her side. His breath came mescal-laden. In the moonlight she saw his face. He slept in peace, almost smiling. She kissed him on the forehead. He snored, slept on.

On the cot before her, Serena's hair picked up the moon-rays. Amara coughed and turned. Nobody woke. Willy stretched her leg high into the air to relieve the cramping in her foot. She must get some good strong shoes to support her feet for standing, thick-soled and broad.

When she first went back to go to bed she had hoped Pat would be awake. She wanted to count the money. She had waited to do that with him. But now she was glad he slept. Tomorrow they would count the money; tonight she would rest and think.

The last thing Bill Lester had done was to give her his pistol and his cartridge belt. He must have seen the envy in her eyes. He had said, "Wanta give you a little present. A feller died an' give it to me." He unbuckled and handed her pistol, belt, and all. "Keep it close. In the daytime by the money; when you're sleepin', by your bed."

She had said, "Thank you." She loved the feel of the pistol as she took it in her hand. She had to have a pistol. Something to grab quickly. The next time Dubose came she'd make him stand still long enough to write down on her order Winchester and shotgun shells. Ammunition is what it takes, in a gun or in yourself! Ammunition and plenty of it! Those awful days and nights when she had so few bullets! That awful journey through the sand! She turned over and determined to quit thinking.

Pearl nickered. Willy jumped up, grabbed the pistol, and stepped out the back door. The moon shone bright in its half quarter. She ran to the corral. Pearl hung her head over the gate and nuzzled, then she arched her neck and nickered in a wild-horse way, unfamiliar even to herself.

Willy walked around the store. She saw two men riding across the railroad track. She looked closely. They were Bill and Pepe. She ducked back to hide, but Bill saw her. He kicked Chiquita to a run and was alongside in a second.

"What's wrong?" His voice was low and hoarse.

Willy backed close to the wall to talk. She thanked God for his full domestic nightgown. She felt clothed, covered up, but timid to be caught.

"What's wrong, Miz Westall?" Bill was on the ground. He stepped up close. Willy felt his breath, hot, mescaled, but steady.

"Nothing," she said. "Pearl just nickered."

Then she remembered she had the pistol in her hand. Bill was gazing at the pistol and at her.

A tense silence followed; then Bill spoke. "Where's the money?"

"In my bed."

"Hear any noises?"

"No. Just Pearl. When she nickers, I always see what it is she wants."

Pepe rode up then, he and his horse silhouetted in the moonlight. Pearl nickered again in that unfamiliar way. Fuego answered. For the first time Willy noted that his horse was stud.

She said, "Don't worry. It's nothing wrong in particular."

Fuego pawed the ground; Pearl lunged at her corral.

Bill remounted slowly. "Rode down to check up on camp. Come by to see how things was here. Always keep a sharp eye when too many folks're 'round. These grubbin' Mexkins're new here now." He pulled up his rein and smiled down at Willy.

"Good night," he said. Chiquita galloped off. Pepe followed.

They rode north.

Pearl pawed and stomped at the corral. Fuego answered in the distance. Willy walked around the house. She set herself to thinking. The hard cool steel in her hand helped greatly.

She went up to Pearl. The mare was nervous, rearing. She snorted and pulled backwards.

"I'll be damned!" Willy said.

18

The next morning Willy got up at five.

She milked the goats, cooked breakfast, and swept the store. She finished the gallery with a flourish. Mexicans crossed the railroad track. She wanted to be standing by the money drawer ready to cash in.

When she turned her head she saw Bill riding in from north. Pepe wasn't with him; another Mexican was, a boy about sixteen, maybe twenty.

"This here's Chico," Bill said as he swung off his horse. "He'll buy groceries. Charge 'em all to me."

That opened Conchita's credit, the first account the Westalls had.

Bill tied Chiquita to the gallery post, and walked in.

"Well, let's get started," he said. "This is Saturday. We've gotta pitch right in." His eyes were clear and steady, his shoulders square and straight. When he stepped in the door, things seemed to swing to balance. The sun set to steady shining, the dust settled on the floor. Pat began to sing "Rock of Ages."

Willy went about filling Chico's order. It was simple: rice, beans, lard, flour, sugar, coffee, and a bottle of vanilla. The vanilla told the story. Willy flinched a little when she wrote vanilla. It spelled out something she couldn't see.

"Some things we know but never will believe," she blurted.

"What's that, Miz Westall?" Bill was whistling "La Paloma," and pitching cans onto the shelves.

"Nothing," Willy answered. "I was asking Chico what about some eggs. It takes eggs to make a cake."

Bill looked straight at her a moment but said nothing. He kept on whistling.

Willy hurried then with Chico. She wanted to get busy with the store. That's what mattered. All this other stuff was fancy thinking.

Bill was right. The day turned into a whirlwind. By ten o'clock that night they had sold everything in stock. Willy telegraphed Corpus Christi for the order in duplication. When he sent the message, Sam Logan drank a bottle of mescal. Mr. Dubose wired back "Good luck!" He doubled the amount and shipped it on open order.

Business boomed. Money jingled. Willy rang it on the counter and put it in the drawer. She forgot that she found little time to eat or sleep. She opened up each morning at six and kept open until twelve or one at night. The big rush came after dark, when the Mexicans finished work and walked in from camp to trade. As they called for items, she added them to her stock. Mr. Dubose came from Corpus Christi and took her order for everything she asked: coal oil, lanterns, blankets, shoes, socks, work pants, shirts, hats, horse collars, rakes, shovels, calico, aceite Mexicana, and vaselina.

Mexicans poured across the river. The town grew; a strange crowd of people from everywhere on earth. It grew stranger every week with each land-seeking party Conlay and Fogg imported and with every train the chuggy engine pulled into the depot, to say nothing of the influx that came by wagon, horse-back, and God-knows-how: cowboys, scraper crews, canal riders, doctors, and lawyers by the dozens, all trying to get in on the ground floor.

Every day Pat met the train. Down the deep dust of La Lomita Boulevard he limped, escorting all newcomers to the store. Nobody escaped the Westalls and no dead beat overlooked the chance of asking loan or credit; no homesick adventurer missed Pat's Irish smile and Willy's warm encouragement; no wayfarer lacked a welcome. La Tienda Caballo Blanco was the center of Mission.

It seemed a little too much of a center to suit Bill Lester. One day Willy overheard him talking to Pablo and Pepe, giving them directions. He told them to take turns at keeping a sharp watch on the store. The thing to worry about was the hundreds of strange Mexicans coming across the river—the shiftless moving pelados that wandered here and there looking for work. They might be tempted to gang up to rob the store. It was full of groceries and nobody there but a woman; besides, she might get hurt. Pablo and Pepe were to keep down any kind of trouble. He didn't want Miz Westall scared. At that point Willy lost track of the conversation, for Bill spoke almost in a whisper. She did hear the words "trouble" and "Weissschmidt," then something about stirring up resentment against the Americans in the grubbing camps.

Willy never spoke of what she had overheard, to Bill or to anybody else; in fact, she thought little more about it. The thing to do was to take things as they came. The chief consideration was that new people kept on coming to the Valley.

At first the newcomers were mostly men. They lived in tents, to get crops in, build houses, and then send home for wives and children. Many of them were old people—rich, retired, weary of the hard Iowa and Nebraska winters, willing to pay fancy prices for land to get the blessing of Texas sunshine. The minute dark came on they all made for the store to trade and talk and plan. The Mexicans swarmed; the Americans sat back and watched. Willy and Emelio led in clerking. Bill and Fanny came in to help. Pablo and Pepe lingered on the porch. Pat and Father Michael led in conversation. Tom Jones quoted the classics to illustrate their points. The big topic was land sales and new crops. Grapefruit was brought in from California. Nobody liked it, but Mr. Conlay said it should be planted. Oranges and lemons were being put in by forties and even sometimes by eighties.

"Make her blossom! Make her blossom!" Mr. Conlay said.

Tom Jones was the only cynic in the group. He was apprehensive about the Mexican situation across the river. Father Michael was the only one who would talk about it. He did it only to be kind to Tom. When Madero and Pancho Villa took Ciudad Juarez and started south to the City of Mexico, Tom got plainly scared.

"They're gettin' too close to us here on the border!" he said one night.

"No, they're just starting at the Rio Grande and working down." The priest's words were quiet and assured. "They're not coming over here. Cortina tried that back after the Civil War, but we had cattle then. Mexicans don't want grapefruit or oranges to eat."

Tom left the men to their grapefruit planting and came over to Willy at the counter.

"It may mean revolution," he said. "I'd hate to see it!"

"Well , let it come!" Willy said. She was busy. Why worry about something that hadn't happened? Too much had already happened. After all, what was a little shooting compared with what she knew of quiet and the prolonged misery of thirsty nights, cattle lowing in the dark for water, a sick baby tossing out her pain, tears swimming in the eyes of one you love, a trackless journey over desert sand, a gun beside you with every cartridge gone. No; she'd take a revolution if there was to be a choice. That would be quick and easy in comparison and she'd have a chance to win. It's a cinch to fight if you can find the thing to shoot at. It's that fighting in the abstract without a soul in sight that takes a man to do it.

Late that night Bill sent word to Willy that he and Pepe had to take a trip.

The next night when he came in, Bill was hot and sweaty.

"Where have you been?" Tom asked. "What's the meaning of your friends Pancho Villa and Madero starting up a fight?"

"Nothin' a'tall! Nothin' a'tall!" Bill grinned broadly.
"What d'you mean, 'nothin' a'tall'?' Explain yourself."

Bill kept on smiling. "That feller down there named Madero is goin' to topple old Diaz off his throne."

"You mean a revolution?"

"No. It'll be the best thing that ever happened."

"Say that again! You mean overthrow the Government down there?"

"Sure! But it's not what it sounds like. It's their business; it's not ours. I know them fellers well. They want freedom for their people just like we got it for our own. Pancho Villa is a special friend of mine. We done some minin' down in Seralgo together not long back and he told me what they'd planned. Madero's a dreamer, but Pancho'll keep him straight. Just give 'em a little time and they'll calm things down. All they want t'do is get rid of old Diaz and give the under dog a chance. He's beat 'em down now for thirty years or more."

John Sanders got up and clicked his old army boots. For a moment he thought he was back in the Philippines. He called Bill to one side and talked. Very soon they left the store.

Before the week was out news came that President Diaz had had to flee the country and Madero had taken his place. His triumphal entry into Mexico City headlined the nation's papers.

"Just give 'em a little time to settle down," Bill said. "It won't be long."

Tom Jones, however, began saving his money to move on. He had his doubts about the Rio Grande Valley with a Mexican revolution across the river.

But the sun shone on. The fertile delta plus irrigation turned the desert into a garden. Whatever was planted grew into giant proportions in the growing season of twelve months a year. Oranges, grapefruit, lemons, palms—date and palmetto—canna lilies, roses, ferns, banana trees, pecans. They all beautified the country while truck brought in the money despite the cutthroat market system and bad shipping that seemed beyond control.

And people kept on coming to the Magic Valley of the Rio Grande. Among the many were the Mr. and Mrs. Peterson whom Pat and Willy had met in Austin. Late one afternoon they walked into the store. Willy was glad to see them.

"Brought my wife to Mission to live close to you, Miz Westall. I'm on the Valley freight run now. That keeps me out at night," Mr. Peterson announced.

"Yes, since Ivan came I'm not so well. I just can't get my strength back," Mrs. Peterson put in. "I'd like to be close to you, Mrs. Westall."

"Is that your baby? The one S'rita's age?" Willy asked. The child she saw before her was undersized, thin, and pale. He wore glasses; his mouth hung open.

"Yes, that's Ivan," Mrs. Peterson replied. "He's not well either, never has been. He just can't get over birth. I almost died, you remember!"

At that moment the back screendoor slammed and S'rita came running through the store. Her hair was flying. She held a cooky in her hand.

"S'rita, honey!" Willy called. "What's your hurry? Stop and speak to little Ivan Peterson. He's just your age, almost exactly. Do shake hands."

S'rita stopped, but she gave a quick glance behind her. She looked up at her mama and tried to smile, but her eyes were shifting here and there. She walked straight up to the little boy and stuck out her hand. "Howdy," she said, a little grimly.

The boy hung back. He grabbed his mother's skirt and held on tightly.

"Well, I'll be damned," his father said.

"Do speak to the little girl," his mother admonished.

S'rita reached out the cooky to him. "Take it," she said, "Fanny'll give me another one." Then she looked behind her and began to fidget. She stared up at her mama, but Willy didn't see her—she was talking loudly to Mr. Peterson about a house or something. The man was frowning. The woman was stooping down, talking to her son, trying to get him to take the cooky.

S'rita jumped when she heard the back screendoor

slam. If Mama would only look down at her! If the boy wouldn't take her cooky she'd have to try something else and get going. She rammed her hand in her apron pocket and brought out a sharp metal spike.

"Here, take this," she said. "It's a spur. Pepe puts it on Pepitón to fight. He's a rooster and fights like hell."

The woman drew back and stared at S'rita. "You shouldn't use such language," she whispered.

The boy still hung back and clung to his mother's skirt.

S'rita was getting mad. Mama had asked her to be nice and shake hands. She'd done the best she could. The boy wouldn't take a thing she had to offer, and now the woman scolded. Fanny was coming and she knew it. She'd heard the back screendoor slam. She'd get a whipping if Fanny caught her, for she was supposed to have her hair washed and she'd run off when Fanny wasn't looking.

"Little girls should never swear," the woman went on whispering. Willy kept talking loudly. Her back was now turned to the children and Mrs. Peterson. The man was scowling.

S'rita crammed the spike back in her pocket. She gave one quick glance backward and saw Fanny reach down and grab a strip off a crate. The Negro swung wide to make a mighty wallop. S'rita gave one lightning glance out front. Pepe was riding up on Fuego. He would save her! She was standing between Fanny and Mrs. Peterson. Just as Fanny whizzed the box top through the air, S'rita ducked and flew. The board came down wham on the stranger woman's bottom.

"I'll teach you to run off," Fanny shouted.

Willy jumped and looked around, and Mrs. Peterson screamed.

"My God!" Willy murmured. She and Fanny stared at each other.

"Excuse me, Madam," Fanny choked; then she arched her neck and walked on out the door.

Willy caught a glimpse of S'rita flying out front. Pepe flung out his foot, she grabbed the stirrup, he clutched her hand. In a second they were off. She held the reins, shouting, "Ándele, Fuego! Let's run!"

Mrs. Peterson gasped weakly, "Who's that woman?"

"She's a friend. I couldn't live without her," Willy answered. "She helps me raise my children. I just haven't got the time."

There was a moment's silence; then the man said, "You've got children worth the raisin'." All at once he broke out laughing wildly, almost insanely, pointing at his wife and son.

Willy reddened. What could she say! S'rita and Fanny had acted awful and she knew it, but she couldn't do anything about it now—just couldn't. She felt so sorry for the woman. She cleared her throat and coughed.

"Why, Papa!" Mrs. Peterson exclaimed.

He kept on laughing.

Pat walked in at that minute. One glance told him something had gone wrong. The woman's eyes were bugging, the child was crying, and Peterson was acting like a crazy man.

"Come on, Peterson, let's have a drink," Pat drawled.

"I need one, God knows it!" The man stopped laughing as he and Pat went out together.

Willy turned to Mrs. Peterson, who was weeping. Willy put her arms around her.

"What will I do, Miz Westall! He's gettin' worse. No wonder I'm not well."

Willy patted her shoulder. "Now don't you worry, Mrs. Peterson. When he comes back you'll never know it happened. That's Pat's business; he smooths out kinks for other people."

Father Michael walked in and Willy introduced Mrs. Peterson and Ivan to him. Willy gave him a side wink and he started at once talking about the boy. When Emelio asked a question, Willy went behind the counter and busied herself with the trade. She heard scraps of their conversation—about operations and the place of human suffering in God's plan of things. She felt relieved when the priest came over to the counter and told her he was taking Mrs. Peterson and her son to the land office to see Mr. Conlay about a lot on which to build a house.

Willy felt sorry for the poor woman and the child, and she felt sorry for the man. Somehow it was a lot of wrong all mixed up together. Sometimes things are just like that. The trade grew heavier, and Willy kept on thinking as she scooped up beans and rice. Mexicans swarmed into the store. It was just after work time and they kept coming. Willy watched the women and the men together. Simple Indians though they were, she sensed a oneness between the couples. They didn't confuse themselves with reasons; they just lived. She thought back to the Rancho Seco and that pretty Mexican woman with all the children. Yes, Mexicans had a way with things she wished she understood— she and all the Americans in the world.

She felt very peaceful. She had a lot of things to learn but she would learn them. At the moment she was weighing a pound of lard for her washwoman. She gave another dab onto the tray and said, "Pelon, I wish I could give you fifty pounds for the service you give me in that washing! And you brought me luck—you were my first customer."

Of course the woman didn't understand a word Willy said, but she smiled broadly.

A gun was fired outside and they both jumped. The lard fell on the floor. For a moment there was silence; then the Mexicans began to chatter and to push toward the door. Willy stuck her head out the window.

Pepe held a pistol in his hand. Bill was slapping him on the back.

"What happened?" Willy asked.

"Pepe shot an hombre," Bill said.

"What for?"

"A bunch of smart fellows decided they'd gang up and rush your cash drawer and stack themselves with lard and beans and stuff, but Pepe spotted the leader and got him."

"Not your Mexkins!"

"Well, not exactly."

Bill smiled at her, then turned to Pepe. Willy knew then that she had asked enough questions. Bill had a way of letting you know that he was through with a subject.

The shot hombre disappeared into the twilight. The Mexicans milled about awhile, then the trade went on as usual. When it cleared out a bit, Bill said something to Jesse Parnell and they left. Mr. Peterson came in drunk and happy, and went off to get his wife and child. Pat went back to bed. His hip was hurting; his scanty strength was spent.

Later Bill and Jesse came back looking tired, breathing heavily, faces red. Bill's hands seemed swollen.

He waited until everybody had left before he talked. Pepe and Pablo lingered on the gallery, watching. Bill and Willy were alone. She asked no questions. She stood waiting. His face looked stern.

"Guess I'd better tell you so's you can be on watch," he began. "Somethin's brewin'. Cain't find out just what. 'T'ain't like Mexkins to get stirred up. They're quiet and peaceful. We pay 'em plenty. That oughta be enough. Watch Pearl. Somebody's stealin' horses. 'T'ain't you they wanta hurt, but the store's the place we Americans all get together in."

She stared frankly at his hands.

"Yeah!" He frowned. "Took them bad hombres out an' beat 'em. I been watchin'. Some come over that never want work. Somebody sends 'em, I believe. Or somebody's here who stirs 'em up. We gotta beat 'em!"

"Beat 'em?"

"Yeah, betterin' shootin'. Tied 'em up to trees. Jesse helped me. Word has to get around that we Americans're watching. This store'll be our point." Then he smiled and looked straight at her.

Willy studied the blueness of Bill's eyes, clear, deep —not light, swimming on the surface. They had a curtain out in front. It held you back. You came so far but no farther. He knew things that were his to keep.

"Wanta swap guns with you," he was saying. "That one you got may fail. Keep your shot-gun loaded, and the Winchester too, for Emelio and Mister Westall."

He unbuckled, handed her the belt and pistol. She reached down, got hers, and exchanged it with him.

"Thanks!" she said. "Lucky you got lots of guns."

"Yeah" He smiled. "Fellows die and give 'em to me."

"I'm glad!" She held out her hand. He took it. He took both her hands. They both looked down at the shaking. All four hands were hard, calloused, dirty, tanned—and strong!

19

The day they counted out the first five hundred dollars' profit Pat said, "God, Sweetheart, but your hands're gettin' rough. It won't be long now till we'll be on easy street again and you can take things easy and get out your diamond ring to wear."

Willy didn't look at her hands. She said, "This'll pay the note in Austin."

Pat wrote out the check and leaned back proudly in his chair. The desk was new. He had insisted on a swivel chair. Willy hadn't argued. It gave Pat poise to have a desk where he could sit and transact business. It made her glad.

"Damned crazy sendin' money clear to Brownsville. Guess I'll start a bank."

Pat loved money—not to keep, but to touch it. It gave him a sense of strength and ease. He liked to hand it out, to take it for granted, to feel it in his pocket.

But Lon Stone beat Pat to the banking. Lon came in one day on the train. Pat met him and brought him to the store. He was a white-faced fellow from Chicago.

"Want to get out of Chicago. Cold," was all he said.

He went straight to putting up a brick building next to the land office. There he opened up the First State Bank of Mission.

"That's progress!" Pat said. They were drinking to Lon's health. "Now, Bill you ought to start in business!"

"What kinda business? Sendero cuttin' an' ditch-diggin' is all I know."

"Any kind of business just so's you get started in on the ground floor."

Every train brought in lumber to build houses. Pablo's hammer and a dozen others like it pounded a steady rhythm from sunup to sundown, not only in Mission but in every little town up and down the sixty miles of the Rio Grande Valley.

"It's a hymn of faith to growth and dreams," Willy said to Pat.

"Pure contagion," he answered. "That's all it takes to make a business. Just get one started; the others quick will fall in line."

Bill bought the lot next door to the Westalls, built a saloon, and hired a man named Kinney to run it for him. They called it "Bill's Place."

Willy felt surprised. She wondered why he did it.

"Got a buildin' spree on," he said, "Cain't seem to get enough. Caught the fever from ever'body."

He built himself a three-roomed house to live in just one block west. It was a replica of Fanny's. "So's to be close in an' next to Fanny. Wanta keep caught up on grub."

Willy felt relieved for him to have a home. That would be an anchor, make him steady. Those were her words.

He slept in one room, Hal Eubank in the other; the third was the guest room of the town. Every visitor of importance slept there when they came: railroad officials, newspaper men of all denominations, irrigation experts, and engineers. Many came to see the country and speculate on what it ought to do.

Fanny went over once a day and cleaned up Bill's room. S'rita was always with her unless she was off with Pepe. 'Mara stayed with Mama. She sat on the counter and listened to the grown-ups talk, or measured beans and rice into little sacks for rush trade. S'rita wanted to be out in the sunshine.

Willy was not happy about the children when she took time out to think about them. That was the point; she had not time to give them. They were growing up alone. She got them up in the morning and cooked their breakfast, but after that they just darted in and out. What she did for them was on the run. And yet the real reason for everything was the children. But what could she expect? After all, Pat was Pat.

Amara was no problem. She stayed very close at hand, but S'rita didn't like to stay inside as long as it was daylight. She wanted to ride a horse. Pepe loved to take her, and Willy didn't mind except without permission. She tried to keep the rule of S'rita's minding Fanny. She talked to Pepe. He said, "Sí, Señora," but when S'rita begged him, he could not resist her smile.

Fanny objected to the riding.

"The exercise is good," Willy reasoned.

"Yes, but he might steal her."

"But Bill trusts Pepe with anything on earth. His devotion's like a dog's."

"Not with a S'rita." That was as much as she could state.

Just to be certain, Willy spoke to Bill about it.

"Just as safe as God," he said. "Fanny's jealous; so is Pepe. They both want S'rita every minute. It's a feud. Let 'em have her; between the two they'll watch her an' do it right."

Willy had to let Fanny have her way, Fanny watched the children's diet, corrected them, set up standards for them. She fed them dinner and supper separate from the boarders. Willy paid the board bill; that was all. She started once to offer Fanny some extra money, but she caught the Negro's eyes. They were tragic.

"I've never had any children. To think now I've got a white and golden baby!" She began to cry.

So Willy never mentioned money. Fanny's service to her was one money couldn't buy. For dinner and for supper Pat joined Fanny's boarders. Willy always meant to get to the table, but she couldn't. Food was unimportant to her. What a comfort it was, though, to know her family was well fed.

"Let's eat sardines today," she'd say to Emelio in a lull time. "Or salmon—or maybe a can of peaches—

anything for food. When a person's hungry, anything is good."

"As long as you've got plenty of water," she always added.

Everybody bought drinking water from ox-cart peddlers who hauled it from the river; but there was plenty. Sometimes Willy woke up in the nighttime thinking, "There's a river just three miles south of Mission and it's ours!"

It was Bill who was much concerned about Willy's eating. He seemed to be the only one except Amara. The others were just too taken up with their own doings to remember that she hadn't eaten. Every day 'Mara came running in with a plate of something from Fanny's, but Willy seldom stopped to eat at the moment.

"It's gettin' cold, Mama," 'Mara always pleaded.

"In a minute, Honey. Have to fill this order. The man's waiting." But she took time to reach down and pat the slick black braids. It's sweet to be remembered even when you're busy.

'Mara worried about why things had to be so different with them. People sat down and ate at tables except Mama—Papa always sat at Fanny's table, and Mr. Conlay and Mr. and Mrs. Peterson. Why couldn't Mama sit sometime, somewhere? Why did she have to be so busy always—especially for eating? Papa wasn't.

But Bill Lester had a way of making Willy do things. When he brought in venison or a mess of quail or white wings he went into Fanny's kitchen and brought the dish to her himself. He set it on the counter and pulled up an onion crate before it.

"You set down an' eat, Miz Westall; I'll do the clerking." She always minded Bill.

"Why won't Mama let me clerk so she can sit down and eat the things I bring her?" asked 'Mara, a little jealous of Bill's prowess.

"Because you can't reach the counter yet. That's all, Honey. It won't be long, though, the rate you're growin'."

Amara stood up very tall. "Do people change a lot when they grow up?" she asked, frowning.

Bill didn't answer, but he reached down and got her and set her on the counter.

'Mara loved to have Bill pick her up. He was the only person who ever thought to do it. Mama was too busy. Papa couldn't. All the others picked up S'rita. She didn't blame them. She wished she could, herself, but she was glad Bill remembered her. She and Bill always talked together. He paid attention. She often felt so troubled; so many things seemed wrong. Papa acted funny when he smelled like whisky. What made it? She loved Papa, but she didn't like to kiss him when he smelled. He always kissed and hugged so much. Things like these she told to Bill. Sometimes he frowned a little. Then she was sorry and talked about Chiquita or Pepitón.

"You're a good kid," he often told her. "Just like your mama."

That pleased 'Mara most of all. She wanted to be like Mama. That was her greatest worry. Mama's hair was curly and hers was straight. Everybody talked about it. Something must be wrong. "What pretty hair!" they'd say when they'd look at S'rita. Even Fanny's hair was curly; so was Mrs. Weisschmidt's, a little; and Mrs. Peterson's, around her face.

"Do people change a lot when they grow up?" she asked again.

"Now what's worryin' you?" he asked her.

"Will my hair curl when I get grown?"

"What difference does it make?"

"I can't wear braids when I'm a lady. My hair's too straight to do like Mama's. Will mine curl like S'rita's when I get grown?"

Bill leaned over on the counter. Their faces were very close together.

"See here, Honey"—he spoke very slowly—"you don't judge folks by hair, whether it's straight or curly, gray or black or yellow; it's by eyes you judge folks altogether."

'Mara interrupted. "What color is the best, Bill?"

"It's not the color, 'Mara; it's the look you see inside 'em."

'Mara stared very straight at Bill. "Are mine all right, you think?"

"They're perfect. They're like your mama's."

She kept looking. He slipped his arm around her, and she put her hand in his. It looked so lonesome. A moment later she felt something wet dripping on her shoulder. She threw her arms around his neck and hugged him and kept on hugging—a long, long time it seemed to her.

Willy walked up and found them there together. Bill dropped his pistol and scuffled on the floor to find it. When he stood up at last his face was very straight and white.

"There goes Pepe. I've gotta see him." he said quickly and hurried out the door.

'Mara reached for her mama's hand and held it. That always helped so when she felt excited, when things went wrong and shaky. Even Mama looked a little funny.

"Always be sweet to Bill," Willy said.

"Yes, ma'm." Amara wanted to explain what had happened, but a Mexican boy came in the store. Willy had to go up front.

It was Chico who came for groceries for Conchita.

"Conchita say he want sandía," he started out the order.

"What's sandía, Emelio?" Willy said.

"Watermelon, Madama."

"Watermelon! Well, I'll be damned. Tell Conchita to grow a watermelon if she wants one."

"The hussy!" was what she felt like adding, but maybe Chico could understand. Mexicans are too polite to give an insult. Maybe Chico was Conchita's brother. She could ask Fanny, but pride prevented. That would be prying. She remembered one question about Pablo's freckles and Bill's quick answer. After all, Conchita was not her business. Bill's life was his; she had so much to think of besides gossip. Just the same, she'd like to know the reason for this woman— Bill so kind, so thoughtful, so sweet to children—gentle even. If he loved the woman, why not marry her? There had to be a reason. Conchita must be a siren —unnatural maybe.

"She's got him in her clutches. He can't get loose. Maybe that's why he drinks mescal and whisky."

Then Willy thought of Pat and blushed a little.

"Some things're past explaining," she concluded. And then the rush began. Beans, rice, lard, garlic, and onions occupied her; no time for fancy thinking.

Bill was in and out of the store that evening. Mr. Conlay got him in a corner for a talk; then Mrs. Peterson took him to task to get her a washwoman like Mrs. Westall's.

Willy caught Bill's eye and gave the signal not to barter off her Castro treasure. What a comfort to see 'Mara and S'rita in clean panties every day, and just a dollar for the whole family washing!

Bill smiled back assurance. That was the only direct conversation they had that day.

At closing time Willy couldn't find Amara. She looked underneath the counter where she always slept on the quilt stack, but she was missing. Willy and Emelio searched everywhere. It was late and they were tired.

"If 'Mara'd just go on to bed with S'rita when Pat goes," Willy said a little crossly.

"She want to stay weeth Mama," Emelio ventured.

"I've got to make her mind me. I'll whip her when I find her. This is crazy."

"No, Madama, pleeze." The boy seemed so distressed.

Pepe ambled in for some Bull Durham. "Go find Bill," Willy said, "I've lost 'Mara." The Mexican bowed and left.

In a minute Bill rushed in.

"What's wrong, Miz Westall?" His eyes took in the room as he said it. "I was just across the street talking to Sam Logan."

"Bill, I can't find 'Mara." Willy's voice was tired and frightened.

He laughed loudly. "Well, just look straight ahead in front." He pointed.

There Amara slept, in the showcase, down underneath with the tobacco.

"Well, I'll be damned," Willy exclaimed. "Why would she do a thing like that!"

"Maybe tryin' to curl her hair," Bill said. "That's what was wrong today, poor young'un."

Willy thought it over. She looked up at Bill very squarely. "Was that the trouble?" she asked flatly.

He peered out across the street a moment.

"No," he said. "No, it wasn't."

An awkward silence followed.

"See you tomorrow," he blurted. And he was gone.

Willy didn't whip Amara when she woke her up, but she asked her shy she got into the showcase.

"I had to tell you something, Mama. I wanted us to be alone."

"But why the showcase, Honey?"

"At night nobody comes to the showcase."

Willy decided not to bother until morning. Then she'd correct her, maybe whip her to make her mind her.

"But you must tell me where you are, Amara. Always remember!"

"I wanta tell you, Mama!" The child began to whimper.

"Then tell me and we'll talk some more tomorrow. Be quick! It's late!"

'Mara caught her mama's hand. She looked up, her eyes swimming, her lips trembling.

"Mama, Bill cried today; he cried and cried!" She clutched her mama's apron and burst out loud in tears.

Willy stooped down and took her in her arms. She nodded to Emelio to go on and leave them.

"Now don't you trouble, Honey," she kept saying as the child sobbed out the spasm. "Don't trouble! Just be sweet to Bill."

Willy slept that night on 'Mara's cot. The little girl snuggled close beside her, with her head upon her shoulder.

Next morning Willy got up tired. Emelio was late in coming. She started sweeping with a limp. Her feet were hurting; they always hurt, but very seldom she took time to bother about them. She saw a roach and made a dash to get it. Always have to kill the big ones to keep the hatching down. She stooped to stomp him. When she looked up, she saw a woman. It was very early for a customer, but there she was.

She was a Mexican woman of about Willy's age and stature, except a little plumper in the bust and middle. She was very different from other Mexican women Willy had seen. She reminded Willy of Mrs. Longoria at the Rancho Seco, the mother of the many children. Her dress was black, but that was unimportant. She wore a lace mantilla of exquisite design. She pushed it back a little and wiped her brow. Then Willy saw her hair. It was raven black, slicked straight, like 'Mara's. Two braids fell down her back. Her eyes shone round and big. Her skin was fair, much fairer than Willy's, more like S'rita's.

Some rancher's wife, no doubt. Willy hadn't seen her enter. She wondered how she came so early in the morning. People always rode up or drove up out front and hitched.

"Good morning," Willy said.

The woman smiled. She didn't answer.

"Qué quiere?" she tried next. She was glad that Spanish now came without an effort. She wanted to talk to this pretty creature. She liked her face; it looked frank. She looked so cared-for, so protected.

"Qué quiere, Señora?" she asked again.

"Sandía con su favor," she answered.

Willy's mouth flew open. She dropped the broom.

"You mean you want a watermelon?" Willy gulped.

The woman nodded her head and smiled. Willy bucked up a little and went back to Spanish. She questioned with great care. The woman had come to get a watermelon; there was no doubt. Then the woman picked up the conversation and rattled on in Spanish. She'd sent Chico for a sandía but Chico didn't bring it. He did not understand what Meeses Westall said. There was confusion; she'd come herself.

Willy leaned on the counter to listen. The woman spoke very fast but softly; a lot of words blurred into others. Willy didn't even hear her. She was looking at her, thinking of her, taking off her clothes to see her. Here stood Bill's reason. She had to get it before the woman left her. "Pure curiosity," she told herself, "but after all I'm just a woman and here's another woman I've thought a whole lot about."

The Mexican was young and bright and pretty— sweet and lovely by her manner and her voice—not what she'd imagined. Willy went back to Fanny's sentence, "Conchita's good and treats Bill right!" Well, what about it? Bill would marry her in the natural course of things. But she kept looking, thinking.

The woman talked. Once she flung out her arms in gesture. Willy stared straight at her hands. They were very soft and white—but naked; no ring touched a single finger. They were bare.

Willy straightened up and said in Spanish, "You shall have a watermelon! For certain, on tomorrow; maybe I can get it yet today. Send Chico. But please don't tell a soul about it."

Conchita clattered out her "Thank you" in many different ways. In the middle of a sentence she stopped short, caught her breath, and murmured, "Qué niñita!"

Willy looked down beside her. There stood S'rita. She'd come up front for Mama to button up her dress.

The big black eyes mellowed; the Mexican reached across the counter and stroked the yellow hair. S'rita gave a scramble and pulled herself on top. She reached up and kissed her mama, then stared at the woman. The Mexican barely touched the child's cheek, and then stepped back and looked.

"Dios te guarda!" Her eyes shadowed. She quickly crossed herself.

"Come over closer," S'rita said. "I like to smell you." She held out her arms and smiled.

Conchita reached over and cupped the little face in her two hands for just a moment; then she left.

"Mama, who is the woman?" S'rita asked a little crossly. People didn't leave her often, and she loved the smell; it was sweet, like nothing she had ever smelled before.

"She's a friend of mine," Willy answered. She busied herself with S'rita's buttons, her back turned squarely to the door. She wasn't certain why she did it, but she knew she didn't want to look. She lifted S'rita off the counter.

"Come on, Honey, let's get breakfast. I've put the oatmeal on to cook. Papa and 'Mara are sleepy-headed. Run on fast and get them up."

S'rita shouted, "I'm a steer!" dashing foward. Willy followed, very careful to avoid a single backward look.

S'rita landed on Amara's stomach, and with hands and feet began to bounce.

"I'm a steer! I'm a steer!" she kept on shouting until 'Mara tumbled on the floor. Then they had a tickling match.

Willy leaned over Pat and kissed him.

"Get up, Darling," she whispered. "The oatmeal's done. Breakfast's ready."'

Pat's eyes opened very blue and smiling. He drew her to him and kissed her warmly. Willy was very glad he did it; yes, she was very, very glad this morning.

Soon after breakfast Willy set about getting the watermelon. Maybe the Allens, on the river, had some. She had to get it. Conchita hankered maybe for watermelon. Most likely she was pregnant. No baby could be born wanting watermelon. No, first she'd telegraph Mr. Dubose in Corpus Christi.

Mrs. Peterson came in early. Willy asked her if she knew of any watermelons. She said, "Yes, Mr. Peterson spoke of some at Laguna Seca." But who could go to Laguna Seca?

Bill came in smiling, whistling "La Paloma."

"Why, Bill'll go get it for you," Mrs. Peterson spoke up.

"Sure, be glad to. What is it? Where?" Bill questioned.

"Oh, no," Willy sputtered, frowning. She turned some chickens and some settin' eggs. Emelio's to bring them to her from the ranch."

"Oh," he said, and went on back to see Pat.

Mrs. Peterson gazed at Willy dumbly. "What's wrong?" she asked. "Bill's going to Laguna Seca. I heard him talking to Ted Tolliver just outside the door."

Willy stepped over close and whispered, "Don't tell a soul. It's a secret! I'll tell you after."

Willy thanked God she hadn't told Mrs. Peterson why she wanted the watermelon. In fact, that was something she knew she'd never tell a soul. It was her secret. After all, a person has a right to keep a secret with herself.

As Mrs. Peterson went out the door, Mrs. Weisschmidt came in. Next to Fanny, Mrs. Weisschmidt was Willy's pet. There was a wholesomeness about her big red face that made Willy feel that all was well. There was a grace about her that spoke heart. On this particular morning that face said watermelon.

"Sure, in my yard I got plenty. De vatermelons like de river. Dis afternoon I bring you a nice pig one," she said.

Mrs. Weisschmidt brought the watermelon and Chico came and got it when he called for the mail. Nobody knew why it came or where it went. Willy kept her secret. On her order book she wrote "garden seed," for Mr. Dubose on his next trip in.

That afternoon, right after the train ran through, when everybody gathered around to read his mail, Sam Logan pulled into the store and sat down. He came to announce the arrival of a box-car labeled Patrick Westall, at the depot. It was the furniture Jim Nelson had sent in from the ranch.

Pat and Willy stared at each other. They couldn't believe what they were hearing. At last Jim Nelson had remembered something. He never sent the rent. Seemingly he just forgot it; he never wrote a letter. Willy jogged Pat up about it. He promised to dun him, but she was never sure Pat did. The furniture didn't matter, really, but they could use the ranch rent. Now Jim'd got the cart before the horse and sent the thing they didn't need. They had no use for furniture. They had no place to put it.

Pat and Bill hurried out to get a drink. When they came back, the plan was finished. The Westalls were to have a house to live in. Bill took time out to build it. He left Henry with the scraping, and in four days he and Pablo had a warehouse put up back of the store. Above it they made four rooms connected by a hall, for the Westalls to live in. An inside stairway they couldn't manage, so they added it outside. Boxing plank, non-stripped, unpainted, it glistened in the sunshine, a two-storied monument to progress.

They finished it on Saturday and moved the furniture in while Willy was at her busiest in the store. It was to be a big surprise for Willy. Pat, Bill, and the children planned it. Fanny came and helped. When Willy closed the store, Bill was to bring her up to see everything in place and pretty. Pat and S'rita, even 'Mara, would be asleep in bed. This was a sacrifice for 'Mara, but she did it. She did so want to be with Bill when he brought Mama up!

"It's her house and her family," Fanny said. "Let her see it once in perfect order like people're supposed to live, not sleepin' around under counters in a store." So 'Mara went to bed as part of Mama's gift. But she wasn't very happy.

The trade was heavy. Willy and Emelio worked until after one. Bill and Pepe came in to help from eight to twelve; then they left to get a drink.

All day Willy had sensed something in the air. She knew Bill and Pat and the children were planning something special. She blessed them all. What surprise she'd show—as if she hadn't suspected a single thing.

Then something happened that sent her plans spinning in the air. About six o'clock Mr. Peterson dashed into the store and called Willy to one side. He whispered excitedly in her ear, "The fever Ivan has is smallpox. Must have come from the Mexican wash-woman. Probably'll be a plague. Look out for 'Mara and S'rita!"

Willy was stunned. Why had she never thought of smallpox.

"There'll be a plague!" Mr. Peterson kept saying.

"What does Dr. Jeffers say?" Willy asked.

"Haven't called him yet. He's gone to Brownsville, anyway. But my wife will call him."

"Your wife?"

"Yes, I'm leaving tonight on the late freight train."

"You're leaving? Why, Mr. Peterson, who'll do the nursing?"

"My wife. She wants to do it."

"But alone? You said this was smallpox!"

"Well, I have to attend to business to keep us fed. Lot of special freights now for cabbage. Have to do it. You'll keep your eye skinned, Miz Westall? That's why I came to tell you. Want to get out of town before they miss me. Old Doc Jeffers might try to catch me in a quarantine. I couldn't afford that!"

In another second he was gone. Willy was glad he left so quickly; otherwise she would have had to slap him. She knew how S'rita felt when she had to stomp. She felt so helpless. Dr. Jeffers should have vaccinated everybody, but he hadn't. She'd been too busy thinking of the store and money to have him do the children. Of course Mrs. Dunbar's sister lost her arm from vaccination back in Franklin. That had scared Willy. But with all these Mexicans she should not have taken the chance of smallpox. Maybe Dr. Jeffers was afraid, too; or maybe he was just too old to hurry into preventive measures. Of course he hadn't been in Mission long enough to start a public health campaign. The fault was hers. She should have asked him about it, got things started. At least she could have taken her children to him.

Well, she'd have to wait until morning to do anything about it, since Dr. Jeffers had gone to Brownsville. Tonight she wouldn't spoil the celebration for the children. Maybe by daylight she wouldn't feel so desperate; then she could think of something to do. After the celebration she'd ask Bill. Then Bill walked in the door. He looked excited, almost childlike, certainly boyish in his swagger and his mien.

"Got a little celebration on, Miz Westall. I've been elected to head it up. Let's shut up the store and get started. Remember now, you've got a house to live in —not just the back end of the store."

Willy tried to match his smile and humor. She wouldn't disappoint them all if she could help it; at least she'd try to be surprised and happy.

"Go on home," Bill said to Emelio. "Miz Westall and I have got a celebration on."

Emelio grabbed his hat and left, smiling. He knew that sitting upstairs on the table was his little gift of flowers for the house and the Madama. He wished he could see the Madama when she saw the flowers, but nobody had thought to ask him to come up. She'd tell him tomorrow. He felt tired and was glad to be going home.

When Pat and Willy walked out the front door, Bill locked it.

"When you lock up from the outside, Miz Westall, it's progress. You can walk around the store now to go home."

Willy took a deep breath and looked straight up. The stars were shining, millions of them.

"Plumb pied, ain't it?" Bill said. "I like the stars. Moon's tricky. Awful bad for fightin'."

"For what?" Willy turned her gaze to him.

"Fighting. If you're goin' to jump on a feller, do it when you can see him in the moonlight. I learned that across the border."

Pearl heard Willy's voice and nickered.

"I'll have to go out and see Pearl first. Let's do it before we see the house."

"Sure!" Bill said. "Got to keep your eye on horses."

They walked along in step. Willy liked the feeling of just swinging in the air. Walking is such a contrast to standing. You hit a rhythm; it gives you power, like horses trotting. Your legs have an understanding with each other; they clip along together. She thought of

Pat—poor darling. How awful to lose the feeling of your legs beneath you! No wonder he drank whisky; it evened up the short one, made him forget the jerkiness in step.

"When's the delivery wagon comin'?" Bill was asking. "Pearl's gettin' awful fat."

"Sure," Willy answered. "I ordered a delivery wagon from Mr. Dubose."

"Yeah, I know, but when's it comin? That feller livin' over by the feed store was askin' me today. His wife gets in tomorrow. Wants to be sure his groceries will be delivered." He laughed loudly.

So did Willy. It seemed so funny. They kept laughing until they got to Pearl's corral. They leaned against it and looked up at the stars a minute. Pearl laid her chin on Willy's shoulder. Bill slapped the palomino's neck.

"Progress," he said finally to the horse. "You have to pull a delivery wagon, Pearl. I guess they'll hitch me to a plow." Again he started laughing.

"That's not the half," Willy said. "Pearl'll deliver groceries to people living yet in tents. But Mr. Conlay's getting an automobile to sell 'em land right out in the brush."

"Yeah," Bill bellowed, slapping Pearl. "Plain old monte like your ranch."

"Don't forget the irrigation."

Suddenly he went silent. He turned to Willy. She smelled whisky on his breath. "Yeah, that's right. That makes a difference, but I don't like it. It's too progressive. I've been thinking—"

He broke the sentence. With firm quick pats he stroked Pearl's shoulder. In the starlight Willy caught the twist that turned his face. He looked grim—in that instant no longer boyish.

"Such slight difference between tears and laughter," crossed her brain.

"You've been thinking, Bill? What were you thinking?"

"Too much progress here for me. Too many people. I like horses."

Pearl nickered softly. Bill stroked her nose and rubbed her neck.

"Pearl speaks English just like a Mex," he said very dryly. Then he laughed.

Willy didn't make the effort to laugh again. Why try to make it? Life was not a laughing matter. You had to face cold facts. They piled and mounted. You had to meet them; they made you meet them. Maybe Bill could laugh at a danger but she couldn't—well, not without him.

She turned to him quickly. "You wouldn't leave us?" she said sadly.

Pearl moved a little. Bill's hand fell and landed on Willy's shoulder. For just a second he didn't move it.

"Hell, no," he answered. They were very silent for a moment. Then Bill said, "Come on, let's go see your house."

Willy tried to thank him for the assurance; but somehow words wouldn't come. It was dark. She just walked along beside him. They hurried to the steps and up the stairs.

The plan was for Pat to wake the children just at twelve. Willy was to see them all in bed; then they'd all jump up and eat the cake that Fanny'd made them. But when Bill and Willy stepped inside the door they heard Pat snoring.

"Pat forgot to wake the kids," Bill whispered.

"Then let's not wake them either. Let them sleep; they're tired."

Willy and Bill were standing very close together. She smelled his breath. She saw the flowers on the table, jasmines with Ponderosa lemon blossoms.

"Who did it?" she whispered.

"Emèlio brought the flowers. S'rita bossed and Fanny done the work," Bill answered.

Willy couldn't keep back the tears. The Brussels carpet on the floor, the bird's-eye maple and the folding bed, the stove and ice-box in the kitchen, the candelabra on the table where she and Pat first sat together—all old friends she had almost forgotten.

She stood there listening to Pat snore—another life, ten thousand years ago—another person even maybe.

She looked quickly up at Bill. "I wouldn't exchange places with her," she said softly. He said nothing but she kept on talking.

"In those days I hadn't lived."

"Mighty nice, I think," he answered.

He was looking at the folding bed.

"Of course, it's lovely—everything is lovely! But let's get together on our conversation."

He frowned a little, then turned squarely to her. "Why not tell me what's wrong tonight, Miz Westall? What's happened? You're not yourself, I notice."

Willy dropped into the chair beside the table. She looked white. Bill grabbed a glass of water and gave it to her.

"Come on and tell me," he admonished.

"It's smallpox, Bill. I'm scared."

"Who said you had the smallpox? By God, I'll shoot 'im!"

She smiled at that. "No, not me. It's that little boy of Peterson's. I'm thinking of the children. I should have had them vaccinated. But I've been living away from people for so long I guess I forgot about diseases. I was too busy with the store and making money."

Then Bill laughed and sat down at the table, slapping his own knee.

"If I got scared of smallpox I'd never do no good. Mexkins always have the smallpox. The point is, don't get scared."

He cut the cake and they ate a slice or two apiece. They tried to talk a little, but they couldn't. At last Bill said good night and left.

Willy went to bed, but she couldn't sleep. She felt disappointed. The children had missed the celebration they had planned; so had Pat and Bill. She didn't mean to do it, but it was the smallpox that had scared her. She hadn't got the spirit they had. But she couldn't help it. Smallpox was awful; so were a lot of things together. She began to count up all the bad things one by one. "Plain crazy," she told herself just as the day was dawning. Then she set to planning what to do. She would arrange their lives, get things in order. She'd been too easy, too splapdash in method

—just too grateful to get back to things and people. Dr. Jeffers would take the smallpox plague in hand; she'd see to that. And while she was at it, she'd straighten out a lot of things. The four furnished rooms gave her a method. She had a house now, away from covered wagons. She'd make the business match it, check up on Pat, impose stricter discipline on the children, get more sleep and rest herself. She'd been too lenient with everybody, including herself.

She turned over and stretched a little, then started on the business. She had to keep a stricter hand on that. Pat handled all the money because it was the only thing he could do. When she had time to watch the cash drawer she saw that much money came in, but much went out again. The bank balance rose in slow proportion to the intake. Credits were mounting. She went off to sleep counting money.

S'rita woke her by bouncing on her stomach. They had their celebration at the breakfast table. But Bill was missing. She felt guilty, but determined that she would use the lessons of her resolutions made in the night.

21

_In_ the middle of the morning Pat and Tom Jones went into "Bill's Place" to get a drink. Soon after, a man walked into the store. He was old, and well dressed.

"My name's Wright," he said. "I wanta buy some groceries on a credit."

"When do you think you can pay, Mr. Wright?" Willy asked.

"Maybe never. I might as well be frank."

"Are you hungry?"

"Oh, no," he laughed, "I've bought some land. I'm just a little short on cash."

"Well, go down and see Mr. Stone at the bank. We

just run a little store here and haven't got the capital to finance people."

The man left. Willy felt very businesslike and smart. She sat down and wrote a letter to the banker in Austin. Would he please go to the pawnshop and ask about her diamond ring.

Pat came hurrying back, glaring at her, white with rage and insult.

"What made you turn down that man's credit?" he demanded. "I sent him in."

"But, Darling, I didn't know you sent him!" Then she got mad herself. It was the anger in his eyes that did it, and she was tired. "We can't run a business the way you do it. We'll be going in the hole."

"The hell we can't! How can you settle up a country unless you help folks settle? They spend their cash in outlay. All they need is time." His voice was high, strained, and trembling. He turned and left the store.

A customer came in. When she left, Willy went outside to look. Bill's horse was tied to the gallery post in front. Pepe sat on the saloon steps. The Weisschmidt buckboard stood in front of the Rio Grande Hardware; that was all. She wanted to see Mr. Wright and fill his order. She wanted to apologize to Pat.

She called to Pepe, "Look in and see who's in there and tell me!"

"They dreenk," he called back. "Meester Westall and Meester Beeley."

Just then Dr. Jeffers stepped out of the feed store. Willy called him and they went into conference over the smallpox. In the excitement she forgot about Rufus Wright and Pat. The doctor had quarantined the Petersons; everybody had to be vaccinated; even Willy. The town was all upset. Fanny took charge of 'Mara and S'rita for vaccination and for the day. Pepe sulked around in jealous anticipation of a break for S'rita, but Fanny kept her guarded.

Later that afternoon Pat staggered into the store looking red and bloated. Willy took time off to get him upstairs to bed. She sent Pepe up once during the evening to see about him. That night when she got home she found him rolling and tumbling, talking strangely of Oklahoma—Siver City—Doc Riley—Sweetheart—S'rita! She rushed down again and got Dr. Jeffers in a jiffy. The doctor looked at Pat and shook his head.

"Not just whisky; it's some kind of fever," he pronounced.

"Not smallpox?" Willy shuddered.

"Can't say. May be!"

"But he's had it once. His parents died of it when he was just a boy."

"Time'll tell." Dr. Jeffers shook his head again.

The next two weeks were a nightmare to Mission. The smallpox scare froze people. They condemned themselves for their negligence. The bright sunshine and lazy Mexican way of living had made them forget the rules of civilization. They had all been too busy to think about a plague. Just too busy was the only excuse that any of them could give. Nobody came to the store but Mexican grubbers. They sensed something wrong but what it was they couldn't figure out. The Americanos were very strange about things in general, so much hurry and loud speaking—all this cutting up of cactus and planting of onions—so much more than they could eat.

Even Emelio seemed puzzled. "The smallpox weel cure," he said to Willy.

Pepe stomped about in rage. Fanny was loco. Why did she keep S'rita shut up in her house? It was not good for health and body.

"She's afraid about the smallpox, Pepe." Willy tried her best to make it plain.

"Smallpox, bah! The smallpox cure," he snarled.

But Pepe proved a prop. Through the awful days that followed he never left the store. Pat rolled in his bed, talking wildly. Willy spent her time running up and down the stairs. Fanny sent food to everybody. Bill was in and out and everywhere. So was Dr. Jeffers.

But Pat didn't have the smallpox. It was something different—maybe fever of the brain. They couldn't clear his head. Sleeping and waking, he kept talking.

The things he said clutched at Willy's heart and crushed her: Sweetheart with diamonds—servants waiting on the table—cotton machinery and round-bale gins—both his children educated—Patrick Westall in big business—walking on two good legs at last.

Through the nighttime Willy knew she'd lose her reason, but every morning she came back to grips with things.

On the tenth day Pat stopped talking; the next two he slept in silence. When he woke, he looked up at Willy and tears ran down his cheeks. For a long time she held him in her arms and rocked him. They said nothing. He rolled over eventually and went to sleep.

"Out of danger," Dr. Jeffers pronounced. "Go on about your business, Miz Westall. I'll watch Pat and the Petersons. That's my business."

"And how are they today?"

"I've never seen the like," was all he said.

That night Jesse Parnell rushed into the store white and shaking. A man had been found dead on his cot over back of the canal.

"Smallpox?" everybody asked at once.

"No, he left a note."

Tom Jones read the note aloud. Everybody listened, taut. It said: "My name is Rufus Wright. I have no friends or people. My money I paid for land. I came to start out afresh with God's earth and sunshine, but I find it can't be done. Without money I do not eat."

"Damn fool!" Tom Jones exclaimed.

Willy shuddered. "What made him die?" she asked.

"Starved was Doc Jeffers' diagnosis."

"Plumb crazy," Bill drawled. "Starvin' in this country. Cattle can live on cactus even, and all this truck we raise!"

"Was loco afore he come," Sam Logan said. "We get all kinds down here now, with this irrigation."

Willy leaned against the counter. She was shaking. She knew she'd killed Rufus Wright; not his body, but his spirit. She was responsible for him just as she was for Pat, sick upstairs on the bed.

A pall fell over everybody. Death came as an intrusion. Their business here was life and growth.

"What're we to do, Miz Westall?" Jesse questioned.

Willy stood up straight and squared her shoulders. "Why, bury him, of course. You boys can make a coffin. The bill came in today for Pearl's delivery wagon. It ought to come tomorrow. We'll have a funeral and that can be the hearse."

"But where'll we bury him? There ain't no graveyard."

Everybody gulped and sputtered. Nobody'd thought about a graveyard.

Tom Jones rushed out for Mr. Conlay. Soon he came puffing in.

"Just tell me where you want the cemetery, Mrs. Westall, and I'll draw the deed right up."

All eyes turned to the land plat on the wall. Bill jerked his forty-five from his pocket and shot into the map.

"That's where it is," he said.

And there is where it is.

The next afternoon Pearl delivered Mr. Wright to his grave, dug out in the bristle of cactus and scrub mesquite. Father Michael was out of town. For a funeral service Tom Jones read a few verses from Willy's Bible. Nobody could pray out loud. When the grave was filled in to the level and then humped up, Bill Lester invited everybody to come on up to Bill's Place and have a drink.

"It's savage," Willy thought as the men filed past the store.

Then Pat's tired eyes danced crazily before her as they used to. She wished she could join the men and go get drunk herself.

"All because of money," she said, dryly. Her voice was bitter. She felt tired and old and broken down herself—mean and wicked, murderous almost like the time she shot the buck.

That night Willy left the store to Pepe and Emelio and went on up to be with Pat. Bill made her do it.

"Go on to bed. You need rest, Miz Westall. Won't be much trade tonight," he said.

Bill had been so faithful through Pat's illness; so had Pepe, Pablo, Emelio, Fanny. She'd try to make it up in time to everybody. Dr. Jeffers sent word he wouldn't be around that night.

She was so glad she had come home. It seemed to make a lot of difference to Pat. When she got into bed, he murmured, "What about the store, Sweetheart?"

"It can go to hell," she answered.

That seemed to make all the difference to his tired eyes.

The next morning Fanny told her something had happened. Mrs. Peterson and little Ivan had both died in the afternoon. Bill and Dr. Jeffers wanted to get them buried in the nighttime so people wouldn't be so scared. Bill had made all sorts of plans for everybody, to keep them busy.

"Did Mr. Peterson get here?" Willy asked.

"No," Fanny stormed. "The sonuvabitch just wired from Brownsville. I think he's glad." She stomped a little, then added, "Or maybe just scared for his own hide."

People gathered around in huddles, discussing tar and feathers. But Willy spent the day feeling sorry for Mr. Peterson. No matter what the reason, he'd regret it. He had used his brain in dealing with the contagion. He didn't want to take the smallpox. His presence couldn't help his wife and son, he'd calculated. That was the point that would drive him crazy. She knew what she was saying. Pat had taught her. You can't sell out your heart for health or money. Reason tricks you. You make plans; then something happens. In the morning you have to comb your hair. Your face will taunt you; your heart won't stand it. She knew; she'd looked at Pat. When she set out to run the business and manage credit she had robbed him of his manhood. He had a right to service. She could work and lift and push; he couldn't. His body wouldn't let him. She had to find a way now to get him back in harness, to let him feel his muscle and his worth.

That afternoon she caught Tom Jones sober and

talked to him at length; then she talked to Bill. Father Michael was her greatest help.

"Just a little setback," he said. "Pat's very weak and frail. He goes on spirit solely. We must find some service he can render that will occupy his thinking and let his body rest."

"Dead easy," Bill spoke up. "I'm ridin' over to Chapin to see the Judge an' Asa Hall today."

The result of the conference was a new title in the town. Pat was elected Justice of the Peace.

He got out of bed to take the oath of office. Willy put him into his gray suit. Fanny did up the shirt for him to wear. The ceremony ended in Bill's place, with drinks on the house to Patrick Westall, the new judge.

When Willy helped Pat back into his bed, she studied his eyes as doctors look at people's tongues. The gleam was there—faint, but it was there. S'rita and 'Mara smoothed Papa's sheet. The three of them made a pretty picture as she looked on.

No, she'd never interfere. She felt happy, gay all over—young again. Bring on the work; keep it coming —that's what matters. Aunt Ann always said it: "Work hard, Willy, do your best, and you'll get ahead."

That night when Bill came in he brought two Mexicans with him, a woman and a man.

"Come on, S'rita, you and 'Mara. We're gonna have a weddin'," he announced.

"A what?" Willy asked.

"A weddin'!" Bill stopped short and looked at her in a brazen sort of way. She stepped up close enough to smell. No, he hadn't been drinking.

"The Judge is gonna marry these two people!" He looked at her again; then he went on upstairs to Pat.

The children loved the wedding. The Mexicans looked so scared. Papa sat up in bed and rubbed his eyes and cussed.

"How much you charge for marryin', Judge?" Bill asked.

"Hell, nothin'! But what in God's world do I say? Go ask Mama, 'Mara, Sugar, quick!"

'Mara ran down to get Mama. Willy was busy with a customer, but she excused herself and left. When she got upstairs Bill was translating a ritual of his own making: Would the woman promise to wash his clothes? Would the man vow to breed the woman freely? Would they swear to name the first baby Patrick Westall, the second one Guillermita—"little Willy"? Pat was laughing.

Willy stopped him short. "It's wicked!" she said coldly. "This is sacred. Do it right or not at all." She felt angry through and through.

"Why, sure, Miz Westall." Bill flinched almost as if she'd hit him. Pat straightened up his face. "They don't know the difference. They don't know English."

"But I do. Say the ritual. I remember every word the preacher said." She began to repeat it. When she came to "Love, honor, and obey," she turned quickly and went downstairs. After the second customer, her anger cooled and she planned to apologize. But Bill stayed upstairs with Pat; so did the children.

Fanny was slow in coming, but when she did, Willy sent her up to take a look.

"Bill's settin' with S'rita an' 'Mara on his knees, tellin' cowboy stories and he's entertainin' the Judge a lot more than the kids."

Bill waited late that night to leave. The customers were all gone, even Emelio, when he came into the store.

"I'm sorry, Miz Westall," he began.

"So am I." Willy turned very red. "I don't know what made me such a fool. It just made me mad to hear you making fun of marriage."

"Yeah, I know," he said.

"I'm awfully sorry," she went on. "You've been so kind and good. You've done so much for all of us. Marrying is a fine new job for Pat. He'll love to do it when he catches on. This justice business is exactly what he needs."

Bill stared at her frankly. "No, I done it for myself. There come times, Miz Westall, when a feller's not himself. There's times when he gets to thinkin'!" He kept on looking straight. "Then's when he oughta drink," he added.

Willy reached and took his hand in hers and held it, gripped it firmly.

"No, Bill, start something new." She looked up at him. "Let's start a church," she said.

22

Before she went to bed, Willy wrote to several mission boards about a preacher. A week later she received an answer from the Presbyterians. They would send down Brother Raymond Renfo on a missionary project.

When she showed Bill the letter, he turned red for just a minute; then he said, "That's fine. Whatta we do next?"

"Just back me up tonight when I tell 'em all about it."

They shook hands and smiled.

That night Willy read the letter to the sitters in the store. Everybody shouted "Yes" before the vote was taken. It was the finest idea anybody had thought up yet. The time was set, two Sundays hence. The only place in which they could hold the service was the pool hall; not exactly what the preacher would expect, perhaps, but the tables could be moved and benches improvised from nail kegs and boxing planks.

The coming Sunday service was talked of in every household. The church excitement overcame the smallpox scare. The whole population met the preacher at the train. Young and shy, Raymond Renfro was staggered by the greeting. A Mexican string band played as the congregation filed into the pool hall and sat down for the service. Willy and the children were right down at the front. Pat, the last one to enter, limped down the aisle to join them. When Bill passed out the songbooks that Brother Renfro'd brought along, Pat rose with judgely poise and said, "Now, come on, folks, let's show this preacher how; no weak-bellied singing; let's open up our lungs."

When they bellowed forth together, Ray Renfro turned sick and pale with stage fright, but by the time they finished "When the Roll Is Called Up Yonder," he had overcome his fear. He began his sermon in a voice that was low but clear. The people sat enchanted at every word he said. He was just warming up to his sermon when suddenly a drum was heard to beat. A road show from Mexiquita was parading down the street. Pat jumped up and limped out to send them back to Mexiquita while the Americanos worshipped God. Pat returned to his seat and Brother Renfro's voice mounted as he lost his nervousness and picked up the vision of the task he'd set out to do. As Pat listened to the message of faith and hope and love, his emotion welled in surges with the whisky in his stomach until with the closing prayer, he was weeping softly to himself. At that moment again the beating of the drum sounded up the street, pounding out its bellow and drowning out the benediction. Pat's emotion transferred in a second to a fury in his brain. He forgot about his crutches except to wave them in the air as he scrambled down the aisle in lurches, shouting as he went, "You goddamned sonsuvbitches, get down across that track!" Then he charged the drum in anger and smashed it with his crutch.

"This concludes the service," Brother Renfro said quietly.

After a moment's silence Bill Lester spoke up, "Well, come on, everybody; let's all go have a drink!"

Willy stepped up to the preacher to shake his hand. It was soft and warm, almost like a child's. Hers felt hard and dry within it. She felt wild and wind-blown before a city man, his suit correctly tailored, his linen far too white. She began talking fast to forget herself. She explained that as yet Sunday was just a day. Everything stayed wide open to accommodate the trade. In the fast-growing country there seemed so much to do that nobody took time out except to eat and sleep.

"And these lovely little children?" Ray Renfro said, before he thought.

"Yes." Willy turned her head a moment. "But that is why we're here. A little hard to begin with, but we've come to make our place. That's why I sent for you."

"But what about a school?"

"That's coming next," she said.

Ray Renfro stayed three days, to get Willy's story and learn a lot of things as he sat in the store listening, and talking some himself. When time came to leave, he talked to Willy alone.

"This seven-day work is killing, Mrs. Westall. You need some rest. You're too young and pretty to kill yourself so fast."

"Not yet." She smiled. "I'm not far enough along. There's got to be a school and music."

"Sunday school's my job, remember," he cut in. "I'm coming back as soon as the settlers bring in children so we can form a class. Promise you will write me if somebody tries to get in first." He shook her hand and started for the door.

"One thing more, Mrs. Westall." He stopped very quickly. "Will you tell me about your shoes? What is the size you wear?"

"My shoes?" Willy crimsoned and looked down at her feet. "They're sixes—but—"

Something stabbed her in the heart. What had he asked that for? To insult her? To make her feel ashamed? For a moment she thought she would shoot him. Her eyes flashed fire and blazed. She added crisply, "And my hat's a John B. Stetson. What's yours?"

Bill Lester almost bumped into the preacher as he was going out. His companion stole his thinking from his legs.

"Miz Westall, want you to know Don Lea," he began. "Just run into him an' his folks, an' thought I'd bring 'im in."

Willy saw before her a manly little fellow with gray eyes and tow hair. He wore cowboy boots and held a wide-brimmed sombrero in his hand.

"His folks have come down to put a restaurant in. Drove in from San Antone. I met 'em on the road. This little hombre here sorta caught my eye. Speak to Miz Westall, Don," he said.

"Howdy!" The child stuck out his hand. Willy reached down and took it. She was angry, hurt at what the preacher said. The small hand made her want to cry. Bill fixed his eyes on something far across the street a minute.

"I'm so glad you've come," Willy said at last. "Have you any brothers or any sisters, Don?"

"No, ma'am." He sidled over close to Bill.

Willy said, "Bill, we've got to start a school." Her eyes began again to blaze. She was thinking of the preacher and her shoes. But he was right, she had to do something about the children. They were growing up. Somebody had to take the time to teach Serena how to mind and not to cuss.

"School teachers're not my specialty," Bill said. "But I can rake up something for the kids to learn by."

Next day Bill brought in Judge Woolcott, an old Scotsman, who had wandered in from somewhere south. Bill found him at Roma living by himself, reading Shakespeare, studying Greek, and thinking back through his past which he had opened to no friend. Before the week was over they started school in the back end of the pool hall, with the Judge as teacher.

"It's a helluva place for a school," Pat frowned.

"Yes, it is," Willy admitted frankly, "but it's the only place there is."

The school added much to Mission. Judge Woolcott was a contribution they never could have done without. He had Tom Jones' culture minus all the whisky. He lived in a one-roomed house Bill Lester built for him. His special charge was Don. Bill Lester made that so. Willy overheard them talking one night in the store.

"Just lemme know what Don needs. I don't know myself. He's a fine kid all right. I like the way he thinks. Likes horses. Cain't beat a man on that. Ain't got no chance with that maw an' paw of his."

"What's the trouble there?" Judge Woolcott questioned sharply.

"Blood, I guess," Bill said. "Miz Lea's all right. Works like hell cookin' in that restaurant over there, but she pays no attention at all to Don. That man of hers I oughta shoot. Brought his family down here chasin' a woman across the track. Poor Miz Lea worries her head plumb off about it. Cain't mix kids up with stuff like that." Bill's face was serious; the curtains on his eyes were down.

"You're right." Judge Woolcott spat across the floor.

"You keep your eyes on Don. For expense, just let me know," he said.

Willy was glad she overheard the conversation. It answered a lot of questions in her heart and in herself.

"That's mighty fine," she said to Bill.

He looked at her and smiled. "It's mighty fine of you, Miz Westall. You told me to go out an' take a hand at somethin' new, remember?"

'Mara and S'rita took Don straight to heart. He was exactly what they wanted, not a whining, crying loco like that little kid called Ivan. They weren't even sorry when the child died. Don was different. He was taller than they were. He could reach things. He could even saddle a horse in a pinch. S'rita liked him extra special because he could ride a bronc. Pepe wouldn't let her ride one, but she could watch. Don and S'rita did most everything together, but they were good to 'Mara. Now 'Mara felt less left out. When they did their tricks on horses, she was there to clap her hands. When Pepe and S'rita rode off together, that left her and Don. He told her lots of things she didn't know about cows, and horses, pigs, chickens, javelinas —every kind of thing on earth.

One day she said to her mama, "Why didn't Don come long ago?"

It was one of those strange occasions when things went queer and wrong. In place of smiling, Mama cried a little.

"God was too busy, Honey, maybe. I don't know."

But just the same 'Mara knew her mama felt very happy over Don.

Everybody loved the little fellow. He was strong and manly. Willy blessed the day he came. He gave a balance to her little girls. He was better than Serena and not half so good as 'Mara. That evened matters up. The three together swore and rode, grew lithe and tall and tough.

Judge Woolcott came every day to trade and to talk about the children. Bill managed to be there often when he came. The old teacher talked little but managed to say much.

Bill and Willy listened. From what he intimated rather than said they got the drift that the children were a little rough perhaps but had a lot of fairness planted in them. "Real values," he said. "We'll teach the fundamentals. That's all there is to teaching. The other you pick up. The thing of most importance is that they've never thought about being poor."

The day Judge Woolcott made that statement, Willy did a lot of thinking. Who was to say who was poor and why? Certainly she would like to have a son like Don. Maybe she'd been cutting edges, taking all of life too hard. Conchita came back to taunt her. Conchita had a way of living. She looked happy and contented despite the obsession for watermelon. She often wondered why the watermelon. Had the woman had a baby? Nobody would ever ask about Conchita. Her name was never mentioned. That was because of Bill. Willy didn't like even to think about her; but she did. "She serves a female function," she often thought. "But so do all women for some man or other." Of course Mexicans had a way about it. They took nature in its stride, didn't fight it, served their purpose, had their children, let money ride. Maybe she should bear and keep on bearing and trust the bringing up and raising just to God. That's what Mrs. Lea had done with Don.

But it took a little money. She remembered back to Austin when Serena came. She ventured to the desk and picked up the bankbook. After all, she had a right to know. She hadn't questioned Pat about their balance since his illness. It didn't matter really since she'd got the letter that her diamond ring was sold. She knew they had business, plenty of business. It was Pat's job to keep the books.

But once seated, with the bankbook in her hand, she began to take a look. She kept turning through the ledger. Nothing balanced; not a single bill was paid; the bank account was very low. She looked up and saw Pat coming. He musn't catch her, for she was spying. He wouldn't like it. She got behind the counter and was busy with an order when he came in through the door.

"Are you ready to take this order, Darling?" she asked sweetly.

"What?" he questioned, a little crossly.

"The red-light order," she replied.

"Oh, hell!" he sputtered. "Let Emelio take it down today. I'm busy."

Don was coming in the door.

Willy's eyes began to flash. "Let's say no more about it, Darling. Get in and take it or I'll have to go myself. This is our one customer who pays cash."

Pat frowned sharply. "What the hell!" he muttered. "Why do you pay Emelio?"

Willy came around the counter. "See here, Pat, I don't send Emelio to a red-light house. You know it. He's just a boy." Her face was burning. Pat knew that she was mad.

"But I'm busy, Sweetheart." He started smiling. "Don and I're on our way to Conlay's. Somethin's comin' off."

"Well, can't it wait?" she snapped.

"Guess it'll have to," he grumbled, picking up the basket. "Come on, Don."

"Don can't go with you where you're going. Are you crazy?"

"The hell I am!" Pat shouted. "Come on, son; Pearl's already pawin'."

The boy scampered out the door, leaped into the delivery wagon, and grabbed the lines. Pat followed.

Willy walked to the front door and watched them. Pearl looked back at her. Willy thought she smiled. For that moment she was glad she didn't have a son. But when Don and Pat got back, she felt ashamed and guilty. Men have their ways with men; women can't understand them. Every husband needs a son.

She saw them drive up, get out of the delivery wagon, and hurry down the street. Then she heard Pearl snort. She rushed to see what was the matter. Emelio beat her to the door. She heard an awful clatter, and people shouting. Pat's voice came clear, ringing, "Look out, Don, the damn thing'll run you down!" Dust was flying down the street.

"What ees eet, Madama?" Emelio murmured, drawing close to Willy's side.

Willy wasn't very certain, but she answered, just to assure the Mexican boy, "It's the automobile they've talked about. I knew Mr. Conlay had bought one, but I wasn't sure just when it would get to Mission."

The puff and splutter was heading straight for the store. Willy ran out and held Pearl's bridle. The horse was snorting, whiffing air. Dust blinded everybody. People came running from everywhere. In the great confusion, Willy got the general notion that the automobile had stopped. She coughed and spit and fought the air. At last she got her breath. She wiped her eyes on her apron and finally got them clear enough to see before her a beautiful shiny thing full of people. They all had on linen coats and hats and veils.

Mr. Conlay was speaking. The people were getting out. He brought them up to Willy. "I want you to meet the woman who got here first. You'll never be able to remember Mission without her because there was no Mission until Mrs. Westall came."

"Yes, and I'm here to stay forever." Willy coughed again.

"Do you really mean that?" a pretty young woman asked. When Willy looked again, she saw tears glistening in the big, round eyes before her.

"This is Mrs. Randolph," Mr. Conlay said. "She's

a bride who has come down to join her husband. He's putting the telephone system in the Valley. And this is Miss Lizzie Shuman who is to work for the company."

He turned to the women. "Want you to know Mrs. Westall. She's Mission. Everybody is her friend."

Then he turned to Willy. "Met these people in Harlingin and drove them down myself so they could see the country as they came."

"It's beautiful!" Willy murmured. Now she could see the thing before her, red and shiny even through the dust. Everybody was crowding in it. Pat was sitting at the wheel pulling and pushing at many levers, telling everybody how to run it. Don was at his side asking questions.

"Of course it's beautiful," Mr. Conlay answered very loud. "This is the Magic Valley of the Rio Grande. God himself has kissed the earth and made it Eden."

"Let's go have a drink," somebody shouted.

"Dirt's got me choked plumb down," another answered.

"It ain't safe. It's too fast. Smallpox is sure to break right out again. Too damn dusty."

"Is there water?" a voice whispered close to Willy. It was the pretty Mrs. Randolph. Tears had puddled mud around her eyes.

"Of course there is," Willy answered. "Come on in; excuse my manners. Mr. Conlay surprised us all with this automobile. We haven't seen one. We're all excited. We were not prepared."

"Us neither," Miss Lizzie said. "You'll never get me to risk my life and legs again."

The two women followed Willy into the store. They took off their linen dusters and shook themselves while Willy got the water.

"And you really like this country?" Mrs. Randolph asked again. "My husband brought me. I had to come!"

Willy looked again at the youthful woman there before her. She saw herself back in Oklahoma City, big-eyed, expectant, dream-laden—hanging on her love like a fruit upon its stem. She felt very sad for this young person who had so much to learn.

"Yes, I like it," was all she said.

"It looks like hell," Miss Lizzie added. "Nothing but a lot of brush."

Willy laughed; Mrs. Randolph didn't.

"Don't mind Miss Lizzie," Mrs. Randolph said politely.

"That's the point about this country; everybody speaks his mind. Trains are leaving every day to go on," Willy answered.

Miss Lizzie looked at Willy, frowned slightly, and nodded toward Mrs. Randolph.

"But, oh, what plans we have," Willy added. "This is going to be the garden of the world."

Willy liked the gesture from the big buxom creature to the younger woman. Her heart must be gentle. She knew she'd find her very kind.

"The fun is building. You'll love it when you get the swing." Willy went on talking. "Every day we're building something. What about your church?"

"My church?" Mrs. Randolph raised her head. Miss Lizzie caught Willy's eye and smiled. "I'm Baptist."

"Well, we've just got one church started, but we all claim it. We'll put you in charge of Sunday school when enough children get down here to start one. Now that'll be a service you can give my children."

At that moment 'Mara and S'rita came racing through the store. They wanted to see the automobile out front. Willy stopped them long enough to meet Mrs. Randolph and Miss Lizzie; then they went sailing on to Don.

"Of course there ought to be a Sunday school," Mrs. Randolph said. She smiled sweetly.

Willy and Miss Lizzie winked at each other.

Before Mr. Conlay came in to get them, Miss Lizzie called Willy to one side. "You saved her, Miz Westall. I want to thank you. She was desperate. But seeing you and the children has bucked her up a lot."

"It's always hard to begin with," Willy answered, "especially on a bride."

"Yeah, I know. I come up hard in Oklahoma where it's rough. It's tough on pretty women who're soft.

Glad to know you, Miz Westall." Miss Lizzie stuck
out a big, firm hand.

Willy took it. She felt strength in the shaking. Somehow she knew she'd found a friend.

23

Miss Lizzie was the telephone in Mission. The first
thing she did was give out numbers. She started with
Mr. Conlay and counted straight up La Lomita. The
Westalls got number nine. She brooked no interference
from anybody, not even from Mr. Randolph.

Mrs. Allen called in from the ranch. She didn't like
her number. It was fifty-two. "I'm superstitious about
numbers. I like threes and sixes. They sound pretty.
Give me thirty-six or sixty-three, please, Miss Shuman."

"Can't do either," Miss Lizzie snapped. "You'll
have to keep the one I gave you. We're not up to
sixty-three as yet."

Mrs. Allen argued. "Why not skip a number? Do
they have to be in order? Why not give me thirty-six?"

"It's give away already."

"Then exchange it."

"I told you no already."

"Well, don't get mad about it. Whose got thirty-six?
I'll call and ask myself."

"If you have to know it, the red-light house in Mexiquita," Miss Lizzie said.

"Red-light house!" Mrs. Allen gasped. "I didn't
know there was one."

"Well, you ought to!" Then Miss Lizzie hung up the
phone.

The story of the conversation got around. Everybody began to whisper.

"That's what telephones are good for!" Willy said to
Fanny. "Now there'll be gossip, all kinds of gossip going around."

"Yeah," Fanny said. "Phil Allen's had that woman put up down there all this time and Miz Allen didn't know it. But watch and see, she'll know it now."

But nobody ever spoke to Miss Lizzie about what she had done. Nobody dared. She lived in the telephone office and took charge of the town. She knew everything that everybody said and straightway told it to everybody else; hence Mission achieved a social unity almost overnight. The sitters sat around the store at night and talked about what had gone by wire the day before.

Frank Dawney and Ed Nickel were having some gay poker parties on the river with some women imported from up the Valley. Mr. Weisschmidt carried on some strange conversation with San Antonio and New York. Phil Allen called Thirty-six every night. Mr. Fogg was having a little legal trouble in Minneapolis; Hal Eubank's girl had called him from California. Mrs. Randolph's mother had pneumonia. Bill Lester— But Miss Lizzie didn't give details about Bill Lester. He was her pet. She was a judge of people.

Bill Lester was the leading citizen of Mission and she knew it. Many others ranked him in importance but none in merit or in prestige. She noticed that when something was needed to be done, Bill Lester did it. He was the leader of any group that gathered. Mr. Conlay, Mr. Fogg, Hal Eubank, Jesse Parnell, Mr. Randolph, Sam Logan, Mr. Weisschmidt, one and all they stood back and let Bill Lester take the lead. It was Bill who always stepped up to the bar and said, "The drinks're on the house." It was Bill who shouted, "Get in line, men, the flume's broke. We've all got to pitch sandbags." It was Bill who went around at Christmas time and took up a collection for the Mexican children at the Oblate Mission. It was Bill who quietly whispered in the back room of the saloon, "Hell's goin' to crack across the river soon; we've got to keep a sharp watch now."

Miss Lizzie knew, like everybody else, that he had a Mexican woman living three miles north of Oblate. But she noticed that no one ever said a word about his mistress. They needed his kind of man and they took him as he was.

It was such astuteness in the woman that drew Willy to her. At heart she was devoutly kind. She rendered to everybody every service that she could. Several times a day she called Willy just to pass the news along. "Miz Weisschmidt's comin' up today. She just called up the depot. She's bringin' 'Mara and S'rita a German book." Or "Land excursion's a little late. Conlay got word from Fogg. The Judge won't need to meet the train," Or "Tell Phil Allen to hurry home. Irene's sick. Miz Allen called Dr. Jeffers." Often she rang and said, "Keep Don there with you. His mother and father're raising hell." And more often, "Don't let Don ride down to Thirty-six's with Judge Westall today. Old man Lea is down there to see his gal."

Miss Lizzie and Willy dovetailed into a city service for the town. People depended on them to make all kinds of strange connections. Bill Lester told them to keep their ears to the ground for horse news.

"Is there any special reason?" Willy asked.

"Just horse sense," he answered, laughing.

The next day Miss Lizzie called and said she'd heard a funny conversation about some horses across the river.

"In Mex or English?" Willy asked.

"Spanish; but I don't think it was a Mexican talking."

Somebody came in and she had to hang up. It was about six o'clock when Miss Lizzie called. Pat had just gone out to unhitch and feed Pearl. Don went along to help him. She expected Bill in every minute and she'd tell him what Miss Lizzie said.

The trade got heavy very quickly and she worked in circles, filling sacks with rice and beans, and scooping lard. 'Mara always helped her with the lard. That was the job she loved. Lard was so slick and white and greasy. S'rita always dabbled in the sugar. Both got in the way, but Willy never let them know it. As long as they thought they were helping, she liked to have them work behind the counter. It gave them a sense of service that they must learn.

The telephone rang and 'Mara answered. It was Miss Lizzie saying the flume had broken and the river was rising out of its bed. Mr. Weisschmidt had just called up that they would soon be cut off on their high spot on the bank. 'Mara told her mama what Miss Lizzie said and Willy tried to listen, but Mexicans kept flocking in. She watched for Bill, but he was late in coming.

She heard a noise at the back and told Emelio to go see about the rattle. In great excitement Pat and Don were pulling at the screen door. When Emelio unhooked it, they dashed up front, both talking at once.

Willy stopped and listened. Together they were saying, "Bill is lost! Pepe has just walked in from the river! Now he's gone into the saloon!"

Willy turned sick in the middle. "Quit talking both at once and tell me what's happened," she said sharply. "Start at the beginning. Let me get it straight."

Pat was fighting air in great confusion. He shouted, "Hell, I said Bill's lost. Don't you speak English any more?"

"Don't talk crazy! Bill Lester lost? Not unless somebody shot him. He knows this country like a book!"

"That's just it, he's drowned in water."

Willy gasped, "My God!" She remembered Miss Lizzie's news about the river out of banks.

"He and Pepe were down past Gran Geno," Pat rattled on. "Bill walked on ahead and left Pepe to watch the horses and a crossing. The river was rising fast and they knew it, but that fool Pepe was drunk and went to sleep. The last time he saw Bill he was on the bank; when he woke up the whole country was full of water. Fuego and Chiquita had run off and there was no hide nor hair of Bill. He must have drowned or got picked up by quicksand."

"And how did Pepe get to town without Fuego?"

"Swum most every lick, he says. Sorta kept above the water, hangin' on to mesquite bushes. The water rushed him, but he made it to the second-lift rise and walked on in."

"What time did he last see Bill? Does he remember?"

"About two o'clock, he thinks."

"Let's hurry! Get started hunting! Go get Pepe! I'll call Dr. Jeffers. Don, you run find Hal and Jesse."

"Hunt? How in God's name? How? The country's full of water."

The telephone rang three times in quick succession. Willy answered. It was Miss Lizzie. "Bill Lester's lost, Miz Westall!" she shouted.

"Yes, I know," Willy said. "At the second-lift pumphouse there's a boat, I think. Call and see. Rome brought it up to fix it. I got him the paint. I'll send the delivery wagon to get it in a jiffy. Call me back." Willy hung up.

She turned to Pat. "Go hitch up Pearl and go get the boat. I'll find Hal and Jesse. Bill might be just somewhere stranded. We've got to find him alive or dead."

"Hell, yes," Pat said. "Don, come on."

The two hurried out the back door as Pepe walked in the front, wet and drabbled. Pablo was with him. Both of them looked like dead men walking—ashen pale, almost unbalanced.

Pepe stared at Willy, his wet hair straggling, his eyes pleading. "Bad mescal," he said. "I sleep like dead, Madama."

Willy tried to smile assurance, but it was hard. "Get on upstairs. Pat's pants're in the dresser. You've got to hurry! You've got to find him!"

Pablo smiled a little; Pepe didn't. They both went out.

Pat and Don dashed in the back, both shouting, "Pearl's gone! Pearl's gone! Somebody stole her!"

"In God's name!" Willy breathed. "Not Pearl!"

S'rita raced out on the street and hollered, "Pearl's gone, Pearl's gone! Somebody stole her!"

The whole town came running. In a minute all of Mission stood at Pearl's corral with lanterns, looking, babbling, cursing, making guesses. They found big shoe tracks and Pearl's broken halter.

Willy clasped the halter as she muttered, "She put up a fight, God bless her!"

"By God, I'll kill the bastard!" Pat shouted.

'Mara cried; Don and S'rita walked up and down like Hal and Jesse.

Pat limped back and forth explaining, gesturing wildly. "They got her just as we left her! They saw us go up to Pepe and start talking. They heard the news of Bill and knew there'd be excitement!"

Willy was the first to calm. "Who's got a horse?" she asked. "We've got to get the boat and get started out for Bill."

Tom Jones said, "I'll run get my pintos."

"My horse's hitched out front," three people spoke at once.

Pablo edged in close to Willy. "Use Fuego, Madama!"

"Where'd he come from? Is Chiquita with him?"

"They come in to me wheen the water get too deep and Pepe ees too drunk asleep."

A dozen hands grabbed Fuego's bridle to unsaddle him and get him hitched to the delivery wagon. "Luck!" everybody shouted when he pulled off.

Pat did the driving. Hal Eubank, Jesse Parnell, Pablo, and Pepe got in the wagon. Everybody wanted to go along, but Willy wouldn't let them.

"Pepe knows the place! Pablo can swim! Hal and Jesse can row the boat." She couldn't think of a reason for Pat right quickly but she knew he had to go—just had to, that was all. "Pat can drive the wagon," she added "and bring back Fuego."

"And bring back Bill?" 'Mara was crying. This awfulness she couldn't understand. Something hurt her in the middle. They wouldn't let her help. She was too little. And Mama looked so strange and far away, somehow.

"Of course, Honey, they'll bring back Bill." Willy took 'Mara's hand and squeezed it. That felt better. Nothing in the world mattered now but Bill. Salita crouched close to her feet and shivered.

"Listen, everybody," Willy shouted. "Pearl's gone but spooks didn't take her. It was a man. Bill says they're stealing horses across the river but not my mare. Twenty-five dollars to the finder. Get the word around. Somebody bring her in!" Then she went back into the store. The crowd broke up.

That night nobody slept in Mission. The river kept rising. Once it jumped its banks, it filled the resacas and pushed up backwater. The first-lift farmers had to get on higher ground. All night they kept coming into Mission.

"Just like I told you," Mr. Conlay stood on the street and announced to everybody. "It's a tricky river. Right on its banks you're safe. It's the backwater that gets you. That's why I put Mission on this hill, even if it is expensive to lift the water a second time to irrigate us."

Willy didn't even go to bed. She kept the store open. Fanny brought over hot coffee for everybody. People came in and went out. There was a moving and milling all night long. Willy called Mrs. Allen. Everything was fine right on the river, just marooned was all. So was Mrs. Weisschmidt.

But no sight or word of Bill.

About midnight Pat drove Fuego in. Pepe and Pablo had taken the first turn rowing. Hal and Jesse went out next. But in the dark they could do no good. They were all resting. At daylight they would start out again.

Pat went to bed about two o'clock in the morning. Mrs. Randolph came down to the store. Her husband had been called out on the telephone line and she was afraid to stay at home by herself.

"I've been praying for Mr. Lester," she said to Willy. "Remember Noah in the Bible. They had a flood."

"Yes, I remember."

"He found an ark. So can Mr. Lester."

"No," Willy said. "Noah made an ark and so will Bill if something hasn't tricked him pretty badly."

Mrs. Randolph's face fell at the correction. Certainly she had meant well.

Willy put her arm around her waist and added, "But you keep on praying, Mrs. Randolph. Find him something to make an ark out of in all that water."

At daylight Pat, Willy, and Mr. Conlay drove

Fuego in the delivery wagon down to the flood edge. What they saw was a still sea of water—hot, bright, glistening, without a house or tree above it.

"Good God, I'd never have thought it!" Pat exclaimed. "In this damned desert!" He turned to Willy. "Plenty of water, Sweetheart. Look at it. Let's get out and get a drink."

Willy tried to smile a little, but she couldn't.

Mr. Conlay sighed. "What a waste! What a waste! And the land so dry and thirsty."

"Not thirsty now," Pat said.

"It's Nature's way," Mr. Conlay continued. "God gives the water. We just don't know how to use it. Some day there'll be gravity irrigation. There'll be a dam that will hold flood water. Then when it's dry the land can use it."

Pat began to listen. "Well, now, that's right," he said. "You've got something, Conlay. Why don't you do it?"

Mr. Conlay laughed loud and long. "Can't beat the Irish, Judge Westall, but I'm not that good. I'm smart all right but not that rich. But some day the Government will do it. Just watch and see. In the meantime, we'll prove our country and keep on dreaming. Amara and Serena will live to see it."

Fuego jerked up his head and nickered. They all listened. They heard brush crackle. A horse snorted.

"Hello!" Pat hollered.

"Be quiet!" Willy sh-d-d-d him.

In a minute a man rode out of the mesquite thicket that edged into the water.

"It's Ted Tolliver," Willy whispered.

"He's out early," Pat said.

"Good mornin', folks," Ted drawled, as he rode up. "Got any news from Bill?"

Willy shuddered. She felt cold. Something about Ted Tolliver always chilled her. She felt trapped when he came near her. There was no reason for it. He was an old-timer, like Phil Allen, but as different as beans from cabbage. When he rode a horse he didn't sit it; he was like a snake, he slunk and slid.

Pat said, "What're you doing out so early?"

"On the lookout for Bill Lester. Saw Pepe and Pablo around that bend."

Willy leaned forward. "Is there any news down there?"

"No, they been ridin' in that boat. Nowhere to look, to tell the truth. Can't find things in water. Heard you lost Pearl, Miz Westall. Got any news from her?"

"Not yet." Willy looked at Ted. Her head began to work. "Reward is fifty dollars, Ted," she said.

"Last night they told me twenty-five. It's goin' up."

"Yes, fast. It's now a hundred." She turned to Pat. He smiled.

Ted squinted and spit hard at a close-by cactus. "Well, so long, folks. I'll see you later," he drawled, and rode off.

When he was out of earshot, Pat spoke. "Well, let's drive on back and count out the hundred dollars. You've got your man all right, Sweetheart!"

When they got back, Pat joined Tom Jones for their morning drink. Willy got the children off to school. She and Emelio cleaned up the store, then filled the morning orders. The excitement of the night dulled into bleak terror. The hot bright sun beat in the facts. Bill and Pearl were gone; the river crops were in flood. That meant the farmers couldn't pay their bills. Willy sat down on a barrel. She wasn't sleepy, but Lord, how tired! Drowning, they say, is easy. Rest and peace must be delicious. She felt jealous, wildly jealous. Bill had mentioned moving on. He could do it, for nothing held him except Conchita. Then suddenly she thought, "Poor Conchita! Nobody's told her! I'll get into the delivery wagon and go myself. That is the one thing I can do for Bill.'"

She jumped up and grabbed her Stetson. "I'll be back," she called to Emelio. She ran out front and untied Fuego. When she touched him, he reared and snorted. A high clear nicker answered back. Willy looked.

There came Pearl. She wasn't leading; she just walked along beside Ted Tolliver. When she saw Willy, she hit a trot. They met together in a gallop.

Willy hugged the mare and kissed her. "Pearl Pearl!" was all she said. She was crying. Pearl nickered back.

Mr. Conlay was watching from the Rio Grande Hardware steps. "Heart is heart whether horse or human when they beat like that," he said, and walked back into the store.

Ted Tolliver didn't look. He slunk into Bill's Place like a rat.

Don trotted up on Chiquita and got off. Fuego snorted and pawed the ground. Pearl nosed him a minute, then followed Don and Willy. They went to the corral and measured out the corn. Pearl chomped and stomped a little as she ate. Don peeped to see if they were being watched.

"What is it, Honey?" Willy asked him.

He whispered, "I know a secret. Pablo let me have Chiquita to go hunt Bill. I rode out west by the water. I saw Ted Tolliver in the brush. He had Pearl tied to a mesquite. He came and got her. I followed every step."

"Now that's good work," Willy said. She put her hands on his shoulders and looked at him. How could his parents care so little for this son, tall and straight, alert to duty, righting wrongs and helping people— just like Bill Lester, she was thinking, when he spoke.

"And Miz Westall, there's somethin' else I want to talk to you about now that we're here all by ourselves." He blushed a little.

"Sure, go on; what is it, Honey? Let 'er shoot!"

"Pearl's gonna have a colt. I told Bill to tell you. Did he?"

"Why, no, he didn't. Are you sure?"

"Yeah, I saw 'em, Pearl an' Fuego. It was once at Thirty-six's. She broke loose from the delivery wagon when Judge Westall and me went to take the groceries in. Fuego had jumped the fence to get loose."

"Yes, I remember about the wagon, but Pat didn't tell me about Fuego."

Don looked down a second a little guilty. "It was our secret, but she's been stole now. You're a woman. You'd know better. I want the colt to be all right."

Willy felt impelled to kiss him, but she knew that wouldn't do. "That's fine," she said. "Now that I'm in on the secret I appoint you watchout man for Pearl. You tell me the minute you see signs of birth."

"Oh, sure," he said proudly. "I'd do that anyhow."

Ted Tolliver walked up, saying. "Found Pearl at Peñitas, tied out. Waitin' for a crossin', I guess, Miz Westall."

"A deal's a deal," Willy snapped. "No explaining. Come on in. I'll give you the hundred dollars."

Ted looked kill-dog as he followed. They walked on into the store.

Pat wasn't there to write the check. Willy wanted to get rid of Ted Tolliver quickly. He seemed like a louse she had to crack. She opened the checkbook and wrote the date; then she looked at the balance in the bank. A hundred and ten dollars was what they had. Her heart sank for just a second, but she jerked it and it leveled.

"Thank God I can cover what I said," she breathed, then dashed off a hundred dollars and signed Mrs. Patrick Westall. She turned to Ted and handed him the piece of paper. "That evens us up completely."

"Sure does," he said, and went on out.

S'rita and Fanny dashed in the door. S'rita was screaming. "Mama, Mama, here they come!"

"Who's coming, Honey? Don't talk so loud. Why aren't you in school?"

"Judge Woolcott let us out! We saw 'em coming across the track.

"It's Bill!" Fanny sputtered through her tears.

Willy rushed to the door. Bill was on his way in. 'Mara and Judge Woolcott were at his heels, with Pablo and Pepe. The saloon emptied to the man. People came running from everywhere to give Bill hell for the awful scare. They grabbed his hand and slapped his back. He thanked everybody and waved his hat.

"Awful hungry!" was about all he said. "There's Fanny yonder, she'll get me grub."

He got loose from the crowd and finally made the store. 'Mara and S'rita grabbed his knees, but Don stood back like a grown man.

Fanny kissed Bill, sobbing, "Raised from the dead, or I'll be damned!"

Willy stuck out her hand and shook his.

Pat rushed in; then Hal and Jesse, Mr. Conlay and Tom Jones.

"Tell us a little," Pat exclaimed. "You've scared us. We've earned the story."

"Awful easy," Bill replied. "I was standin' on the riverbank lookin' down. Somethin' crumbled and I fell in."

"What in God's world were you doin' there?"

Bill looked at Pat straight and long. "A little business," he replied.

"Then what happened?" Jesse asked.

"I swum like hell as long as I could. Then I caught to a willow on the edge and pulled to a mesquite and lodged myself. When Pepe found me, I was plumb wore out."

Willy cut in, "That's enough." She turned to Fanny, "Take him and feed him and get him to bed."

The Negro was smiling through her tears. "Get out of our way and let us go."

"Me too, Fanny?" S'rita asked.

"Not now, Sweeter. My business's Bill." She grabbed Bill's arm and out they went.

S'rita lips began to pucker. She ran to her papa.

Pat said, "Well, I'll be damned. Come on, Baby, let's go see Pearl!"

"Pearl!" all three children screamed, and away they ran, Pat behind them, and Tom Jones.

Willy looked at Emelio and smiled wanly. She rang the telephone a good long ring.

"Wonderful, ain't it?" Miss Lizzie said, her voice unsteady.

"Yes, thank God. Give me Mrs. Randolph, please."

When the voice answered, Willy said, "Your prayer is answered. Bill Lester's back."

"He is?" she gasped. "Do you think my praying helped?"

"Think? I know! He said so himself. He was worn out when the ark came up and he gave a grab and got aboard."

Mrs. Randolph laughed. "You are so sweet, Mrs. Westall. You make me feel like I'm some account."

"You are—if you only knew. Good-bye. We'll talk later." She hung up and just bowed her head. Now she wouldn't have to tell Conchita.

Pepe slipped inside the door. He looked pale and worn, frowzy, in Pat's clothes. His eyes were wild, like a hunted thing.

Willy went over and put her hand in his. "Go get some sleep now and don't forget—mescal's no good to mix with friends. You can't go to sleep when you're asked to watch."

24

The river went down slowly. Cabbage rotting in the loblolly sent up a stink that made Mrs. Randolph take a trip back home. S'rita and Pat got off their food. Fanny imposed sulphur and molasses and made them take it.

Most people kept on eating on Westall credit. They couldn't pay, for they had no crops. Having paid big prices for their land they were stranded for cash. Nothing was coming in. But Mr. Dubose shipped Willy's orders. He never questioned.

"That's the wonder of the country," Mr. Conlay reverberated. "In no time at all you'll have the next crop. They come just as fast as you can put them in. Remember this is the Magic Valley of the Rio Grande."

Pat motioned Mr. Conlay to one side. "Then you'd better do something about it. We're runnin' deep in debt. Get new folks down here with new money. Do somethin' new to start a show. Those Mexicans raisin' hell across the river's not helpin' us a bit."

Mr. Conlay took the tip and got busy. There was a lot of telephoning back and forth. He urged everybody to get flood land replanted.

The sun shone on the rich earth drunk deep with water. Seed sprouted, grew overnight, blossomed. Before people knew what had happened, they looked out and saw their paradise again: cabbage, onions, cantaloupes, tomatoes ready for the winter market.

Mr. Conlay looked out and smiled. He had his scene set for the trick card in his pocket. He would draw homeseekers by the thousands to the Magic Valley. Prominent visitors would visit her in grandeur. Land would sell at rising prices. By the thousands Mexican grubbers would cross the river; new stores would spring up overnight! Everybody would talk free silver. Business booming! World attention would focus on the Rio Grande.

He walked into La Tienda Caballo Blanco to announce the news. All the sitters gathered round.

"Land party will be down on Tuesday," he started out. "Fogg called me from St. Louis. Fine crowd of people, all rich, wanting sunshine. He's heading up the party with William Jennings Bryan."

"My God," Pat shouted, "Bryan's comin' back at last?"

"How can he do it?" Judge Woolcott asked. "How can he spare the time?"

"Wants a dose of sunshine and Valley cabbage," Mr. Conlay answered, puffing out his vest.

Lon Stone snarled a little. "Why does he fool around like this? He's got more important business!"

"The hell he has," Pat snapped.

"And that's not all," Mr. Conlay continued. "He'll have his wife along, and his daughter, too."

John Sanders looked at Hal Eubank and Willy looked at Bill.

Pat jumped up and began limping back and forth. "Well, let's get started and be ready. Tuesday's not far off." Then he began on orders of what every man should do: cut the weeds, plant palms along the streets, paint all store porches, put out some water barrels. "Can't look like we're all still ranchers when the big bugs get down here."

Phil Allen got up and left the store. Bill smiled at Willy and lit a cigarette.

Willy went outside to take a squint at Pearl. She always took the pistol, because Bill had told her to. Pearl snorted—she didn't nicker—when her mistress slammed the screen. Willy stopped and listened. She heard a rustle, like footsteps, in the crib. Since the moon was shining, Pearl was plain to see; but dust was blowing up. It blurred Willy's vision, but she aimed her gun and shot. Something shuffled. She ran to see. She heard footsteps, and something jumped the fence.

"Hope I got him," she said to Pearl. She patted the mare's shoulder and went back into the house.

Pat had just finished giving orders. The crowd was going home. When dirt began to whirl into the store, everybody hurried to beat the dust storm.

That night Pat kicked and tumbled. He didn't sleep a wink. Dirt was rolling and it was hard to breathe.

"What is it, Darling?" Willy kept asking him.

"Just thinking," was all he said.

The next morning he announced he felt very sick. Willy knew he didn't. But he said he believed he'd take the train and run over to Corpus Christi. Dubose had said that Dr. Farr of the Pasteur Institute had set up a private place for stomach trouble. He'd go over and take a look. Might take S'rita later. Their stomachs were always weak.

Willy didn't argue. She never did with Pat. Anyway, expense or no expense, she was glad for him to have the trip. The wind kept blowing; dirt came pouring in. They were in for a regular blow. It was best to have Pat gone. He hated the choking and stifling that went with dusty wind. The last storm made him sick. She asked him to take S'rita with him. He decided to take all three children.

Willy was glad they went. The town was in a bustle, getting ready for the Bryans. But the dirt kept blowing and there wasn't much they could get done. But on Monday morning, when the sun rose bright and clear, everybody set to work. It took the day just to rake off dust.

The train brought Pat and the children home. All four were dressed up in new suits, ties, stockings, shoes, dresses, hair ribbons. Don wore a red silk shirt.

Willy didn't mention expense; she just stood back and
raved. Pat's eyes were shining. He had to do it. She
knew that very well. He was the host of Mission and
Bryan was coming in.

Pat kissed her warmly.

"Tell me about Dr. Farr," she said.

"Didn't get time to see him," Pat replied. "I was
buyin' you a hat, Sweetheart, and S'rita stopped me,"
he said. "She vowed it looked like hell. We'll all go
back up there soon and dress you up," he added.

"Sure!" Willy said. She kept assurance in her voice,
but she remembered the bank balance.

Pat kept on talking. "We decided on a surprise! It'll
be up in a minute."

When it came, Willy almost fainted. Puffing up in
front of the store rolled a car; not a long, red, shining
automobile like Mr. Conlay's, but a short, black, one-
seated wagon without a horse.

"It's a Brush," Pat said proudly. "The latest thing.
Got it to deliver groceries in!"

"But Pearl!" Willy gasped.

"She's gonna have a colt, remember," Don whispered.

"Well, she's done her part, Sweetheart," Pat said.
"She's like you. She needs a rest."

When Pat insisted, Willy got in. Pat had bought the
thing; she might as well ride in it; but it scared her,
not the speed but all the sputter.

"Turn the corner. Don't let Pearl see us," she
screamed to Pat. Once around the block she asked to
get out. Pat could have the Brush; she'd keep Pearl.
They'd have two delivery wagons.

That afternoon all Mission took a ride. They felt
ready then for William Jennings Bryan.

The next morning Willy and Emelio snatched and
grabbed to get the store in order. 'Mara swept the
porch. Don curried all the horses. S'rita brought in cactus flowers. Fanny dressed the children and herself,
then came over to help Pat.

He put on his new suit and hat. Father Michael
came early. He and Pat were the official committee to

meet the train. Pat got out the Brush and they sat out front, waiting. The crowd gathered.

People flocked into the store. Willy and Emelio stayed on the job. She meant to leave every minute and get upstairs to dress. 'Mara came running in and begged her to come out front and look at all the people, and she did. Fanny and S'rita and Don were standing on the porch.

Bill rode up and hollered, "Howdy!" Chiquita glistened in the sun. Bill wore a white shirt and tie. His boots were brand new, Justin's best.

"Mighty dressed up," Willy hollered.

"Had to keep up with the Judge."

He was smiling. So was Pat.

Mr. Conlay chugged down the street. Chiquita reared. The automobile choked and sputtered. "Too slow driving," he explained. People gathered around to take a look at this strange critter. It was shining, bright and red. Pat's face clouded for a moment.

The whistle blew. The whole town made the depot at a run. The saloon door popped open and men poured out. People came darting out of doors. Everybody went running toward the train.

Willy watched them go. All at once she looked down at herself: big broad shoes, her apron far from clean, her shirt ripped a little in the sleeve!"

"And my hair! I meant to change, and comb my hair, and now they'll be here in a minute."

She rushed back, grabbed Pat's blue coat and put it on, and socked her Stetson on her head. Since there was no glass to look in, she didn't try to look. She heard a noise and turned around.

Ted Tolliver sidled in. His arm was in a sling. He looked surprised to see her.

"What can I do for you?" she said.

"Nothin', Miz Westall. I'm jest waitin' for the crowd." He leaned against the counter.

"Why didn't you meet the train?"

"Not feelin' well. Had a little trouble with my arm."

"Yes, I see. Had a little trouble myself the other night. Had to shoot a scoundrel in Pearl's lot."

"Yeah, I'd like to talk to you about it. Thought you

might need a little help." His eyes beaded. He stepped up close enough to her to touch. He smelled body-sweaty and like carbolic acid.

"This is jest for you an' me." His eyes narrowed to a line. "Things're gettin' pretty shaky. I'm in on a lot of things, you know. Me an' my family're old-timers in this country. We like you folks a lot. Hate to see you put upon. Now this is straight." He stepped up closer still.

Willy held her breath to keep from smelling. She held her ground.

"Wouldn't dare to tell this to the Judge. His head's too hot. So I'm tellin' you. I know you put a lot of stock in that mare of yores."

"You ought to know!" Willy snapped.

"Well, she'll be stole!" he went on.

"What're you trying to say?" Willy shifted her weight and frowned.

"I kin watch her for you. It'll cost ye somethin' like twenty dollars every month!" He bent down toward her, his eyes cutting.

She wished she were behind the counter near the gun.

"Do you think I'm crazy?" She looked at him straight.

"But you don't know the half. I'll do your shootin', an' you'll need shootin' pretty soon."

"Look here, talk sense to me and tell me what you mean." She knew now she felt scared.

He laughed a little and leaned back on the counter. "You'll say in a minute you'll tell Bill Lester."

"Well, I will at that."

"Yeah, now that's the point." He leaned over her again. "Do you know about Bill Lester? Where he come from? What he works at when he goes across the river? Why he keeps that Mexkin woman?"

Willy felt her heart clench. "Tollivers're cockroach cattle rustlers!" Bill had said.

"Do you know what?" Ted's breath came vile and close. "I'm tellin' you to protect you, mind you that —Bill Lester's headin' up a bandit gang across the river that's gettin' ready to raid the border. That's what he does with. Pablo an' Pepe with him all the time. They gang up at that woman's! They're out to steal an' raid an' kill. He's warmin' up to you because the people all come here. That's why you need me around, to shoot when the shootin' starts."

Willy reached up and slapped with all her might. If she had had a gun she would have shot. Ted stepped back stunned. He held to the counter's edge. Willy gained the middle of the floor.

"You yellow-bellied coward," she screamed. "If I had a knife I'd cut your black heart out and carve those words in flesh!" Her hands were on her hips; her feet wide set; her curls straggling from underneath her hat. She darted for the counter. She'd get the pistol and kill the bastard.

But she stumbled and fell. Salita squealed and backed off. Willy lay there flat on her stomach for a moment. All she could see was a snarling line of teeth and tusks in the javelina's mouth. The hog looked wild and frightened, as she did that time Willy tried to stab her.

"I don't blame her," Willy thought. "When you're mad, you're mad and you can't help it. You've got to protect yourself. Nobody'll do it for you."

She felt a hand reach down and grab her arm. It was Ted Tolliver. Well, he couldn't help her do anything on earth! She pushed him away and sprang to her feet at one bound.

When she stood upright, she saw Father Michael leading the land-seeking party into the store. In a minute the store was full of people, Mr. Conlay and all the land crowd. Willy looked at them straightly, but she felt giddy. Faces danced before her, crazy faces white with veils and hats.

"This is my wife," she heard Pat say proudly. That cleared her mind a little. "Sweetheart, this is Mrs. Bryan."

Willy reached out her hand and shook. She wasn't very sure of what she was doing. All she knew was that the next hand was big and soft, but it shook strong.

Pat spoke again. "This is his honor, William Jennings Bryan." His voice was poised, very proud.

Then she looked up into a big, kind face. Her anger and confusion faded. She jerked herself to reason while some more things happened. Pat was introducing William Jennings Bryan to the crowd. He was speaking. Everybody listened. She dropped her pencil and heard it fall.

Bill came in the door with Don. She looked around for Ted Tolliver, but he was gone. But she spotted two familiar faces—Mrs. Baxter and Mr. Thornton, who had spent Christmas with them on the ranch.

"Well, I'll be damned!" she said.

When Mr. Bryan finished talking, he looked down and picked up Amara and held her in his arms.

"I do wish you could understand, my dear," he said.

"Yes, sir." Amara looked at him just as if she did.

Mr. Conlay came forward. He spoke a few words of greeting to the crowd, then stepped up to Willy. The Bryans wanted some provisions to take out to their place. "Please fix up what they need and do it fast, Mrs. Westall."

"I want a rake, Mrs. Westall, for the garden," Miss Bryan said.

Willy reached and got one and handed it to her. But Miss Bryan stood with her arms folded.

"Please wrap it up," she said.

"Well, I'll be damned." Willy never knew whether she said it or thought it to herself.

William Jennings himself reached out and took the rake. "My children aren't all as smart as I am," he said, and everybody laughed.

Willy and Emelio hurried with the order while the people talked and milled around. Bill, Pat, Father Michael, Don, and Amara served as hosts to the reception.

Pat was everywhere. 'Mara was talking to the women. Bill sidled in a corner with some men.

S'rita stayed out front with Pepe on the steps. He held Pepitón in his lap. The snow-digging women questioned, but Pepe sat there as if he couldn't understand. So did S'rita. Fanny came forward as the mouthpiece and talked on any subject anybody asked.

"Why does he hold a rooster in his lap?"

"It's a religion with the Mexkins."

"Is the beautiful child with him Mexican?"

"Yes, pure blood."

"Why won't she talk?"

"Born dumb from birth."

A schoolteacher from Iowa stood by listening. She grew suspicious and went inside. Willy was dashing up and down behind the counter, but the schoolteacher didn't care. She had to get things straight.

"Who is that woman outside, talking? Is she black or white?"

"She's a Negro with the whitest heart on earth," Willy answered.

Mrs. Baxter edged over close, to talk to Willy.

She was still lovely, wearing a long linen duster and yards of veil.

"And you pretty young creature! Still in this awful country, seeking land, I guess."

"Well, what are you doing?" Willy snapped.

Mrs. Baxter leaned close to whisper so Mr. Conlay could not hear, "I'm just on a little lark, my dear. I get so bored staying still."

"And Mr. Thornton?"

"He's interested, of course, in buying. He always is. He just lets me come along. We've been so many places!"

Willy felt as if she'd have to slap her for that Christmas visit. "Yes, I know," she said. "We leased the ranch to Jim Nelson."

"I'm so glad, my dear. This place is bad enough, but that was worse. The children are beautiful. You really must do something about yourself. You look too quaint with that man's hat and those big shoes but, of course, in time you won't. You'll grow older. Remember what I've told you."

Mr. Thornton called and Mrs. Baxter joined him.

Willy stomped her heavy shoe on Emelio's toe.

"Qué tiene, Madama?" The boy looked up in surprise.

"Nothing, Emelio. I guess I'm mad and jealous of a

pretty woman who manages to wander around with a man and has no worries."

The Mexican stood puzzled as he looked into Willy's eyes. They sank deep into her head, circled around with shadow. He wished he could say something that would help her.

But he couldn't. Nobody could help the Madama. She somehow always helped herself. These Americanos were so queer. One was screaming at the moment. Mexican women never scream. It was Mrs. Baxter. When Salita snapped her on the leg, it was like a gunshot to the crowd. Women scampered, ran, and got on chairs.

Mr. Conlay, always sensing the dramatic moment, used that incident as a signal for departure. He hustled the party out front into buckboards, all drawn up, waiting. Bill, Hal, Jesse, Pepe, Pablo, Tom Jones, even Judge Woolcott did the driving. Mr. Conlay took the Bryans in his automobile, with Father Michael. Pat lent his Brush to Mr. Fogg. He stood there watching as they drove off to view the wonders of the Magic Valley of the Rio Grande.

Willy thanked God when they were gone. She felt confused and tired enough to die. The javelina came and hid beneath her skirt.

"She's tired of people too," Willy said.

Then she and Pat began to talk about the javelina and why she had begun to snap.

"Got to get rid of her! She's gettin' wild," Pat said.

"I wish there were some way to turn her loose so she could go back to her pack," Willy said.

"That's damned foolishness. She'd be killed in no time because we've had her since she was a pig. No; I'm goin' to send her to Dr. Riley in Oklahoma City. He can give her to the Zoo. This is the day to do it before somebody sues us for a bite. We'll just have time to catch the train coming back from Fordyce."

They called the children and then all went outside together to build a shipping crate. Pat noticed that Willy's eyes were by far the saddest of them all.

"Go on inside, Sweetheart, and let me do this job," he admonished.

And she was very glad to shift the responsibility of so hard a task. She loved Salita almost as she loved Pearl. In another way the pig had served her just as well. She had entertained the children when there was nothing for the little girls to do. Now to put her into discard just because she would not smile seemed disloyal, weak, and human, and she couldn't help but hate herself.

Pat waxed eloquent in his reasons to the children. They knew javelinas now by association and it was only fair to let other little children see Salita in the Zoo.

'Mara cried while Papa hammered shut the crate. Don went off so he wouldn't have to look. S'rita stood there almost gritting her teeth, but she did keep back the tears until the train pulled out with Salita on it; then she grabbed her papa's knees and wailing to the heavens shouted, "Papa, it's a goddamned shame!"

That night after the land seekers were put to bed on the Pullmans and all the crowd had cleared out home, Judge Woolcott came in with a little puppy as a gift. S'rita named him Mutt and set about to teach him tricks. But 'Mara went to Papa for the answer. "How'll Salita live in Oklahoma City, Papa?" She felt so troubled.

"Why, Sugar, she'll be bringing people from everywhere to see her behind glass casings. She'll be a queen," he answered.

Willy didn't listen, but she couldn't help hearing them talk, and she couldn't keep from thinking. "The wilderness beating out her heart. We betrayed her and she knows it, javelina though she is."

25

The following night the sitters all gathered around to talk about the land excursion.

"Best sales we've ever had," Mr. Conlay announced. "Just wait and see! With Bryan established here, the world will come to us. We'll have them at our feet. These folks we sold this trip will boom business for us all."

Lon Stone interrupted. "What about the ruckus across the border? Getting in the papers an awful lot these days. Folks are writing me from home."

Bill frowned and spit. "Nothin' to it. All we have to do is quit talkin' about it and let 'em all alone down there. They don't butt into our business, you can see. Things are goin' strong. Just give Madero and Pancho Villa time and they'll get things steadied up and runnin'."

"Yeah, but what about the fight at Torreon?" Hal Eubank put in.

Bill's face turned red. "It's folks like you, Hal, that make a revolution. All you do is talk. If you know so much about it, do something and do it quick or else shut up or leave!"

Hal jumped up. Pat grabbed him. "See here now, boys; calm down. Can't have a fight among ourselves. Too few of us," Pat said.

Mr. Conlay interjected, "Judge Westall's right. Anyway, we have no worries. People're coming to the Valley every day. Every mail is full of letters. Had six inquiries about stores moving in."

"What kind of stores?" Willy asked.

"All kinds—a fancy grocery, two dry goods and a drug store, a millinery—all kinds! But don't worry. Competition's the life of trade, Mrs. Westall."

"Oh, sure," she said. "But tell them to open up for strictly cash."

Pat frowned at her. She felt a little bit ashamed. She had no business interrupting when the men were talking.

Don dashed in and called her aside. "Pearl's gonna have the colt soon, Miz Westall. I was at the corral watchin'. You'd better hurry up." His eyes were bulging.

S'rita and 'Mara rushed up to ask a lot of questions.

"It's somethin' you can't know," Don snarled.

"Go on!" Bill said to Willy. "I've got a lot of talkin' to do to 'Mara. We're behind with talkin'. S'rita can listen. I'll see you later." The girls both landed in his lap.

Willy gave Emelio a few directions, then she got out the lantern. She and Don hurried to the corral. Pearl's eyes were wide and frightened. She nickered softly when they came up.

Willy put her arms around the mare's neck and rubbed her nose and ears. If she could only help her —but she couldn't. She did a lot of thinking while she talked to Don. They waited and watched nature as it performed its function.

The colt stepped out into the world long-legged, big-eyed, a little Fuego in form and line and color.

"Swell!" Don said when they looked him over. "Let's name him something really swell, Miz Westall."

"Prince," Willy said.

She was thinking of a horse pulling a buggy with rubber tires. A man was driving, head up, chin stuck out, pale-blue eyes focused to the front. His two good legs braced him against the dashboard as he drove.

Don shouted, "Just watch Prince suck!"

Willy caught Pearl's eye in the lantern light. She wanted her to know she understood. Suddenly she heard footsteps, then a voice.

"Good work, you hombres," a familiar voice said. She turned and saw Bill walking toward them.

"Mustn't let Chiquita see this feller. She'll get jealous." He smiled widely.

So did Willy. "You ought to let Chiquita have a colt," she said. "She's been faithful. Every woman wants a child."

The smile faded. "Yeah, I know," he said. "But I'm too busy. We'll have to put an extra guard now on this young'un. What'll you call the colt?"

"Prince," Don spoke up.

"Well, Ted Tolliver'll have an eye for Prince now. We'll have to keep Prince guarded."

This was the chance that Willy had been looking for. She had not spoken of Ted Tolliver to anybody. That was the perfect way to get Ted killed. But she thought about him and all he said. Just a dirty horse thief. But there was something strange lurking behind his words. She had to talk to Bill about it. She couldn't just then because 'Mara and S'rita came shrieking. Bill had slipped off and left them. They had looked for him and spied the colt, and here they came! Then Emelio and Judge Woolcott—and Fanny. S'rita ran for Pepe on the saloon steps. Pablo came along. They all stood around and rubbed the new colt's head and back.

"Fuego oughta see him," Don suggested. "He'll be awful proud!"

They all laughed then and left Pearl with her baby colt.

Willy got up once after she went to bed and went out to the corral to see if all was well with Pearl and Prince.

Willy didn't know how long she had been sleeping when somebody woke her, calling.

"It's me," Bill hollered. "Let me in!"

She jerked on her skirt and lit the lamp. When Bill stepped inside he looked excited.

"That damned Dr. Jeffers!" he said in his first breath.

"He went to Brownsville."

"Yeah, I know. I've just come back from there."

"Brownsville?"

"No, the Weisschmidts'. I come for the doctor an' the damn fool's gone."

Willy caught her breath. She knew what it was to have a baby by herself.

"Can you go, Miz Westall? I just happened to pass by. She's awful sick. She's there all by herself! I brought Fuego for you to ride."

Twenty minutes later they galloped across the railroad track and headed south. Mr. McIntire was on his third watch for the night. He tried to stop them but they rode on.

"Something's wrong," he said, "or they wouldn't be ridin' off like that."

He watched the two mustangs flash in the moonlight. In a minute they were gone.

There was no waiting for the birth. Willy got there just in time to receive the child as it cried first. In her hurry she cut her finger together with the navel cord.

When she presented the little girl to Mrs. Weis-schmidt, she said, "You did a fine job of that."

"Vat ve muss do, ve muss do." Tear were swimming in the fagged blue eyes.

Willy understood the meaning of those words too well. That awful walking back and forth in the ranch house wondering where Pat was. She didn't ask Mrs. Weisschmidt about her husband. She just sat and held her hand.

Once he knew the baby had been born, Bill rode back to town for Fanny.

The German woman went to sleep. When she woke up, she looked at Willy and smiled wanly.

"Her name iss Guillermita—little Villy—for you, Mrs. Vestall."

Willy leaned over and kissed her on the forehead and whispered, "Go on back to sleep."

When Fanny got there and took charge, Bill and Willy rode back to town. The sun was rising as they left.

"Let's let the horses walk," she said. "It's so nice and cool and clear. I feel like I'm back again on the ranch!"

Then neither of them spoke for a solid mile. In the clear cool morning the Gulf breeze made it good to think.

Willy was the one who started talking. "Where is Mr. Weisschmidt?" she asked.

"Yeah, that's just it," Bill said. "We've been trailin' him for days. That's what I was doin' on the river. Was snoopin' aroun' the house when I heard Miz Weisschmidt groanin'."

"We? Who do you mean we?"

"Pepe an' me an' Dutch an' Duke."

"Those boys from the Stewart ranch?"

"Yeah. Asa Hall sends them out on real shootin' deals. They ain't so old but they can shoot, an' they suit me fine."

"Shoot? What's all this about?"

They rode on in silence for a minute, then Bill said,

"Well, I don't like to tell you. It might scare you some."

"I guess I'll have to know it all in time."

"That's just the point. This damn German livin' on the river's got somethin' up his sleeve. He's runnin' a truck farm for a blind. Folks like them don't come to no place like this to live. Did you notice how swell they've fixed up them jacales?"

"Well, I was too busy to notice much about the house. I was thinking."

"Yeah," he said.

They rode on. Neither spoke.

"Did you see that picture above the bed?" Bill finally asked.

"Yes; a man with a mustache and a sword."

"That's the German Kaiser, Duke says."

"Well, that's natural. They're Germans."

"Yeah, but this trouble I been havin' with the Mexkin workers I've traced back to Weissschmidt."

"What does it all mean, Bill? Make it simple so I can understand it."

"Just this. For some reason them Europe countries wants to get us mad at Mexico; maybe get us into war. It's the time to do it because the Mexkins've been blowin' up. This German here goes off down there an' works 'em up agin' us an' pays some ratty white trash on this side to do the same."

"Ted Tolliver, for instance?"

Bill's face grew taut and cold. "That coyote. I'm gonna kill him some day. The trouble is the women an' children here on the border might hit it a little hard."

She didn't mean to ask a question, but he had given her the lead. "What's your interest in all this?" she asked. "You risk your life crossing the river, trailing Germans. You could be making money in some business." She emphasized the *some*.

"Yeah, I know," he interrupted. "But I don't!" He was looking far down the road ahead of him—out into the distance—maybe backward, Willy thought. Why did she have to mention money? She could have cut her throat.

The horses' hoofs rang out. They had hit the railroad track. Willy looked up, to see La Lomita Boulevard in front of her.

Bill straightened in his saddle and kicked Chiquita to a trot. "Oughta plow up this street and pave it with cement."

Fuego picked up his pace and kept alongside. The sun was up and hot.

As they dismounted, Willy said, "Mrs. Weisschmidt named the baby Guillermita."

Bill smiled. "That's what I'd 'a named it." He looked at Willy frankly just a moment, then walked into the saloon. His eyes were circled, deep set, lonely. His step seemed slow and heavy; it lacked his certain swing.

"He's tired," Willy thought. "And so am I! Lord, how tired!"

As Willy went about her work she noticed that her cut finger began to swell. At noon she squeezed off her wedding ring and put it in the money drawer. The wide gold band was sinking in her flesh. That night when Dr. Jeffers got back from Brownsville he found her with a fine infection in her hand. He bandaged it and told her to go to bed. Of course she didn't. She kept right on at her job, except for washing the breakfast dishes. She put 'Mara and S'rita at that task.

S'rita washed. She insisted that she wash. 'Mara had to dry. But when 'Mara put down a glass not well polished, S'rita raised a fuss and Willy spanked her. Pat had to finish the dishes.

Every morning something happened. The children fought and cried. S'rita always got a whipping. Pat announced he'd eat breakfast with Mrs. Lea at the restaurant until things got straightened out.

Every day Willy said to Dr. Jeffers when he dressed her hand, "It's just a finger. Why all this bother?"

"But fingers are important members of your body, Miz Westall, especially yours. I'd get run out of Mission if I let anything happen to your hands. We need them to take care of all of us. I'd be like that feller Peterson and the smallpox."

"Poor fellow, have you ever seen him?" Willy asked.

"Yeah, in Brownsville the other day, dead drunk. Railroad's fired him."

"What for?"

"Drinking."

"I don't blame him. He has to forget that awful picture that he wouldn't see."

Dr. Jeffers dropped the bandage and looked at Willy strangely. "You don't blame him for drinking whisky? You? I'd think you would, Mrs. Westall!"

Willy's face turned red. "Well, I don't," she said firmly.

She felt like hitting Dr. Jeffers after that. Doctors ought to understand; they ought to see motives behind acts. Dr. Jeffers should know better than to judge. He should look to see what went behind escapes and broken bodies.

Years ago, in Austin, Dr. Farr had understood. He saw the fear of money in her face. She smiled a little. She'd ask Mr. Dubose about Dr. Farr. She had heard that he was in Corpus Christi. Maybe he could be persuaded to move to Mission. With the big new Bryan boom he'd do well to get in on the ground floor. The town needed another doctor.

She felt a little mean about her reaction to Dr. Jeffers, but every morning she remembered what he had said about the whisky. When he took off the bandage and pronounced her finger cured, she felt relieved. She laughed a little at her hand. It was white, almost soft, as it used to be in Oklahoma City. She went to the money drawer to get her wedding ring and put it on again. To her surprise it was not there. She took out everything and looked. She couldn't find it. She asked Emelio. He searched and searched.

"The Madama couldn't think he took it?"

"Of course not, Emelio! It's just slipped out or into some crack or crevice."

Pat looked. Bill looked. So did everybody who came into the store. But it wasn't anywhere. The children went out and felt in the dirt all around the house. The ring was lost. They simply couldn't find it.

Pat was frantic.

"Don't worry, Darling," Willy said, "My hands're too rough and too ugly now for rings."

"The hell they are! The bestlookin' pair of hands on earth. Put on your diamond now and wear it some."

Willy worked hard to get him off the subject of her diamond ring. It was one she didn't like to think about herself. As long as she had the wedding ring the diamond didn't count. But now they both were gone. She looked at her hand and felt cheated—as if Pat had slipped away and left her or divorced her or found another woman.

"It was just a piece of gold," she kept saying to herself. Yet it was more than gold and she knew it. It was their hopes and dreams in retrospect. It held her back to Sugarland and Oklahoma City when she and Pat were just budding through the earth.

"Now, we're full-grown mesquites," she said. "But I'd rather think of us as cactus."

She never spoke of her wedding ring again, but she missed it like a front tooth that is gone, or a leg when you have lost it.

Mrs. Randolph was the one who kept talking about the ring. "How do you stand it? I'd die if I lost my wedding ring," she said.

"Well, I've lost mine and I'm not dead," Willy laughed.

"But it's not right and I can't understand it. That time I prayed for Mr. Lester can't compare with what I've done for this; yet we can't find the ring. It makes me lose my faith in prayer."

Willy put her arms around Mrs. Randolph. She always had to put her arms around this woman. She seemed to need arms around her; she had to have them.

"Now see here, Mrs. Randolph," Willy said, "prayers're always answered. Always! Sometimes one way, sometimes another. Now in place of praying for me and Bill, you start praying for yourself."

"Why, Mrs. Westall, I do pray for myself."

"But not enough. You've got a job to do that you haven't even started."

Mrs. Randolph looked up guiltily. "The Sunday school!" she gasped. "But what do I do to start a Sunday school?"

"Just round up the children. I'll get Brother Renfro to come down to help you organize."

"Who is Brother Renfro?"

"He's a preacher who came here once and held a service. He wants to come back to start a Sunday school."

"Is he a Baptist?"

"Well, no, Mrs. Randolph, not exactly; and yet he is —like John the Baptist—a preacher of God's word out in the wilderness. That's how he came to us."

They both laughed.

"How you do baby me," Mrs. Randolph said. She called 'Mara and S'rita right then to tell them about the Sunday school. 'Mara listened, but S'rita wouldn't. Judge Woolcott's school was bad enough. She didn't want a new one to start in. They'd figure out some new reasons to whip her. She slipped out the back and left.

Mrs. Randolph gave 'Mara the job of telling the little Allday girls and the Dunbar boys when they came in from the river, and the Henderson child, the Allen children, Don, of course, and maybe a few Mexicans. She'd talk to all the mothers so they'd all be ready for the start.

Willy wrote Brother Renfro in San Antonio. Four days later she got an answer. He would be down for Sunday a month from then.

As a regular mission worker, Ray Renfro was eager to follow up his beginning in the lower Rio Grande Valley. The Presbyterians were eager to get churches started throughout the Southwest. He felt very grateful for the invitation. He had thought so much about them all. From all he heard about the Valley they'd been too busy making money to think about Sunday school.

Willy fired up a little when she read the letter. She remembered that remark about her shoes. But she had

promised him the chance for a Sunday school and she
had kept her word. Now more families were moving
in and for the new children they had to make provi-
sion. She'd show that preacher a lot of things before
he left this time.

26

Willy and Mrs. Randolph went into detailed preparation for the preacher's visit. So far, church had been
just a series of prayer meetings here and there. Willy
had never had time to attend them, so she had got out
of touch.

"He's right," she told Mrs. Randolph. "I've been
too busy making money. I'm going to light in now and
take up a collection for a church. When Brother Renfro gets here we can have the building ready."

Willy started out in earnest and kept at it. She
talked to everybody who came into the store about the
church. They were all enthusiastic. While they were
about it, they began a school fund, too. Mr. Conlay
made a big contribution of both building lots and
money. Bill corralled all the carpenters he could find.
He worked himself, so did Judge Woolcott and the
Stewart boys. Tom Jones helped a little. Pat did the
bossing. Both buildings went up at once. They were
not much to look at—one-roomed box structures—but
they were painted white. The children could talk of
nothing else.

'Mara said every morning when she left, "Please
come see the new school today." S'rita was partial to
the church. It had a little steeple and a bell.

One afternoon Willy decided she'd take time to
look. She'd go to see the church first and then come
back by way of the school. That would please the
children.

When she got near the steps, she heard voices. She
hesitated just a moment before she entered. Bill and

Pat were talking. "Smuggling" was the word that made
her stop and listen.

"Sure it's smugglin'," Bill said. "You have to call
things smugglin' that're against the law. But it's the
law that's wrong. Our people just can't understand the
Mexkins, never have I've noticed. It started back in
the beginnin', with Austin and Sam Houston."

Pat interrupted. "Maybe the Mexkins don't quite
get us?"

"But they was here first, remember. We're the ones
that butted in."

"Well, go on," Pat said.

"If we had sense now we'd understand their reason,
but we don't. They've got a chance for freedom like
we fought and got, but we won't help 'em. We make
it against our law."

"Your man Madero's in the saddle. What're you
kicking for?"

"Yeah, he run old Diaz off and got hisself all set up
in Chapultepec; but that don't end the story. Everybody wants his job. If it wasn't for Pancho Villa on
the watch, they'd put him out today. Huerta is the
snake. Got Madero to make him Commander-in-Chief
of Federal forces, and that's not safe."

"What's special wrong with Huerta?"

"He's plain coyote. I mined gold with him once.
He'll sell out for money or anything on earth. Madero
oughta give that job to Pancho Villa. Hell'll break
loose now, just wait and see. Might come across the
border and take a shot at us."

"What about Pancho Villa?"

"Pancho's just a ignorant fellow that's had it awful
tough. Saw his father hung for nothing. Decided he'd
light out and right a lot of wrongs. People love him,
for he's helped 'em everywhere he's gone. When
Madero started out to help the poor peons, Pancho
joined right up. He's a fighter. He don't want to be the
President. We've talked about it. But he wants to keep
Madero in; can't let these other fellows get the upper
hand. They'll lose everything they've won."

"You smuggled guns to Pancho Villa, Bill?"

"Sure, that's why we done it, just to help him. He

sent me word. They had to get a start. I got John
Sanders to go in on the deal, for smugglin' guns's a
two-man business. But John Sanders's and me can't
work together. Since I'm quittin' him I wanta team
up, and Judge, you're sure my man. You got connections to get Winchesters and I can deliver 'em to
Pancho just like I done for John. The damned Germans're runnin' guns to Huerta to put Madero out.
I've got that straight. Don't ask me how I know it."

"Well, how do you know it?"

Bill smiled a little. "It's that Weisschmidt on the
river. I've been watchin' him. He's been down in the
interior for months. Oughta follered him myself. Sent
Dutch, but he lost track. Weisschmidt's mighty hard
to foller. I keep a watch on his missus at the river.
She gits messages across. I ain't figgered out her system."

"Have you reported all this?"

"My God, yes, a dozen times. It ain't done no good
at all."

"I like Mrs. Weisschmidt. I can't believe she'd do
us harm."

"I ain't sayin'—I ain't figgered out her system. She's
got one!" He hesitated. "A damned nice baby, that
Guillermita," he finally said.

"But what's Germany got to do with wantin' Huerta
as President of Mexico?"

"They don't give a damn. All they want is to keep
things stirrin'. They won't let the people settle down.
Father Michael and me do a lot of talkin'. He says
things're boilin' up in Europe. They want to keep us
busy over here. If they can make a ruckus across the
river, we can't cross the ocean in a pinch."

"You mean Germany wants to fight?"

"Father Michael says it's certain. But they'll fight
England, not us. They want to keep us busy here, to
keep from joinin' in. They're now just layin' plans.
Mexkins're just like children and the Germans know
it. That's why I've pitched in to help. You see, I know
Mexkin people, knowd 'em a long, long time."

"Yeah," Pat answered quickly.

They were silent for a moment. Willy knew she'd

have to stay and listen. Her heart was pounding. She dropped down on the steps.

Bill said crisply, "Well, that's my business for the Mexkin people as I see it."

"You deal straight with Pancho Villa?"

"Well, yeah, but my business is on this side. His is to do the shootin' over where he is. Seldom see him; haven't now for months. But me and Pepe're to meet his man in Reynosa tomorrow night. I'll take you with me."

"Sure," Pat said. "But how do we get the guns across the river?"

"Swim 'em jest like sheep. Tie 'em to a pole an' a boy pushes, down at Gran Geno crossin' where the river's narrer and shaller enough to swim."

"I can see your point," Pat added. "Have to help strugglin' people. I'll be with you. Glad to have the chance. Might protect my children."

"Well, tomorrow night in Reynosa we can settle on the money dealin' and the price."

The children came running, hollering, "Mama!" Willy went to meet them. They all walked back to the store together. Willy said nothing then or later about what she had overheard, but she worried. It was daring, complicated, against the law. And Pat and Bill didn't tell her. She was hurt.

Evidently they carried out their plan. Next day Pat announced that he would go to Corpus Christi to see Dr. Farr. That night Pablo came to watch the store in place of Bill. That was the day the preacher got to town. Mrs. Randolph led the procession to the train.

Willy couldn't go—or said she couldn't. Her heart was heavy. Pat and Bill had ruined her celebration. All she could see was smuggled guns to mix up with Sunday school—and people called that civilized!

'Mara felt very troubled about the way her mama looked. She spoke to Emelio. He shook his head. Emelio always shook his head about the Madama.

Ray Renfro ducked Mrs. Randolph as quickly as he could and came rushing to the store. He was glad to be in Mission. He had thought a lot about the town and about the woman who had given him the invitation to come back.

When he walked in, Willy forgot the guns and Bill and Pat. She made herself forget them. She smiled and shook the preacher's hand. It was still warm and soft. Hers was hard and dry. His clothes were as before, too well-tailored; his linen far too white. But his face was different. She saw him for the first time as a man.

They started in talking about the Sunday school, then went on to crops and floods and new settlers in the country.

"What about the Mexican revolution across the river?" he asked.

"It's still across the river," Willy said, and they laughed.

Mrs. Randolph drove up to take him to see the church. Pat had let her have the Brush. It chugged out front. As the preacher turned to leave he put a package in Willy's hand. He blushed a little.

"I brought you some arch supports. They ought to help your feet for all this standing. I had to get these sweaters for the girls."

Willy looked and gasped. She remembered all her shooting impulse when he spoke about her shoes. "Thank you, Brother Renfro!" No more words came. She stood there trying to decide the proper thing to do. Should she offer to pay him, or accept his service as a gift? After a moment she walked over to the showcase. "Pat and I decided we wanted you to remember that benediction to your service by wearing this John B. Stetson hat," she said proudly.

He put on the hat, and left. She liked the way he looked. The Stetson did the trick. It took away his shyness, evened up his hips, gave him the Texas swing.

Pat got home next day in time for church, but he didn't go. He and Bill got drunk. 'Mara came upon her mama crying in the warehouse by the stack of flour. It was after church. It had been such a lovely service. Everybody came. She and S'rita sang. She liked Brother Renfro. He said her hair was pretty.

Mama seemed so pleased, and now she found her crying. She felt frightened. She didn't run up to her; she slipped away and didn't let her know that she had seen. She went upstairs and cried, herself.

Willy saw Amara, but she didn't let her know it. She felt ashamed. There was no reason really for her to cry. She hated crying. These tears just came. Why would Pat and Bill get drunk? Of course they always did a lot of drinking. She didn't like it, never did, but she didn't think about it. Yet today she did. At her big step in progress they desert her—like the guns. Outlaws, smugglers, prison, disgrace, children pointed at in shame; such words went spinning in her brain.

When night came she felt better. People began coming in. There was much talk about the church and Sunday school. Brother Renfro was the center of attention. They had invited him to come down for preaching when the Presbyterians could let him include Mission in his trips through Texas.

Pat staggered up to bed. Bill came in late. His face was bloated, his eyes swollen. Don was with him. The boy wore a pistol on his belt.

"Well, it's gonna be a helluva row now!" Bill said in a quiet way. "Pancho Villa can't be pushed around."

The crowd flinched; some cringed; many got up and went straight home.

Bill unbuckled and put his pistol down. He walked over to the money drawer, picked up the forty-one, and replaced his forty-five.

"Better shootin'," he said to Willy.

Ray Renfro went over to him. "Start at the beginning, Mr. Lester, and tell us what has happened. Why the fight?"

"Very simple," Bill replied. "We're gonna have a war. Huerta's in the saddle down in Mexico. He's sold out to foreign power just to have a war. The only peace now is in jail."

"What's that?"

"Madero! They forced his resignation and locked him up in jail. Huerta's the President."

"What about Pancho Villa?" Tom Jones asked.

"They ain't got Pancho Villa and they won't get 'em. He's too smart. He knows the people an' they'll foller 'im an' fight!"

Bill walked on out. Willy didn't see him for a week. She tried to keep calm and unworried, at least before other people.

There was much to do with the preacher in the store. People came and went, but Willy wasn't very certain what they did. She went about her work as usual with her body, but her mind focused on the guns and what Bill had said about a war. Drunk or sober, Bill said exactly what he meant.

One night she saw some strange long boxes sticking out from underneath the bed.

"Some tools I'm gettin' from the Murdy people in Oklahoma City for Mr. Conlay's irrigation pump," Pat woke up to tell her. But she saw "Winchesters" printed plain in red.

The next morning she called the children out of hearing distance and told them sternly to tell nobody about the boxes.

"But what are they, Mama?" S'rita asked.

"I don't know," she said. "I haven't looked inside. It's Papa's secret. When he wants to tell us, he will tell us; and until then we must not ask questions. And don't ask Bill."

"Yes, Mama!" they both replied.

'Mara had told S'rita about Mama's crying. S'rita cried too, bitterly. They sat on the steps and talked a long, long time. Things were funny and they knew it. Papa, Bill—now Mama—and those funny boxes! Don came along and joined them. He too thought things were strange. If only grown people would tell children what the trouble was!

Don told the girls about his parents. They were always funny. He couldn't remember that he ever saw them kiss. His mama cried all the time in the kitchen. He hated to see her do it. That's why he hated the damned old restaurant and stayed away from it. It wasn't fun like Thirty-six's and 'Mara and S'rita's store. Once he told his mama he went with Judge Westall to take groceries to Thirty-six's and she whipped him. It made him mad as hell. After all, he once saw his dad down there with a gal.

Willy called the children in. Brother Renfro was leaving on the train. They must say good-by.

'Mara stepped up and thanked him for her pretty sweater. She had it on. It felt good, too, for a norther was blowing in. S'rita didn't thank him but she smiled and handed him the steel rooster spur in her pocket. Ray reached down and kissed both little girls.

"Can't you say something, S'rita?" Willy said.

"It's thanks enough to see her hair against that blue," Renfro replied.

"Forgot this little hombre here!" He took out his pocketknife and handed it to Don.

The boy's eyes glistened. "Gracías, Mr. Renfro," he exclaimed. "Come on; let's go carve 'Prince' and 'Pearl' on the corral!"

S'rita was the first to make the door, Don next, then Amara. They were gone.

"Purpose!" Ray Renfro rather murmured.

"Yes," Willy answered, very loud. Her voice was screechy. She heard it and hated the ugly sound.

The preacher looked at her very squarely. "If I can ever serve you, Mrs. Westall—"

"Well, you can. Bring me a music teacher when you come back next month. I decided that in church. Have some firm send prices on a piano. The children are growing up; they must have lessons."

The preacher frowned a little sadly.

"What's wrong?" Willy asked.

"Are you sure you want to buy a piano?"

"Of course. Why have a music teacher if no piano?"

"I was thinking of the revolution across the river. You might be leaving."

"Leaving? What for?"

Ray knew she hadn't heard the news. He noticed that she never read the newspaper. When it came in on the train, Pat grabbed it. Miss Lizzie told her what she knew.

"Things don't look so good," he continued. "Bill Lester's man got killed!"

Willy gasped. "You mean Pancho Villa?"

"No; Madero. Heard it just as I walked up. Killed him on a pretense of escape. Shot him down. Cold murder. It'll cause an awful row. They hate Huerta. He's one of the old crowd."

"Well, how did he get to be the President?"

"Money strictly; foreign money—even Father Michael says so. Trickery from start to finish. They trapped Madero in his office, pointed a gun, and made him sign his resignation. The Minister of Foreign Affairs then served as President. He kept the office just an hour. All he did was appoint Huerto as Minister of Government, then resigned. That left Huerto 'it.' "

"Why, it's an outrage!"

"Worse than that! No need to kill Madero."

"What made them do it?"

"Because people love him. He's a savior. They'd storm the prison to get him out. Bigger brains than Huerta thought of that."

"But why Huerta?"

"They can buy him off. That's why. They've bought him to keep things in a muddle everywhere in Mexico."

"Is Bill really right about Pancho Villa?"

"Of course I don't know the man. He does. But he was loyal to Madero. That leaves him in the fight. There's not only Pancho Villa, but Obregon and Carranza. They're all heading up revolts. Looks like it'll be a bloody fight. Mexicans got a taste of freedom from Madero. With guns and money from foreign sources they'll light in and cut each other's throats."

Willy sighed. "Just like children!"

"That's the shame of it. And we work to civilize the world!"

They both sighed.

The train whistle blew. Ray grabbed his Stetson and put out his hand. Willy shook it very firmly.

"Just the same, I want the piano and the music teacher," she said.

"I'll bring them both when I come back," Ray hollered from the door. He had to run to catch the train.

Willy and Emelio talked about what the preacher said. The boy knew nothing more than he had heard. Ranch Mexicans get no news.

About four o'clock Bill came in. His face was swollen and his eyes were red.

"I've been drunk, Miz Westall," he announced.

"Yes," Willy answered, "so I see. You and Pat are crazy. Why do you do it? It makes you sick and it doesn't help a thing."

"Yeah, I know." He sat down on a crate. "But you don't understand." He sat there looking at the floor.

"Well, nothing's worth it. That's all I've got to say about it."

"Did you hear about Madero?"

"Yes," she answered. "Brother Renfro told me."

He didn't go on. He kept looking at the floor.

She said, "Did you know Madero, Bill?"

"Yeah, he got me out of jail. It was in Seralgo when I was just a boy." He choked a little. "This is my fault really. I should 'a been there. Me and Pancho could have stopped it!"

"No, don't think that. They say there's a lot behind it—foreign money and all that."

"Sure there is! But they didn't have to kill him. At least we could 'ave saved his life."

Willy started talking. "They'll do something. Don't you worry. Brother Renfro says there're three revolts already—Obregon, Carranza, and Pancho Villa. Which one do you think will win?"

He didn't answer at once, but when he did he said, "Pancho Villa."

"I hope he will," said Willy.

Bill looked up then. His eyes were burning. They flashed arrows. She was glad.

"These poor Mexkins need a leader!" he exclaimed. "They need a man with spirit! A shootin' leader who can batter down this foreign money—all those foreign people goin' in there to make the Mexkins footstools for Europe, and against us here! The French done it back in Juarez's time. The idea now is to get us into war here at home so they can do what they want to in Europe."

Willy felt relieved to see him mad.

"So Villa is the leader that they need?" she asked him.

"Sure! He's the only one who can really lead. Pancho knows his people an' he loves 'em. Give him a little help an' he'll straighten out the country an' stop all this war."

"But has Pancho Villa got a chance to win?"

"Hell, yes! He'll be the President; an' when he is, he'll stop this foolishness for good. I know the way Pancho Villa works."

"But what about Carranza and Obregon?"

"They'll kill them if we'll just give 'em plenty of guns."

Pat came in and he and Bill went out to get a drink.

That night Willy checked up on her ammunition. She made two night calls on Pearl and Prince before she went to bed. When she fed them, she made a point of locking the corral.

The next morning early two new settlers came in to buy groceries. They were talking wildly as they entered. One was saying, "I want to make a killing in this onion crop so's I can get on back to Iowa."

The other answered, "No, cabbage is the quick money. Put your acreage in them. That's what I'm doing so I can go home and see some New York snow again."

Willy listened as she put up the order, and finally she had to ask a question. "But why go back? Didn't you come down to help us build the country?"

The fat man cringed. Willy's smile was hard to face when she set her mind to make you face it.

"Sure, sure!" he said. "Couldn't pull me away from this Kingdom of the Sun!"

"And rattlesnakes and tarantulas and fleas and lice and roaches!" snarled the tall one. He was a pious man from Kansas City, who despised the country for the forty thousand dollars he had lost in the land deal.

"But the climate, Mr. Maxwell, makes up for everything. No ice and snow, no long dark winters to bog through."

Mr. Maxwell's eyes gleamed with pent-up anger. "I'll tell you, Mrs. Westall, I'm going to cut my throat if this goddamned sun doesn't fail to shine one day."

"But we've got irrigation. That's why we can enjoy the sunshine and not hope for rain." Willy meant to comfort the exasperated man.

"Well, you can keep it, Mrs. Westall; it's too much sun for me," he said coldly as he marched out in rage.

Willy understood that the man did not mean to be unkind or rude; he was simply scared. Everybody was. Everybody hurried to beat time itself, it seemed. Even the Magic Valley, producing eleven months a year, was slow for what they dreamed. Underneath the nervous tension was a subtle sort of fear. Nobody would admit it, but he felt it just the same.

27

Before Ray Renfro got back to Mission with Navasota King, the music teacher, a lot had happened in a very little while. General Blanco struck out for the Border to gather up some horses for the Carrancistas, so he announced. His focal points were Reynosa and Matamoros. That meant that the Rio Grande Valley was to know the smell of war. Just across the river from Brownsville down to Mission he bribed and fought and stole. He took Reynosa, then marched on to Matomoros, taking as he went.

The stack of half-burned bodies on the plaza of Matamoros began to smell and rot. Buzzards swooped by the thousands and circled up and down the river, from Brownsville to Rio Grande City. Half the state of Tamaulipas moved across to Texas to make their homes. Ranches were looted. Horses disappeared, property was confiscated, shots came across the river, people were killed. Our government told all Americans to leave Mexico. Governor Colquitt ordered out the State Militia and the Texas Rangers. He requested the Washington Administration to send down 25,000 soldiers to guard the border.

The day Ray Renfro and Navasota King arrived in Mission, the Texas Militia got off the train. The whole town was down to see the soldiers come in. Nobody paid much attention to the preacher, except Willy and Mrs. Randolph. Willy tried to make up for the others' indifference, especially to Navasota.

"You're just what we need," she said. "A pretty girl to take our minds off the war!"

Navasota King was small, quick, Irish; with red hair and blue eyes. One glance told her what she had to do. The first thing was kiss the women and children at the depot. Then she announced that she had come to teach the fine arts one and all—piano, violin, singing, dancing, roller skating, needlework and china painting.

"That's the kind of girl for you," Mrs. Randolph said to Brother Renfro on the side. "Pretty and very smart."

He didn't answer. He only frowned at her.

The piano came in on the same train. Willy had bought it from a firm in San Antonio, to be paid for on the installment plan. Bill and Ray Renfro hauled it to the store in Pat's Brush.

"Where'll we put it, Miz Westall?" Bill shouted above the splutter of the car.

That had been the question up to now. S'rita wanted it upstairs. She cried and begged to have it there. 'Mara didn't say a word. Willy's problem was how to get it there. She feared the steps. They were very shaky. Then, too, it was to be used for lessons for all the children in the town. Pat had to have his daily rest. Piano thumping would drive him wild. She thought of the back end of the warehouse, which could be a studio for Miss King.

"A pretty funny combination," Navasota said.

"But it's a start, and in this country that's all it takes, my dear."

"Take it to the warehouse," the girl hollered out to

Bill. The Brush started up in a burst of smoke and noise.

Willy jumped. Then she felt ashamed. She hated nerves, and hers were growing by the day. She thanked God S'rita wasn't there. She wouldn't have to squelch an arguing spell.

The children were with Pat. They had met the train, then gone down to see the soldiers' camp. The whole town was there to watch the miliia pitch their pup tens in Mexiquita, just across the railroad track. Willy would have gone herself except for Brother Renfro and Miss King.

It was a day of great excitement in the town. Everybody had done his best to offer what he could to this influx of soldiers who came just overnight. The day before, they held a meeting in the store and elected Pat chairman of arrangements. Pat chose Father Michael as his aide. Judge Woolcott they put to keeping books of contributions. The first thing to provide was water barrels along the street, with tin cups strung along the sides. Pat filled them up with ice. For the evening's entertainment they planned a dance.

Willy suggested that the women bring in cakes and pies for the soldiers' supper that first night. Pies and cakes started coming in the morning and by the time the train came in the store was full. Pat was to take them down when he came back from helping set up the tents. As chairman he felt that he must be right on the job for everything.

When they escorted Navasota into the store, she saw only cakes and pies, and she was hungry. The pastry seemed to mean a lot more to her than the new piano, Willy thought. She stood and gazed at one particular chocolate cake.

"Suppose we eat a piece or two," Willy said. "Mrs. Allday will never know it. Anyway, we have too many."

"Not too many for that trainload of soldiers," Navasota said. "I've never seen so many people in my life. What will you do with all of them in this small town?" She looked around the store.

Willy tried not to notice. "They'll rush us a little, maybe, but we'll get used to them in time."

Navasota got up very close. "And they do make me feel safer. Tell me, Mrs. Westall, aren't you scared? Brother Renfro assured me, or I never would have come; but now I'm here, I'm afrad."

Willy laughed a little. She put her arm around the girl. "You'll get over that," she said. "Come on, let's cut the cake!"

Willy called Bill and the preacher to the back and they were cutting cake when Pat and Judge Woolcott came in, talking loudly.

"Why don't you put the girls in school in San Antonio for a while?" Judge Woolcott was saying.

"Why, what's wrong? Aren't they learnin' as they should?"

"Oh, it's not that. They're learning right along. It's safety I'm thinking of. The girls are very dear to me, and I'd hate to see them hurt."

"Well let me tell you somethin', Judge Woolcott, they mean a damn sight more to me and I'm not sendin' 'em away to any school. I'll protect my children an' my home. I don't need you to tell me what to do!" Pat shouted.

The old teacher turned and left the store.

Pat came on back and joined in the party. Navasota very quickly cooled down his wrath. She stood very close and stroked him on the chin. Pat told her all about the dance that night. Who would come and why.

"Just wait until you see Dutch and Duke! You'll love our Valley then," Pat said, giving a little sideways wink at Bill.

It was getting late. They had to get the cakes and pies down to the soldiers before supper. Willy hurried Pat off in the Brush, with Navasota. Bill took the preacher home to change his shirt.

When they had all left, Willy felt relieved. She could see Pat liked Navasota. That would help a lot. They could do things together. Maybe Pat would cut down some on drink. The girl would take the pressure off. Willy needed pressure off. Pat needed entertainment. He loved music and pretty things—just like S'rita. So did she, but she kept so busy! And she was tired. Navosota would add a lot.

She sat down just a minute to rest her feet. Mrs. Randolph came hurrying in with a punch bowl and cups. She was in charge of refreshments for the dance. The Hallam girls were to help, but they forgot to come. They drove down to the army camp in the Conlay car. Willy saw them pass with a captain and two lieutenants, but she didn't tell Mrs. Randolph. She herself pitched in to help.

'Mara came in the back looking very hurt. Willy was sure that Don and S'rita had run off and left her; and they had. They had gone down to watch the soldiers feed their horses at the camp.

'Mara and Mrs. Randolph finished making the punch. It was to be served in the store. The dancing was to be upstairs next door, in the K. of P. Hall over the new Goldstein Dry Goods Store.

When Pat and Navosota came back from the army camp Willy went with them to Mrs. Allday's, where Navosota was to board, just to introduce her and make her feel at home.

Everybody was dashing about getting ready for the dance, even old Colonel Cunningham. Willy knew, for she was sold out of shoe polish before dark.

Fanny came over to dress the children and tie Pat's tie. She wore her black silk dress and white apron. She was to serve the punch. The children were excited. Nothing had ever been such fun. They had new dresses—linen embroidered in scallops around the neck and sleeves. Fanny had made them. S'rita's hair ribbons were blue, Amara's pink.

"What'll Mama wear?" S'rita said to Fanny.

Fanny didn't answer. She went on talking about the punch and how S'rita should behave herself. She and 'Mara and Don were to pass out the cups to everybody. Fanny made it sound exciting. She had to in order to avoid Serena's question. She knew Willy had nothing to wear except her store clothes and apron. That's what she always wore. Nobody thought of her dressed up, like Mrs. Randolph. But this new music teacher would make a difference, and these Hallam girls, moved in from St. Louis. Fanny felt a little sad for Willy.

But Willy didn't mind it. She never thought of clothes. She didn't have the time. Emelio called her to the telephone. It was Mrs. Allen on the river.

"Miz Westall, I want to ask a favor," she began. Her voice was strained and overwrought.

"Sure," Willy said.

"Will you call Thirty-six's and tell Daddy to come home? Dr. Jeffers has just been down. He says the baby's comin'." She started to cry.

"Who's there with you?"

"Miz Weisschmidt," she sobbed.

"Now don't you worry. I'll get hold of Mr. Allen for you."

Willy hung up the receiver and rang Miss Lizzie for Thirty-six.

The usual sweet voice answered, "This is Thirty-six." That was what she always said. It was a voice that challenged Willy and always had—sweet, well-modulated, poised. When Willy took her order every day she never failed to wish that she could see the owner. Now she'd like to wring her neck.

"May I speak to Mr. Allen?" she snapped.

There was no hesitation. "Certainly; just a moment, Miz Westall."

When Phil Allen answered, Willy let go her temper. "You must go home at once," she shouted. "You've got a baby coming. Don't you know it?"

"Sure, but don't you worry, Miz Westall," he said.

"You'll go, won't you?"

"Sure!" Then he hung up.

Willy turned to Emelio, her eyes blazing. "Well, I'll be damned!" she said. "Why can't men be home when women have them babies? Why do they always manage to be away?" She stomped her foot. Mutt tucked his tail in and ran.

Poor Emelio couldn't answer. He just shook his head. The Madama acted in so strange a way. At times she made him tremble. These questions he did not know. She looked at him as if she saw straight through him, and spoke so loud. At other times she smiled so sweetly, was so gentle. He saw changing lights come to her face when she talked with the little girls and Don; great sweetness and compassion when she was near the Señor Westall; much concern and wonder when she conversed with Meester Beeley Lester. He watched carefully always then because the two faces together were a joy to see. It was like dancing with a girl. They swayed in rhythm to the music. There was no give or take. It was a melting into one.

"I'm sorry," Willy turned to him and said.

It had been a long, hard day, and she was tired. She kept thinking of Mrs. Allen, poor woman— Thirty-six and Conchita—all kinds of things. But when people began coming in for the dance, she felt better.

Everybody came. All the settlers and ranchers were there plus the army crowd. Some officers from Brownsville rode down, and some from Fort Ringgold at Rio Grande City. The Mexican string band came up from Hidalgo.

The evening started well. Everybody seemed gay and ready for a frolic. Navasota shocked Mrs. Randolph just a little by the low cut of her dress, but Mrs. Weisschmidt said it was very stylish. Her sister had written her from France. The Hallam girls topped Navasota with their split skirts. The captains with them looked around in pride, but one saw Navasota and made a dash for her. Hal Eubank beat him to it and asked her for the dance. When it was over, Navasota sought out Pat and took him to one side.

"This is my first night," she said. "I might as well start right. Tell me, Judge, which man am I to marry?"

Pat reared back and smiled. This was the kind of thing he loved, people all dressed up having fun— pretty women, pretty music, things hitting off to time. Even if he couldn't dance he was in the swing.

"Well," he said, "of course I like the preacher for a girl like you, my dear."

"But Mrs. Randolph has him cornered," Navasota said.

"If you really want to know," he whispered, "the best catch in the country is Bill Lester."

"But he doesn't even notice that I'm living. Look, he just stands there at the door watching other people dance. Why doesn't he take part?"

Pat straightened up his face and spoke in earnest. "Well, girl, he does, but he does it in a way that's just his own." The string band struck up "La Paloma." Old Colonel Cunningham bow-legged over to claim Navasota for the waltz.

Just then Dutch and Duke walked in. Navasota looked at them and lost her heart. They were the kind of men she had read about in books, just boys really, but tall and straight and fair. When Pat introduced them, Dutch took her in his arms and they whirled away in music.

Willy came in to take a look. She slipped away from the store now and then to watch the dances a minute. She didn't dance herself. Aunt Ann had never let her because it had been against the church rules, but now she liked to watch the others. She sat down by Pat. He reached over and took her hand and they sat there smiling as the dancers whirled by them.

"Doesn't Eva Hallam cut a wing with that captain?" Pat remarked.

Willy whispered back, "But look now at Duke and Navasota. Duke can waltz a lot more smoothly than Dutch. Those long legs were really made for dancing."

And then—Mr. McIntire's pistol rang out five times in fast succession—the danger signal—that meant fire or raid.

The dancing and the music stopped with a jerk. Everybody rushed toward the door. Pat and Willy got there first, for they were sitting closest to it. As they ran down the steps, they saw Miss Lizzie stick her head out the window.

She was shouting, "The outpost just called in! They're shootin' hell outa something near Reynosa."

The dancers came as one, pushing and shoving down the stairs. The thing to do was get home quick and check up on fire and horses. Everybody rushed for the street. The soldiers broke and ran for camp.

Willy ran into the store and called Miss Lizzie. "Miz Allen can see the shootin' from her gallery. They're just across the river, she said."

"Is Mr. Allen there?" Willy asked.

"No. Miz Allen asked me to tell you that he wasn't."

"Then call Thirty-six," Willy said. But no answer came.

"Keep on ringing!" she urged Miss Lizzie.

Pat, Judge Woolcott, the preacher, and the children hurried into the store. Fanny put out the lights. There was a great running back and forth on the street, horses being unhitched and cars being cranked, everybody taking off.

Bill walked in. He seemed calm and undisturbed.

Willy hung up the receiver. "Bill, get down to Thirty-six's and make Phil Allen go on home."

He didn't seem to hear her. "Have you seen Pablo an' Pepe?" he asked.

"No, not tonight," she answered.

He took out a paper and began to roll a cigarette.

"But Mrs. Allen's sick!". .

"Yeah." Bill kept on rolling until he had finished; then he looked up at her. "Don't you worry, Miz Westall. That's where I'm goin' now. I'll get Phil home all right an' mighty quick at that."

In a second he was gone.

She rushed to the door and shouted, "Be careful." He was going straight to the shooting. In a pinch how cool he kept!

The street was deserted now. All lights were out. In the stillness and the darkness they heard the soldiers trotting out of camp. Pat had the Winchester, Judge Woolcott the shotgun. Willy edged over close to the cash drawer with the pistol underneath. They all waited. For what they didn't know.

They stayed in the store until midnight; then they went to bed—everybody but the preacher. He sat on the gallery until daylight. Willy came down then to take charge.

At sunrise Don and S'rita climbed Bill's windmill and watched the Reynosa fire.

That day the newspaper carried the heading, U. S. MARINES JAILED IN TAMPICO, MEXICO. Willy read it and sat down a long time to think.

The train left that day full of people going "back north," home.

That afternoon old Mrs. Leonard came in from the Kant Ranch. There was no special reason why she did it, but she began talking about the Cortina bandit raid on Corpus Christi long ago and what happened to the girls and women.

"Especially blondes," she said. "They like blonde women, and when they're crazy mescal drunk they turn brute savage."

"Damned old fool! What made her tell me that?" Willy faced Emelio.

The Mexican boy shook his head. He did not know the answer. He saw pain written on the Madama's pretty face.

That night Bill called a Vigilante meeting and gave directions. At five quick shots all women and children must go to the land office and lie down flat on the floor. Every man in town must have a gun; every place of business must have a guard. Volunteers could go with him and Dutch and Duke to ride the river and check up on troublemakers in grubbing camps.

"Especially among the whites," he said.

"Meaning vat?" Mrs. Weisschmidt spoke out.

"Exactly what I said. These Mexkins won't cause no trouble without some help. They're like children. You can stir 'em up. There's folks among us I don't trust."

"Ya, you are right," she said.

Willy pulled Judge Woolcott out of earshot of the others.

"You'll take care of Don?" she asked.

"And the girls too if you say so."

They shook hands.

She called 'Mara and S'rita aside for serious talking.

"Listen, children," she began. "You heard what Bill just said you should do when you hear five pistol shots together?"

"Yes, Mama," they both answered. Mama looked so strange they felt afraid.

"For once I'm going to ask you to disobey. When you hear five quick shots, no matter where you are, you come to Mama. Run fast! Don't stop for anybody! No matter what they say, just keep on running! And don't tell anybody what I've said—not even Papa. Not even Don!"

"Yes, Mama!" they both replied.

Late that night after they were all asleep Willy slipped back down to the store to catalogue her ammunition.

What she did was count up her Winchester and pistol cartridges and stack the boxes of shotgun shells close underneath the money drawer.

"How safe it makes you feel to have a plenty," she said to herself as she shined the Winchester on her apron and sighted several times down through its barrel.

Then she cut a square of calico and carefully sewed a pocket underneath her skirt. In it she hid two cartridges for her pistol and pinned them tight inside with safety pins.

"Just in case," she said quietly to herself.

Next morning Mr. Conlay came in early. He looked worried. He waited until they were alone to talk. "Buy some life insurance today, Mrs. Westall; tomorrow'll be too late," he said.

"What's wrong?" she asked.

"Just ordered not to write any more. Lon Stone told me on the side."

"Does that mean real danger?"

"Well, they think so in New York!"

They laughed together.

"What is it, Mr. Conlay? I'd like to get it straight. The Mexicans are upset across the river, but that's their business. They don't bother us! These soldiers? The marines in Tampico? All this excitement? What's behind it all?"

Mr. Conlay sat down on a crate. He spoke slowly. "The trouble is plain misunderstanding. This man

Huerta, the President, has a notion that we don't like Mexico. From what I hear he's been made to think so by European people who would like to get us into war. And to make it worse, we poke our heads out to get slapped. This Tampico trouble could have been avoided if we'd been more careful. Some of our marines go ashore and get in jail. Their commander feels insulted and demands that Huerta salute our flag. Huerta won't do it because somebody's there to tell him not to. So our marines march in and the American people go simply crazy. We're ordering out warships and soldiers. There's no telling where it all will end! We're playing right into these Europeans' hands."

"And we're the border country," Willy said.

"Yes, we'll get the brunt! I had such hopes of what we'd do." His voice was sad.

"Mr. Conlay, it won't ruin us, will it?"

"Well, it's hard to say. I've kept things quiet, tried to ward it off. Sales are falling; people aren't paying up; they let land go back. Fogg can't get people to come down here on excursions any more. Now I get this news about insurance. Let that get around and see what happens."

"But we're safe here," Willy said. "Nothing's happened."

"It's the news that gets around, Mrs. Westall. It'll ruin our country, I'm afraid."

Don came running in pale and frightened. Would Miz Westall please come quick. Bill wanted her out back.

Willy excused herself and went.

She found Bill and Pepe in the warehouse. Pepe was lying on the floor, his head bloody, his shirt open to the waist. Bill was stooping near him.

"What's wrong?" she said. "You always ride up front!"

"Nothin', Miz Westall, but hurry. Pepe's been bad hurt. Can't look up Doc Jeffers because we don't want this knowed."

Willy ran upstairs and got the turpentine and was back in a minute. When they looked closely, they found a bullet wound, just in the flesh. They got it dressed and Pepe upstairs on a pallet in the kitchen before Bill tried to tell her how he had hurt himself.

"Shouldn't have never done it, but of course he went and did. He an' Pablo was in Matamoros courtin' a couple of girls when they started shootin', an' they couldn't cross the bridge. Then I don't know what happened except what he has said. They killed three hundred men an' Brownsville's aswarm with wounded an' they're still a-shootin' now. When they got the mayor cornered there was nothin' left to do but swim the river, an' the fool can't swim a lick; so Pepe an' Pablo crossed him and Pepe got damn nigh killed."

"But, Bill, tell me what you think?"

He didn't answer.

"Mr. Conlay has just been talking about Tampico and the marines."

"Yes," he said. "I told you, you remember, about Weisschmidt and all these spies around. Well, now the world's got proof. A German boat full of ammunition sailed right into port down there. 'Twas signed to Huerta. That proves the side he's on. Our marines had to stop it and shot up the town. Things like that don't just happen; they're planned."

"Why would Huerta want to cause trouble for his people? Mexicans like Americans. We're all friends."

"Pure coyote. I know the man. He don't give a damn about the people. War's all right for him. It gives him glory. Just the kind of fellow Weisschmidt'd find to do his business for him."

"Then, Bill, you think we're in for trouble?"

"Yeah, I know it, for Pancho Villa's still alive and kickin' and he'll fight. He loves his people. He'll do his best to keep 'em out of war. He's an ignorant fellow, but he's honest. He's always for the underdog. He's no double-crosser. He does exactly what he thinks is right."

He stopped talking for a minute.

"Maybe it won't be so bad," Willy said.

Bill got up to leave. "Keep the kids in close where you can find 'em in a minute. Don't let Don an' S'rita ride. Things'll be gettin' a little shaky for a while."

He looked taut, muscled up. His face was set and cold.

"I oughta shot Weisschmidt an' said it was for cattle thievin'!"

"I've wondered why you didn't."

"I would have—" he said quickly. Then he looked at her. "Except for that little Guillermita."

She took his hand and held it. Neither of them spoke.

28

Willy learned a lot from Pepe while they nursed him. So did the children. She came to know the Mexican people as a race. She felt grateful. It came at a time when she needed her faith renewed.

So much happened all at once. In place of depending on Miss Lizzie or the general talk, she grabbed the paper the minute Don brought it from the train. For the first time in her life she became conscious of the world. Somehow these strange things that happened far away came straight home to her.

One day headlines glared: ARCHDUKE FRANZ FERDINAND KILLED IN SARAJEVO. Willy didn't even know the place, but Judge Woolcott shook his head.

Tom Jones said, "Just wait and see! Hell'll break loose sure over the whole damned world."

The next time she was alone Willy tried to figure it out: Mexico had changed Presidents and shooting had started across the river close enough for her to hear. Settlers left the Valley every day. They couldn't pay their bills because they didn't have the money. They were scared and they were running. Pat even lent them money, money that he didn't have. She did good business, but all on credit. The bank account was low. She owed for the piano. She was afraid to ask about the Brush. Dubose shipped groceries and never said a word; but she worried—she couldn't help it. When he came, she felt ashamed.

The marines had done some shooting in Tampico, and the Valley overflowed with soldiers. She was grateful, but she worried day and night. And Mexico kept on changing Presidents. Huerta fled the country. The marines burned him out. Carranza and Pancho Villa both made a dash to take his place.

Willy talked to Bill about it.

"Nothin' to it," he assured her. "Pancho will whip old Carranza if he can get the guns."

"But they keep on fighting," Willy said. "This fellow Blanco just hangs here on the Rio Grande. Why doesn't he go on and join his forces and make his efforts count? All he does is ruin our Valley, making news for papers everywhere. People keep on leaving every day. Except for soldiers we wouldn't have a bit of business. Somebody ought to kill that fellow!"

Bill laughed. "Leave that to Pancho. He's got Blanco on his list. We got rid of Huerta for him; he'll take old Carranza out. The Mexkins need a leader who can ride and fight like Pancho, not an old fellow with a beard."

"But can Pancho win?" Willy asked him.

"Just give him time and plenty of ammunition. That is all it takes."

That was all Bill said.

But the Mexicans kept on fighting. In fact, the whole world started fighting.

The paper came in bearing headlines: GERMANS MARCH THROUGH BELGIUM INTO FRANCE.

"Why, that's war!" Willy said to Pat.

"God, yes!" he answered.

She looked at him. His eyes were shining, his shoulders lifted, his chin stuck out in front.

"I'm gonna start a gin," he said. "We'll make a killin' in cotton with the world in war."

"But the outlay? How about the money for the gin machinery?"

"To hell with money! It's the intake that's gonna count."

Pat got up and left the store.

Later Lon Stone came by to tell Willy that Pat wanted to borrow money at the bank.

"Well, let him have it," she said.

"With a mortgage?"

She looked at him. "If it takes a mortgage, yes."

Lon went on out to get a drink.

The war in Europe made little difference on the border except that more soldiers kept coming.

Before the month was out Pat started building his gin. He even cut down on his whisky and threw away one crutch.

That made all the difference to Willy, and there was a lot of difference to be made. She couldn't help seeing the long boxes that kept coming in and going out in the nighttime.

Bill was out now much more than he was in. He and the Stewart boys rode the river every day. Asa Hall made deputies of all the ranchers so they could carry guns. Jesse Parnell and his rangers came in muddy every night. And General Blanco across the river kept up his pillage, shooting, killing, stealing horses.

Willy called in the children and gave directions. When they took off their clothes at night, they must put them on a chair where they could get them in a minute. Don was to check on Judge Woolcott and see that he did too. "Especially shoes," Willy said. "Be sure that you can get your shoes with one grab."

She herself checked up on Pat's things every night. And she took an extra round before daylight at the corral.

"You're looking awful tired, Miz Westall!" Fanny said. "You've got to get more sleep. Can't live without sleep, Honey."

"Yes," Willy said, "I guess that's right. But if you have to I guess you can all right."

Nursing Pepe made Willy think about many things. He gave her an understanding of the human heart. The world itself could crash and crumble, but qualities remained. Pepe was grateful and she knew it. His spirit touched them all. He stayed up in the kitchen until he could ride. Bill and Pablo came to see him every day.

"Can't have folks see him comin' in and out while he's bandaged," Bill said to Willy. "Fanny's got all them boarders, and my house—well, it just won't do at all!"

The children loved having Pepe in the kitchen. It was a secret. Nobody knew it but Don and Fanny. Fuego was in Pearl's lot. They liked to have the horses all together. It was like all of them together.

"Mama and Papa and Prince," 'Mara said.

Don thought that was silly, but Pepe didn't. For once he stroked Amara's hair. S'rita sat very close and held his hand. He told them all kinds of stories about horses, steers, and roosters—bandits, rattlesnakes, and guns. Pepitón was always the hero in his stories. He won money, killed rattlesnakes, sent men to fame and fortune. They felt very sorry when he could ride out with Bill again.

"He's a different person," Willy said to Pat.

And to himself he was.

Pepe never disobeyed Bill Lester. Service to the Westalls had been service to Meester Beeley who got him out of scrapes. But now it was all different. It came from his own heart: la madama and las niñitas had rubbed his aching head and fed him by the spoonful, never asking questions of why he chose to fight in Matamoros. Each time he hitched his Fuego he found in his morral a yucca blossom, or aguacates or petayas or cactus flowers for "th' cheeldreen," he always said. Once it was a Guadalupe done in glass.

That was what decided Pat to get a cook. They ought to be fixing up the house a little. The children were growing up. They ought to have a family table so they could sit around and talk.

Willy thought so too, but how to do it was the question.

"Leave that to me," Pat said. Of course she did; she had to.

One day he brought in a Mexican man named Juan. He was a cook from the Mercedes Hotel, he said.

Willy was busy with the soldier order when he came.

When she got through she meant to run upstairs and tell him what to cook for supper, but before she finished she heard 'Mara scream.

"Mama! Mama! Pepe's got a knife!"

She left the order and dashed upstairs. Pepe was pinning the new cook to the wall, his machete poised for a stab. Willy grabbed him. In the tussle, Juan escaped without a scratch.

"What happened?" Willy asked.

Pepe slumped down in a chair.

"Pepitón! Madama, Pepitón," he murmured.

Willy saw what had happened. Sitting on the table was a platter full of chicken fried for supper and a plate of something she took for biscuits. She figured out the rest. Pat and Pepe had gone down to get a drink and the cook, anxious to do his duty and with no directions, had killed the rooster in the coop.

There was nothing she could say to help. She put her hand on Pepe's shoulder. He clasped it and showered it with tears. Maybe it was kisses. She didn't stop to think. She tried to translate her thoughts into Spanish so he could really understand, but she failed; so she went on back to work.

The children set about preparing the funeral for late that afternoon. Don dug a grave behind the Spanish dagger in the yard. Papa, Mama, and Judge Woolcott came as audience to 'Mara's Scripture reading and Don and S'rita's prayer. Together they all sang "Rock of Ages," and everybody cried.

Pepe sat on the steps and refused to budge an inch. S'rita crept up close beside him and slipped her hand in his. Pat stumbled straight to bed. When Willy found time to go out back to talk to Pepe, she found him still sitting on the steps, with S'rita sleeping in his arms.

"It's my fault," she said. "I should have let you kill Juan and you'd feel better now."

He looked up quickly. His eyes lit up with fire. "No, Madama, es la vida." He tried very hard to smile. "Eet ees the life! Pepitón ees my fren. For me he fight lak hell. I make beeg mohney. Why do they steek heem een the back?"

Since she couldn't answer that question, she went

on to bed, feeling very helpless about everything in general.

The next day Willy saw Pepe on the gallery watching through the windows in a funny sort of way. At last, when all the trade had gone, he ambled in.

"Thees ees for you," he whispered, and handed her a package which contained a black mantilla and a Spanish comb.

"Beautiful!" she cried as she spread the handmade lace across the counter.

"For your hair," he said. Willy turned away to stick the comb into her curls and drape the lace across it merely by doing, not by looking, for there wasn't any mirror.

"Que bonita! Exquisita!" Pepe breathed.

"Thank you, Pepe, for so grand a gift. Some day I'll dress up and you and I shall dance, just to do justice to this mantilla and give ourselves a fling." Willy laughed out loud to lighten the mood.

Of course, Willy knew that she would never wear the lace because she had no place to wear it, but she loved it just the same because it was a definite creation —like S'rita's hair—gossamer, almost disembodied.

"Like friendship," she thought. "You know it's there and you can't touch it; yet you can see it if the light is clear. Some day S'rita can wear it to a dance."

She went upstairs and hid it in her trunk.

As she came down, she heard voices in the warehouse that made her forget the lace and comb. Pat and Bill were talking very loud. A bottle of mescal was pasing back and forth. She sat down on the steps and listened. It seemed to her that she was alway listening in on Bill and Pat. If they would only tell her things— like the guns, for instance! Why did they leave her out? She never argued, never crossed their paths. She felt hurt and guilty, but she listened just the same. Bill was speaking.

"By God," he said, "I told you he'd do it and I knew he would. You can't beat a fellow like Pancho Villa when he sets out to right a wrong. Now he's got the Federal government over he'll stop this fightin' and settle down to peace and give the people back the land."

"But can he hold Mexico City with the force he's got?" Pat put in.

"He's got plenty of force; all he needs is guns. If that last shipment of ours got through, he'll hold it."

"What about Carranza and Obregon?"

"They're plumb whipped. They'll quit fighting and lay down arms."

"And Weisschmidt and his crowd?"

"Them warships of ours at Tampico learnt them a lesson they won't forget."

"Yeah, but I don't like Weisschmidt around so close. I don't feel safe."

Bill laughed. "That's my job, Judge. Don't worry. Pancho's got Obregon and Carranza. I've got just one to get."

At that, Pepe galloped up. Bill came out and got on Chiquita and they rode off.

Willy tried to talk to Pat about the whole situation as she had heard it, but he wouldn't talk.

"It's over," was all he said. "Bill knows these Mexkins like a book. What we want is cotton growin'. That's the stuff for war. I'm gonna make a lot of money so you can quit this work." And he went on to the gin.

When Ray Renfro came for church, she felt relieved. He would talk to her. He loved to talk, it seemed. He told her all about himself—how lonely he had been since his mother died and left him, what this Valley meant to him, how he looked forward to his trips. They planned the children's education, talked of world events. He explained the *Lusitania* sinking in great detail, just what it could mean to the whole world.

"You mean it might get us into that European war?" Willy asked.

"It might," he said. Then he went on to Pancho Villa and his campaign against Carranza and Obregon.

Willy felt tempted to ask him about the guns, but she didn't. She did ask around the subject to see what he might think. What were people in San Antonio saying? Who would win?

"Well, we seem to be in favor of Carranza since we sent our representative down to talk with him," he said.

"But why Carranza? It seems to be an even fight. It's certainly their own choice, not ours."

"It's the style to take sides with neighbors in a fuss," he said. "Somebody just pitched a dime, I guess, and it came out Carranza."

Ray saw Willy's face cloud a little, so he hurried on to lighten up the conversation. He spoke about a Dr. Farr who had moved to San Antonio and remembered the Westalls. He had recalled the mad-dog bite back when he was in the Pasteur Institute in Austin years ago. "Plans to come down this way and see you, he says."

Willy smiled. "Tell him by all means to come," she said. "Tell him to come and settle. We need a doctor." Then she added a little wanly, "We did need another doctor before this revolution sent all the settlers home."

That trip of Ray's was spoiled by his concern over Willy. She looked pale and haggard, thin and worn. Her big eyes stood out in her face, apart, as though they did not belong. He knew that somebody had to help her and help her quickly. He tossed all one night, got up the next morning, and circulated a petition to close all stores on Sunday.

"That's wonderful," Willy said when he presented her with the list. "Now I can go to church and hear you preach, and so can everybody else."

"Oh, no, you won't. You go to bed. You're sick, Mrs. Westall, whether you admit it to yourself or not."

But when Sunday came, Willy postponed her resting until she could cook a chicken dinner while Pat and the children went to church. To surprise them she got out the Oklahoma City china and set the table. S'rita had brought in some cactus flowers. Willy told Don to be sure and come. Once they had eaten, she planned to fall right into bed. Lord, how tired she felt!

But Pat came home with Navasota to spend the day "and catch up on our visiting," he said. "I tried to bring the parson too so he and Navasota could do some courtin', but he wouldn't come."

"That's what you think, Papa," 'Mara said. "He's comin' up the stairs and he looks awful mad."

When Ray Renfro walked into the kitchen, his face was white. He looked at Pat as if he'd like to hit him, crippled as he was.

"Do sit down, Brother Renfro, and have some dinner. We're all just ready to begin," Willy said.

"No, thank you, Mrs. Westall. I came to wash the dishes and take Navasota home so you can go straight to bed. Your family doesn't seem to realize that you're sick and need some rest."

Willy looked up at him in such a way he couldn't add another word. Pat didn't seem to listen. Willy pointed to a chair and Ray sat down. He took a bite or two and frowned into his plate.

"Now, here's your chance, Navasota," Pat whispered on the side. "The parson's a good catch for any pretty girl."

The next day Navasota went to Father Michael for consolation.

"Ray Renfro's the queerest man! He didn't even eat. All he did was sit there and look at Mrs. Westall in the strangest sort of way. If the Judge hadn't had so much to drink he would have noticed it himself. He's the first man I ever saw who wouldn't give me one faint squint."

"You're forgetting Bill Lester, Navasota."

"Oh, Bill Lester doesn't look at anybody, not even the Hallam girls."

The old padre smiled.

When Ray got back to San Antonio he looked up Dr. Farr.

"Want you to take a trip to Mission," he said, "to see our friend, Mrs. Westall. I'm worried about her. She's really sick. All that work and worry plus this Mexican trouble and the country going on the rocks is killing her. Go down and see her just on a trip and make a diagnosis while you're there."

Dr. Farr asked a lot of questions. He had never forgotten Willy—so vivid and so alive—and so uncomplaining at such a difficult time in her life. He liked Ray Renfro's suggestion. The friendship with the preacher had revivified his first impression of the big-eyed girl who brought her baby to him with a mad-dog bite. They had talked a lot about her every time they met. He knew now that he would find a reason to go down to the Valley. All the articles in the papers made that little strip of sixty miles along the Rio Grande, from Brownsville to Mission, stand out in everybody's mind.

A few days later the *San Antonio Star* announced a boosters' meeting to the Rio Grande Valley. The San Antonio merchants would take the train and go down to visit the new towns and boost the new trade to San Antonio, in place of Houston. The railroad planned the rally, arranging to stop for forty minutes only in every town. They were to turn around at Sam Fordyce and go back.

Dr. Farr arranged his schedule so he could go. He always managed to do anything he decided on. But the joy he got out of this decision was the impulse that prompted him to do it. Since his work at Pasteur Institute, he had done many things on impulse. Some had been good and some had been bad. He had managed to make a lot of money and to rise in his profession, but twice—through his own fault—he had cracked up emotionally.

He did a lot of thinking on the train that night while the other fellows sat around and smoked and talked, doing a lot of drinking on the side. He thought back through the reasons for people's funny actions in the world, especially his own. Why had he loved those two women and why had each left his heart so empty? What made that pretty young Willy Westall cling to that crippled old man? He finally went to sleep, halfway hoping he wouldn't have to wake up.

When the train got into Harlingen the next morning, he slipped away from the party. The train went on

down the Valley to Brownsville and he hired an automobile to drive him the forty miles up to Mission so
he would get there first and see Willy before the boost-
ing crowd arrived.

He had the man put him out at the depot, to avoid
suspicion. He wanted to walk in casually and catch her
on the job.

When he had paid the driver, he headed for the
store.

"My God, how does she stand it!" he said as he
walked down the street.

It was two o'clock. People were home asleep. The
street was shoe-top deep in dirt. Two army trucks
chugged along, fogging up the dust. Six soldiers trotted
along behind. Dr. Far coughed and spat a lot. Two
cowboys walked their horses. They were talking loudly
about "them sonsobitches" or something of the kind.
One was older than the other. He wore a sheriff's
star. The other was square-cut and sturdy. They both
wore Stetson hats. One of their horses was cream-
colored, just like another one hitched to a delivery
wagon he saw in front of him.

Those were all the people he saw. He was glad, for
the men made him feel out of place and queer. He
wanted to apologize and get back on the train. But
dismal as this place Mission was, he meant to see the
woman he had come to see. How could she stand this
row of box houses on two sides of a dusty street! Nothing was painted any color; lumber, earth, and human flesh seemed to bleach together in the sun.

When he walked into the store, Willy was there
with a Mexican boy and two old men buying groceries.
She was still very little, weathered and lithe. Her black
curls tousled on her head. Her eyes were big. Her
clothes were nothing; clothes couldn't matter, good or
bad, on such a woman. But he saw a pencil in her
hair.

She looked up and said, "Why, Dr. Farr!"

That instant recognition gave him a feeling he had
seldom had before. He reached over and took her
hand and held it. He didn't let it go. To him it was a
blessed time together, before the crowd arrived. The

old men went out and she sent the boy to stack some flour in the warehouse.

He told her why he came. Renfro had sent him; yet it was of his own accord he did it. Then he told her why. He knew a lot of women. But he'd never found the glimmer that he saw that day she came into his office with a baby bitten by a dog. She'd remained a legend in his mind; loveliness tied up to life, fighting all the forces by herself. He'd come to offer her some help.

"But, Dr. Farr," she said, "I don't need a thing. I have the world itself. I have my business; I have my husband and my children and my friends."

"You need a doctor," he replied.

She blushed a little. He kept on talking. "It's not tuberculosis or diabetes or a cancer or any of the things our preacher thought. You're pregnant and you know it. Why didn't you tell poor old Renfro and save him all this trouble?"

Willy tried to talk, but he wouldn't let her. In that hour before the train came in he told her everything she ever knew about herself. He praised her and condemned her and threatened her with death. She felt alarmed. She couldn't stop him. But no one came in and she was glad of that. He made her promise she would come to San Antonio for a complete examination.

"If I could ever find you when some man has not just had you!" he exclaimed.

She would have shot him, but he put on his hat and left.

She leaned on the counter almost in a faint. She felt exhausted, insulted, and disgraced. If she hadn't felt so bad she would have done something—it didn't matter what; but for the first time in her life she felt completely weak.

She looked out front at Pearl. Bill was riding up. She blew her nose and wiped away the tears.

Bill was very hot and sweaty. He looked almost old, very worried, angry, at loose ends. Dr. Farr was well groomed, with a trim mustache. Bill's boots were muddy. He was covered up in dust. A spot of blood was on his shirt, another on his hat. "But God, the difference!" Willy said.

"Who's that fellow?" Bill asked her. "I saw him as we rode off a little while ago."

"A Dr. Farr from San Antonio, a friend of Pat's and mine."

She pointed to the blood spot on his shirt.

"Yeah, Chiquita stumbled."

"Where?"

"At Cavazo's Crossing. They sent for me and Asa Hall. Havin' trouble there!"

"What happened?"

"Mexkins come across the river. The soldiers sent for us!"

"You mean they came over on our side, Bill?" She forgot about Dr. Farr and all that he had said. "There was killing?"

"Just a little." He sat down on a crate. "I hurried back to be here for the boosters. Thought they might rush the trade."

Willy came around the counter and dropped down on a box. "Why did they cross the river?"

"They came to loot; but who sent 'em is what I'd like to know."

"But if they cross the river, Bill, what will happen then?"

"We'll have to send 'em back." He got up slowly. He stood there looking straight ahead. He seemed puzzled, uncertain what to do.

"You're lookin' awful tired, Miz Westall."

"I am a little. Can't get much sleep these days, with McIntire shootin' check-scare every night or so."

"An' you go out to that horse corral and break your rest a lot."

"Well, I don't want Ted Tolliver to snatch Pearl and Prince."

"Don't Pepe watch?"

"Sure! I just don't sleep so well. I go outside to get some air."

She tried to smile; instead she cried. Bill flinched, reached out his hand, then took it back; but Willy grabbed it and held it for a moment.

"Thank you!" she said, to cover up the gesture. She just wanted to feel the strength of that strong hand. Now she faced another vigil. Bill couldn't help her.

"You're sick," he said.

"No, honest, Bill, I'm fine." She pulled her face into a smile, but it was forced and twisted. Her eyes looked up at his, deep in her head, circled, troubled, tired.

"Yeah," he said. "You are!"

They stood there looking at each other.

Finally Bill shifted from one foot to the other, hemmed and hawed a little; then he said, "Could we deposit a few things in the warehouse, Miz Westall?"

"Of course, anything you want," she answered.

As he went out, Asa Hall rode in. He came by just to check up on the Westalls and to greet the San Antonio boosters. Willy questioned him about the Cavazo's Crossing fight, but he got around the answers. He talked on about Dutch and Duke and Bill.

"Wouldn't trade that trio for a whole army of soldiers," he said. "They're free to go and do just like they please. All the soldiers do is drown in the river, swimmin', waitin' for their orders. Bill and the Stewarts shoot first, then talk later. Important business these days, Miz Westall. How's your ammunition?"

"It's fine, Mr. Hall. I'll never get caught short again. How's the bandit situation? Are we in for trouble?"

"Of course not," he said. "Nothin' to be skeered of. Just keep your powder dry."

S'rita ran in shouting. "Go upstairs quick, Mama; Papa's raising hell."

Willy excused herself and rushed up to see what was the matter. Pat was throwing things out of dresser drawers right and left, looking for a letter from Dr. Riley in Oklahoma City. It was about a Mr. Hollis he had recommended to the Murdy Gin Company.

Willy went to her trunk and opened it. In a second Pat was throwing things again. There lay the letter right on top of the comb and mantilla, Pepe's gift.

"Where in God's name did you get this?" Pat asked, grabbing up the lace.

Willy looked at him a second; she knew she had to

lie. It was like the time on the ranch when Bill rode in. So she said, "Mrs. Weisschmidt gave it to me."

"What for?" he asked sharply.

"To wear, I guess," she said.

"Well. I'll be damned," was all he said.

But Willy felt his implication. She was hurt.

The mirror was before her, but she deliberately kept from looking in it lest she should see her tears. She went downstairs. Asa Hall was gone. The trade was fairly heavy. Everybody came to town to greet the San Antonio merchants.

When the train came in, the men jumped off, handing souvenirs to everybody. They walked down the street shouting "Howdy" and shaking hands. 'Mara and S'rita and Don stood out front serving ice water from a barrel. They loved the little trinkets they got —pins and needles, pencils, all kinds of whistles, and colored balloons. Many of the men stopped to pick up S'rita and hold her a minute, but only one man noticed 'Mara especially. He said, "I like your black braids a lot, little lady!"

Willy, standing there shaking hands, heard him and smiled gratefully at him.

The forty minutes proved very short. As quickly as the crowd got off, they got back on the train. Willy saw Dr. Farr across the street. He waved at her and she waved back. He didn't come over to say good-by. She was glad of that.

When the children came into the store to compare their presents, 'Mara and S'rita showed a dollar bill apiece.

"Who gave you that money?" she questioned.

"A man with a mustache," both said at once.

Willy frowned. "Listen, children," she said firmly, "never take money from people, never! Now don't forget it. And put that up for Sunday School."

The girls felt very puzzled, for Mama looked so strangely at them.

Before Willy closed up she found reason to go back to the warehouse. Nothing unusual was in sight. She began to poke around to find what Bill had hidden. Finally she felt something hard underneath the flour stack. It was a gun, some quaint old kind she had seen only in picture books. She looked up farther.

Just as she pulled the door shut, she heard a whisper.

"Miz Westall!" It was Ted Tolliver, standing very near.

"What do you want?" she said. Her voice trembled.

"I been watchin' you." He stepped up close.

She drew back. "I told you, Ted—"

"Can't we talk some?" he interrupted. "I'd like to be your friend."

Willy steadied herself. "Whatever you've got to say, say fast. I've got customers in the store."

"I'm just tryin' to help you. Remember, I warned you about Bill Lester."

"That's why we can't talk. He's my friend."

"That's what you think. He's got th' Judge in on this smugglin' deal. No good's gonna come outa that. He joins up with th' Stewart boys for a blind, because their folks're friends of Asa Hall's. That puts th' law behind him. But notice, ever' now an' then he ducks off with them Mexkins. That's when he does his dirt. I foller him. I know. I told you about this revolution, recollect? This Pancho Villa is a bandit, nothin' else."

"Shut up!" Willy shouted. "Bill's my friend!"

"Yeah, I know! I've noticed that." His voice implied a lot. He ducked around the corner of the house.

Willy made a turn out to the corral to look in on Pearl and Prince, and then walked back into the store.

She felt smothered, choked. It had been a hard day from start to finish.

Willy's days were growing harder. Dr. Farr had guessed her secret. She was pregnant again. She guarded her fears until she was very sure; then she told Pat and had to meet a further conflict in herself.

He was rapturous that he had begot a son. "What a fellow! We'll name him Patrick Westall the Second and teach him how to ride and cuss!" He kissed her.

And that was all he said or did.

Willy tried to figure ways and means for this new baby. Pat couldn't run the store. He was too frail and too impatient. The hours were long, the tasks mi-

nutely taxing. The bank account was low. Credits
mounted. Business slumped. Settlers swarmed back
north.

When she went to bed, she couldn't go to sleep. Ted
Tolliver's words walked through her brain. Dr. Farr!
How strange men were! How strange! She hated herself for what she was thinking. Poor women! Mrs.
Allen! This new baby of hers made six children in ten
years. Phil Allen slept with thirty-six. Mrs. Weisschmidt mixed up with a spying husband. Willy Westall with another baby! Her little girls neglected as they
were!

"The price is just too high," she thought; then she
tried to go to sleep.

But she kept searching for the answer no woman
ever finds when she's been married and served the
man she loves. The pink-satin wrappers, the black-
alpaca skirt, her hands too good for dishwater, the
thin batiste for gowns; now unbleached domestic that
Pat refused to wear, calico for dresses, a Stetson for a
hat.

"And he doesn't even notice!"

The thought plumbed too deep for tears.

But for the physical exhaustion that blurred her
reason as she finally tumbled into sleep, she would
have purged herself for thinking, "But Pepe said, 'Que
bonita! Exquisita!' And I saw the doctor's eyes!"

29

In the days that followed Willy had no time to think
of herself or the coming baby. Things happened too
fast in the Valley of the Rio Grande. The Mexicans
shot across the river at Hidalgo, then at La Feria,
Progreso, and Mercedes Pump. Army patrols shot
back. Raiders crossed the border. Rancho Tule and
Paso Real were robbed of cattle. A store at Sebastian
was looted. A Brownsville railroad bridge was set on

fire and burned. At the Norias Ranch the rangers shot and killed four bandits. Carrancista deserters crossed at Hidalgo. Sheriffs and deputies chased them back. Fresnos' pumping plant was burned. Men named Smith and Donaldson were shot.

Bill rode out with the Stewarts. Pepe stayed close in. When he went out, he went in haste. He always galloped in on Fuego lathered hot. The old mañana dreaming changed to a snake-like sharpness in his eyes. He seemed to be looking everywhere at once. Pablo came and went only after dark.

McIntire shot check-scare almost every night. That meant get on your clothes; there's a chance of fire or raid. Everybody watched for fire. Always on moonlight nights Willy let the children sleep with their shoes on. Those were the nights the bandits rode across the border. She checked up on her ammunition. Every day she wore the skirt with the bullets sewed inside. Now that the fight overflowed the Rio Grande and ran up and down the Valley, every life changed its tempo, every face changed its expression.

Willy noted a confused determination in Bill. He never spoke of Pancho Villa or the raiding. Nobody dared ask him a question.

Suddenly Dutch and Duke grew into men.

Willy slept less and less; she watched. Dr. Farr wrote her a letter about the examination she had promised. She tore up the letter and didn't answer it. She'd meant to speak to Pat about it, but he was too busy with his cotton and his many friends among the soldiers. He was too happy to disturb.

"Just gettin' started," he said every morning as he left for the gin. "Next year I'll pay out and lift the mortgage on the store. That war in Europe makes the chances better every day. Need lots of cotton for ammunition. Just need more cotton planted in this country. This season'll show 'em. Next year we will."

Willy always said, "Oh, sure!" She never told Pat what she was thinking. She doubted if there would be any people left in the Valley to plant cotton. Soldiers kept coming in. People kept going "back north" home. They were scared.

The undercurrent of excitement was electric. "What's the news?" everybody asked everybody else he met, for news came up from the river the day it was made, and the newspapers came down from San Antonio and Houston the next day. Miss Lizzie was the one who gave out the news first hand. When messages came in for help, she would pass them on to whoever called in next. As for Willy, she always took time out to call Miss Lizzie. Willy welcomed the news, because she wanted to know what was going on, but the added responsibility weighed a little, for she had to sift it out to other people.

One day Mrs. Randolph dashed into the store just as Willy had hung up the receiver. Miss Lizzie had said briefly, "Bandits raided the train coming out of Brownsville just now. Tell you more about it later!"

Willy looked at Mrs. Randolph. Something had happened! Willy herself felt a little frightened.

"They've killed my husband—on the train—coming right out of Brownsville—on his way home!" Mrs. Randolph wailed.

"But how? Tell me more about it!"

"They shot him in cold blood!"

"Who shot him?"

"Pancho Villa!"

Willy got her arm around Mrs. Randolph, seeking to calm her down a bit. Then she called Miss Lizzie to get Brownsville and find out who was killed. A few minutes later Miss Lizzie reported that the two men killed were from Brownsville and that Mr. Randolph was unhurt. A bandit band had derailed the engine, hopped aboard, shot several passengers, and killed two.

It took several minutes to reassure Mrs. Randolph, and to help her get over her fright.

As she was leaving, Bill came in. Willy was glad to see him. She saw him so little nowadays, except as he rushed in and out.

He stood and waited until Mrs. Randolph had gone before he began to talk.

"How many hours did you sleep last night, Miz Westall?"

Willy laughed a little. "About the same as you!"

Then they laughed together.

"Want to talk to you a little," he went on. "You're not scared, are you?"

"No," she said. "Why?"

"Lots of talkin' goin' on, an' all this raidin' this side the river." He hesitated. "I want you to understand. Somethin's gone awful wrong. It's our own fault." His voice began to mount.

Willy knew the reason. She'd never asked him. Nobody dared. The day the United States recognized Carranza in place of Pancho Villa as First Chief of Mexico, Bill had got very drunk. Nobody had seen him for a week, not even Pat. So now she was glad that Bill had come to talk to her about the situation. If he had only talked to her about the guns!

Bill went on speaking. "Folks say Pancho's doin' all this raidin' along the border. Well, he's not! We done him dirty. I wouldn't blame him if he was, but that's just not his kind!"

"I'm glad to hear you say that," Willy said.

"Sure I say it, for I know it. I know the man. He's a ignorant fellow, but he's smart. He's got a purpose an' he fights to win it. He joined up with Madero for the common man. They kill Madero, and Huerta gets in the saddle and damn nigh sells the country to the Germans until we step in and put him out. Old Carranza's been down there fightin', I admit; but so has Pancho. Why should we pick out Carranza to recognize?" His voice was loud and harsh.

"What will Pancho Villa do?"

"He'll find another way to win. He'll start in Morelos or some such state and work from little up to big."

"Have you seen him?"

"No, not for months. Not since things have been gettin' hot. He's down there in the center where things is goin' on. And I've been here."

"Yes, of course; I know."

Neither spoke for a minute. Then Bill said, "But this means the war will go right on."

"You mean this border raiding?"

"No, Miz Westall. These bandits're just ridin' on

their own. People blame them on Pancho Villa because he was the loser in our draw."

"But how will Pancho take our recognizing Carranza as First Chief of Mexico?"

"He's mad as hell, I know. But he wouldn't shoot across the river at us. He'd come on across himself. But that's not what he wants. He wants freedom for the Indians. He wants to give them back their land."

"But what about these border raids? They've got to stop. Our Valley can't stand the strain. We're too new and undeveloped."

"They'll stop, don't worry. It's just a little splutter. A few fellows want to ride and rob, but Pancho'll come up here himself and bring 'em back across."

When Bill left, he shook Willy's hand. She felt better. He had talked to her about the border situation. That took away the strain. She'd shoot the next person who said a word behind Bill's back. No matter who was First Chief of Mexico, Pancho Villa was Bill's friend.

That was the day Ray Renfro came back to Mission for the Sunday service at the church. He came early because he liked to be in Mission. He liked to play around with 'Mara and S'rita. He took time to teach them a lot of things they ought to know—Bible study, catechism, manners of all degrees and kinds. He found out they learned the fundamentals from the store.

Willy talked to him about the children often. How she hated to have them grow up without training. Nothing normal, like other children! No mama at home to see about them. Just a place to duck in and out!

Ray always told her not to worry. The store was the best education they could get. He saw them learning how to live with people in the open. They learned the kindness of human contact. They knew no difference in people as they come. "Like their mother," he added. "People are people and that's what's important," he always told her. "You know that." Ray always brought the conversation back to Willy when he could.

This trip he brought her an ultimatum from Dr. Farr. She had to come to San Antonio. Her health demanded attention. If she didn't, he promised nothing.

Willy blushed when Ray told her. She knew the men had talked together. Ray knew what the trouble was. The baby in her body jerked her. She winced and shifted weight. He saw her and pushed a chair beneath her. Then he went behind the counter and started waiting on the trade. Of course she didn't sit there very long. Mess-Sergeant Turney came in and she got up to help with the order for the soldiers.

That afternoon Sergeant Shonert rode in from the Ojo de Agua outpost to get supplies. Willy saw him and Pat duck into Bill's Place about one o'clock, to make their weekly celebration at the bar. At four, when they had not yet come out, she called bartender Kinney to send Pat home. At five she rang again. Ray Renfro started for the door.

"Oh, no, you mustn't, Brother Renfro!" Willy said.

"Oh, yes, I must!" He went out.

When the preacher stepped into Bill's Place, all the fellows at the bar turned and gazed. He walked up to Pat's swaying body and took him by the arm.

"My God, it's the parson!" old Colonel Cunningham exclaimed.

"Yeah, 'tis!" Bill Lester said. He looked twice to make sure; then removed his Stetson and bowed shyly in respect. Every hat in the saloon came off.

"By God, we've got Jack Potter back again," Tom Jones shouted.

Pat and the preacher walked on out the door.

"No, we've got Ray Renfro, and that's enough," Bill said. "Now, come on, fellers, let's drink to this parson who does the thing Miz Westall wants. We drink with the Judge. He takes him home."

Willy stepped out front to watch. When Sergeant Shonert got on his horse, she knew he was too drunk to ride the five miles to his post.

"Why not take a nap and sober up a bit?" she asked him.

"Thanks, Miz Westall, but 'twould be neglectin' duty," he managed to say.

"Let him alone, Sweetheart," Pat drawled. "Sarg can ride drunk better'n most men sober."

The soldier whammed the horse with his hat. It broke at a gallop.

Willy worried through the afternoon, but she and Ray didn't talk about what they were thinking. She thanked God Pat was upstairs in bed, asleep. She knew the sergeant was somewhere in the brush half killed. Bill didn't come into the store at all.

Mrs. Randolph came and took the preacher home to supper. She had a party planned for Navasota and the Hallam girls. Fanny was doing the cooking and the serving. She had invited the army officers from Mission and some stationed at Fort Ringgold and Fort Brown. Ray didn't want to go, but Willy made him. Mrs. Randolph would be awfully disappointed if he failed her. She'd been too excited lately, with all the bandit scare.

"She's not so well," Willy said.

"And you aren't either," Ray replied.

Willy frowned a little and Ray knew he'd better not keep up the conversation. He'd go and eat, then hurry back. But he didn't. Mrs. Randolph wouldn't let him.

As Willy looked back upon that day and night, she realized it had been strange from beginning to end: Ray Renfro entering the saloon, Pat upstairs drunk, Sergeant Shonert staggering on a horse, Bill's absence from the store, no sign of Pablo anywhere, Hal and Jesse at the Vigilante meeting; only Pepe lurking on the gallery with a queer jerky peering through the windows as if to make sure she was there.

Trade picked up after supper. She noted an unusual influx of Mexicano sombreros, with huaraches, and tight pants.

S'rita stayed down in the store with 'Mara. She was very mad. Don had gone with his dad to a poker party at the soldier camp. He wouldn't let her go along. She didn't go upstairs to bed with Papa. "He stinks," she said.

A little after midnight, when the store had cleared out and Emelio had gone home, Pepe stepped inside.

Willy looked up at him wanly; she felt sorry for herself.

"You don't forget me, do you, Pepe?"

"No, Madama, no!" His dark eyes flashed, then smoldered, as he reached his hand to his left-side pocket.

"You haven't gone to shooting left-handed, have you?"

"No, Madama, no!" His face flushed. He dropped his head, and touched his pistol in the holster on his right hip.

"Here, how about a little Bull Durham," she went on, to change the subject. "Sometimes I wish I smoked myself; you men seem to get such a comfort from tobacco."

But when she handed him the sack, she noted a strange shadow in his eyes, tears almost brimming. He stood there holding to the sack, gazing at it as if it were a live thing in his hand.

"Where's Bill tonight?" she said.

"At Conchita's," he answered in a whisper.

"Conchita's? Bill never goes to Conchita's on Saturday, especially when it's moonlight. He rides the river then."

"Tonight he go! I meeke sure he go!" Pepe kept his voice low. "He ees very drunk!"

Willy suddenly saw danger in the Mexican's eyes. "What's wrong?" she said quickly.

He leaned over the counter as he spoke. "Leeve queeck, Madama!" he pleaded, all restraint abandoned. "To the monte weeth S'rita and 'Marita! Stay steel. Do not tell! They keel me queeck!"

"What is it, Pepe?"

"Pleeze, Madama!" was all he said, his eyes imploring and adoring, as he darted out the door, cramming the Bull Durham in the pocket of his shirt.

Willy ran after him shouting, "Pepe!" but Fuego's hoofs clattered down the street across the railroad track through Mexiquita, south.

"Well, I'll be damned!" she said. "He knows something!" She ran to the telephone to ring Miss Lizzie. Then she recalled Pepe's words, "Do not tell! They keel me queeck!" She hesitated just one moment; then she frowned and rang the telephone bell with all her might. No answer came.

"What in God's name!" she exclaimed. "Is it a conspiracy? What's happened to everybody? 'Mara! S'rita!" she shouted.

It was the noise of her own voice that quieted her. She began to reason. "I'm scared! Scared of a Mexkin raid! And here I've been bragging about how I'd meet one. I'm acting like a woman!"

She straightened her shoulders with a shrug, reached for her pistol, and slipped a box of cartridges into her apron pocket. Then she felt for the two bullets in her skirt. She found the children sleeping underneath the counter, and shook them into waking, slapping S'rita because she cried. Mutt wagged his tail and barked.

"I'm sorry, Honey," she said. "Mama's acting like a fool tonight, but open up your eyes and stay awake! Come on, we're going across the street to see Miss Lizzie."

As she led the girls out the door, Miss Lizzie stuck her head out the window shouting, "Raid on the river down about Ojo de Agua. Word just came in through Peñitas from Capt'n Scott. They're shootin' hell outa the outpost from what they hear from there. He called in for us to send help down."

She pulled the children back into the store and slammed the doors, locking and barring them almost at a stroke. Then she put out all the lights.

This was what Pepe had tried to tell her. Where was Bill? Ted Tolliver's words flashed through her mind. "I'll be damned!" she thought. "Sergeant Shonert! Did he make it back to camp?"

She reached down to feel the cartridges in her skirt. She gripped the pistol in her hand.

"What is it, Mama?" 'Mara asked.

"Where's Bill?" S'rita cried.

"Bill will be here any minute," Willy said. They went out the back. She hustled the children up the stairs, Mutt leaping three steps at a time. "Hush!" McIntire's five quick shots of warning rang out. Dead silence for a moment. Then the clamor of shouting, running, frightened people came up to them from the street.

"Just stay close to Mama," Willy said to 'Mara and S'rita. "There's nothing to be scared of; just stay close to me!"

The next moment she was shaking Pat. "Get up, Darling! Mexkins are attacking Ojo de Agua. I know Sergeant Shonert didn't make it to the camp. Get up and go find Bill and see what he can do."

Pat opened his eyes, sober. "My God, they'll court-martial Sarg if he's off duty in a raid. Where's Bill?"

"He hasn't been in yet tonight."

"Out at that damned woman's! Saddle Pearl. I'll go find him!" Pat grabbed and snatched and scrambled into clothes. The children helped him.

Willy ran out to the corral. She did not saddle Pearl; she hitched her into the delivery wagon and drove her around front. "Just in case!" she said as she climbed out. She stood there holding Pearl's bridle.

The soldiers galloped out of camp on the river road. People pushed and crowded, horses nickered, children cried. Judge Woolcott walked up near her.

"Don's with me. Where're the girls?"

"They're upstairs with Mutt."

"Shall I take them to the land office?"

"No. I want them where they are."

He was gone. Then Fanny came. She asked the same questions.

"No. I want them where they are," Willy snapped. The Negro said something back. She sounded hurt. She left.

Willy felt faint and giddy. She looked for Bill. All she saw was moving shadows of frightened people running in all directions, and Pearl's palomino coat leaned up against her for support.

Pat was climbing into the wagon.

"What are you doing?" she cried.

"Goin' to find Sarg and get him on the job."

"But you can't go alone!"

"Who said I couldn't? Gimme the whip!"

"No, Darling, no!" Willy begged. "This is going to be a fight. Pepe warned me—or tried to." She was holding to his leg.

"Don't be such a fool," he shouted. "I don't need nobody to help me fight them sonsobitches."

"Not by yourself!"

Somebody edged up close again, very close. She was lifted from her feet, held maybe for just a second. The smell was clean, not like whisky or tobacco or even body—clean, like fresh sheets in the sunshine. Then she was set down on the gallery very gently. Pearl gave a stomp and snort.

Ray Renfro spoke. "I'm going with the Judge, Mrs. Westall!" He climbed aboard with Pat.

"Watch out for fires," he hollered back. Pat raised the whip for Pearl to see, gave her the rein and shouted, "Ándele, girl! Ándele!"

Pearl broke at a gallop. Willy stretched up on tiptoe to watch them as they went. When they crossed the railroad track, all she could make out was a streak. Pat stood up. He flaunted his whip, but he never touched it to the mare.

Willy took a look around for fire, then went upstairs to watch from the window, but not for bandits really. She watched for Bill. The children tumbled into bed fully dressed.

Thoughts tugged and pulled. Willy put up her fight. She tried to reason, but reason made her doubt. The safest thing to do was feel. She saw a tall, lank figure edge round the saloon. She jerked out her pistol and took a shot in that direction.

McIntire called up from the street. "You up there, Miz Westall?"

"Yes, I am. Why?"

"Girls with you?"

"Yes, of course!"

"All the other wimmen're over at the land office. Maybe you want me to go over with the children."

"No, thank you. We'll stay here," she said.

"I thought so," she heard him mumble.

Willy never knew when she fell asleep, but she must have because she woke startled to hear pistol shots and

McIntire yelling "F—I—R—R—E!" Mutt was barking wildly. When she looked out the window, flames were leaping from the back door of the saloon.

By the time she woke the children and got them out across the street, the store gallery was blazing. Fanny ran up and snatched S'rita and 'Mara by the hands.

"We'll see about the horses," she shouted.

"They must have oiled it," Willy shouted back. She dashed in and got the ledger; then back upstairs. Everybody ran to help her. She didn't notice who was who. Smoke thickened. Flames spread.

First she grabbed the feather bed and threw it down to somebody standing there to catch. Two men struggled with the folding bed.

"Leave the bed and get the machine," she hollered.

She grabbed and snatched. She gave commands. Suddenly she remembered the piano in the warehouse. She dashed downstairs. The warehouse was burning. Flames leapt out the window. She rushed up to the door. It was locked. She struggled with it. Somebody pulled her back.

"For God's sake don't go in there, Miz Westall."

"I've got to get the piano! It's not paid for!"

She jerked loose. She grabbed at the lock again. The door gave way and she darted in. The smoke stifled her. She pulled with all her might. The piano would not budge.

"God held me!" she pleaded. Her legs wobbled. Her head spun. Her skin blistered. She mustered all her force and pushed. The piano sped across the floor.

"Thank God! Thank God!" she screamed.

At the door she sensed two other hands on hers. They were pulling. She looked up in the brightness. It was Bill.

Then people ran to help them. They got the piano out across the street. Bill and Willy leaned against it as they watched La Tienda Caballo Blanco and Bill's Place crumble into ashes. The crowd went home to check their horses and watch out for fire. Fortunately two vacant lots intervened to the north. The wind suddenly changing in that direction thwarted the bandits' plan for burning up the town.

"I was awful drunk tonight," he said. "When I headed north I thought it was awful late. Did I come to the store at all?'

"No, not since noon. I was worried."

"I'm sorry! I was a fool, Miz Westall."

She hurried on to tell him what had happened. "Something's funny, Bill," she said. "Pepe came—"

Bill cut her short. "Yeah, I sent him." The fire held his eyes in a focus. He evidently missed the import of her words.

Willy didn't answer. It didn't matter. There would be time later to talk of Pepe. She felt so tired—so heavy. The flames before her mixed her up.

She and Bill were silent.

He spoke at last. "Sorta like tobacco in a cigarette."

"Or like bubbles in a dream," she added. "We work to get something we can see and touch, and think we've done a lot. I'm beginning to believe—"

She did not get the sentence finished, for suddenly the world began to swim before her. She saw 'Mara holding Mutt. Fanny clasped S'rita to her breast. Don clutched Prince's bridle as the little pinto pranced. Three times they circled her; then black was all she saw. Everything dissolved into a pain that centered in the very middle of her life. The children, Fanny, Mutt, and Prince sailed away; the fire went up in smoke.

For just a moment she sensed the feeling of Bill's strong arms around her.

The next thing Willy knew the sun was coming up. When she opened her eyes, she looked into Fanny's face.

"Take it easy, honey," Fanny said.

"But where am I? What's happened?"

"You're at Bill's house. He carried you here last night. You moved the piano outa the warehouse and had a little mishap. It was a little girl again."

Willy blinked her eyes. She tried to get back into the world. "Where're the children? Where's Pat?"

"The girls're at Miz Randolph's and the Judge hasn't come back from the river. Bill's gone down to get him."

Poised between reality and oblivion, Willy's mind

picked up only consequentials. Bill Lester's arms, his strong hard hands! Pat prancing down the walk in Sugarland! A fig tree in the moonlight! Oklahoma City —he held her on his lap! The ranch house—she paced the floor—her heart wailed in desolation! The white, white bed in Austin—S'rita slipped into the world! Where was Pat? And now Fanny's dark kind face to take his place—her hand unheld as always, her burden having to sustain itself.

"Thank God!" she said out loud to Fanny.

Before she went to sleep, she gave directions for Emelio to see about the groceries scheduled to come in on the train.

"We'll get a building somewhere and start a store today."

30

The Ojo de Agua raid was well-planned, quick, and bloody. Drunk as he was, Sergeant Shonert rode safely back to his detachment. His men were billeted in a two-roomed box house on the edge of the Ojo de Agua Village, between the military road and the river. In the early morning a volley woke the soldiers. The telegrapher fell dead, a bullet through his chest. The others made for the open, dropped down on the ground, and fought as best they could.

The bandits rode in circles, shooting wildly in Indian fashion. The soldiers kept on shooting until all of them were down. Then the bandits dashed back across the river and were gone.

When Captain Scott and his cavalry rode in from the Peñitas outpost, he found all the Americans killed or wounded. Only one man escaped to the river and lived to tell the story. Four Mexicans and one well-dressed Japanese lay dead. The moon was shining bright. Horses nickered, men screamed and moaned, groveling on the ground. The village Mexicans chattered wildly, running back and forth.

Captain McCoy's detachment galloped in from Mission. Pearl and her delivery wagon were not far behind. Everybody began to grab and render service as best he could. Ray Renfro helped Pat to the ground.

"Sarg!" Pat was screaming, "Sarg, where are you? Answer me?"

Pat was dashing everywhere. Underneath the gallery floor he found Sergeant Shonert, lying in his blood, with a bullet through his head. He still clutched his pistol in his hand.

Pat's heart swelled. "Goddamn them sonsobitches. I hope to God you killed your share, Sarg, before they shot you down!"

Then he spied the Japanese, with a new Winchester in his hand. It was the very kind he and Bill had sold to Pancho Villa.

"My God!" he cried. He reached to Ray Renfro for support. His body shook. His eyes filled with tears.

"Our men didn't have a chance! We sold the sonsobitches guns!" The preacher gripped his hand.

Tears streamed down Pat's face. He reached down and stroked the Sergeant's hair.

"I would have done it for you, Sarg! I'm all crippled up and you was goin' strong. We got drunk, but you got back and died the way you should."

Ray Renfro walked over to the barbed-wire fence.

"Come here, Judge!" he shouted. They looked down close at a body on the ground. Ray struck a match. One bullet had pierced the heart.

Pat gulped. "In God's name, it's Pepe!" They leaned over closer. "In God's name!" He stared down into the still, dark face. "In God's name!" he said again.

"Pepe fought against our soldiers," Ray Renfro said.

"Yes," Pat answered. He kicked the corpse. "The dirty coward! I hope your soul's in hell. I'd like to have shot you with a Winchester you sold to 'em for us!"

"Don't say it! That puts murder in your heart," the preacher said.

Pat paced up and down. "But he was our middleman," he kept saying, "the one we trusted to deliver goods. He knew it all. I'll bet he planned this raid himself. Old Diaz had the right idea! Ought to 'dobe wall 'em all! Castrate the sonsobitches, earmark 'em an' brand 'em like Mustang Gray!"

Pat kept on swearing. He was everywhere at once, giving orders, poking, kicking, cursing out his wrath.

The Ojo de Agua Mexicans stood around in wonder as the soldiers bound up wounds, stacked the dead, shot crippled horses.

Ray Renfro stepped aside to vomit.

When Bill Lester galloped into Ojo de Agua, Pat stood over Pepe's body cursing Pancho Villa, Bill, Pepe, himself even, for being such a fool!

All Bill said was, "I'd rather hung him myself." He turned to old José and made arrangements for Pepe's body to be kept untouched until he could return later in the day.

Then he told Pat about the fire. He saved the shock of Willy's collapse until he could get him home.

Pat paid no attention to what Bill said. He swore at Pepe for double-crossing his best friends, at Bill for trusting Mexicans and getting him into the smuggling deal!

"And to think we sold 'em guns to come over here and murder us with 'em in our beds! It's that damned Pancho Villa that's done the dirt. Pepe wasn't smart enough for that! And you said Pancho was your friend!"

"He is," Bill said. "Plenty good men make mistakes. The store's burnt down, Judge. You'd better get on back to town."

Pat paid no attention.

"What's a house or so compared with wholesale slaughter right at our own front doors! We won't need houses if these sonsobitches're goin' to run us in the river! I thought we were doin' right to help Pancho Villa get his guns so he could settle his own fight! You told me that an' I took you on the level in the deal."

"Sure, Judge, sure; or we'd 'a never done it!" Bill's voice was quiet. But Ray Renfro saw the conflict going on inside.

Captain McCoy asked Pat to drive the wounded men to town.

It was a painful journey. Ray drove. Pearl galloped. The soldiers groaned. Pat cursed right on into Mission.

Pearl pulled up in front of the smoldering ashes of what had been La Tienda Caballo Blanco and Bill's Place. Pat climbed down from his seat, shouting, "For God's sake somebody help the preacher and me with these half-dead men!"

The whole town ran to help them get the soldiers into the drug store. They stood and watched Dr. Jeffers probe and bandage.

When Pat turned his attention to the debris where once had stood the store, he suddenly missed Willy and the children. His fevered brain convinced him that everything was gone.

"Where in the hell is Sweetheart?" he demanded of the ashes before him. "This goddamned wilderness's got no right to do a man like this! You go to help your friend and when you get back your business and family have turned right into dust!" Helpless, bewildered, sick, he looked at the preacher.

Ray hurried him up to Bill's house. Willy took him in her arms. He collapsed.

Ray looked at Willy lying there in bed. His heart despaired. "What can I do?" he asked.

She told him every detail and he carried them out: He found Lon Stone at the bank. They made a deal for the pool hall. He and Emelio took out the tables and nailed in shelves. Bill got back in time to help them. Fanny came over to boss a bit. The train brought in an order of groceries which they stretched out over the new store and with them started business.

By noon the town milled with people. The whole Valley came to take a look at what had happened at Ojo de Agua and to talk about the prospects of the country under border warfare. The majority went home to pack up wives and children; many made their plans to leave, themselves. When the train pulled out that afternoon Sam Logan counted his money. Passenger fares topped the record for the history of the railroad.

"Country can't stand this," Tom Jones said, shaking his head.

"Damn good riddance," Phil Allen spit far across the street and smiled.

About six o'cock Ray and Bill were standing in the store.

"Go on, I know you've got a lot to do," Ray said. "This happens to be one of the few ways I can help. I can run a store."

"Thanks," Bill said, and left.

Ray remembered the genial face that had bowed to him the afternoon before in the saloon. Twenty-four hours later it could never have been taken for the same. It looked lost, almost as if an eye or the nose were missing.

"Something's hit him awful hard," Ray said.

Just at sundown Bill Lester drove Pearl back into the village of Ojo de Agua. Her delivery wagon bore the burden of a cheap black coffin, the best one Mr. Allday had in stock.

As Bill directed, Pepe had been omitted in the bandit burial. His body lay just where it had fallen, covered with a torn and faded serape, blood-soaked in one spot.

Old José came up and told him the grave was ready. Bill handed the Mexican ten pesos for the labor.

"You dug it by the church like I said?" he asked him.

"Sí, Señor! Cómo no?" The old man smiled.

Not an eye peered when Bill approached Pepe's body. Out of respect for the well-known feeling between the men the jacales of the village suddenly swallowed up its people.

Bill smoked three cigarettes before he pulled back the serape to look into Pepe's face—drawn, distorted, mouth open, eyes glaring. His left hand, flung across his breast, clutched at his shirt pocket. Beneath his fingers dangled a round Bull Durham tag. The one bullet that hit him went straight through his chest. It left a wide circumference of blood-soaked shirt and flesh.

Bill reached down and smoothed back the tousled hair.

"What made you do it, Pepe?" he said sadly. "If you had to, why did you get hit so's I'd have to find it out?" He spoke as if the dead man were a child he sought to comfort.

When the stench of dry blood reached his nostrils, Bill unbuttoned his own shirt. "Can't bury you like that, old feller. You was always a fool about your clothes."

He struggled with the stiff body to remove the shirt. His face clouded; he frowned in awe. In the left side pocket he felt something hard. It proved to be a large green brooch. Bill held it in his hand a moment and then put it back.

He said. "It's a shame to be cut short like this. Pepe loved life!"

He pulled the Bull Durham out of the shirt pocket. Five hundred pesos fell out. Bill sank down as if the Mexican money had shot him to the ground.

"My God!" he breathed. Tears filled his eyes. "You done it for money! Such a damned little bit at that! Why didn't you tell me you wanted money? Why didn't you make Pancho pay you a decent price to do it? He would have, for Pancho's the kind of guy that pays for what he wants."

He sat silent for a while. Then he straightened up and scrutinized the growing shadows in the twilight, his eyes shifting quickly from the jacales down toward the riverbank.

"Better get this job done with because this ain't all that's gonna happen. Pancho Villa don't plan no *little* deals."

He pulled the shirt from Pepe's body. He caught his breath. There shone from 'round Pepe's neck a silver chain. Two emblems hung from it. He looked closely. One was a Guadalupe medal of the church. The other was Willy's wide gold wedding ring.

"Well, I'll be damned!" he said. He disengaged the

chain. "Why would you do a th
stared at the cold dead face.

He held the ring in his hand. Tears
"Yes, I think I understand why you done
think she'll understand it too." He carefully place
ring in his pocket and clipped the Guadalupe aroun
the Mexican's neck.

"You keep the money, Pepe, but I'll give her back
her ring!"

Quickly he pulled his own shirt onto the dead body,
crammed the five hundred pesos in the pocket, lifted
the corpse into the coffin, and drove Pearl to the little
chapel on the riverbank. Old José was waiting to help
him with the grave. They worked fast, in perfect silence. Bill kept one eye focused on the shadows in
the brush along the river.

"Who killed Fuego?" he asked the old Mexican
when they had finished.

"I keel heem. They shoot hees leg!" He shrugged
his shoulders and looked off.

"Yeah, I know. I burned him along with the army
horses!"

"Sí, Señor! Cómo no?" The old Mexican shrugged
again.

A little later Bill walked into The Palace of Sweets
in Mission and ordered whisky.

"We don't carry whisky, Mr. Lester," the quiet little owner said.

"Well, start carrying it right now. My place's gone.
We've got to have a good saloon because I've got to
have a drink," Bill said with such conviction that Mr.
Bingham knew he had to do it.

From somewhere a quart of mescal came. Bill
called Tom Jones in to join him in a drink. Liquor
kept coming. Both men drank until they held on to
the soda fountain to stand up.

"We'll just call this Bill's Place and serve ice cream
along with whisky!" Tom Jones hiccupped a time or
two.

"No such thing! We'll call this Bingham's Palace,
and I want it over here across the street! My place's
gone like a lot of other things. It's gone forever like

e keepin' names when

d to Brutus." Tom hic-

iouted. "I'm gonna give it
ie done it, but I swear I'm

om stepped up close to ask.
Bill shook the counter with his
fist.

"Oh, yes. wed deeply. "You're speaking of
Desdemona. I a. ys thought Othello should 'ave
given her a ring. A handkerchief's not enough to get
killed over, after all."

Next morning the first customers in the new Westall
grocery scared the preacher. Bruce McElroy, the emi-
nent, white-haired old rancher from the Agua Dulce,
walked in and asked for cigarettes.

"Where's Miz Westall?" he said.

"She won't be down today. She's sick." Ray turned
a little red.

"Sick? Miz Westall? There must be some mistake!"

"She'll be back in a day or two." Ray turned redder
still. "May I serve you?"

"Well, I want to buy three coffins," the old Scotsman said.

"Three coffins?" The preacher's mouth flew open.

"Yes, three coffins. I knew Miz Westall'd know,"
the old man said again.

At that moment Bill Lester walked in the door. He
looked strangely drawn despite the puffiness in his
eyes resulting from his drunk. So changed he seemed,
that Ray stepped back in amazement. Emelio gazed
into his face.

Without ado of any kind Bill said, "Let me do it for
you, Mr. McElroy. You go on and catch the train for
Corpus Christi. When you get back it'll all be over
with and done."

The two men looked at each other for a minute.
The old man said, "Thank you, Bill," and shook his
hand. "It'll lift a mighty burden off my mind."

"Yeah, I know," Bill said. "I buried Pepe last night at the river. Come on over to Bingham's Palace an' let's get a drink."

They walked out together.

Ray turned to Emelio. "What do they mean? Three coffins! And did you notice how they looked?"

"Cómo no?" Emelio said with a shrug. Why did these Americanos always question him about things he never knew?

31

The Valley Vigilantes and the Texas Rangers corralled all banditti suspects up and down the Lower Rio Grande. They gained confession of a Mexico-hatched plan for raid attacks from Fort Ringgold to Fort Brown. All were to strike at once. Burning, plundering, and killing, they were to drive the border troops and American settlers back to their note-writing government for safekeeping. That government chose to recognize Carranza as First Chief of Mexico while other men were in the field who could deliver messages with shot and shell. The Ojo de Agua and Agua Dulce Ranch fights were the only two that got through. But much damage was sustained by fire.

That night the Mission Vigilantes held a meeting in the store. Pat and Willy were not there. Ray Renfro served as host to all the crowd. There were no arrangements; people came. They were scared. The thing to do was get together and talk things over and present a solid front.

Tom Jones led the charge. Liquor made him shaky, far from brave. "Cold-blooded murder," he kept saying.

"Well, it's war," Judge Woolcott answered.

"It's worse than war! In a war you make your plans and send soldiers out to fight. This is sticking in the back. You don't know where to hit them. They stay in hiding. It's pure Indian, the way they do it."

"Of course it's Indian," Lon Stone said. "Pancho Villa is pure Indian. What do you expect?"

Somebody answered, "Square-shootin' from th' whites!" Everybody turned and looked. Ted Tolliver was coming in the back. He kept on talking. "Bill Lester's not an Indian an' Bill's th' one that's done th' dirt."

"Don't say that, Ted!" Father Michael spoke. "That's not right."

Ted grinned and sat down on a box. He looked around the crowd. Willy and Pat were absent; so was Bill. This was his chance to talk.

"Then let Bill speak in his own behalf," another voice spoke out. It was Mr. Maxwell, the building contractor from Kansas City who had lost so much in land. He jumped up and began to scream and shout.

"You did this thing to all of us!" He pointed at Mr. Conlay, sitting on a crate. "You brought us to this Godforsaken valley on a pretense of great gain. You sell us land at prices we can't pay. We raise the stuff but we can't sell it. The land goes back to you. You're getting rich. We're going broke." He stopped to get his breath. His voice began to break. "I haven't got the money to get my family home. This Pancho Villa comes across the river and shoots us in our beds. Good God! Good God!" His head bent despairingly to his hands.

All eyes turned to Mr. Conlay, sitting on the crate. He didn't say a word. His hand went into his pocket and brought out a roll of bills. He got up, walked over to Mr. Maxwell, and pressed the money into his hand. Then he left the store.

Ted Tolliver coughed and spit.

"As I was sayin'," he began, "the man to blame is Bill! Now where is he tonight?"

Nobody spoke. They looked around the store. Bill was not there; neither were the Westalls. It wasn't Mission any more. The crate crashed beneath Hal Eubank. Navasota screamed and jumped. Mrs. Lea grabbed hold of Don. Her husband slapped her. Don kicked his father on the shins. Lea shouted, "Murder!" Everybody cringed.

"Let's all go have a drink," Tom Jones exclaimed. "We've got the jimmies all right."

"Jimmies, hell!" Sam Logan said. "We're damned nigh scared to death. Besides, these's no saloon. Bill's Place is burned!"

Ted cleared his throat again. "As I was sayin', Bill Lester is to blame. He's ganged up with Pancho Villa in this war. He's used these Mexkin boys as blinds. Got them killed on purpose because they knew too much on him. He's got all the plans made up. It's Villa's time to strike. He knows our country like a book. Now the shooting will begin."

Ray Renfro cut him off. "See here, my friend, don't take this thing too far."

"Just wait and see," Ted said. "Bill Lester'll leave the Valley now. You won't see him any more. He's got his pay. He'll fight across the river! Just wait and see I said right."

"You'll see the swellest guy on earth," Don screamed.

The boy jerked loose. His mother shouted, "Don!" He made a lunge and landed in Ted's lap. His knife was open in his hand. He drew it back and struck. His mother screamed. His father made a dive to catch the knife. The old priest grabbed the boy; Ted jumped back. Ray took Don in his arms.

Mrs. Randolph dabbed her handkerchief at the blood. Ted clutched the gash across his neck. Nobody spoke. They all looked toward the door. Bill was walking in.

Father Michael stepped up to meet him. Bill stuck out his hand and shook. He looked around the crowd and said a little hard, "I see I'm late."

They all got up and left.

At the door Bill stopped Don. Mrs. Lea was crying. "Just like his father," she wailed.

"No, by God, he's not," Bill said.

Lea pretended not to hear.

Bill turned to Don and said, "Thanks, compadre! Thanks!"

The boy smiled and pointed. "The preacher give me the knife," he said proudly.

When all were gone, Bill and Ray sat down on the gallery steps and talked about the weather and the crops. They were careful to discuss nothing that touched them both. Then they fell into a silence. Both were thinking.

Ray concerned himself with Bill. What was going on inside that head? What was the meaning of all these things the people said? What was important to a fellow of Bill's sort? Where was he aiming? What would be his end?

Bill got up to leave. When he was on Chiquita he turned and said, "Sorry I caused trouble, Parson. I should have hurried on. Rode out to the Agua Dulce. Chiquita got tired comin' back. I let her walk a lot!"

Ray tried to answer but he couldn't. Bill was riding off.

That morning Bill Lester had driven into the Agua Dulce yard. He had three coffins in the wagon. He saw the ranch house bullet-riddled, three dead men and a horse close by. He knew Pablo would be among the corpses. He had read the funeral notice. It was in the eyes of Bruce McElroy.

Old Lupe was there by herself. She was the cook who had loaded guns for McElroy to shoot with the night before. The Mexicans rode in upon them when they were there alone. She helped Bill dig the graves.

When he lifted Pablo into his coffin he noticed that his freckled face was scraped and scarred, his nose broken and pushed sideways. His whole head looked stomped.

"What happened here?" he said to Lupe.

"Meester McElroy keeck en th' face."

"After Pablo was dead?"

"Sí, Señor! Cómo no? He say hee come heere to keel heem en hees house."

"Oh, I see!" Bill said, and went on with the graves.

Bill Lester was the only other person in the world who could see the meaning of that high-heeled Justin boot stomping in that freckled, blue-eyed face after it was dead. Bill Lester was the only other person who knew why Bruce McElroy chose to buy coffins for three men who tried to murder him in bed. Bill Lester was the only other person who understood the old rancher's reluctance to do the burying himself. And Bill Lester was the only person who comprehended the old Scotsman's dying delirium, a year later, when he screamed, "The skulls! The skulls! The blood!"

For Bill Lester was the only other person who knew that Pablo was Bruce McElroy's own son.

Nursing Angelita through the smallpox at Rancho Bravo, he had learned her story before she died. But he kept it as she had lived it, and he felt proud to be the one to bury Pablo as she would want it done.

32

The next morning Bill walked up and knocked on his own bedroom door. Fanny let him in. His step was heavy, tired, short.

"How's Miz Westall?" he asked.

"Fine! She wants to get down to that store an' I'm havin' a time to keep her in."

The Negro put out his hand to Bill.

Willy spoke up from her bed. Her voice was tired more than sick, her face was drawn and pale. She looked like a boy lying there in Bill's nightshirt, buttoned at the neck.

Bill shifted his weight from one foot to the other. He tried to look away, but he couldn't. Finally he stood frankly staring.

"Just come by to tell you about a deal I made with Pat. I owe you all for groceries and now you all need a house; so we swapped an' I'm movin' out."

"But that won't do. You need a place to live."

"Well, not just yet. I'm goin' on a trip."

Willy sat straight up in bed. "Where to, Bill? What for?"

"A little business; but I'll be back." He turned to Fanny. "Get me my other boots and chaps."

The Negro set about opening bureau drawers.

"But tell me, Bill, I've got to know!" Willy said.

He walked over close and looked straight down at her.

"Sit down," she said.

"No, I ain't got time." He looked straighter still. "I don't wanta go, you understand. But this is something I've got to do. I've put it off now long enough."

"But your scraping gang?"

"Henry'll take care of that. The preacher'll help you with the store. Hal an' Jesse'll do your watchin,' Dutch an' Duke'll do your shootin'."

"But you, Bill?"

He dropped down in a chair. Willy saw tired wrinkles. Age had settled in his body overnight. He looked almost old sitting there.

"A lot has happened," he began.

"Yes, I know," she said.

"Caught me short." He looked down. "Oughta been here for that fire. You can't stop watchin' for a minute. If you do, you're caught."

Willy said, "Forget what's happened! We'll start over."

"Some things you can't start over!" He hesitated, then he added, "Pepe's dead!"

Willy couldn't say a word. She tried hard, but she couldn't. There was no answer—no question coming.

Bill went on. "Why Pepe done it I don't know, but he done it. I found the money." Then he glanced up, grabbed his pocket, caught Willy's eyes, and kept on looking. She dropped hers, for just an instant. When she looked back, he was staring at her hand, the left one. It lay on his nightshirt, calloused, rough, amost dirty. She gazed at it herself a moment. Then their eyes met. They kept on looking.

"I don't want to go, you understand—I've got to!" His hands dropped limp. He was silent.

Willy sat up straighter. She forgot the burning spot

inside her. Bill was drooping there before her. Something flashed and stung her.

"If you've got to, then you've got to," she said firmly. "Don't worry. Just go on and do your duty. When you get back we'll have things straight here in the Valley."

He looked up and smiled a little. His eyes were blurring. "That's why I've got to go," he said.

Then he leaned over. His hand gripped the footboard. He talked fast. "Don't want to scare you, but we're in for trouble and that fast. Last night Dutch got back from Monterrey. I sent him scountin' on Weisschmidt with a word to take to Pancho. I ain't seen Pancho. Been busy here myself. Things are shaky. I wanted him to know."

"Of course," she said.

"But somethin's happened—somethin' awful. Dutch couldn't see Pancho Villa right there in his hotel!"

"Did he know you sent him?"

"That's what Dutch told 'em, but they said he sent word that he was busy—couldn't see him!"

"What does it mean, you think?"

"It means he's bein' guarded and don't know it. He never got that word. We're friends, you know. I know Pancho Villa and he knows me the same. When one sends word, the other answers. It's always been that way."

"Of course."

Bill smiled faintly. "Yeah, them guns! You found 'em? I told the Judge you would find 'em."

"It didn't matter."

"Not now, but then it did. Pancho sent me word to send him guns. I sent 'em. I send Dutch to talk to him. He says he's too busy. No, that's not Pancho Villa. Somebody's in between."

"Who is it, Bill?"

"Weisschmidt and that coyote gang of his."

"But what's the reason?"

"That's why I've got to go see Pancho. I'll bring you back the reason."

"But, Bill, this raiding on the border?"

"Yeah, I know. That's it. They said Pancho shot

them Americans on the train in Chihuahua. I was sure
he didn't do it. I told you so, remember? But now I
know he did."

"And Pepe?"

Bill looked down again. "Pablo's the one that proves
it much better than our guns. There may be reasons
for Pepe to fight against the soldiers but not for Pablo
at the Agua Dulce."

He lit a cigarette. Willy sat there and watched him.
She felt frightened. Bill seemed so far away.

He spoke on from the distance. "Nothing could
make Pablo raid the Agua Dulce. Somebody talked
him into that."

Willy asked no questions, but she wondered.

"Somebody done some snoopin'—somebody in our
midst. They made him think he'd been done some
awful wrong. It all worked together. They meant to
hit at once!"

"Bill, did Villa plan it?"

"Yes, I think he did. That's why I got to see him.
He needs a friend to tell him how he's wrong. These
fellows use him. They've pumped him up with air."

"About Carranza and Obregon?"

"Sure! He's mad as hell at that. They come in and
sick him on the border."

"Do you think so, really?"

"Weisschmidt told Dutch himself. Dutch got him
drunk in Monterrey. They picked out Huerta to get us
into war. We pinched that in the bud. So they hop
Pancho. They stay right with him and make him think
we've insulted him. They give him money. They give
him guns. They keep him hot on the trail. They stay
right with him. They don't give him time to think at
all. That's why I've got to see him. He'll listen when
I tell him what they've done."

"They've done it all to get us into war?"

"That's the point. Pancho could make terms with
Carranza and he would. Weisschmidt wants to keep
us fightin' over here."

Willy sat up straighter still. Her face took on a
frown.

"Bill, what'll we do if war does come? Thing're bad enough the way they are."

He drew up closer. "That's what I came to talk to you about." He spoke bluntly. "Ain't there some place somewhere you folks can move to for a while?"

Willy winced. "Move to? No, there's not. If there was, we wouldn't be here."

He crossed his legs and rolled another cigarette.

"I was thinkin' of the kids. Don can take it, but girls're different."

"Yes, I know." Willy sighed.

He saw the weight settle on her heart.

"But what is it I can do?" she said.

They looked at each other. Neither spoke. Then Bill said, "Yeah, I know."

"It's a great country if we can live it through," Willy said. "Somehow I can't turn back, Bill. It's for the children. I want them to have the start we never got, so life won't be so hard."

"Yeah, yeah; I know!"

He got up. "I oughta been here for the fire," he said. "Don't wanta ever be caught that short again."

Willy reached up and took his hand. She cried softly. He groaned sharply.

Fanny slammed the door to let them know that she'd gone out.

After a time Willy said, "You'll be careful, Bill?"

"Yeah! But remember, I can't write."

He buckled up his belt a notch and looked toward the door. "You'll keep your eye on Don?"

"I will," she said.

He snatched up his boots and chaps, shot one quick glance at Willy, and in no time was on his horse.

"The old washwoman's got your shirts," Fanny shouted from the porch.

"Yeah, thanks," Bill hollered back.

Willy heard Chiquita's hoofbeats. She closed her eyes and said, "God, help us all—and him!"

Bill galloped down the street, Willy's ring still in his pocket.

She tried to go to sleep but she couldn't. The windmill squeaked. Her thoughts were confused. She concentrated on the concrete: that was money. It was the safest worry, the most urgent at the moment. Where would she get the money for a store? The lot was mortgaged for the gin. The gin wasn't paying profit yet. They owed Dubose for the stock that burned. They had to have more groceries now to sell.

She was thinking still when Judge Woolcott came in to see her. Fanny let him in and then went down to the store. The old teacher seemed excited—in a hurry.

"Want you to be thinking about a little matter, so I hurried on and came. It's the girls, Mrs. Westall. It's not safe to have them here. I saw old Mrs. Leonard down the street. She came in from the ranch just to see you. Miss Lizzie told her no. So I came on up myself."

"Thanks a lot," Willy said. Her head kept whirling. Bill had said the same. There must be danger.

"Isn't there some place that you could send them? To an aunt's or uncle's or a friend's?"

Willy took a long, deep breath. "No, there's not!" she said.

At that moment they heard a screaming, then a bursting through the gate. It was Don. 'Mara and S'rita came running close behind. Don saw his teacher and flew into his arms. His eyes were wide and wild.

"They've killed my dad, Judge Woolcott. They just brought him in!"

S'rita said, "The blood's all running in the kitchen!"

'Mara went close up to Willy and whispered softly, "Mama, I begged S'rita not to look. He hasn't got a head."

"Who killed him?" Willy asked, as calmly as she could.

"He got shot at Thirty-six's! They all said a soldier shot him." Don sobbed and shook.

"Oh, Thirty-six's!" Willy and Judge Woolcott said together.

"Where is he now?"

"In the kitchen at the restaurant. They just brought him in."

"Who brought him?"

"Soldiers!" S'rita shouted. "Millions of soldiers!"

Willy gasped. "Where were you children?"

"At the depot," 'Mara said.

"Why the depot?"

"Mutt chased a dog. We followed."

Willy sat up in the bed. "Go see what's happened, Judge Woolcott. Children, you stay here with me!"

Judge Woolcott hurried out the door. Don fled to Willy's arms. His sobbing shook him. Willy held him tight. "There! There!" she kept saying.

'Mara and S'rita stood by and watched them. They felt frightened. The world had turned so strange so fast. Everything was gone. The store was different. They had no clothes. Pepe and Pablo didn't come. They saw Bill riding fast. He saw them and stopped quick. He jumped off and kissed them both and got back on. Then he galloped off. And all the blood! The soldiers cursing and Don crying! They stood very close together and held each other's hands.

Don looked up at Willy. "Mom says she's gonna take strych-nine! I saw the bottle in her hand."

Willy pushed him back and got out of bed. "Find my clothes," she said to 'Mara. "I'll go see Mrs. Lea myself."

The children helped her. In a jiffy she was dressed. She felt a little wobbly, but she didn't stop to think about it. She was at the restaurant before she knew it. A crowd had gathered, gazing at the bloody sight before them. Willy pushed through the center of it and got to Mrs. Lea. She was sitting by the stove. Her hand clutched a bottle. Her eyes looked straight ahead.

"In God's name!" somebody hollered. It was Fanny, very near Willy. "Get on back to bed!" she yelled at Willy. "I turn my back and you slip off like S'rita. Let one thing happen in this town without you, honey! You'll kill yourself!"

"Hush," Willy whispered. "Look at Mrs. Lea. She's Don's mother. We've got to help her." She edged on over and sat down. She grasped the clammy hand and held it.

When Mr. Allday came and got the corpse, the crowd cleared out. Fanny and Willy stayed. They made coffee, but Mrs. Lea refused to drink it. She just kept saying, "I knew he'd do it! I knew he'd do it!"

"But remember, you've got Don," Willy answered time and time again.

The woman didn't seem to hear her. Eventually Willy got hold of the bottle and slipped it in her pocket. Fanny took Mrs. Lea home with her.

Willy walked toward the store. She could not seem to keep her thoughts sorted out. This poor woman! Pancho Villa and Bill Lester! Poor Conchita! Little Don! Her own problems all in one—money was all she needed. That was simpler. But now she had no ring to pawn—once this seemed so little—now it seemed so much; but it was just the same in measure —meaning safety for her children, life and love for Pat.

She walked into the store. Ray Renfro and Emelio met her at the door. The preacher's collar stood open at the neck, his sleeves were rolled up. He looked dirty, tired, disheveled, like everybody else, but young and happy. She looked around her at this makeshift store in the pool hall. "It's lovely!" she exclaimed.

Emelio brought up an onion crate for her to sit on. He looked grown in stature over night.

The phone rang. Willy got up to answer it.

"Have you heard the latest news?" Miss Lizzie said. "Conlay and Fogg took the bankrupt law at last!"

"You mean they're gone broke?" Willy caught her breath. "But what about our irrigation and our country?" Her head seemed almost detached from her body; she felt a little sick.

"Hell, I don't know. I'm just givin' you the news!" Miss Lizzie hung up.

That night Willy slept very little. Her body ached and burned. Her thoughts formed in zigzags, squares, and circles. She had to figure out the ways and means. Bill's words came back. "Why don't we leave the country? There must be somewhere else to go."

She asked herself the question. The answer came

itself. "I've ne̶
made my stand̶
cut right off in spa̶

Before daylight a̶
bage froze; the citrus t̶

That morning Pat s̶
drooped in his chair. "We̶
the damned country. It wo̶
dry and then it's cold. Then t̶
you to the ground. An' now it ̶
a thing to sell."

"We've got the sunshine," Willy sa̶

"Well, you can keep it!" Pat storm̶
Tom Jones joined him on the street.

When she opened the mail, she found a̶
Edinburg—compounded delinquent taxes.

"But why didn't you pay the taxes when t̶
due?" she asked Pat when he came in.

"Well, by God, we didn't have the money!"

"Take the bankrupt law," Tom Jones said.

"The hell I will. We've got children growin' up! N̶
Westalls jump their debts."

"But you've got to make some money. Let's put in
a saloon. Bill Lester's left the country and somebody's
losin' cash."

Pat limped up and down, swearing. "Do you mean
to make me mad? I thought me and you was friends?
I can drink this goddamned whisky, but I won't sell it
to other men."

Willy put on her Stetson and walked to the First
State Bank. She looked at Lon Stone and didn't bat
an eye. "I want to borrow money and pay you the interest charge. I've no security, but I've got to have
some cash."

"Why, sure, Mrs. Westall. How much do you
want?" He wondered why he said it, but he did.

"It's for the children. I've got to send them off to
school. You know we can't afford it with business as
it is, but it seems they've got to go."

"It's the only thing to do. Best loan I've made in
years if you never pay it back."

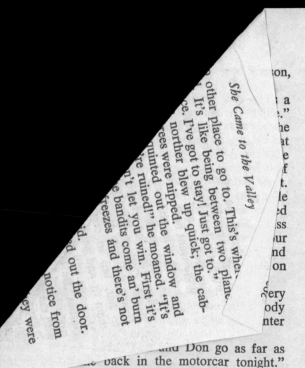

…on,

other place to go to. This's when
It's like being between two plane…
…ce. I've got to stay! Just got to."
norther blew up quick; the cab-
…rees were nipped.
…quinted out the window and
…ruined!" he moaned. "It's
…n't let 'you win. First it's
…e bandits come an' burn
…reezes and there's not

…d out the door.

…notice from

…ey were

…and Don go as far as
…back in the motorcar tonight."
…ssed the electric train, known to them all as
'the motorcar," that brought down the mail from
Harlingen and the Brownsville paper with the latest
news.

The train was leaving. Don jumped on and Pat followed. 'Mara and S'rita were glad they did. They
didn't feel so strange. They all stood on the back plat-
form and waved. Miss Navasota said to do it. "Like a
ship voyage," is what she said.

'Mara's eyes were blurring; S'rita began to cry. They
saw all the people but only two stood out—Fanny crying on her apron; Mama smiling and waving.

From the train Willy went home with Fanny. While
the funeral was going on she wanted to stay with Mrs.
Lea.

"I couldn't stand it to see him buried," Mrs. Lea
had sobbed. "Don can do that much for me!" She
wept on Willy's breast.

Willy kept on talking about the future, what they
had to do. The border raiding meant real danger. She

had to watch out for Don. She didn't tell her where Don was. When she began to ask for him, Willy said she had sent him down to Weisschmidt's with some groceries. Little Guillermita wasn't well. Mrs. Lea complained then about Don's slowness and his neglect of her. Willy answered by saying that Don was driving Pearl and Prince was following. He couldn't rush a colt. That calmed her. Finally she went to sleep.

Willy went back to the store. The funeral was not over. Emelio was there alone. Mr. Conlay was walking in. He looked old and broken. His face was pale and drawn. He took off his hat and wiped his forehead, then dropped down on a box.

"You've heard the news?" he asked.

"Yes," Willy said.

"I came to say good-by. I'm going home, to rest up awhile and maybe try again."

"Of course. But can we do without you, Mr. Conlay, while you're gone? What about our irrigation? We've got to have it to keep the Valley up."

Mr. Conlay smiled. "Phil Allen's glad to see me going. He says I've been a curse. We ought to leave this country to the ranchers like it's been."

"But I'm no rancher," Willy said.

Mr. Conlay got up and walked around the store. His eyes beaded. He looked out far ahead.

"That's just the point," he said. "You're my kind of people, Mrs. Westall; right or wrong, you're it. We got the vision; we came and tried. They've hit me low on money; that's all it is. To turn a desert into a garden without governmental aid is no small problem, but we'll do it some day! There's plenty of money. I just haven't got my share. It takes money for pumping plants and gins. People think we're crazy. But when we get them started, they'll all rush in and shout!" He was pacing back and forth.

"But in the meantime?" Willy asked him.

"That's up to you," he said. He stopped quickly and looked straight at her. "You'll do it somehow, Mrs. Westall. You'll make the grade between. That's the kind you are."

Willy tried to smile. "If the bandits don't smoke us out," she added.

"Bandits're just a moment's notice. They'll come but they'll go again. You'll somehow go on forever. You're the bottom; I'm the top. They strike me off but you keep growing. That's the fundamental law."

"I wish I could believe you, Mr. Conlay."

"Just wait and see, Mrs. Westall. At least your children will, or their grandchildren. You plant a dream and you can't kill it. Visions have to grow. It's inward. They sustain themselves."

He leaned on the counter and pounded with his first. "The day will come, Mrs. Westall, when gravity irrigation will take my place. They'll dam up water in floodtime; then when we need it we can get it without pumping plants. This fertile Valley will yield its increase as a natural gift of God. The old ranchers showed us how to do it with their gardens. Now they blame us."

"But we can't help it," Willy said.

"No, we love the country. We have to make it blossom. That's our vision. We can't give it back."

He grabbed her hand and held it.

A whistle blew. The motorcar! Pat and Don were in it. Willy hurried. She felt nervous.

"You're leaving, Mr. Conlay? Could I help you? I mean with railroad fare. A hundred dollars, say, for instance?"

Mr. Conlay reached over and kissed her. "No," he said, "I'll walk!"

He went out quickly.

Willy knew that she was crying and she couldn't help it. Mr. Conlay meant so much to her. He was the moving spirit of the Valley, the one who came and saw and built. He was greenness in the wasteland; he was water in the well; he was buckboards full of people buying land and paying cash. He was William Jennings Bryan in person, whooping up and handing out. He was Mission in the making. What was left when he was gone? Could they hold the thing together? Could they bridge the gap between? Without

Bill and Mr. Conlay could the Valley make the grade? She asked the questions straight to God.

When Pat and Don walked in the door, she looked up and squared her shoulders. Pat was so drunk he staggered on his crutches. Ray Renfro was following close behind. When Ray made excuses to take Pat home to bed, Don went home to his mother and Willy set about the evening trade.

Soldiers straggled up to town to buy cigarettes and go to the new picture show. It was a long-drawn-out evening. About nine o'clock Ray insisted that Willy go on home to bed.

"Farr will shoot my brains out," he remarked. "You're looking very tired."

"Please don't tell him," Willy said. "I'm grateful, very grateful to him for his interest. He means well and so do I, but I just have to; that is all. When these things happen, we have to meet them. It's the in-between that's hard," she said.

"The what?" Ray asked her.

"Mr. Conlay said I had a duty and this is it!"

Ray frowned darkly. "If I were Pat I'd say, 'Duty be damned.' You've got a body, Mrs. Westall."

"Well, it behaves!" she said.

When she got home Pat lay snoring loudly. Mutt wagged his tail and barked.

"Poor darling!" She stopped and stroked Pat's hair. "I hated to do it to you but I know that Bill knows best. He says we're in for trouble. I had to make them safe. I guess I'm a little jealous. Whisky's your release. Maybe I don't blame whiskey as much as I did once."

She went on out to the horse lot to check up on Pearl. Prince snorted and Pearl nickered to Willy's call.

"Who's there?" she hollered when she saw a shadow on the fence.

"Me, Miz Westall," a boy's voice answered back.

"What're you doing, honey?" Willy took Don's sweaty hand.

"Just lookin' an' thinkin'." His voice trembled at her touch.

She put her arms around him. They both looked up at the stars.

When she tried to go to sleep that night, she couldn't. She hated what she thought. "If I'd have had the money I'd have sent Don with the girls—yes, money! It resolves itself to money, no matter how I think. I didn't come for money. I came for love and water and things money couldn't buy. But I had to have some money to save my children's lives."

She got up and ripped the pocket from underneath her skirt. Two cartridges fell out. She put them in a box.

33

Ray Renfro stayed in the Valley a month on that special trip. Then he went home and came again. So much happened! He had to be around! In San Antonio he couldn't eat or sleep. He grabbed the papers and gobbled up the news. He skimmed through the European war news. Pancho Villa was the headline that made the earth beneath him burn his feet. Who cared about the Germans and the French? That was Europe. Let them cut each other's throats. This was different. He knew the people. He knew the country. He knew their purpose there.

"The border of a nation is where people fight and die," he said to Dr. Farr.

"You're getting trite!" the doctor answered back. "The French and English are proving that in blood."

"But the Valley is our border on the south. That's where we'll spill our blood if this doesn't stop."

The doctor said, "It's spilled already."

"Of course, but more and more will run when we have to fight these devils in a war."

"You're duller still. Blood doesn't have to run to spill."

The preacher blushed. He changed the subject to trench warfare and poison gas. He found it hard to talk to Dr. Farr about his Valley trips.

When Mrs. Randolph wrote him that they had hired a regular preacher, it seemed he didn't care. But when Pancho Villa rode into Columbus and shot up the soldiers there, he headed for the Valley train.

The nation's papers blazed with Pancho Villa's face. This raiding had to stop. President Wilson quit his warnings; Congress backed him up, and Pershing was ordered to cross the river and chase the bandits down. The Punitive Expedition marched across the Rio Grande and started the hunt for Pancho Villa. Ray read the headlines and went to cash a check.

"One-way to Mission, Texas," he told the ticket agent at the station.

"Can't go tonight. State Militia's got the train," the old man answered.

"All right; tomorrow night, and save a place," Ray said.

He stood back and watched the soldiers get aboard. They pushed and shoved and shouted out as they scrambled on the train. "Viva Americanos!" " 'Dobe wall th' cowards!" "Naturalize 'em all!"

"Pure Texas Militia," Ray said to himself. "They're Zachary Taylor and Sam Houton on the march!"

The day after, when he arrived in Mission, he found the Second Texas spread about in town. They were hot and tired and dusty and in an awful mood. Arguments arose with regular soldiers. There were many fights.

Pat was everywhere at once. He met the train and drove Ray to the store in his Brush.

"What about Pancho Villa and this raiding?" Ray asked him on the way.

"War for certain," Pat said. "We've got to whip the sonsobitches to calm 'em down at all."

"Well, Carranza's calm enough."

"Don't trust him any more than Pancho Villa!"

Ray didn't answer. Pat went on talking. "We need some practice in a fight. This note sendin's got to stop. Them damn Germans submarine our boats and all we do is write to Kaiser Bill."

The Brush chugged three times and stopped. Ray looked up and saw the new store. It was brick, with plate-glass windows. "Westall Fancy Grocery" was painted on the front.

Ray gasped and looked again. "When did you do it?" He stared at Pat.

"Just moved in. See the date?" Pat reared back and pointed at the concrete sidewalk in front of them.

"How did you get it done so quickly?"

"You can throw up bricks as fast as lumber in this country. Had to build it in a hurry," he went on. "Too many soldiers here. More comin' with this war. Cotton prospects good to start with. We'll make a killin' on the summer crop."

"How's the acreage with so many farmers leaving, Conlay broke, and all of that?"

Pat smiled broadly. "Can't kill dogs with butter," he replied. "I've got the Mexkin ranchers plantin' cotton now. Jim Neal's got the whole back country full of cotton!" Then he leaned forward. "That's not the money end," he added. "It's cotton brokerage that counts!"

Willy saw the Brush and came out front. Ray looked at her and sighed. She was thin and drawn. She looked trapped and withered, almost as if her youth were burning out.

Ray got out. Pat saw Father Michael and drove on down the street. Ray and Willy walked into the store.

"What's happened?" Ray began.

"Nothing," Willy said. "We've just been living pretty fast."

"But I turn my back a minute and you run off and leave me. I don't even know the town."

"All these Militia soldiers make a difference overnight."

"But the store?"

"It's Pat's!" She sighed slightly. "He had to do it. He can't live without the children. He kept crying. Lon Stone let us have the money on the gin."

"And you've worried?"

"Well, a little! Not about this building. It's the cotton futures I'm afraid of. And this war."

"Who started the cotton futures?"

"Jim Nelson mostly. It's a gamble on the war.

They're plunging. They think they'll make a fortune, and they may."

"Is Jim Nelson good with money?"

Willy smiled. "Well, not exactly. He's never paid us ranch rent yet."

"What made you let Pat do it?"

Willy smiled again. "I had to do it. There was no let about it. I saw him drooping. Even Lon Stone saw that it was best. It started with the shooting at Las Cruces."

"Las Cruces? Why so quickly? All this has happened overnight!"

"Has it? It's seemed to me a thousand years ago."

She closed her eyes a minute. Ray almost grabbed her hand.

He spoke bluntly. "This little while has made an awful toll, Mrs. Westall. It's not right. It's made you almost old."

She said nothing. He got up and walked across the store. Emelio nodded to him and he walked back again.

"Is there word from Bill Lester?" he started off this time.

"No," Willy answered.

"Not even through the Stewarts? Or Asa Hall?"

"No, no word at all."

"And all this raiding!"

"Yes, all this raiding!" Willy frowned and got up.

Mutt ran out and wagged his tail. She reached down to pat his head. Emelio motioned to the preacher to be quiet.

"How're the children?"

She looked up and smiled at him.

" 'Mara's fine. She likes school. She loves her teachers and all the things the girls do together. She writes us every day. But S'rita's not. She hates it all. She cries often, 'Mara says. She wants to come home and ride with Don. 'It's the indoors,' she writes home. They won't let her out. She hates dark and books and lessons. She loves the sun and light." Willy's voice began to quaver. She turned to Ray. "But what can I do? How can I have her here?"

Ray hemmed and hawed; and then he started out on Pancho Villa just as Mrs. Weisschmidt and Guillermita came in the door. He looked over at Emelio and gave a sigh.

Willy stepped up to meet them. She shook hands with the German woman and picked up the small blonde child.

"And how is my little namesake?" she asked her.

"Mrs. Vestall!" The small hand patted Willy's cheek.

Ray saw tears fill Willy's eyes.

"We bring you de birtstag cake." Mrs. Weisschmidt smiled.

"But it's not my birthday!" Willy answered.

"Ya, ve know; it is Guillermita's birtstag. Dat's vhy de cake iss yours."

"Oh, I see!" Willy kissed the rosy cheek. Then she set Guillermita on the counter and went to the candy case. She filled two sacks very full and handed them to her.

"Not two!" Mrs. Weisschmidt said.

"Yes, one from 'Mara and one from S'rita. That's your birthday gift. Don'll bring his down himself. He'll bring Prince, and you can ride."

"And your chiltren, Mrs. Vestall, how are dey?"

"Just fine, thank you." Her voice trembled. "Both just fine!" she said firmly.

The German woman reached across the counter and took Willy's hand. "You are lonesome for your chiltren!" she said kindly. Willy broke down then and cried.

Ray and Emelio walked back into the warehouse for a while.

Finally they heard Willy talking. "Be grateful as you can be for Guillermita," she was saying. She spoke firmly. "It's hard to let them grow up by themselves. It's the only cross I've ever felt. My children ran loose as babies. Now they're off at school. Of course I miss them. It's all right for 'Mara, but S'rita hates it all." Then there was a silence. Finally they heard. "But what can I do, Mrs. Weisschmidt, with all this bandit shooting and war right on our doorstep? I have to make the money to keep them out of here!"

"Don't say it, Mrs. Vestall!" The German woman spoke.

The screen door slammed and Don rushed in. Ray and Emelio came back into the store. The boy's eyes were bulging with news. Tom Jones had told him bandits had crossed at Ranchito. A big fight was going on. Fifty cavalry soldiers had chased the bandits back across the Rio Grande, had swum the river and kept on chasing south.

"Mom says that I can carry my pistol now!" He pulled out his father's gun and showed it to the preacher.

Willy put her arms around his shoulders and drew him to her. "You stay here with me," she said.

Mrs. Weisschmidt's blue eyes clouded. She said good-by and left. Mutt came out and licked Guillermita's hands in parting. Willy kissed the child.

Mrs. Lea walked by and called to Don to come on home. Sergeant Turney came in for his evening order. Willy filled it, with Ray and Emelio helping as they could.

That night everybody came to town. One by one they dropped in the store and started talking. To Ray the crowd seemed strange. Bill Lester was missing. Pepe and Pablo were not there. nor Mr. Conlay and Mr. Fogg. Mrs. Randolph had gone home to her mother. Jesse Parnell was on a Ranger watch. Ray missed the children. S'rita always bobbed from lap to lap. 'Mara slept beneath the counter. Now even Don was gone. He followed Willy's bidding and stayed at night with his mother.

"Where're Dutch and Duke?" Ray asked Willy.

"Riding the river at this hour."

"And yet they get no news?"

"No!" she said shortly.

Navasota came in with two captains and a major. The Hallam girls were with her. Their escorts were two lieutenants. Other soldiers came. Tom Jones started off the war talk. Everybody joined in. Ted Tolliver had told Hal Eubank a big tale about Peñitas.

Logan knew that the soldiers were all worked up over Roma. Pershing and Pancho concerned Pat chiefly. That meant war, and cotton on the boom. German submarines made Judge Woolcott join in the conversation.

Lon Stone said, "Better hold on to your money. Times're going to be harder and harder."

"Yeah, they've robbin' and killin' and holdin' for ransom down there," Tom Jones said.

"Don't cross the river for nothing," a captain put in. "It's just as good as your life!"

Ray looked at Willy and saw her sigh. "It's better to have them off at school," he said softly.

"Yes, Bill told me, and I did it!"

The next morning Ray helped Willy fill the shelves. It was all he knew to do to help her. It was cold comfort and he knew it, but he couldn't reach the sore spot in the wound.

Jesse Parnell came in to get some Bull Durham. His eye was bandaged.

"What happened?" Willy asked him.

"Bullet came across the river at Peñitas," he said shyly.

"Did any go back to get it and keep it company?"

"Well, several!" He smiled widely. "I sent across a few for Bill."

When he was gone Ray turned to Willy. "What did Jesse mean by that?" he said.

"Just joking. He and Bill're always joking. Bill jokes about the Rangers and he comes back with Bill's Pepe and his rooster." Then she stopped and began stacking cans again.

"Any word come through about Pepe or Pablo?"

"No," she said.

Ray wrinkled his brow. "It's all funny business when you stop to think about it, Pepe at the Ojo and Pablo at the Dulce, both turning rebel without a seeming cause. You, for instance. They acted like they loved you and the girls."

"Of course they did!"

"But they would have killed you!"

"No, they wouldn't. Pepe warned me."

"But too late if their plans had carried through."

"But they didn't. That's where right wins out."

"And Bill Lester's got up and left to boot!"

Willy dropped the can she was holding. She stepped down off the ladder to the floor. Her eyes shot sparks a second.

"Who told you that?"

Ray turned crimson. "Well, everybody—if you want to know. The Alldays, Al Randolph, old Cunningham, Ted Tolliver—"

She stomped her foot. "Damned liars to the man. Deliver that word from me in person."

Ray sat down on the counter. Emelio slunk out to the back.

Ray gulped a moment; then he said, "No offense, Mrs. Westall. Thought you'd want to know."

"Yes, of course," she answered. "Thanks a lot. How else could I protect him? That coyote Tolliver started it. I'll kill that man just out of pride."

"He's said a lot, but so have other people. It's the subject they talk about when you're not listening."

"What do they say?"

"Well, that it was Pepe and Pablo who started it— the meaning of Bill's burying them and all that, then leaving without a word to anybody. Negro Henry won't tell a thing, and you won't either. The Stewarts don't seem to know. People're not afraid to ask them."

She looked up at him, helpless. "But I don't know, Brother Renfro, except that he went to find Pancho Villa to make him realize what he is doing!"

"But that's just it. How can he do it? What can one man do to stop a war after all the shooting's started? Maybe he's helping to keep it up. They fight right on, even worse. Tolliver brought in a big tale about the Tigre raid last night. The soldiers're all worked up over the Roma scrap."

Willy leaned against the counter. Pain was in her face. A dream was dying and she fought to hold it.

"Sorry!" Ray held her eyes to his.

Willy straightened up and squared her shoulders.

"Thanks," she said. "I'm glad. If you hadn't told me, you would have failed me as a friend. You see, I know what Bill Lester's doing, whether the facts square up or not."

Her voice lowered, calmed. "Tell me one thing further. Do they say he went off with Conchita?"

"Yes, of course."

Willy didn't bat an eye. She said, "I know Conchita's gone—Chico doesn't come for groceries but—that doesn't prove the point."

Ray's heart warmed. What a fight she was making! "Gossip never reasons," he said gently. "It just flows; especially when people are all worked up. They want to blame somebody."

"But you don't believe this, do you, Brother Renfro?"

He looked at Willy. "No," he said.

In that instant she caught something in his eyes.

He got up and looked out the door. "It's just because of you. It grieves me to see you run these chances. Life's too sweet, you know."

"Chances?" Willy said.

He turned quickly. "Do you have to stay in the Valley?" He had to say it. Maybe it would lead to a solution. And it did.

"There are so many other places. There are so many other things!"

"I have to stay. I've settled that," she said.

Somehow he knew she meant it. He was whipped.

They worked on in silence until they had finished the task; then he walked out to the street and joined Pat.

Everywhere there were groups of men, greatly excited. News had just come in that Major Anderson with Troop E and machine gunners had crossed the Rio Grande at Tahuachal. They marched eastward toward Matamoros, chasing bandits.

"My God, right here at our door—American soldiers across the river. This means war!" Pat cried out.

"Yeah; at last we're goin' after 'em," Tom Jones quietly answered back.

"Not only here but everywhere on earth. When the election's over we'll settle down to fight. Can't avoid it with all this submarining by the Germans."

"But Wilson's all for peace, just like William Jennings Bryan."

"Then why did Bryan quit the Cabinet?"

"That was a personal matter."

"No, he saw war comin'. That's why he walked out.'"

Ted Tolliver and Mr. Maxwell joined the group.

"Where's Bill Lester?" Ted Tolliver spoke up very loud.

"Hope the soldiers kill the coward!" Mr. Maxwell screeched out. "Wish I'd never left Kansas City!"

"Why, you little fool!" Pat grabbed him by the neck. "Take that back! I'll brain you with my crutch. You're just scared without him! Bill Lester's the whitest man that ever set foot in the Valley."

"Well, where is he? We need him here to fight. He's turned yellow like his Mexkins." Maxwell choked and squirmed, but Pat held fast.

Men rushed up to see the fight. Pat's fights were always worth a show, but their sympathy in the quarrel was for Maxwell. They all agreed that Bill's absence was pretty queer. Probably, like Tolliver always said, Bill was down in Mexico kicking up the row. Pepe and Pablo had done their share; now Bill was working at his bit with Pancho Villa. Nobody ever knew anything about him. Even his woman had moved out.

Pat drew back his crutch. "You're gonna fight yourself, you dirty croakin' crook. I'll make you eat your tongue and spit out teeth and lick Bill's boots."

Ray caught Pat's arm and disengaged his crutch. Maxwell ducked and ran. Pat lunged forward, stumbled, fell. Everybody grabbed to catch him. Arms and legs got scrambled; curses split the air. When they straightened out, Tom Jones led Pat in to get a drink.

Ray looked for Ted Tolliver, but he was nowhere to be seen. He walked back into the store. Willy looked at him very straight.

"I'm glad you told me," she said. "I'll run down this tale and make somebody eat it. Bill keeps his business to himself. He's served this town, shot and fought and whipped to make it safe. He was a fine fellow then because they needed what he did. Now

he's doing twice as much but they can't see him do it;
so they think the worst about him. Ask the people who
really know him—Phil Allen, the Stewart boys, Asa
Hall!"

"And you?"

"Yes, me!"

Willy's face flung stars. In that moment something
snapped in the preacher's heart. It was like a taproot
cut, the flower doomed, the wither to set in.

Willy kept on talking. "He's done so much for us.
If I could only do some little thing to help him now
when people are against him!"

"But you do, Mrs. Westall, just by being you." Ray
swallowed hard. He rolled down his sleeves and buttoned up his collar at the neck. With conscious effort
he became the preacher once again.

He said firmly, "With Pancho Villa turning bandit
and Pepe and Pablo joining in for pay, he may lose
the foothold to his faith. He had it placed in people.
He hasn't learned to look to God. As yet he has only
you to hold to."

"Me to hold to?"

"Yes, you; because you're strong. Weak men like
me and Pat and Bill have to have strong women."

"I don't understand you, Brother Renfro!"

"I know you don't, Mrs. Westall, because I spoke
without a right." He looked straight at her so there
could be no doubt.

34

When the train pulled out that day, Ray Renfro was
aboard. He told the Westalls he'd got a message to
come home. He told no one where the message came
from. That was the secret in his heart.

When he got back to San Antonio, Dr. Farr asked
him much about his Valley trip. Ray answered little.

The doctor ordered liquor for himself and coffee for his guest. Then he led the conversation in a different way.

"You're a preacher, Renfro," he started off. "You ought to know a lot of things. I'm a doctor. I'm supposed to doubt. What makes things so uneven? What is the rule for that?"

"Balance, I suppose," Ray said. "It takes the low to even up the high."

"Yes, I know that much myself. I mean in human lives! For example, that pretty woman in that Mission town. What put her there? What keeps her there? What clips her every chance? And these women who come to me to doctor them—rich and petted— What makes the difference? It's not fair!"

"It's the quality that counts."

"But, hell, where's the reward?"

Ray sat silent. The doctor went on, pounding the table as he spoke. "I know what your answer is, 'pie in the sky,' you say."

"It's not that easy," Ray replied.

"Then why the complication? Answer that! What mixed her up? What got her off on the wrong foot?"

"Her own unselfishness, I should say!"

"Yes, I know—but don't say that to me."

"Well, maybe her reward is something we can't see." Ray leaned forward and pounded some himself. "You're a doctor. Some things you ought to know. What makes us talk about her when we meet?"

The doctor frowned. He didn't answer.

"She's not your patient and I'm not her preacher. You have a hundred women to treat—she's only one among them. And I—I have my mission work."

"Well, she's a different sort," the doctor said. "She's on an awful spot." He beat the table. "And, by God, she doesn't whine! She gives away her youth and comfort—never knows she's done a thing—never says a word!"

"And you remember?"

"Yes, by God, I do!"

"Is it the contrast? I mean with the others?"

"Call it what you want to. No word is good enough!"

Ray sighed, sipped his coffee. The doctor downed another drink.

"How about that booted hombre I saw there on the street?"

"You mean Bill Lester?"

"I guess so. All I remember is his face."

"People are saying that he turned bandit, left the Valley, crossed the river, and fights now with Pancho Villa."

"What does Mrs. Westall say?"

"Nothing! And she'll scratch your eyes out if you try to. She thinks he's off on some big mission to stop the fighting on the border."

"Good God! The fighting's getting worse each day."

"Sure, that's just another burden on her shoulders."

Then suddenly the conversation turned to Pancho Villa, with General Pershing on the hunt.

After that evening the two men never spoke of Willy Westall when they met. Each pretended to the other that Mission, Texas, didn't count. But each searched the daily paper. In detail they followed every movement of General Pershing across the border. Pancho Villa burned the front pages. He was reported wounded at San Geronimo, but fought again at Parral, then at Tomachi and at Ojos Azules! He crossed the Rio Grande at Boquillas, then at Laredo, and at Glen Springs. Bandits swam the Rio Grande from Brownsville to Columbus. They stole horses, shot at soldiers and civilians. Soldiers and Rangers chased them back. People left the Valley every day. Wilson ordered out all State Militia to guard the border and get in training for the war.

Ray Renfro and Dr. Farr read the papers and talked about the news as it concerned the general European war. They met often and argued over France and England's chance to win. Could they keep fighting without American intervention? With Mexico on the rampage, could the United States afford to cross the ocean for a fight? But each concerned himself with Mission, Texas. Was it safe for people there?

Ray wrote to Pat and Willy every week on Sunday afternoon. Once he went to see 'Mara and S'rita at their school. That letter Willy answered; to the others Pat replied.

Pat loved writing letters. He had new paper at the gin engraved: Patrick Westall Cotton Brokerage. He liked writing on the paper and he liked the preacher. Sometimes he wrote him twice a week. He gave him all the news about Peñitas, Gran Geno, and Madero. Somebody stole Pearl and Prince again and he paid big ransom to get them back. Often he bragged about his business. He'd bought new machinery at the gin. The cotton crop was coming. It didn't matter about the settlers leaving. Truck farming was too big a gamble. He meant to make a killing in cotton, close up the store, and leave the Valley. They'd move up to Dallas, maybe, and put the children in Mrs. Llewellyn's private school. Lately his Sweetheart was looking awful tired and old. She'd worked so hard and been so brave. Both of them were worried about Bill Lester. Nobody's heard a single word from him. He wished to God the fool would write. It worried Sweetheart so. Ray never tore up Pat's letters.

When Ray wrote about his visit to the children, Willy grabbed a paper sack and scratched a note back to him. He had told her all about their teachers and their work; how well they played the piano; how they stayed together and seemed to cling so close there among the other girls. But he didn't mention how they looked. Willy wrote three sentences and asked him please to tell her that.

Ray answered quickly that they looked very well. Their blue suits fitted snug and trim. They looked a little quaint in square-tops marching off to church. He preferred to see them riding Pearl and Prince. Their skin had bleached from indoor living. He wrote a paragraph on Serena's face and hair.

"I really never saw the child," he wrote, "until she sat before me that at school. I sat up on the stage with Dr. Haldy and the faculty for chapel and looked down at that room full of girls. In that sea of faces there was only one that stood out. It was S'rita's. She looked like a golden brooch upon a dress. Her skin was clear like china. I could almost see the veins. Her eyes have darkened, I believe; maybe that was because she gazed downward. I didn't see them really."

Willy read the letter and tore it up. She wished she hadn't read it. Certainly Pat mustn't know about it —not yet. He was unloading new machinery for the gin. When he got that erected, he must go to Belton and check up. He could do that before cotton started coming in. Something was wrong with S'rita. 'Mara's letters hadn't told it all. The skin paleness didn't matter, maybe; but the eyes were different. They should be dancing, looking up.

She meant to sit down and write Ray Renfro a long letter in reply to thank him, and to see if he had a suggestion for making S'rita happy there in school. But that afternoon a troop train pulled the New York Sixty-ninth Militia into Mission. The town changed overnight, as did every other settlement up the Valley. From all the states Militia came: green, raw, unused to heat and dust and fleas. They cursed the country and begged for water in their tents. Their khaki scratched and they needed baths. When the Texas soldiers laughed, they started fighting.

The Mission people met together that night and appointed Pat and Father Michael to take charge of the soldier situation. They made Willy chairman of cakes and pies.

"But that's not the problem," Judge Woolcott said. "We need a supply of water. A few hundred people increased to thousands overnight is a challenge. We have to meet it."

"Well, there's the river," Tom Jones said.

"Yes, but we're three miles north and we're a town. We need some wells. All we have to do is drill them."

"The Judge is right," Pat said. "We'll meet tomorrow afternoon and vote. I'll have a driller there."

That night Willy had no time to write to Ray Renfro. The store was thronged with soldiers. They bought everything in sight. Fanny got behind the counter; so did Don. Three times the water barrels ran out and had to be filled up.

A Texas corporal asked for a Dr. Pepper, and a New York sergeant laughed. "Who's Dr. Pepper?" he asked. "Maybe he's de guy who gives us drinks in dis ratty town!"

The Second Texas had been waiting for just such a chance. They ganged up on the side and rushed the Yanks. The corporal grabbed the sergeant; then both sides got into action. They threw onions and potatoes, anything they could snatch. In the tussle a hard pineapple hit the big mantel lamp in the store. It exploded. Willy jerked off her apron and beat out the flame. The soldiers kept on fighting in the dark. Willy screamed, "Stop it, boys!" They paid no attention, or they didn't hear her. "Big-headed Yankees!" "Rough-neck Texans!" "Go back where you come from if you don't like it!" split the air along with anything they could throw.

As Fanny reached for candles to light up, Willy stooped down to the Dr. Pepper box. By the time Fanny got the candles going, Don was on a sergeant's shoulder beating him with his fists. Willy swung a Dr. Pepper bottle in her hand. Just then Dutch and Duke came in and shortly straightened out the row. Eventually military police marched their men off to jail. That night Texas and New York guardhouses were filled to the limit.

Dutch and Duke came back to the store. They sat on the counter, dangled their long legs, and talked. These days were very busy. They didn't have much time. They just ran in and out.

"It's a helluva job, Miz Westall. These soldiers're so green and dumb!" Duke spoke with polite disgust.

"Damn fools," said Dutch. Then he apologized for swearing, as the Stewarts always did.

"But we must be patient. They've been sent to help us," Willy said. "It's so hot and we haven't enough water for five thousand men. That's our next job. We've got to dig some wells."

"Well, we give 'em water as well as they can fight. All they do is wait for orders and grumble about the sun. All we do is keep busy settlin' the North and

South. That Second Texas was itching to fight the New
York Sixty-ninth! Well, we oughta be ridin' on the
river. Bill'll be back and give us hell!"

"Haven't heard from Bill, have you?" Willy asked.

"No, Miz Westall. Our dad's known Bill for years.
He says nobody hears from Bill. He just comes and
goes and does. He never sends a word."

Duke spoke up. "But don't you worry. We'll do your
shootin' for you and keep a check on Pearl."

When Navasota walked by with a New York major,
the Stewarts remembered there was a dance. They
dashed upstairs to waltz a round or two before they
took their river ride. Duke begged Willy to come along
with them, but she said no, she had to write a letter;
besides, she was too tired. Also a little trade kept up.
Soon Pat went to bed. At midnight Fanny left, and
then Emelio, at one o'clock. Don stayed with Willy. It
was after two when she closed up and Don went
home.

Willy walked along alone. She thought about the
New York soldiers, the fight, and all the mess, and
then about the cotton crop. Pat's gin! Could he pay
out? Would this new boom of soldier trade get them
out of debt?

She loved this one block of walking home. It gave
her time to think. The stars shone out. She liked to
think of them. The same stars were shining on her
babies. She felt near them for a moment. All things
were near and close and very dear. She heard a horse.
It turned the corner. Phil Allen spoke.

"It's a little late, Miz Westall, to be gettin' home to
bed. Soldiers got you on the run?"

"Yes, I guess so," she called to him. He trotted on.

She knew he was going home from Thirty-six's.
What an hour to break his sleep. Well, in his life he
left out nothing, not even for one night. That's what
Bill always said about Phil Allen. He can do more'n
any any other livin' human bein' and do it all at once.
How Bill knew people! He knew them all, it seemed,
up and down and inside out—except perhaps himself.

How could he go away like this and never send a
word! Henry said his scraping had gone straight to

hell. With no new contracts the mules ate themselves
up in feed. He'd go off after Pancho Villa and let his
business go! She knew he had thought he could stop
the raiding by making Pancho see the light, but he
hadn't. Since the raids were worse than ever, she felt
sure he hadn't got to Pancho. Maybe he was dead! So
much could happen. She felt a little faint. When she
passed the alley she saw the flutter of a dress and a
uniform. It was white against the Rio Grande Hardware wall. She speeded up and didn't turn her head,
but she heard the talking. It was Eva Hallam's voice.

"Oh, Sug, don't!" it said. "That hurts. Kiss the other
one awhile."

Willy hurried on, looking straight up at the stars.
Somehow she saw S'rita's face up there. The eyes were
downcast and the skin was pale. Then two hands
reached and cupped S'rita's chin—soft, swarthy hands
that caress skin. She heard S'rita murmur, "Don't
leave! You smell so good!"

Willy walked in the gate and sat down on the steps.
"I must be tired as hell," she said. She leaned back
against the gallery post and smelled. A night-blooming
cereus gave its fragrance to the air. It was a little like
that perfume Conchita wore! S'rita liked that perfume;
so did Bill.

She sat up straight and said, "I'm a fool! Bill rode
off on a horse. Of course Conchita could have met him
somewhere for the trip. But he couldn't look for
Pancho Villa with a woman on his hands!" Then she
laughed.

"Tomorrow, if I live, I'll ask Fanny. There's no need
to be so proud about your friend. Besides, there's nothing to it. Bill has a right to his woman where he wants
her; and I have a right to know. He gives her a house
and pays the bills. He doesn't meet her in dark alleys
on the sly. He lets the world know what he's doing. He
pays the price for that."

Then she set to thinking. Why hadn't she asked
Fanny? She couldn't find the answer, for pride was not
enough. It was true that nobody talked about Bill to
anybody else, but she and Fanny talked about every
kind of thing. She mulled over it a little; then she said

to herself, "I might as well be frank and tell myself that I am afraid to know."

She looked up and saw somebody running. It was Don. She got up and met him at the gate. He threw his arms around her waist. He wasn't crying; he seemed just stunned.

"She went and done it, Miz Westall! She said she would!"

Willy held him very close.

"I found her in the kitchen when I got home. The strychnine bottle was on the table. She is twisted up and dead."

Willy took Don into the house and woke up Pat. She left them together and went for Fanny. They hurried to Mrs. Lea. She lay on the floor, stiff and cold, with her sandy hair tousled about her face. Just her mouth was showing. It was open; her teeth stuck out.

"She looks like a coyote in a trap," Fanny said.

"Well, she was!" Willy answered.

One knotted hand clutched a piece of paper. Willy got it loose and read: "I couldn't stand to live without my husband. He was kind and good. I'm going now to find him. My son will be better off without me. Dora Lea."

"Well, I'll be damned!" Fanny said. "She calls that Myrtle at Thirty-six's sweet and kind, I guess. She's got a big buck sergeant now that old man Lea is dead!"

Willy said, "Well, let's hope they are together and find it better going on this trip. At least Myrtle is separated from them for a while. But that sweet child!"

Willy looked at the woman on the floor. "Yes, you fool," she said. "And you did this to find a man!"

"Bill told us, you remember, when they came to Mission?"

"Did he?"

"Well, he told me."

"I guess Bill tells you a lot of things he doesn't tell other people."

"Well, yes, he does," Fanny said.

Willy looked at her a moment, then went to the telephone and called Miss Lizzie to get hold of Mr.

Allday. When he came and took charge of Mrs. Lea, Willy and Fanny sat down on the restaurant steps.

"I guess it wouldn't be decent to leave her by herself," Fanny said. "But you need rest, Miz Westall; you ought to go to bed."

"No, we'll wait," Willy said. "The poor thing needs some attention. This is the last that we can do. I'm afraid Mr. Lea disappointed her for the meeting she had planned. Besides, she is Don's mother."

"Yeah, I guess so; but I can't believe it. So far he's as nice a kid as ever lived."

"Well, that's because of Judge Woolcott and Bill!"

"And you and Judge Westall."

"Not me, Fanny. I had to send my children off to school to raise them. I've been too busy."

"Makin' a country for them to live in!" Fanny started crying. She always cried when the children's names were mentioned. Life without S'rita was a thorny cross to bear.

"Well, we've all done the best we could do with the light we've had to work with at the time."

"God won't find no fault with you, Miz Westall. You gave S'rita to the world."

"And 'Mara! Don't forget Amara!"

Willy knew she had to change the subject, and she did. Fanny's crying was too much. She was tired. She might cry, herself.

"What do you think has become of Bill?" she asked.

Fanny blew her nose on her apron. "He's either dead or doin' business," she replied.

"But what about this Pancho Villa business? You don't think he's in it?"

"Hell, no!" Fanny said. "I know Bill's not in it."

"These damn people! They say such awful things! With Pepe and Pablo gone, Bill goes off and sends no kind of word! And the raiding's worse than ever. He hasn't stopped it!"

"Well, I never thought he could. But he thought Pancho Villa would listen to him when he talked. Lord, I'd like to hear that conversation. I'll bet he told all about you and 'Mara and S'rita—can't kill women and children and all that kind of thing."

"And Conchita?" Willy asked.

"Yeah, what about Conchita?" Fanny looked at Willy very sharply.

"Well, where is she? She's not here. Is she in Mexico with Bill?"

"I can't answer that, but I do know a little bit about it."

"What?"

"The night after Ojo de Agua, Bill an' Conchita had an awful fuss. He was drunk when he told me, but a drunk man never lies. The buryin' Pepe an' Pablo sorta hit him below the belt. That night Conchita got awful jealous over somethin' he had done. She accused him of lovin' another woman; so he beat her up. She left next day, but not with him."

"Did she go to Mexico?"

"Of course. Chico told me."

"Then that's the reason Bill doesn't come on back."

"It may be and it may not. Bill's a funny fellow. He always talks to me when he gets good and drunk."

"Did he ever tell you where he came from or who his people are?"

"Not Bill Lester! Honey, you don't know that man. Nobody knows where he come from an' nobody ever will. Bill talks about the present. He leaves the past behind. It's the action of the moment that seems to get him down."

"But he believes in Pancho Villa? That he's the Mexkin people's savior?"

"Yes, of course. But there're other things besides. He worries. That's the reason he drinks."

"Bill couldn't worry, Fanny. He never takes the time."

"That's what you think, honey. Lots of things're on his mind: Pablo, for example. He talked for hours. I never got it straight. But it was somethin' about blood and mixed breedin' and bastard children—all how wrong it is!"

"Not Bill Lester?"

"Yes, Bill Lester!" Fanny reared back a little against the gallery post. "Then he goes from that to marryin' early to a woman of your kind, havin' children of your own!" Her voice began to quaver.

Willy knew she had to change the subject another time.

"That's just whisky talk," she said.

"Yeah. But Bill worries sober. We talk some then besides. Then's when the thing hits him really. He comes and talks for hours—the hell of living like Indians, the hell of lovin' another man's wife—the way of feelin' dirty because you ain't been clean yourself!" Fanny began to cry.

Willy jumped up quickly. "That's enough," she said. "It's too late and we're too tired to talk. It's like being drunk, almost, ourselves. Important talking should be done in daylight—in the sunshine, really, so you can think it out."

Then Mr. Allday came out and said Mrs. Lea was reads. They went in and looked at her in the coffin. Fanny noticed that Willy cried.

As they walked home, the sun was rising, a tiny arc on the horizon, then a beam of brilliant fire.

"It's so much easier in the daylight," she said to Fanny. "We see things plainly. The shadows vanish."

"Sure, honey, sure!" Fanny said.

The Negro dropped down on the bed. She had to sleep a little before the funeral. When she closed her eyes, she was thinking of white people. How they complicated their problems! How they mixed things up!

Willy didn't go to sleep. She couldn't. She went to the kitchen and baked hot biscuits. They had just fixed up the kitchen and bought a stove. At breakfast she and Pat and Don sat down together. Don looked straight and tall and old. His eyes were deep and blue like Bill's. His hair was dark and straight like Pat's. His shoulders seemed to square up to the world.

"You're just made to order, Don!" she said.

"That's what I've been tellin' him!" Pat added.

Don smiled a little, then he said, "But I'll live with Judge Woolcott. He's awful lonesome. Bill and I talked about it once!"

"Well, then, of course that settles it for a while," Willy answered.

Pat turned to Don. "You see, we've never had a son. Always wanted one, of course, and you're it, my boy!"

Willy went for more biscuits. When she got back, they were talking about a trip to Corpus Christi on the train at three o'clock. That settled the problem of the moment.

Willy arranged Mrs. Lea's funeral for two o'clock. The train left at three. Pat and Don hurried from the cemetery to the depot.

Willy hurried to the bank. Among her deposits there were many checks bearing names one seldom saw— Father Duffy, Rupert Hughes, Floyd Gibbons, Vanderbilt. Lon Stone's mouth flew open. "Have you noticed?" he said to Willy. His finger pointed to a check.

"Noticed what? That check's for ten dollars."

"But the name!"

She was unimpressed by Vanderbilt. "I hope it's good," she said.

"Well, with over a hundred thousand troops on the border I guess we're bound to get them all!"

"Well, enough to pay a little on my note. I've paid out the piano now with soldier money and have sent in an insurance check."

"Then something's good about a war," Lon said.

When she was gone, he went to get a drink.

Willy went on to the water meeting and took a seat, the only woman in the crowd.

She felt a little strange, but with Pat away she had to attend.

The driller spoke at length about the need and cost and time for drilling. But Willy saw the men were not concerned. It meant money and they all had had a mighty pull with money just as she had.

"But do we need these wells?" Mr. Allday asked.

"That's why we have this meeting," Judge Woolcott rose and said.

"With the extra soldiers coming to the Valley one town is bound to become the center of the Valley trade. I've come to Mission first," the driller said.

"Who's our competitor?" Mr. McIntire called out.

"McAllen's the next town I'll ask to dig the wells."

"They'll never do it," old Colonel Cunningham spoke up. "They're all broke there worse than we are here."

"We don't need water; we need saloons!" Tom Jones drunkenly broke in.

Everybody laughed.

Willy squirmed and twisted. "If Bill were only here, he could swing it in a minute. Now's the time to make them see the point! They'll do it now or never! It's a point in progress, but they can't see it."

Nobody said a word.

At last bartender Kinney rose and said, "Let's vote."

Willy couldn't stand it. She had to talk. She hopped up quick and said, "We can't afford to let McAllen dig those wells. That'll give them a jump on us we'll never overcome. Two towns can't really grow five miles apart. One will be a big one and the other just a runt. This's our chance to take the lead. The soldier trade will save our business now. We've got to keep it; so we've got to dig these wells. This expense will hurt to start with, but we'll make it up. It's a step in progress we can't afford to overlook!" Then she sat down. The men clapped long and loud.

When Lon Stone rose to speak, Willy held her breath.

"Mrs. Westall's right," he started out. "But I'm the banker in this town. I know the balance of every person in the room. It's not what we want but what we can afford. Business's better and we're glad for that. But do you know what rise there's going to be in taxes this next year? New roads and schools and irrigation bonds since Conlay's broke and all these soldiers here. Think carefully, folks, before you take on something new."

He took his seat. His listeners didn't clap.

Willy didn't rise to answer. She owed the children's money yet. Pat had to have more for the gin. Something hit her in the heart, a heavy lick right in the center. She had to choose between her family and her town. She chose the little girls and Pat.

"If I only had the strength," she thought.

The vote was called. Everybody voted no but Willy and Judge Woolcott; their votes were yes.

As she walked home, Willy's heart felt like a brick-bat in her chest. "If Bill had only been there, he'd have found a way." Bill never stooped to money; he fought for what was right. And money came as money should because it's not the reason. But when you haven't got it, you've got to get it when you have children.

She went on to the corral to check on Pearl and Prince.

"It's like they hit you with a whip," she siad to Pearl.

The mare nuzzled on her neck.

"I love Mission like I love you. Mission doesn't fail me any more than you do."

Pearl nickered softly. Willy rubbed the mare's nose, put her arm around her neck, and kept on talking.

"When I think I'm done for, the village comes through with something new to help me—like this soldier trade when I had to send the children off to school. Now when she has a chance to grow and be the center of the Valley trade they say no. They doom her to be a little town. It's like a plant you fail to water." Willy was talking loudly. "But if Bill had been there!" She grew louder. Pearl gave a whimper. "If Bill had been there it would have been a different story. He'd have thought of something to turn the trick! Yet they think they've made this town. Well, they can't do a thing without him. Mission's his just like 'Mara and S'rita are mine."

Willy went in and wrote to Ray Renfro. She tried to make the letter full of news. She told him about Mrs. Lea and about the soldiers. She invited him to come back and see the Valley in a flush. "It's all so different," she said. "We miss you and Bill and the children, Pepe and Pablo—even the poor Leas." The point she made was about Serena there at school. What could he suggest to lift the child's spirit? Would they let her keep a horse? They could ship Prince up at once. Now that Mrs. Lea was dead, Don was the next consideration. Things were too strange and hostile for a boy without a mother and a home.

She smiled a little when she wrote that sentence. "But a mother is a mother, good or bad," she thought. "Me, for example!"

Willy put her head down on the desk and cried!

35

The following week Navasota married Major Doolan of the New York Sixty-ninth. This wedding proved the Yankees really liked the country and the people. The town showed its appreciation. Mrs. Allday gave a party. Pat and Willy gave a dance. The Second Texas served mescal highballs to the New York Sixty-ninth.

But the morning of the wedding the Villistas and Carrancistas met in Reynosa just across the river for a fight, and set the town on fire. Don climbed the windmill and brought in reports of the flames' progress from time to time. Father Michael hurried the ceremony so people could leave to watch their homes.

"Damned shame to ruin a weddin'," Pat said. He got very drunk in celebration and had to stagger home to bed.

Willy was too busy at the store to see the wedding. Don left the windmill just for the ceremony and ran back and told her about it.

With a Villista army near Reynosa, Willy was all excitement. Bill should be somewhere close if he were living. She expected Dutch and Duke, but they didn't come. Probably slipped across the river to take a look around! Ted Tolliver passed by. She felt tempted to break their no-speaking and ask him what he knew. Then she wondered why she didn't ask him. Probably Bill lay out on some desert space unburied, buzzards picking at his carcass. She'd never know what had happened. Nobody would.

Navasota and the Major came in to say good-by. She felt a little relieved to think of love in place of death for just a minute.

Navasota held out her hand to be admired.

"How pretty your rings are!" Willy said. "Certainly you deserve the best!" She felt impelled to cry, Major Doolan looked so happy with Navasota as his bride. Willy thought of Patrick Westall and the Baptist church in Franklin, Texas—in another life it seemed. Then she saw Navasota looking at her hand.

"I've always meant to ask you, Miz Westall, why you never wore a wedding ring."

Willy reddened. She knew Navasota didn't mean to hurt her. The remark was casual, thoughtless—meant to fill up space; yet it cut.

"I don't know," Willy said with certain fairness. "Just don't know—like you won't know a lot of things a year from now, my child."

The day wore on. The trade was heavy, and Willy tried not to think. People milled around in great excitement. Everybody darted in and out. Don said a dozen times, "Please come out and see how the fire reddens up the sky!"

The moon was up when Willy finally got outside. She felt deserted, broken, robbed of something—something like a friend. Life was going on about her, but she couldn't get in touch. If only Pat had stayed sober so they could talk! She dropped down on the back steps to rest a little. "Just feeling sorry for myself," she said; "and scared with fighting near Reynosa. That's too close with Bill not here to watch."

She looked up at the moon a minute. The fire glowed red against the sky. Somehow God must take care of Bill, direct his steps, and take him where he ought to go—alive or dead. And God must please remember S'rita and calm her heart to indoor living as she tried to go to school—make her happy like Amara. Some day may they both be happy as Navasota was today—yes, Navasota!

She stopped praying.

Yes, Navasota! Why did Navasota ask her about

her wedding ring? As if she lived in sin with Pat and bore children without the rite of marriage. Of course the girl didn't mean it so.

"That's women for you," she said out loud. "Once we get this new gin set up and paid for and the old debts covered, damned if I don't buy myself a diamond ring!"

"A diamond ring?" someone whispered.

She jumped up and stepped back.

"Ted Tolliver? You snooping bastard!" She raised her voice. It rang out clear.

"No, I'm Bill!" the whisper came again.

A man stepped out into the moonlight. It was Bill, dirty, worn, and frazzled, hat crushed, boots muddy, shirt bloody, even smelling. Willy heard a horse stomp, then a snort—a strange horse, not Chiquita.

She reached out and took Bill's hand just to know that he was real. Her heart beat a rattle in her chest.

"Thank God, you're back," was all she said.

He held her hand very tight.

"Fine to see you. How's the Judge? Glad you sent the girls to school." Then he added quickly, "I got to hurry." She heard something to that effect.

When she calmed herself a little, Bill was saying in a whisper, "The brick store's mighty fine. Heard about it down at Thirty-six's."

"Thirty-six's," she heard clearly. She jerked back. She felt glad that moonlight softened shades of color. Fanny said Conchita left because of some other woman—but that was no way for her to act.

"This horse? Where's Chiquita?" she asked sharply.

"Shot." His voice quavered just a little. "Miz Westall, I've got to ask you somethin'."

"Shot? Did you say 'shot'?" she gasped, not hearing his last words.

She reached out and took his hand again. He clasped it tight, but now his grip was different. He gripped her hand against a pain. She knew, for she had gripped Rosita's hand that way when Amara's birth throes hit her. When it passed, he drew his hand away.

She wished he hadn't.

"Found this little mustang in Sonora," he hurried on. "Named him Fuego. Couldn't find a mare on such quick notice."

"Have you been fighting, Bill?" she said.

"No, just followed along behind, got in a little bit too close and they nipped Chiquita in the neck. I had to shoot her. Say, Miz Westall—"

"Bill, I'm sorry! You know I'm sorry!"

Still in a whisper he said, " 'Twas Weisschmidt's fault. He's too damned smart. Won't let me get in hollerin' distance of Pancho Villa. Got Pancho all fed up to thinkin' I'm a spy. Tells him a fellow calls himself Bill Lester but the real Bill's across the river on this side. Pancho's all swelled up himself with all his fightin'. But I'll see him yet, you'll see."

"But you're home now," Willy said. "Stay here and let Pancho Villa go. They'll kill you. We need you here in Mission."

"Ain't Hal and Jesse watched the store?"

"Yes, of course. So have Dutch and Duke, but they're not you!" Then Will gulped, "People don't appreciate what you're doing. You risk your life. It's not worth it."

"Yeah, but we gotta stop this raidin'. It'll ruin the country."

"But Ted Tolliver—"

"Ted won't say much for long, Miz Westall. Don't you worry. It's skunks like him that gets us into war. Somebody's got to get us out. It's him I crossed the river for tonight. I got wind of something down in Monterrey last week where Pancho Villa is. This fightin' near Renosa was fine for what I want. Rode into Thirty-six's to get hold of Phil Allen. Got to do a little operatin' down near the Weisschmidts' an' knew Phil was my man to do it—but—"

Willy took four breaths and dropped down on the step. "Let's sit down and talk." All at once she felt relaxed and easy.

Not so Bill's horse. He snorted and stomped again.

"No, ain't got time. That's why I slunk in here tonight to get hold of you, Miz Westall. Found Phil Allen awful sick. Somethin' hit him like a stroke just as I rode in the gate. Didn't wanta call the doctor at Thirty-six's. Miz Allen wouldn't like it. But he's gotta have a doctor!"

Willy suddenly realized that Bill had been trying to tell her this all the time.

"Yes, of course," she said. "Bring him to the house. I'll run and shake up the feather bed." She jumped up and darted into the store.

"Thanks! Be there in a jiffy!" he called as he rode off.

Willy rang up Miz Lizzie to get Dr. Jeffers and to call Mrs. Allen to come quickly. She ran the one block home and shook Pat and got him up. He cursed a little for the interruption until he heard the story straight. If Phil Allen was sick they had to do something and do it fast. He grabbed the feather bed and began to shake it.

When a car drove up in front, they both rushed out. It was Captain Toddard's roadster.

Bill jumped down and helped a woman to the ground. One glance told Willy she was Thirty-six.

Pat said, "Howdy, honey. Come on in." He turned to Willy. "Sweetheart, this is Thirty-six."

They all caught hold to lift Phil Allen. He was heavy, but they got him in and on the bed.

Willy gazed at the woman she knew only by her voice. Thirty-six was small, blonde, and pretty. Her sport suit fitted snugly. Her blue eyes, swollen red from weeping, warmed when they saw Willy.

"I had to come, Miz Westall. Bill said you wouldn't mind. I know Phil's going to die. I couldn't let him do it by himself."

Bill turned to Willy helpless, and Willy smiled right back.

"Sure, grab an arm. Bill, you take the other. Begin to rub! It's the heat! Mr. Allen's much too fat!"

Their eyes all met and smiled.

Willy ran back to the store and rang Miss Lizzie.

"Call the Allen ranch and hold up some time," she said.

"What for?" Miss Lizzie asked.

"Complications!"

"Oh! I see!" she said. "I'll get Chico to say the car won't start or something."

When Willy got back to the house, Dr. Jeffers was there. He shook his head. "There's nothing I can do." he whispered to Pat. Phil Allen didn't know a thing. Willy felt glad for that. She sat down. Pat got out the whisky bottle and he and Bill got drunk. The blonde girl leaned against the door and watched. She no longer wept. Her eyes set beadlike in her head.

At last the doctor whispered, "He won't last out the hour. It's his heart. Something's hit him like a brick. There's nothing I can do."

"Let's go out on the porch," Willy said to Pat and Bill. She turned to Thirty-six. "I know you want to be alone."

"Please!" she said.

The doctor followed. They all sat down on the steps. Pat and Bill drank whisky. Dr. Jeffers lit his pipe. Phil Allen's heavy breathing came out to them through the door. Somehow they found it hard to talk. Pat asked Bill a few questions about Pancho Villa. Bill didn't answer. They sat there waiting.

"The very devil's going to walk up and grab Phil's soul and scamper off to hell with it," Pat said.

Willy shivered and went into the kitchen to make coffee.

The streets were very quiet. Bill rolled a cigarette and Pat mopped his brow. When Willy came back, Pat was talking. She set down the pot and darted back into the kitchen, but she couldn't help hearing.

"Finest boy that ever lived," Pat was saying. "Never had a son myself, but I wouldn't have had a better one than Don."

"Yeah!" Bill said.

"He's got no business in this country. I gotta get him out. Judge Woolcott says he's mighty smart. He's gotta have his chance."

"Yeah!" Bill sighed.

"With my gin I'm sure to make a killin' with this European war. Jim Nelson says we might strike oil on the ranch. The first extra cash I get sends Don right off to school. Best thing that ever happened to my girls." Pat's voice trailed.

"Yeah." Bill sighed again.

Willy wiped away some tears. She shut her eyes and tried to straighten out her thinking. When she opened them again, she no longer heard Phil Allen's heavy breathing. It had stopped.

She couldn't stand it. She had to go and see. And she saw something she could never forget. The man lay dead—mouth open, eyes glaring. The lamplight on the dresser shone through Thirty-six's hair. It picked up the yellow and made a certain glimmer like a halo around her head. She looked just like an angel kneeling, her hands clasped together in an attitude of prayer.

Willy led the girl into the parlor and sat her in a chair. The moonlight through the window picked up the light again.

"Like S'rita's," Willy thought. "And she looks as much a child. She's a hussy and I know it, but it doesn't seem to matter. It's like the setting to a story one reads in a book."

Thirty-six began to talk.

"I knew you'd be like this, Miz Westall. I could tell it in your voice. Phil told me all about you, and so did Bill and Judge. The way men love you has made me want to know you. I never dreamed I would. Sending the Judge with the groceries puzzles all the girls; I understand myself. He's our friend, like Bill Lester. I can depend on Bill when I'm in trouble. I always have, it seems. He got there just in time to bring me here to you tonight. Now they'll never know the difference. Will they?" Her eyes were riveted on Willy's. "Not Phil's family? Phil's got children. You make it sound as if he was here when the stroke hit him."

"Sure," Willy said. "Don't you worry."

The girl opened her purse. "That's the way he'd want it. Take this fifty dollars and buy flowers, please, for us. Use your name. Mine won't do, of course. That'll count the girls in. They loved to see Phil come. He was always kind and gay. Nobody ever laughed like Phil." Her eyes looked off into space.

"I'll never forget the first time I heard Phil laugh.

I was just a kid. He came to see my father about a
Brahman bull. He was alone then, riding through the
country buying cattle. That was fifteen years ago—"
She paused a moment. "I've loved him every minute of
my life since then—every one, Miz Westall. If things
had just been different!" Her voice trembled for a
moment.

Willy reached out and took her hand.

"What happened?" Willy asked.

"So much!" the girl answered.

"You didn't marry?"

"No, we couldn't!"

"But you loved him?"

"More than life! But I can't tell you about it; it's his
secret and he's dead."

Willy squeezed her hand. Thirty-six got up.

"I'll go now. Thank you, Miz Westall, and I know
Phil thanks you."

"But can't I help you? You seem so young and—
you couldn't—"

"Yes, I am!" The girl held her eyes on Willy's. "I'm
glad to see you close like this, Miz Westall. Life makes
a lot of patterns. Without Phil I don't know—I'll
never think he's dead although I saw him die."

"Yes, I know," Willy said.

"Do you know what Phil was talkin' about—I
mean when he was struck?"

Willy shook her head.

"About our little son. He died! Phil had a heart, a
real heart. Few people have, you know!" She spoke
almost in a whisper.

The gate squeaked open. Willy knew that somebody
came up on the porch, for Pat was talking very loud.
Then Bill ducked into the parlor. He and Thirty-six
and Willy looked at each other. None of them knew
what to say.

"Don't go!" Willy murmured.

"Got to," Bill whispered back. "Crossed the river to
finish up a job. Gotta do it before daylight catches me
in Mission. Remember, you ain't seen me, ain't even
heard a word."

"Of course. But do you have to go?" Then Willy

heard Mrs. Allen on the porch. Pat kept talking. Thirty-six began to cry. Willy looked at her a moment, then at Bill—helpless, searching. What could she do or say to help or comfort? A sharp pain struck her heart. She clasped her bosom with her hand. Bill's eyes followed. He stood there staring at her hand. He looked so tired and old, dirty, smelly—almost hungry, weak. Tears were swimming in his eyes.

Thirty-six grabbed Willy's hand and kissed it.

Bill grasped the other for just a moment.

"But you'll be back?" Willy said.

"Sure! Now don't you worry." His whisper quavered.

They dashed out the back.

Pearl nickered. Willy listened.

"They climbed through the corral!" she said to herself.

She leaned against the wall and hid her face.

When Pat and Mrs. Allen came in and found her, she jerked up straight. They all sat down and began to talk. Willy told Mrs. Allen how Phil and Pat were planning cotton planting right there in the kitchen when the stroke hit. They both had drunk too much and it was hot.

"Daddy always worked too hard," Mrs. Allen sobbed. "Just worked himself to death for us these dozen years."

"How long have you been married?"

"Twelve years in March and six children. Thank God for them," she said, putting her head on Willy's shoulder so she could cry.

Willy tried to comfort her but it was hard. She couldn't forget the picture she had seen: Thirty-six's haloed hair, her adoration at the last. Fifteen years ago and Mrs. Allen had said twelve. Arithmetic was wrong or something; she couldn't see from the figures but that Thirty-six came first. What was the connection in Phil Allen's heart? What relation between these six children and the ghost of that dead son?

She patted Mrs. Allen's hand. She hoped death had brought Mr. Allen release. She thought of Pepe; of Pablo. She hoped they were all at peace. Maybe death was the answer when one was very tired. Yes, maybe that was it!

When Mr. Allday came to take charge of Phil, Mrs. Allen went home. Pat and Don sat up with the corpse. Willy went to sleep in the kitchen. She dreamed of S'rita riding first on Prince, then she saw her perched on Pepe's saddle, her hair flying in the wind, his dark face lifted in his pride.

She woke up and lay there thinking. It was a picture to remember. She liked to think of Pepe and S'rita as two wild spirits, too wild to hamper—of the day Juan fried Pepe's rooster—of Serena in Pepe's arms—his pained face as he rode in, shot, from Matamoros—the way S'rita lingered near him and rubbed his fevered head—that last night, the frantic burning in his eyes when he said, "Leeve queeck, Madama." In so short a time so much had happened. Pepe gone, Pablo, Bill, the children! They scrambled together and twisted in her heart.

The next morning when Willy called Thirty-six, on the telephone, no answer came.

"They're all moved out," Miss Lizzie said. "Left about four o'clock, I think. At least Thirty-six phoned me then to say good-by."

"Did she say where she was going?"

"No, but she was crying."

Willy sighed. "We'll miss her, won't we, Mizz Lizzie?"

Miss Lizzie's reply sounded offhand, "Yeah, but other red-lighters'll soon be movin' in."

36

The next day Willy hoped for some word from Bill; but none came. About six o'clock Lon Stone walked into the store and asked to speak to her alone.

"I've seen Bill Lester," he started out.

"You have? When?"

"He woke me just before daylight. I'm to tell this to only you and Pat."

"Of course; go on. What happened? What did he want?"

"He asked me to sell his saloon lot and all his land."

"Everything he's got?"

"Yes, that's all he owns. The house is yours."

"Don't do it!" Willy said. "He'll spend it all for guns and have nothing to come back to Mission for."

"No, it's to be put in the bank for Don. You're to send Don off to school. He said he'd never thought about it until Pat spoke of it the other night. Don's little yet, but Bill wants to do it 'before Pat gets a chance,' he said. That part I'm not supposed to tell. There's danger here for boys as well as girls, he says."

Willy heard again Bill's different tones of yeah's.

"He asked me to tell you to do as you think best. Send him with 'Mara and S'rita if that school takes boys. You're to tell folks that you sent him off. People're not to know where Bill is now."

"What time did he see you?" Willy asked.

"Day was just breaking when he left."

"In which direction did he ride?"

"South, straight toward the Gran Geno crossing."

"Was he alone?"

"When I saw him last he was."

"Then he *was* alone!"

"Of course, Miz Westall. Of course he was."

"Then say so!" Her eyes snapped fire.

"I just said it." He looked abashed.

She turned and left him standing in the store and walked on to the back.

"I'll be damned," Lon said as he went on down the street. "Never saw her act like that before. She works too hard. Bill's right. Can't live like she does and not crack up. If Pat'd just let her get ahead and take the money pressure off."

When Willy reached the warehouse, she did a thing she couldn't understand herself. She hid behind some crates. Her heart seemed bursting with all the sorrow in the world. She put her head down on a box and sobbed. If somebody had asked her why she did it, she could not have told—except that Bill had left the country and rubbed out all his tracks. He'd sold his earthly goods for investment in a child. This was the end. The page was turned. She faced another blank.

She knew that she was lonely in the way that she had been as a little girl. It was like that day when they filled in her mother's grave and stacked the flowers all on top. They led her home and told her to be brave. That's what she'd been trying to be ever since. But her mama's bed stayed empty. Willy's hand was never held.

When Emelio found her, she was sobbing, "Mama! Mama!"

The boy fell on his knees beside her. "Madama!" he murmured, and he himself began to weep.

Willy put her arms around his shoulders for a moment; then she blew her nose and got up. They walked together to the front of the store.

"Mees Leezey wants to talk," he said.

Willy went to the telephone.

Miss Lizzie said, "Hung Ted Tolliver across the river. He's swelled up like a bull."

"Hung Ted Tolliver? Who did it? Why across the river?"

"Seems like he was a spy workin' both for the Carrancistas and the Villistas, and they caught him with the goods."

"Which side hung him."

"The Villistas."

Willy caught her breath. Emelio crossed himself. He didn't know why he did it—he just saw Madama's face.

"A Mexkin swum the river and brought the news. His family's goin' over to get the corpse. Say they can't get a coffin big enough, he's so swelled up. Havin' to make one out of boards." Then Miss Lizzie whispered, "Chico told me Bill was there."

"Have you seen Dutch and Duke?" Willy asked.

"No, you send 'em up as soon as they come in."

They both hung up at once.

The next day Phil Allen and Ted Tolliver were buried, and not even William Jennings Bryan could have brought together such a crowd. The Allen family arrived from Amarillo, El Paso, and Fort Worth. The Tollivers swarmed in from all the cattle ranches. Friends came from everywhere; they rode in on horseback, by buckboard, automobile, and train.

Father Michael said the service. Two hearses were sent from Brownsville to carry the coffins to their graves.

Willy kept her word to Thirty-six. She wired Mr. Dubose to send flowers—fifty dollars' worth—from Corpus Christi. They bore no card. Everybody wondered at their beauty, a blanket of red roses without a spray of green.

Among the many visitors was Mr. Dubose himself. When the funeral was over, he dropped by the store. Willy saw him, older, uglier, more pinched in at the middle than he had ever been. But now he was her friend, and that made a difference.

He began to talk in a reminiscent strain. "Can't forget the first time I met you, Miz Westall."

"I can't either, Mr. Dubose. I could have shot you then except I didn't have a cartridge, not one single shell, and hadn't had one for many miles of desert travel."

"Desert travel with those children?"

"Yes, they were my reason for coming."

"You didn't say you needed bullets; you said you wanted credit."

"Yes, and I paid cash."

He wrinkled up his face. "Didn't sleep a wink for nights. Couldn't forget your eyes. Where did you get that money? I've always wondered."

"Would you really like to know? Well, I pawned my engagement ring and a watch in Austin for four hundred dollars. That was it."

He dropped his shoulders. "You should have told me."

"That doesn't matter, Mr. Dubose. Too much has happened since. My wedding ring was stolen. I'm glad the other's gone."

"But I took away your ring!"

"No, you made me prove what was important. You proved yourself my friend."

He waited a moment. "That's what I've wanted." His voice was not steady.

"You've never failed me when I asked a favor."

"Except that once."

"Well, we'll make up for that right now. Find me a school to send my son to."

"Your son?"

"Yes, in a way—Don Lea. He can't spend his whole life climbing windmills to watch towns burn. He won't forget what he sees. This pistol carrying and Texas Ranger Camp is too grown-up for him. He's just a boy."

Mr. Dubose sat down on the pickle barrel and lit his pipe. He was silent for a while. Willy leaned against the counter, waiting. At length he said:

"Of course, we're going to have to fight a war. This submarining can't go on. France and England need our help to win. They're doing everything they can to pull us in. We can't tell how things're going to go down here on the border, Germans've got a mighty inroad across the river with the Carrancistas and Villistas at each other's throats. Maybe that's not good for boys, but if Don was mine I wouldn't move him."

"Why not, Mr. Dubose? With all these soldiers and new ones coming all the time? Besides, he needs an education."

"He gets one every day."

"Of course, with Judge Woolcott! But he hasn't got a home!"

"No. But he rides a horse and loves him like a friend. That's more than he'll ever learn in school." He got up and put on his hat. "I'm looking backward through the years," he said.

When he went out, Willy stomped her foot. Emelio jumped. "How that man can mix me up!" she said.

Don left for Texas Military School the next week. Nobody but Lon Stone and the Westalls knew exactly why. Willy told him he must go; Bill would like it.

Judge Woolcott said yes, he must. Pat took him for a long ride in the delivery wagon, then marched him into the Goldstein Dry Goods store and dressed him up.

Don curried the horses until they staggered on their feet. So much had happened so fast! He couldn't understand it all. He'd promised Bill that he would look out for Mrs. Westall. But Bill went off and had never written to him. Now Judge Westall said he had to go away to school. Judge Westall always knew. But he'd rather live with his old teacher and ride Prince with the soldiers if he had a choice. He told Pearl all about it and she seemed to understand. She shook her head the way she did at the Brush when it went puffing out with grocery orders. Horses had a way of understanding things.

On the day he was to leave Pat went out and found him sitting on the fence. Prince's head was near him on the gate. The pinto jerked up and snorted when Pat approached him. He was Fuego in duplicate. Pat looked for Pepe to stick up his head and greet him. Don swung down, said adiós, and started for the train. Pat went with him; that was all.

Willy saw that somehow that was what they wanted. She told Judge Woolcott. She said that she was busy, and they went on alone.

37

Willy set to thinking what she could do to ease Don's homesickness. She knew if somebody met him at the train in San Antonio he wouldn't feel so strange. Not being certain that Ray Renfro was in town, she considered telegraphing Dr. Farr, but she decided not to do so. Instead, she sent a telegram to the preacher, and then started praying that he would be there to get it. It so happened that he was in town to preach a guest sermon at the church. When he got Willy's telegram, he called Dr. Farr and then went down to meet the train.

Don was very glad to see Ray. Being all night on a Pullman gave one a funny feeling to begin with. Then to step off the train alone in San Antonio was a lot for him to manage all at once. Of course he acted as if it didn't matter, but when he saw the preacher coming toward him, something heavy in his middle disappeared.

He felt shy and very strange in the funny clothes that he was wearing. The collar choked; the shoes gave his feet a droopy feeling—the heels were so low and flat, not like his boot heels. The backs of his legs stretched and pained as he walked along with Ray to the church.

The church was lovely. Don had never seen the like before, big with columns. He sat down in front where Brother Renfro left him. People came in all dressed up. Women had on hats and veils and gloves —funny-looking things to wear! They all looked sort of pasty. Their mouths were painted—not like Miz Westall. You wouldn't want to touch them. He wondered why they did it. The men looked funnier still, all buttoned up like he was at the neck. Judge Westall said that he too must wear that kind of clothes; so he did. What he preferred was boots like Bill's, and spurs, a silk shirt maybe, and a bandanna, and a big wide leather belt.

Don stopped looking about when Brother Renfro came out to preach. He listened. The preacher said a lot about doing unto others; but he looked so sad and downcast a time or two that Don expected him to cry.

When church was over, a man came up and joined them. Brother Renfro introduced him as Dr. Farr. He was tall and square-looking, especially about the chin. His clothes too were buttoned up, but they seemed to hang easy. Don decided he'd try to make his look the same way. He admired the doctor's well-trimmed black hair and little clipped mustache. He was glad that Dr. Farr went with them.

They walked to a place down by the river, to eat.

It was very Mexican and pretty. They sat down and ordered, then started talking. The two men asked Don a lot of questions about the Valley. How did the people get along with so many soldiers in the country? Which town had the most and why?

Don knew the answer to that question. He'd heard everybody talk about it. Judge Westall cursed and raved; so did everybody, now that it had happened. McAllen drilled some wells and had lots of city water. They had twice as many soldiers as any other town. Miz Westall said four times the trade.

Dr. Farr said, "I'll be damned!" and ordered beer.

"It's hard to select in the dark," the preacher said.

"It's that difference I was asking you about," the doctor said. "What makes it? Why can't that woman get ahead? She goes to a brand-new country to settle down, and chooses the wrong spot, it seems."

"But Miz Westall tried to get the wells," Don said.

"Of course, she would! Good God!" The doctor gulped his beer and ordered another glass.

The waiter brought the food and spread it before them. Don started eating. He was too hungry to listen much, but the preacher led off a conversation—something about Wilson being elected President again —Germans kept on submarining—that meant war— William Jennings Bryan's resigning as Secretary of State meant it for sure.

Don perked up and listened then. He knew Mr. Bryan. He asked, "Why?"

"Plain fool!" Dr. Farr replied.

"No," the preacher said. "It's against his principles to fight. He loves peace at heart."

"That's what Bill says about Pancho Villa," Don said. "But Pancho Villa fights like hell."

The doctor laughed and slapped his knee.

The preacher frowned. "He won't now. He's dead, they say."

"Not Pancho Villa?" Don exclaimed.

"That's what the paper says today."

"But Bill's with Pancho. Bill may be killed!" Don's heart beat fast. This couldn't be!

The men looked at each other and pushed back

their plates. The doctor put his hand on Don's shoulder. "Don't get excited, little fellow," he said. "It's just a rumor. Papers don't always get the truth. Probably they'll both show up to tell their stories straight."

"I'm afraid they will!" the preacher said.

Don was relieved when the men suggested that they go now to the school out on the edge of town. He felt unhappy. So many awful things had happened. Bill couldn't be a corpse! He'd seen three already—his mom and his dad, and Mr. Allen. He hoped he'd never have to see another person dead.

The minute Don walked into the school, he liked the Texas Military. Through an open door he saw some bridles. That meant they'd have horses to ride. That was the sort of thing that counted in a school.

He stood at the door watching, as the preacher and the doctor left to go back to town. They were talking. Their heads were very close together. The place was new and strange to him, but he felt less lonely than the two men looked.

That night he wrote Judge Westall a long letter and told him all about the school, the doctor, and the preacher. "Brother Renfro looks so sad," he wrote. "The doctor gets so mad! The school is fine. I've got a horse to drill on, but I know how to drill already. I learned that with the soldiers."

Then he went on to ask Judge Westall to explain the European war. One boy got smart and asked him a lot of questions. He set in to telling him about Bill and Pancho Villa. The boy said, "Why, Pancho Villa's a dirty bandit! I'm talking about the war." Then they had a fight. And please was there any word from Bill? Was Pancho Villa killed? Brother Renfro said it was in the paper.

When Pat got the letter, he received another with it. It was from Ray Renfro. He read them both, handed them to Willy, and then went to the gin.

He had bought new machinery. Murdy people sent the best. It was a big outlay for the season, but with the cotton crop they'd make a killin'. Now with Wilson re-elected they were sure to go to war. That meant big money in cotton futures. He had made the plunge all right. But he'd come out winning. He'd end this Valley struggle—all this pioneering! He'd take his Sweetheart where she ought to be at last. He'd dress her up and bleach her skin and soften up her hands. He'd hire servants by the scores. His little girls and Don would have the best of everything. They'd live in a big house and have a picket fence, a bathroom for everybody, breakfast served in bed.

He looked back through the window and threw a kiss to Willy. Then he walked on down the street.

Willy kissed her fingers to him and kept on with the trade. When it cleared a little, she read Don's letter first. While she was reading, Dutch and Duke rushed in to say good-by.

"Goin' up to Fort Brown!" Duke announced with pride.

"What for?" she asked.

"To enlist in the army," Dutch replied.

"But the border—" Willy suggested.

"Leave that to the soldiers. We wanta go to France."

"France!" Willy gasped.

"Yes, with all this submarining we're bound to get in the fight now. We wanta be the first."

Willy leaned over and propped her elbows on the counter. She needed help for this parting. She had watched Dutch and Duke grow from lank boys to hard men—riding, shooting, keeping order, performing their duty as best they could. Now they were soldiers going off to war. This was different! When they rode in every night and hid guns among her flour sacks, that was like a game they played. Now they were leaving to fight with foreign people against another nation, people white in color but strange in heart and action.

A little shooting across the river, burning, raiding, riding wildly, had never made them hate the Mexicans. After all, they knew and understood them better for the close association, like Bill and Pancho Villa. They had a way among themselves, Americans and Mexicans. They worked and fought together as it came. There were close relations that no fighting could ever sever; geography, weather complications, drought, and flood. Like a family, they fought each other, but together they turned against a common foe.

She studied Dutch and Duke. They sat on the counter smoking cigarettes, but she saw a cold, hard glint of hatred in their eyes. It was the lust of war. It spoke murder in their hearts. Then she thought of Mrs. Weisschmidt and little Guillermita. Mr. Wesschmidt's spying across the river. He brought this curse to Dutch and Duke. And only God knew what it meant to Bill and poor deluded Pancho Villa.

She heard Duke saying, "If Bill comes back—"

She jerked her attention to the moment. "Yes, of course, Duke—if I can help—"

"Tell him we hated to go off and leave him, but we're anxious to get started."

"There're plenty of soldiers." Dutch spoke up as if apologizing for a post deserted.

"Yeah, but that won't answer up to Bill. He left us things to do, but this European war has sorta changed the plan. You'll tell him that, Miz Westall?"

"Of course. He'll understand—if he comes back," she added.

"Yeah—if he does! That's why we decided not to wait. With Pancho Villa dead, he probably won't."

Willy didn't try to answer. There was nothing she could say.

The boys eased off the counter and threw away their cigarettes. Willy walked around and kissed them both good-by.

Emelio came forward to shake their hands. Dutch reached in his pocket, pulled out a pistol and gave it to the boy.

"Here's a pelon for you," he said. "Take extra care of the Señora here. I don't trust these soldiers none."

"Sí, Señor." Emelio smiled and bowed to the Stewarts and to Meeses Westall.

"You must say good-by to Pat," Willy said.

"Sure. We're ridin' by the gin right now."

They all walked toward the door.

Duke reached down and kissed Willy. Dutch followed his example, but he held her very close for a minute. She had to pull away.

As they got on their horses she said, "Write and tell me all about it."

"Sure thing," Duke hollered back. Dutch looked straight ahead.

They rode off toward the gin.

Emelio held out his pistol, smiling. Willy examined it with care. She hoped to hide her eyes. Tears hurt the Mexican boy. She hated them herself. He saw them, though, and trudged back into the store.

She stood there a moment looking at the sun. The same sun, the same wind—but what a difference in her heart! So much had left her. Pepe, Pablo, Bill, Dutch and Duke, 'Mara, S'rita, Don! Now khaki and olive drab subdued the brightness of Valley living. People marched in columns. The faces all were strange. She felt alone and frightened. She reached down into her pocket and took out Ray Renfro's letter. She read it slowly; then she put it back.

Ray wrote about Don's school, about his teachers and his work. They had a cavalry unit and taught the boys how to ride. He thought that was very funny, and so did Don. "Wish they took girls. I'd go get S'rita," he went on to say. "Think I'll go up tomorrow and see how the girls are getting on. Amara writes me often but Serena seldom."

"How like themselves their letters are!" Willy thought.

The telephone rang. "Long distance," Miss Lizzie said. "Brother Renfro's calling you from Belton, Texas."

"My God, hurry!" Willy shouted.

"Hello! Mrs. Westall," Ray said. "I'm here in Belton. You got my letter?"

"Yes, today! What's happened?"

"Nothing. I just came to see the girls. I thought you might come up here to see them."

"What's wrong? Tell me!"

"Don't get excited. It's S'rita. She has a fever. The doctor is a little puzzled. It's nothing really, but you should come."

"Of course! I'll be there tomorrow. Watch her closely! Let nothing happen! Thank you, Brother Renfro. Good-by!"

She hung up the receiver. Her heart almost stopped beating for an instant; then she began to organize. The train would be back from Fordyce very soon. She would go exactly as she was. She called Pat at the gin. She just told him to hurry to the store.

In a minute he was there. When she told him what happened, he went crazy. "Get me on this train!" he shouted. "Put my clothes into the grip! I'll go to the bank! Call Miss Lizzie! Get Sam Logan to hold the train! Wire Brother Renfro to find the best doctor in th' country and send him straight to Belton. God, don't let nothin' happen to my baby!"

Blinded by confusion, he hobbled out onto the street.

Willy knew she had to let him go. She didn't even mention that she had meant to go herself. She ran to the house and threw his clothes into a grip. Miss Lizzie called Fanny and she came to help. Sam Logan held the train. They got Pat on.

"I'll call you the minute I get there, Sweetheart," he shouted as the train pulled out.

"Be sure to get some sleep!" Willy called.

She and Fanny walked home together. "I oughta gone myself," Fanny kept saying to herself.

Willy said, "I meant to go, but Pat was so excited. He would have been sicker than S'rita if I hadn't let him go."

"We oughta all gone!" Fanny said.

"It was so quick! We couldn't think! But Pat's hysterical about S'rita. He always is. Once on the ranch I remember—"

"Yeah, but this may be different. I oughta gone myself!"

Willy tried to calm Fanny's fears by soothing her, but she kept wondering why she had let Pat leave without her.

At six o'clock Ray Renfro called long distance to assure her that Serena was much better. The cough continued but the fever had broken and the rash was not so red. When he told her that he had sent for Dr. Farr, Willy felt relieved.

The next day Pat telephoned, just as he had promised. Miss Lizzie listened so she could report to everybody. The whole town took time off from war activities and soldier entertaining to be concerned about S'rita's strange disease. Pat's voice relieved the tension when it spoke. S'rita's temperature was normal. The rash had disappeared. Dr. Farr said she could come home.

"But why come home?" Willy gasped.

"Because she wants to," Pat shouted.

"But can she stand the trip?"

"Hell, yes. That's what she needs. It's this damn school that's made her sick. She needs to ride a horse an' get some sunshine!"

Willy wasn't sure Pat knew what he was saying. "Do as Dr. Farr decides, then," she said. "Take your time. Don't hurry, please!"

Pat hung up. She forgot to ask about Brother Renfro and Dr. Farr. That night she told Fanny to include wisdom in her prayers. She herself went out to look up at the stars.

Her mind skipped back to the ranch—S'rita starving—water—Pat's frail hold on living! Such things as war and money are so unimportant when you face real trouble. Surely S'rita was not in danger; yet somehow she knew she was.

She couldn't sleep that night. She went out to the corral.

Pearl seemed to be waiting when she came. Prince got up to look for sugar in Willy's hand.

"I'm sure you understand," Willy told the mare. "It's my baby. I'm so worried! I should have gone myself—but Pat had to—and the business! All these soldiers—we need the money for the children and the gin."

Pearl nickered. Willy put her face against the horse's shoulder and wept.

On Saturday Pat brought Serena home. All Mission met them at the train. Willy didn't know which of the

two looked the worst. Both were wrung-dry in body,
so bright in spirit.

"My God, you and Fanny look like you've been
sick," Pat said.

S'rita hugged her mama's neck and whispered,
"Mama, can I ride on Prince?"

Willy held her close a minute, then pushed her back
to look at. S'rita's yellow curls fringed her face. She
wore a dark-blue tam. Her skin seemed transparent,
as if the thing it covered was not flesh. She looked
disembodied, just a flash of spirit maybe. No, the blue
military coat was there, brass-buttoned high up at the
neck. Red gloves and shoes were there, but somehow
S'rita wasn't.

Yet she kept saying, "Mama, can I ride on Prince?"
She spoke loudly but instead of jumping up and down,
she stood still.

"No, baby darling. You'd better go to bed," Willy
said. Then her eyes swept past her mama to the
Negro. "Fanny'll let me, won't you?"

Fanny couldn't answer. She was crying. She picked
S'rita up and hugged her body as if she were a holy
thing to touch.

Pat smiled gladly. "I think you can ride, Sugar. Dr.
Farr says exercise is good, just a little at a time."

He turned to Willy. "He and Brother Renfro
stopped off in San Antone. They'll be down next week,
they said. Couldn't have done without that preacher
and that doctor. He says this is a new disease." Pat
went on talking in a fevered manner as they all
walked to the store.

Willy said to Fanny on the side, "Get them home to
bed. They'll let you do it. Don't let them know I told
you. Pat won't like my butting in, but to me they both
look mighty sick."

The afternoon rush started early. Willy waited on it
in a frenzy. It seemed that every soldier in camp came
to town. She wanted to run up to the house and see
how Fanny had quieted Pat and S'rita.

Just as she was finishing Sergeant Turney's order for
the Thirteenth Cavalry mess, she sensed a crowd gath-

ering out in front. Soldiers waved their hats and shouted. People stopped and looked. When she heard a high voice lilting in the air, she left the Sergeant and hurried to the door.

One glimpse told the story. Pat had beaten Fanny at the draw.

"Baby, darling," Willy screamed, pushing through the crowd.

She saw S'rita galloping up and down the street on Prince, snatching soldiers' hats from the ground as they threw them at her. For one second she let each hat sit upon her head; then she pitched it to its owner and made another run.

Willy dashed out, grabbed Prince by the bridle. She jerked him to a stop.

"Baby, darling! Get straight home to bed!"

S'rita's face flushed almost to bleeding. Her eyes danced wildly in her head.

"No, Mama, no! I promised Papa to ride just to the store. I promised I wouldn't ride nowhere else! I wanta ride, Mama! I wanta ride!"

As Willy pulled S'rita off of Prince, she kicked and fought and screamed, but by the time Willy got her home she had calmed a little.

Now Willy took up the watch herself. She hurried Fanny off for Dr. Jeffers.

The red face did not cool; the wild eyes grew wilder still. When Dr. Jeffers got there, S'rita talked deliriously of Pepe, Fanny, 'Mara, Prince.

Pat was too dazed to function, except to call Dr. Farr in San Antonio and shout at him to catch the next train out. He told him that S'rita had suffered a relapse.

Fanny walked the floor and wrung her hands. Pat sat by the bedside cursing, as tears streamed down his cheeks. He kept saying, "She begged so hard to ride! I wouldn't listen to Fanny. Fanny said she mustn't ride!"

Willy tried to comfort him. "You did exactly right. You had to let her ride. Don't condemn yourself. She'd relapsed already. I saw she wasn't right when she got off the train.

Finally Willy called Dr. Jeffers aside. She asked him to slip something into Pat's coffee to make him sleep. He could stand no such vigil as she knew they faced that night.

Through the long hours the fever mounted. The child's breath shortened; she coughed in spasms. As the sun rose, she choked—and death came for S'rita.

Almost to the minute thunder began to rumble; then rain fell in a torrent. The deluge came as a mighty weeping for S'rita's death; as if in grief to give a back-drop for the hush that fell upon the town.

At two o'clock that afternoon the train came in with Ray Renfro and Dr. Farr aboard. Emelio was there to tell them that Serenita was dead. They went straight to Willy.

"This shouldn't have happened—not to you!" Ray said. Then he went to Pat.

Dr. Farr grasped Willy's hand and held it. He tried to talk, but he couldn't.

"We mustn't question," she said to him. "It's all in God's plan."

"I'll leave now," he replied, "and come back later when it's over."

He caught the train when it came back from Fordyce, and returned to San Antonio.

Amara and Don came home together. They got in the next day at two. 'Mara caught her mama's hand and clung to it. Don went out and stayed with Pearl and Prince.

The day of S'rita's funeral it was raining still. The Valley had never seen the like before. Willy asked Pat if he wanted S'rita sent back to Oklahoma City. He said, "No. She always hated school and cried to come back home. I want her buried here."

But they never could have put S'rita in the ground without morphine to banish Pat into oblivion. "Not in the rain!" he kept saying every day. Yet when a week had passed there was nothing else to do.

The washwoman and her husband pulled up all the weeds in the little Mission cemetery, that spot where Rufus Wright was buried, Ted Tolliver, Phil

Allen, four soldiers, and two old people from Nebraska who died of sunstroke—the spot Bill Lester had shot on the land plat with his pistol.

But the two miles out to the little cleared-out square in the brush was deep in mud, the first real mud the settlers had seen in the Rio Grande Valley.

"The hearse can't get through," Mrs. Randolph said.

"Don't bother about a hearse," Willy said. "Pearl will pull us there."

The little casket was in the delivery wagon. The whole town plus the army camp stood lined up in buggies and buckboards and on horseback.

Ray called Willy to one side and said, "I just can't preach the funeral. I've worked and prayed but the words won't come. I just can't is all, Mrs. Westall!" He tried to avoid her stare, but Willy was too steady.

"Don't worry," she replied. "S'rita doesn't need a funeral sermon. Like a sunbeam she's dissolved in light. She danced between the sky and earth long enough for us to catch her for a while. She's just now slipped our hold is all; so there's nothing left to say."

Ray reached and took Willy by the hand. "How do you do it?" he whispered. "You teach me how to preach! How do you learn these things?"

She looked up at him. "Learn? I haven't learned, Brother Renfro; I've just have to live," she said.

Don drove the delivery wagon and Pearl pulled it through the mud.

The sun shone out in splendor the hour the service came.

Fanny stayed with Pat. "I just can't stand it," she cried. "I'll take a drink of whiskey and watch the Judge."

"Yes, please," Willy said. "Make up some coffee, for people'll be coming by after the funeral's over."

She picked up her Stetson and set it squarely on her head. Amara pulled down her tam with an imitative yank and reached out for her mama's hand. Together they walked out to the gate.

"You're to ride with me," Lon Stone was saying.

"Thanks," Willy said.

She and 'Mara crawled into Lon's buckboard and looked straight ahead.

"Ándele!" Don called out to Pearl.

The procession got into motion and pulled the two miles through the mud to hear S'rita's funeral service at the grave.

Ray Renfro caught Willy's spirit and gave it to the town. His words were simple, few but vital, bright and shining like the sun.

"Like's S'rita's life!" Willy thought as they rode back into town.

Everybody came back by the house.

Don saddled the horses. He and 'Mara took a ride.

"Where is S'rita?" asked Don.

"Just gone, I guess," 'Mara said.

"Gone where?"

Amara shook her head.

"She's not underneath the ground. She hated dirt! She hated dark. She loved things light." The boy wiped away his tears.

Amara knew she had to talk. "I guess we'll have to remember all the things she said." Then she began to cry. "I never hit her back, because I loved her."

Don stopped the horse. They both got off. He put his arms around 'Mara. Together they sobbed out the sorrow for their S'rita who was lost to them.

Willy sent them back to school the next day. Judge Woolcott urged her to. "Get them back to work. Here they will miss S'rita too much. Besides, this town's too thronged with soldiers for children to be running around." He hesitated before he added, "Your hands will be full enough with Pat."

Willy felt better to have the children safe at school, for the town went into another frenzy that afternoon when Weisschmidt was arrested as a spy.

The officers finally caught him at home and took him to Brownsville, to jail.

"No telling what will happen with spies right here in our laps. Ought to tar and feather the dirty scoundrel," everybody said.

"But that blonde German baby needs a father," Pat said to Willy.

She put her arms around him and kissed him. "And that woman needs her lover," Willy said.

38

Ray Renfro arranged to stay in Mission for a while. Somehow he felt he had to.

"How can I help you?" he asked Willy.

"By helping Pat," she said.

Pat's grief went through stages of tears and gloom, then condemnation of himself.

"I was too run down to beget a baby when we got S'rita," he told Willy every day. "Look at 'Mara, she's strong and able to hold out against a blow."

Willy bent every effort to lift his spirit. She forgot herself.

"Yes, Darling! But look at S'rita and all the years of love that she gave us before she went away."

"But where is she?"

Willy couldn't answer except perhaps to see the sun.

She saw Pat's blue eyes fading to that far-off distant stare like the ranch days. She knew that she had to find something to pull him into living, against those golden curls that beckoned.

"Maybe some kind of war work," Ray suggested.

"No, he's used to war work. We've always done it here. Try to interest him in church. Some abiding faith might help. He's got to grasp some purpose. The same thing happened before Bill had him made justice of the peace."

Ray set about his task. "It is a sacred duty to my own soul," he said. "Salvation—purging—purifying; I've got to work it out."

He rode with Pat throughout the country. They looked at crops; prospected on the future, and talked of man and God. Each one confessed his shortcomings to the other—earthly loves, failures and successes, hope for heaven maybe after death. Willy watched them closely. They both looked sick and tired.

But Willy too needed help. Bill could help her; he was the only person who ever had. Bill could look at trouble and find the reason. Somehow he always managed to find the cure—beating, shouting, guarding, hanging, planning, helping—but he found it. Even now the bandit raiding was less frequent. Maybe he had made his way to Pancho Villa as he had said he would.

But Bill must be dead, along with Pancho Villa. If he were living, he'd get news of S'rita's death. If he got news he'd come back, for he knew Pat and what a blow like S'rita's death would do to him. How she did need him! Two weeks ago she'd thought she'd whipped the world. Now it had crashed around her head.

One day Lon Stone came to report. He liked to come despite the news he had to bring. He started off by lining up the Carrancistas and Villistas for a look; then he went to money. The Murdy People were raising hell about Pat's neglect of business. They'd sent all this machinery down and he hadn't paid a cent. The cotton season would open and nothing would be ready to begin. They'd kept their contract; they expected Patrick Westall to keep his. Then Jim Nelson had balled up the cottons futures that he and Pat were gambling on. Pat's cash was gone. He didn't seem to notice or to care. The creditors demanded pay. What step should he, Lon Stone, take next?

Willy didn't know herself. She had paid the funeral bill and Pat's first note on the gin. For the rest she asked Lon to stave off the Murdy people as best he could. Another month of store business would give her a surplus to put into Pat's business.

"But should you?" Lon questioned.

"I've got to! Pat would die without his business."

"But can he pull himself together? The preacher hasn't done much good."

That question she couldn't answer. She had to think

of something new to make him do it. That's what Bill would do.

The telephone rang. Willy answered. It was Miss Lizzie—with the latest news. Weisschmidt had been convicted. At the last minute new evidence was offered that broke down his defense and sent him sliding into prison, lucky not to be condemned to death!

"The dirty crook! They oughta hung him," Lon said.

In a minute it was a chorus in the store, then in the town. People met in groups and mumbled.

"Living on the river, spying on us!"

"A picture of the Kaiser hanging on his wall!"

"Tar and feather the dirty coward!"

"Why should we let his wife keep on living here among us?"

"Bill Lester oughta shot him long ago!"

"Why let German children grow up to fight us when they come of age?"

The talk grew wilder as the day wore on.

About dark Pat limped into the store, his face frowning, his eyes flashing. "Get your hat, Sweetheart, we've got to drive down to the river. The Brush won't run."

The store was crowded, but Willy knew she had to go. She gave Emelio a few directions for the clerks and set her Stetson on her head. She and Pat crawled into the delivery wagon. They galloped Pearl much of the way to the Weisschmidt jacales on the riverbank.

Mrs. Weisschmidt came out to meet them. Her body bulged in front.

Little Guillermita held onto her mama's skirt. The woman's eyes were red from weeping.

"That's the German for you," Pat whispered. "They carry on. If he's hanged, she's goin' to supply another man to take his place."

"Hush, Darling, she'll hear you."

Willy climbed out of the delivery wagon, hitched Pearl, walked up and kissed her friend.

"Just came to eat supper with you all," Pat announced as he picked up Guillermita. The little girl threw her arms around his neck. Pat struggled against tears.

They walked on into the house. Mrs. Weisschmidt excused herself to go into the kitchen.

Pat and Willy took seats and looked around. There hung the Kaiser. Fine tapestry covered the other walls. The rug was deep and soft. Candelabra of intricate design sat on the table. German books and magazines lay everywhere.

"Mighty swell," Pat said.

"They were rich in the old country. The children always loved the rugs."

Mrs. Weisschmidt brought in supper on a silver tray, hand wrought, heavily designed to match the coffeepot. The dishes were the prettiest Willy had ever seen; so were the linen and the knives and forks.

During supper they centered their conversation on the children: what 'Mara wrote, Don's progress at the military school, Guillermita's latest pranks, her pets and loves among the animals and plants. Pat sat there taut, as if he were listening for something.

"She has only de animals as toys." Mrs. Weisschmidt's blue eyes clouded.

"Yes, I know," Willy added quickly. "That's how my children came up on the ranch. They had no friends—but they came through. Judge Woolcott says it is the best training."

When a noise sounded, Pat frowned and jumped up. Willy stopped talking and they all listened. Pearl nickered. They knew horses were trotting through the gate. Mrs. Weisschmidt paled.

"I'll do the talkin'," Pat announced.

They sat there waiting.

In a minute Lon Stone walked in the door. He scowled; his eyes burned hate. When he saw Pat and Willy, he stepped back.

"Well, I'll be damned!" he gasped. "I saw Pearl, but I thought there must be some mistake."

"Come on in and sit down," Pat said. "Who's with you?"

"Some of the boys." He eased into a chair.

Mrs. Weisschmidt froze into a statue, but Willy noticed the heaving of her breast.

Willy got up and poured Lon a cup of coffee and started off a conversation about Dutch and Duke.

Horses stomped outside. Men's voices drifted in. Willy recognized old Colonel Cunningham, bartender Kinney, Tom Jones, and Sam Logan. The others blurred. Pearl nickered again.

After a time Pat said to Lon, "Guess we oughta all go home."

"Yes, Pearl wants to get on back to Prince," Willy added.

"Yeah, we ought."

Lon got up and turned to Mrs. Weisschmidt. Her face seemed more relaxed. A little of her color had come back.

"Rode down to ask you to take the Kaiser off the wall," he said.

"Sure," Pat replied. "We'll wait awhile an' help her do it. You boys go on home."

Willy and Pat stayed until day broke, just in case Lon and his crowd came back.

Pat assured the German woman, "They're just scared. They don't wanta harm you. They didn't know nothin' else to do."

"Won't you come up and stay with us?" Willy asked.

"No!" the woman answered quickly. "I must stay here."

"It's all over now," Pat said. "But mind your business. Don't try no fancy tricks across the river. You're a woman. You've got these children to think of first. War is made for men in all its angles."

He looked Mrs. Weisschmidt very sharply in the eye and she looked just as sharply back. Nobody spoke. Minutes passed.

She said at last. "For tonight I vant to make a geeft."

She disappeared. When she came back she held a parrot on her finger, a large green bird with a very yellow head.

"Guillermita's Papa brought him from Mexico," she said.

Willy held out her finger. The parrot stepped over

on it, then walked up her arm onto her shoulder, and hollered "Cacao" very loud.

Mrs. Weisschmidt smiled. "He iss Mexican and talks good in Spanish. I hope he is a friend to you like you have been to me!" Her blue eyes filled with tears.

Willy reached up and kissed her. Pat slipped a quarter into Guillermita's pocket.

Pat and Willy rode home talking to the parrot. Neither spoke of what he knew to be a fact. Mrs. Weisschmidt had her reasons for staying on the river. But she was a woman. She had one baby, another coming. They all were human. They couldn't let her come to harm.

Pearl jogged along, disgusted no doubt at the antics of human people. They'd kept her hitched up all night away from Prince.

When Willy opened the store next morning, Lon was standing at the door. They greeted each other as if nothing strange had happened.

"Have you heard from Bill Lester?" Lon began.

Willy frowned. "Not a word since he left our house that night. Have you?"

"No, nothing yet. But I got some wind that the last-minute evidence on Weisschmidt was something Bill sent in."

Willy dropped down on the steps. Her impulse was to kneel.

"Are you sick, Miz Westall?" Lon asked. "You look so pale."

"No, just tired. I haven't been to bed."

"Yes, of course." He sat down beside her.

She made herself seem calm. "Where did the news come from?" she asked.

"Don't know that either. May not be so at that. The Federal judge let out that the new evidence came from a personal friend of Pancho Villa, a feller who used to live down here in Mission. He's been in Mexico gettin' up the dope. Ed Lane spoke up and said 'Bill Lester'? 'That's him,' said the judge. That's all I know."

"See what you can find out." She cringed a little.

"Damned shame to keep you up like that. Sorry!" he said. "And thanks a lot!"

She looked him squarely in the eyes. "Don't thank me, thank Pat. I didn't have that kind of sense."

"You mean you thought we had more?"

"Well, yes, I guess that's it. You see she's got a little girl."

"Yes, that makes a difference."

His eyes kept riveted on hers. They added meaning as he talked.

"I hope you can forget," he said at length.

"It never happened!" she replied.

They shook hands and turned their talk to Pat's debt at the bank.

Dr. Jeffers came by. Willy got up and went into the store.

"I've decided to have another baby," she said to him.

"You're very foolish," he replied. "You're too run down and too tired out."

"Am I sick?" she asked.

"Not sick, certainly, but awful tired. You might die in the try."

"Well, I'll take that chance!"

"Remember you've got Amara."

That statement made Willy think. She sat down at her desk to reason for a while. Pat was dying from his grief. He couldn't live without his heart. S'rita took that with her when she went. Not that she and 'Mara didn't count; it was just that S'rita's going put out the light. Fire must be rekindled. Did she have the right to gamble on her own life for 'Mara's future against a baby for Pat's love? Which came first? What was duty? Women and children? Men and love? Money? What?

She was trying to strike a balance when Mrs. Weisschmidt came in the door. Mrs. Randolph was passing. Willy noticed that she turned her back. Guillermita carried a basket in her hand.

The parrot on his perch hollered, "Buenas dias,"

and came climbing down to greet them. Mutt stretched, yawned, and wagged his tail.

"Vat a velcome!" Mrs. Weisschmidt smiled wanly.

"We're always glad to see you." Willy got up and kissed her on the cheek.

At the moment Willy felt sorry for the German woman; then jealousy struck her heart. Mrs. Weisschmidt's big body rounded out in front. Willy knew the hard, heavy pull of such a burden, the instinctive dread of childbirth no matter how you braced yourself against it, especially when you know you'd got to face it by yourself. Yet the baby squirming in her body gave her hope against the future. The prison sentence could not damn Herr Weisschmidt. She had a gift to offer, a creation of her making—life's gift to death, an even balance.

Yes, that was the answer. She had to have a baby. That would give Pat back his life, make S'rita happy to know her place was taken, leave her free to dance the clouds—go back to the world she came from— find Pepe maybe.

She reached down and took Guillermita in her arms. She stroked the child's blonde hair.

Mrs. Weisschmidt's eyes filled with tears. "Guillermita vants to tank you," she said.

Willy kissed her. Certainly a strange pattern but a real one. Thirty-six said this the night Phil Allen died. Life makes a lot of patterns—Mrs. Weisschmidt, Pepe, Fanny, the Torres Mexicans, Emelio, Ted Tolliver, even Bill. All were of different colors, races, breeds, and kinds, yet love and friendship transcended blood and past experience. Trouble binds people into bundles, melts their hearts and makes them one.

She looked at Mrs. Weisschmidt's protruding body. Very soon the baby would be born. "Remember, this time you're to let me know. I want to be there from the start."

"Oh, schure!" Mrs. Weisschmidt turned her head.

Pat came in. He took Guillermita in his arms. Tears kept running down his cheeks.

"Sweetheart, let's give Prince to Guillermita when she's big enough to ride. He's trained to S'rita. It's the only thing I can think of that's good enough for Prince."

Willy reached up and kissed Pat very warmly.

"I didn't have the sense to think of that," she said.

39

Willy set to working for conception as she used to work against it, except that now she had to work almost by herself. Pat rallied very seldom to anything.

Ray Renfro went to her for permission before he asked a revivalist to come to town. "For a flood of exultation to counteract Pat's grief," he said to her.

"Anything you say, Brother Renfro. I can't seem to help much, myself." She blushed a little as she said it.

"Keep on trying," Ray replied.

Then he blushed himself and frowned slightly.

Two days later the revivalist came to Mission. The first night Pat joined the church.

The preacher crooned the invitation as the choir sang "Rock of Ages." When they got to: "From thy side, a healing flood," Pat rose. Everybody turned and looked. Overcome with weakness and emotion, he limped down the aisle.

"Just confess your sins to Jesus and He'll wash them all away!" The evangelist stretched out his hand.

Pat grasped it. "I can't, Preacher, there's too damned many of 'em!" He wept, sinking to the seat.

Ray rushed to his side and put his arm around him.

The choir rose in volume on "Let me hide myself in Thee!"

Tom Jones staggered up and gave his hand. Sam Logan followed, then Colonel Cunningham; on and on they came that night to join the church.

The revivalist looked at Ray and shouted, "Hallelujah!" Before he went to bed he said to Ray: "No need to make this a two-week meeting. We're off to such a start I think the whole town will be converted by Sunday night."

Ray smiled a little. "Yes, you can depend on that. When Pat Westall went up that started things in Mission. Next to Bill Lester, he's the leader in this town."

"Who's Bill Lester?"

"He's a fellow I sometimes wish was dead!" Ray's eyes were set far off somewhere in the distance.

Every night Pat sat on the front seat and listened to the revivalist paint the picture of the golden throne of grace and the angels of God's mercy.

"My little S'rita!" Pat would murmur. "And, by God, I'll join her in heaven."

Every day he took Ray and the revivalist to the soldier camp to preach, and urged all the soldiers to come to church. By Friday they crowded most civilians out.

If Judge Westall sat on the front seat they would go to church too, to please him, for after all he was the best guy in the town. He lent them money, bought them whisky, got them out of jail.

The next Monday, when Pat went to the gin, Ray went with him. They started putting up the new machinery. That night Willy saw his eyes and breathed her thanks to God.

Next day, when Jim Nelson came to town, he and Pat went to the bank together. Late that afternoon Lon Stone came by to explain to Willy what they had done. "It's cotton futures. They've both gone crazy. With this war in Europe anything can happen. Very likely they'll get rich. But they may lose everything they've got. I just wanted you to know."

"The homestead law will leave me the house and lot?" she asked.

"Yes, nothing can touch your homestead no matter what you do."

"Well, let Pat alone. Help him. Lend him money. He's fighting now. We've got to help him win!"

"All right," Lon said. He walked on across to Bingham's Palace without even looking back.

When Willy got home she found Pat writing letters. He usually wrote them at the gin.

"Thought of somethin' extra to tell Don and 'Mara," he explained.

The one thing he never neglected was writing to the children. Every day the letters went. Drunk or sober, sick or well, he had in the past written three letters. Now, as faithfully, he wrote two.

"Went to bed and couldn't sleep," he went on talking. "Decided, Sweetheart, we would take a trip just as soon as cotton closes. Gonna make a pile of money. I've just been countin' up. We'll go by and pick up Don and 'Mara for vacation and go on up to Oklahoma City and see Doc Riley and that new wife he's got—and our little javelina at the Zoo."

"That's fine," Willy said. "You'll enjoy the trip; so will the children? It'll be good for all of you."

"Whatta you mean, you? You're goin' too."

"No, Darling, I'll stay and look after things."

"Like hell you will. You're lookin' tired. We'll stop by San Antone and dress you up. Get you a hat with a plume like you had in Oklahoma City."

Willy laughed. "I wouldn't know how to wear it. I'm too used to my old Stetson."

"Just the same, I'm gonna buy it."

He got up, came over close, and took her in his arms. When she looked up into his face she saw the old Patrick Westall. His blue eyes smoldered and swam around in dreams. His arms around her drew her to him. His body pulsed with life. He kissed her, kept on kissing.

She forgot the years between. They walked down the oleander path. They stood before the preacher in the Baptist church. They were alone together on their wedding night.

"I'll dress you up, my little Sweetheart," he was saying. "And you can wear your diamond ring."

The next day Willy called Ray Renfro to one side to say, "I'm grateful! You've done it! The cotton season and religion will pull him through."

Ray's eyes dissolved again. "No, you've done it. You keep us all together and make us work for you."

"You'll stay with him at the gin?"

"That's my job, not yours," Ray said.

Willy knew he wanted to tell her she had a job to do. Something to that effect was on his face; then a shadow followed. He gripped his watch fob and walked out. She felt sorry for him, but her own plans grew.

She'd have another baby in spite of Dr. Jeffers. She'd hire extra clerks and supervise the store during her last pregnant months. Emelio could take charge. Maybe this time it would be a boy. A son would do for Pat what Don had started—and for herself as well!

She remembered Pat and Bill talking on the porch steps the night Phil Allen died. Pat's words came back, "I never had a son!" Then Bill's labored "Yeah's!" The sighing in his voice! She remembered what Thirty-six had said. Phil Allen's last words were about their son. The night Bill quarreled with Conchita he talked of sons that men should have when they were young. Well, she would try for Pat!

Maybe she'd been very wicked to think only of her little girls. She'd needed money. Yes, money had been the problem. She had to keep them off at school. Then S'rita slipped away almost without warning. Suppose the same thing should happen to Amara! Don! Yes, she must have another baby and have it quickly. She made up her mind to that.

She looked up at the clock on the wall. It had been a Christmas gift from Mr. Dubose. She loved the clock. It marked the days off into hours. She looked up very often to tell the time of day; so now she looked again.

She never forgot the hour.

The hands pointed to four and twelve. At four o'clock the rush of the afternoon began.

Willy saw Pat driving by in the delivery wagon. He waved at her, and pointed south. She knew he was going to the gin. As she went on waiting on the customers, she felt comforted a lot. She had to keep her eye on Pat these days. It was the way she had always felt about S'rita: a little uncertain, trembling on the brink of something. She had noticed that, recently, he stayed close enough for her to watch him. Since S'rita's death he never used the Brush. He left that for Emelio and the groceries. Willy knew that he had made a point of driving Pearl by for her to see him.

Pat, driving down the street, was thinking about Willy. Never had he been able to be close enough to his Sweetheart to suit him. She was too busy and he'd spent too much time in the saloon; that thought drove him crazy. All those hours he could have been in the store close to Willy! A man ought to know what's important to him and never let it down.

"Pearl, you've been steady on your job," he said out loud, just as they crossed the railroad track and turned left on the side road to the gin.

Some hint of noise or motion made Pat turn his head. In that instant he saw a whirlwind of dust coming up Mexiquita Street—a horse and buggy tearing in his direction. He heard a scream. Pearl stopped dead in her tracks. Pat squinted his eyes shut, and looked again. "My God!" he shouted. "It's Miz Weisschmidt and Guillermita!"

The buggy was now almost at the turn of the road. Pat jerked up the reins and Pearl, turning, wheeled the delivery wagon in a circle, and started forward. Pat stood up and shouted: "Catch 'em, girl! We've got to!"

Pearl, in a burst of speed, caught up with the frightened horse. Pat was swaying back and forth.

"Just hold the reins, Miz Weisschmidt! I'll catch his bridle," he yelled.

The horses were racing neck to neck, then Pearl drew ahead, and Pat reached over to grab the bridle.

"Don't fall!" Mrs. Weisschmidt screamed. Pat seized the bridle, but he lost his footing and headed over. His hand caught in the choke strap, he fought to pull it loose but couldn't. Pearl stopped, but the frightened horse kept on running, dragging Pat along the street. The flying hoofs struck his chest and stomach as his arm jerked his helpless body back and forth.

In front of the bank Ray Renfro stopped the exhausted horse and picked up Pat. Dr. Jeffers and a crowd ran out to help him, and to lift down Mrs. Weisschmidt and the little girl.

Willy heard the noise down the street and started out the front door to see what was happening. The telephone rang with such insistence that she went back to answer it. Miss Lizzie said very firmly: "Go home at once, Miz Westall. Go out the back way and run. Get the bed ready and put some water on the stove. The Judge's been hurt."

Willy didn't answer; she just hung up. She felt as clear and cool as ice, and just as chilled.

"Judge Westall's hurt," she said to Emelio. He saw her face and shivered.

She ran out the back door and was at the house, with water on the stove, when Dr. Jeffers' Ford rattled to a stop. Ray and the doctor lifted Pat out in their arms. Willy ran to help.

Pat's shirt was bloody and torn, one arm dangled. His eyes were closed.

"My God! Is he dead?" Willy asked.

"No, just doped," Ray answered.

Nobody spoke again until they got Pat into bed.

When Dr. Jeffers stepped into the kitchen, Willy turned to Ray.

"Tell me what happened," she said.

"Horse was running away with Mrs. Weisschmidt and Guillermita. He tried to stop it and lost his balance."

"And Mrs. Weisschmidt?"

"Took her to Fanny's. She's pretty shaken."

"Yes, of course— She's going to have a baby." Then she looked up at Ray and said, "Tell me, did Pat suffer?"

"It was his chest the most."

"What did the doctor say?"

"Nothing yet. They just gave him dope. That's what makes the heavy breathing."

"Yes, I know. I heard Phil Allen!" The scene came back in a flash, the same in essence, differing only in design. She dropped down beside the bed and turned to Ray. "Won't you pray?" she asked.

"I am praying," he murmured.

They both were silent.

Dr. Jeffers stepped back into the room.

"Tell me the truth," Willy said.

"He hasn't got a chance," Dr. Jeffers said. "I couldn't lie to you, Miz Westall."

"He's not in pain?"

"No, not at all. He'll just breathe out as he is."

But an hour later Pat's eyes opened. Willy held him in her arms. The setting sun streaked the pillow. Ray, the doctor, and Father Michael sat beside his bed.

Pat murmured, "Where's Bill?"

"He'll be here soon." Somehow Willy made her voice seem steady. She made her face break into a smile.

"The horse?"

"Brother Renfro caught the horse!"

Pat frowned. "And Pearl?"

"She's all right." She wiped his brow. "Where do you hurt, Darling?" she asked.

"It's so dark!" he answered.

Willy looked at Dr. Jeffers.

He shook his head. "Let him talk," he said.

"When Bill comes, tell him—" Pat wondered off a minute. "Tell him I wanta see him."

"Bill'll be here any minute!" Willy stroked his hair.

He smiled in her direction. She could tell he couldn't see her.

"It's the head wound," Dr. Jeffers whispered.

"Who's that talkin'?" Pat asked plainly.

"Dr. Jeffers, Darling. He came to help us. You tried to catch a runaway."

"Was that what happened?"

"Yes, but you're all right. Don't you want to shut your eyes and try to sleep?"

"I wanta shoot that damned horse. Turn on the light!" he said.

"No, Darling, we can't!" Her voice trembled. "Please try to go to sleep."

"Not time to sleep," he said. "I've got a lot to do. Help me up. I've got to get to the gin."

"Not now, Darling. You stay here. Brother Renfro's taking care of all the cotton. You just lie and rest."

He said, "Yeah, he will. That preacher's a fine fellow, Sweetheart. I've talked a lot to him.

Ray Renfro's eyes began to swim. He bit his lips but tears came rolling.

Dr. Jeffers blew his nose. Father Michael bowed his head.

"Pepe's a good Mexkin, Sweetheart. He didn't mean to do no wrong."

"Of course not, Darling. Now don't you worry. Close your eyes and try to sleep."

"Bill'll take care of things."

"Yes, Bill will."

Ray got up and left the room.

Pat raised his hand a little and began to reach out for something. Willy grabbed it. He smiled and relaxed his shoulders.

"I'm gonna die," he said.

"No, no! Just be quiet and try to rest. You're going to be all right."

All at once his eyes brightened. Willy looked at Dr. Jeffers. The old doctor shook his head. Pat's voice was firm.

"Don't worry, Sweetheart. It's all right. In time we all have to die. People come in two's and two's. S'rita's gone and left me. I knew I had to follow. You an' 'Mara'll come in time. Pepe an' Pablo! Bill an' Pancho. We just do the best we can."

"Yes, Darling!" Willy murmured.

"Things're in an awful mess. I hate to leave you— you'll take care of Don and 'Mara." He gripped her hand. Willy couldn't keep her tears from dropping. They splashed against his face.

"You've got on your rings, Sweetheart?" he said.

"Yes, of course," she whispered.

"I wanted you to wear diamonds in your hair. I wanted you to wear fine clothes. I wanted the world to stand in line to see you." His voice began to quaver. "But somehow I never could!"

"But you have, Darling. You've given me your love. Nothing counts but that."

She hugged him to her. He was comforted by her arms.

"You an' 'Mara'll make it, won't you, Sweetheart? Bill'll help you."

"Of course we will. And so will you!"

"Yeah, me and S'rita. We'll make it."

He looked up at her. She knew he saw her. She managed to smile down.

"In another country—a good country. There'll be servants, plenty of servants—white tablecloths—no damn cactus—plenty of water."

"Yes, yes, of course!" She held him tighter.

Suddenly he pulled back and sat up straight. His blue eyes shone like clear glass beads. He focused them first on Father Michael, next on Dr. Jeffers; then he turned to Willy.

"No hearse!" he exclaimed. "I want Pearl to pull me to the cemetery just like S'rita. We're travelin' West. It takes a heart to do it! The sunshine an'—the light!"

His face twitched, contorted; blood oozed from his mouth.

Willy clasped him to her.

His body twisted; he gurgled, and fell back dead.

When the undertaker came, Willy went outside. The curb was full of people, waiting. Automobiles, buggies, buckboards, wagons, horses lined the streets.

"People who have come to offer help," Ray told her.

"Then I'll go out and see them. There're too many to come in."

The whole town had congregated: old friends of credit days, news friends of war boom—Mexicans, soldiers, women, men, and children. Willy went down the line and spoke to everybody.

The little Peña girl handed her some jasmines; the washwoman brought three eggs. Miss Lizzie rushed up with a funeral wreath of Ponderosa lemon blossoms, to tack on the door. Mrs. Randolph made her drink some French drip coffee she had brought in a chafing dish. Mrs. Allen threw her arms around her neck and kissed her. Lon Stone gripped her hand.

"What can we do?" each one said.

"Nothing, thank you. Just go on home. It's over now. Pat's dead."

But nobody listened.

"She would stay with us," reverberated down the curb.

That night in the house she was alone with Pat. It was the last page in their book. She wanted to read it by herself.

Through the hours she thought of many things, but most of all of the quiet peace on Patrick Westall's face.

His was a life of vivid contrasts, of downs and ups and outs, all bound together by love of men and God. The way he lived was a religion that knows no bound or creed, but writes itself in human lives and gives man peace in death.

"I'm jealous, Pat, plain jealous!" she told him many times that night. "I'm jealous of your rest and all your work complete. Just yesterday I planned for birth; now I wish for death. I'd like to even up the deal and go go with you and try that other side. After all, I'm tired! Tired!"

"And where is the other side?" she asked herself.

The next few hours she tried to figure out where Pat and S'rita were.

At last it came to her: they lived in her; in the wholeness they had given her, in the love they made her know. And she had Amara left.

Thirty-six came back in vivid clearness watching Phil Allen die. They both had prayed to the same God to save the men they loved; thus they were sisters in a purpose. In the last test there seemed no difference except that Willy had Amara. Thirty-six's son was dead.

"But we had our loves," she reasoned.

By the power of the love that bred it to begin with! Like that cactus on the desert that kept on living by the power within itself! Death couldn't stop it anymore than cutting cactus. Pile it up; it keeps on growing. Darkness can't put out the light nor a coffin shut it up. You can't blot out a sunbeam; it is the light itself.

Thus Willy thought through the night as Pat drifted into the big design of love.

40

In the early morning, when Fanny came, Willy put her head on the Negro's breast and cried. Fanny held her tight.

"Miz Weisschmidt had the baby," Fanny said. "Dr. Jeffer's got there just in time. A little boy, named Hans. She sent her love to you and to Pearl."

Willy straighted up and blew her nose, and they went out to the corral to feed the horses.

Neither said anything for a long time. Prince came close to nuzzle Willy's neck as she filled his morral.

"He knows that somethin's wrong. He's smart, like Fuego," Fanny said.

"Yes, Pepe knew good horses and a lot of other things, I guess," Willy said. She was silent for a moment; then she said, "And so Mrs. Weisschmidt has a son."

"Yeah," Fanny said, looking off into the distance.

"Well, we'll give Prince to Hans and Guillermita." Pearl stomped and nickered.

Willy walked over and put her arms around the mare's neck. "I don't blame you," she said. "You don't want to give away your son." She bit her lip a minute. "But we have to give away our sons, it seems —wars, crosses, death, money struggles—we always give away our sons."

Fanny put her hand in Willy's and they went back into the house.

Don and 'Mara came in on the train that day. Willy and Ray Renfro went to meet them. It had been a long, sad journey for the children. Miss Lizzie had telegraphed each of them: "Come home at once. Judge Westall's dead."

When they met at the depot in San Antonio, each asked the other what had happened. "Did somebody

shoot Papa?" Amara questioned. "His letter yesterday
was so very happy. He told me we were going to make
a trip to Oklahoma City."

"If somebody did, I'm goin' home to kill him!" Don
replied.

Don didn't talk much after that. He went to bed
early on the train so he wouldn't have to talk. In all
the world it was Judge Westall he loved most. 'Mara
had her mama. All the boys at school had parents.
Bill Lester'd been a partner, and he went off and
never wrote a line. But Judge Westall wrote him every
day. He was the one who cared about football, hunting, riding, all the things a fellow cares about himself.
He was the one who took him on long rides to talk
over things they never mentioned to anybody else.

Once the dean called him in to question him about
an escapade the boys had gone on.

"But I didn't go," he said.

"That's what I want to know. Why did you refuse?"
the dean asked.

"Because Judge Westall told me not to do a thing
like that."

"Who's Judge Westall?" asked the dean.

"The finest feller that ever lived," Don replied.

And that's the way Don felt.

How he could live without Judge Westall's kindness
and intimate concern Don didn't know. He loved
Judge Woolcott too, but he was different. It was only
about lessons he ever talked or wrote.

That's why Don went to bed early. He cried himself to sleep that night.

Amara didn't cry. She simply couldn't figure out
what had happened. S'rita dead, now Papa! Dead was
such an awful way to be. She looked at S'rita lying
there in white. She seemed asleep, but she touched
her. She shivered yet when she thought of it. S'rita
felt cold and hard like marble. She grabbed her mama's hand and held it tight. It was warm and rough
and—well, just mama's hand was all. She went to
sleep thinking of Mama's hand. Mama wouldn't be
dead when she got back to Mission.

The next morning Don and 'Mara got off the train

for breakfast at Kingsville. Amara's eyes were frightened.

"Don, I'm scared. I dreamed of S'rita. She was ridin' on a horse. Did you dream last night?"

"Yeah, I dreamed Judge Westall was gallopin' west toward Fordyce just at sundown. I hollered, but he didn't see me. The sun was in his eyes. S'rita was with him. They was ridin' fast as hell."

Pat's funeral was just as he would have wanted it. All his friends were there to do him honor. People came from everywhere. In his *Harpoon,* K-Lamity Bonner wrote a special tribute to Patrick Westall, his host for Valley hunting. Other hunting friends read it and sent telegrams and flowers, even William Jennings Bryan. Floral offerings arrived by train and wagon and on horseback. A blanket of orchids and gardenias came from San Antonio. Willy gasped when she saw it. The card read: "Frieda Weisschmidt and her children, to Patrick Westall." "She ordered that from San Antonio!" Willy said.

But no less heartfelt was the washwoman's wreath of bachelors-buttons, the jasmines and crepe myrtle that came by handful, and the cactus flowers, from Pat's Mexican friends—old crippled fellows, widows, children, even families whom he had helped in secret.

The Mexicans came and stood close to the house and waited. They didn't know the custom of the Americanos, but they wanted to be near.

"No wonder I love Mexicans," Willy said to Ray when she went out to shake their hands. "It's their hearts inside that are so right. I'm glad I've been able to know them as I have."

The funeral was announced for four o'clock on Sunday, at the church. By two the crowd began to gather. Jesse Parnell and three other Texas Rangers rode in from Rio Grande. Jim Nelson brought along the Torres Mexicans from the ranch. They rattled in in their new Ford. Benito had grown mature and fat; old Cepriano, old and shriveled—both sorely grieved at their amigo Americano's death.

Navasota was visiting at Fort Sam Houston in San

Antonio. When she read the *Harpoon,* she caught the Valley train. Mr. Conlay was aboard. Father Michael's message had reached him in St. Louis. He welcomed the excuse to see the beloved Valley of his dreams, and Mrs. Westall and Amara.

Mrs. Allen rushed in. "The church'll never hold the crowd," she said. "These old friends'll be disappointed if they don't get in."

"Then we'll go straight to the cemetery as we did for S'rita. There'll be no crowding there. Pat hated cramping, just wouldn't have it if he could help it."

Don had spent the morning currying and brushing Pearl, to make her shine. It was a perfect day, hot and bright and clear. Willy ambled out to the corral. The loneliness of the boy's face rebuked her.

"Can I drive the delivery wagon, Miz Westall?" he brushed with all his might.

"Yes, of course. I know Pat would like to have you drive him just as you did S'rita."

"He was my friend," Don said. He turned his head away.

"Yes, he was! Will you let me take his place?" She tried to make the statement like a business proposition so the boy would listen. He didn't answer.

"I'm not so good at letter writing as Pat was, but I'll try to make up the difference to you and 'Mara. In fact, Pat asked me to, just as he was dying."

Don turned quickly. "Did he?" His eyes lighted.

"Yes, he asked me to tell you to take care of me and 'Mara."

"Oh, sure!" Don blurted.

As Willy walked into the house she heard him whistle.

When Don pulled Pearl to a stop at Pat's grave, the last of the procession was just leaving town.

The two miles stretched out with conveyances of every kind—horses, wagons, automobiles, buckboards. Many Mexicans walked. The two hearses from McAllen and Mercedes carried only flowers. The two combat wagons from the army camp were packed with soldiers. Officers drove their cars. Father Michael brought up the rear on Prince.

The old priest said, "I know Prince wants to be there."

Of all the thoughtfulness people offered, Willy appreciated Father Michael's in a special sort of way—maybe because it concerned her horse.

Had she been asked to choose a man to preach Pat's funeral sermon, she would have said Father Michael. Pat's friendship with the priest was deep-rooted, long and strong. He belonged to the Valley. But Pat had made his choice.

"I'm to preach the funeral," Ray said to Willy. "Pat told me what to say."

"When?" she asked.

"Right after S'rita's death. You'll let me?" His face pleaded.

"Of course, Brother Renfro. I'm so glad you both made the plan."

The time between Pat's death and burial had been torture to the preacher. He had prayed for grace and wisdom and strength to sustain himself when time came to say the service. He looked out on the eager faces at the graveyard and knew he was expected to say something worthy of his charge. To transpose Patrick Westall's soul into words was his obligation. He knew he must fall short. He could repeat Pat's message, but that was not enough. He'd found greatness in the man he represented. He would like to pass it on. There stood 'Mara, Don, and Willy. The town was waiting—even Pearl and Prince.

He knew the outline of his sermon, but his heart raised such a furor. Suddenly the cemetery blurred. Instead of the open grave before him, the flowers, the good earth, he saw himself standing in the pool hall where he preached first in Mission. He heard the Mexican band coming down the street. He saw Pat hobbling down the aisle on crutches. The band blared forth again. Pat scampered, waving crutches, cursing! Bill Lester spoke, "Let's all go get a drink." Two brown eyes came forward. They were Willy Westall's.

That was what bothered him. They taunted, lured him, followed him.

He opened his Bible at the passage he had marked. He couldn't read the print. It was dim and clouded. He tried to concentrate, but circles focused into two eyes, brown and shining. His hands were trembling. In a minute he would fall.

"Shall we sing?" a voice said.

He looked straight ahead of him at Willy. She was holding on to Pearl.

"Rock of Ages," the voice said. It was his voice.

Mrs. Randolph coughed, tried to speak.

"Rock of Ages," he said again. The song began.

He didn't know when it ended, but all was quiet. They were waiting.

"Patrick Westall was my friend!" He hardly knew he spoke. All he did was watch Pearl. The words kept coming.

"I wish I could have been a friend to him. But I couldn't touch him—mortal flesh could never house two men of such proportions. Pat Westall was pure heart. You may have misjudged him as you saw him. You didn't know him as I did. Forgiveness is a virtue few mortals ever learn. Patrick Westall could forgive. I gave him such a test as no man stands, but he stood it—came through on heart."

"Hallelujah!" somebody cried.

Then Ray knew he himself did the speaking. He knew it because the voice was shaking. He didn't try to read his sermon. He tried to tell them—about Pat. Then he said: "Patrick Westall left this message. 'There's only one way to live, and that's to love. Other things're pale and stupid. Fill your lives with love. Mine's been full and brimming. I hope you find my peace.' Those are Patrick Westall's words." He saw tears splash on the Bible. He coughed.

"Rock of Ages," somebody said.

Voices sang. Many voices. Maybe all the angels sang.

That was all Ray Renfro could remember of what had happened at Pat's funeral. When he could think, he was on a freight train. It was night. The train had stopped. He jumped off and walked up to the station. "What's this town?" he asked the agent.

"Kingsville," the man replied.

"Let me send a telegram," he said. With quiet deliberation he wrote out on the blank:

Mrs. Patrick Westall, Mission, Texas.

Had to leave on too quick notice. Knew you were busy with old friends. Have made arrangements to join the army. They promised I could go abroad. Want to clear my brain of cobwebs. Your forgiveness if you can.

Ray Renfro

Willy got the message before she went to bed. Sam Logan brought it over with a lot of others. He sat down to talk. Tom Jones, Lon Stone, and Mrs. Randolph were there.

"Best funeral I ever heard," Sam began.

"So eloquent," Mrs. Randolph said. "I never dreamed that little preacher had it in him, and how broken up he was!"

"Too long was all." Tom said. "Pat liked short, quick service in anything, from drinking whisky to preaching funerals. The preacher drug it out too much."

"I don't think he knew how long he talked," Mrs. Randolph said. "He looked so white and scared."

"But the words kept coming'," Sam said. "God, how he did talk, cryin' as he was!"

"Yes, Pat was pleased, I know," Willy said. "He loved grace and form and feeling."

"I wonder why he announced 'Rock of Ages' twice?" Mrs. Randolph asked. "I had 'Nearer My God to Thee' put down to start with."

"Pat's request, I'm sure," Willy said. "He'd told him what he wanted done. 'Rock of Ages' was Pat's favorite hymn."

41

A week later Willy was sitting at her desk. She was alone. All the stores were closed for the afternoon so the people could attend the rodeo at the park. Everybody went, soldiers and civilians. Even Emelio ventured over to take his mother and his girl. They had come in from the ranch. Not a soul was on the streets. It was hot and sultry; not a breath of air was stirring. Willy got up to open the front door. She looked out for Don and 'Mara. They had gone to ride. A glance at the clock told her it was five. She would work an hour, then go for supper. Fanny promised enchiladas. She wasn't hungry—certainly not for garlic-chili mixtures—but she would eat. Don and 'Mara liked the Mexican dishes. Soon they would go back to school.

She started working with the mail. The one letter she always looked for never came, but she kept on looking. If Bill were living, some day she would hear. She opened two letters that made her think. The third one was a check. One of the two was from Oklahoma City. Dr. Riley announced a birth, the son of his old age, "named Patrick Westall Riley for my best friend on earth, with eyes as blue as his. My wife is very fair," he noted later on the pages.

"I'm glad of that," Willy said to herself, and tore the letter up. "Mustn't keep a lot of things to clutter up my desk. Just keep facts in your heart is best."

But as she pushed back her blotter and her pen, she touched a little box. When she opened the lid, she saw two cartridges grown green with time—"and tears," she thought. She pushed it to the farthest end of the most secret drawer and locked it with a key.

She straightened up and began again. "Well, let's see what's next."

The second letter was from Corpus Christi. It was

engraved Scott and Kidd. Willy paled a little as she read. Scott and Kidd were lawyers. They wrote to tell her that Mr. Dubose was dead. In his will he had left a stickpin to Mrs. Patrick Westall. It held a diamond of two carats, something of his family's, very old, French, from New Orleans. In addition there was money for its setting in a ring. What disposition did Mrs. Westall wish? Could the work be done in Mission? Or should they send designs to choose from and have the ring made up in Corpus Christi? It was the last thing Mr. Dubose spoke of to Mr. Kidd. He died of stomach cancer. He had known he had it but told nobody, not even at the end. He kept on working, went home one night and died the next day at ten.

Mutt barked. He chased a rat across the floor. The parrot on his perch squawked, "Cómo no?"

"Mutt, don't do that! She's got mice!" Willy scolded. "You don't kill the mother."

Then she leaned back in her chair to wonder why she spared the nest of pink things underneath her desk. "Getting queer, I guess," she said at last. "But somehow I can't kill baby mice; they belong to the whole scheme of life. I've seen too much to say, '*You* can live but *you* must die! *I'*ll do this or *I'*ll do that!' For whom am I to say? Life gives the answers yet."

She looked up. Lon Stone was coming in the door. She rose to meet him.

"Glad I found you by yourself," he said.

They shook hands as always. Willy sat down again. He dropped in the chair beside her.

"I thought you might be by yourself. That's why I came by."

"Always glad to see you," Willy said. "Just trying to get some book-work done myself."

Lon smiled; then he frowned as if something hurt him. Suddenly he undid his collar.

"Too dressed up today." He laughed.

"It's not worth your comfort, is it? You Yankees have to come around to our Texas way of living."

Lon lolled back in the chair, but his neck muscles

tightened. Willy sensed great tension in the man before her. He looked boyish, almost in confusion.

"Can I help you, Lon?" she said.

"Yes, by hearing what I have to say."

He leaned forward, began to gesture.

"Pat owes a lot of money," he began. "He's all mixed up in these cotton futures with Jim Nelson. They've bungled. I can't say yet what's been lost."

"Yes, Jim was in to see me."

"Said he might strike oil?"

"Yes, of course. Poor fellow's boots were threadbare, but I'm glad he still has hopes."

"His kind always have, I've noticed; but they never pay the mortgage on their land."

Willy straightened up to listen.

"But they dream dreams. We have to have them."

"Just a gamble! That's all it is."

"So is life—grapefruit, cattle, the grocery business —you have to run your chances. Even in war. It's all a gamble."

"But the families have to suffer."

"Yes, but we have their dreams and visions. Arithmetic alone is killing."

"Yes, but so are debts. I can't stand to see it. I'm getting gray now, watching." He tried to laugh a little, but he didn't.

"Now see here, Mrs. Westall, listen! The Murdy people will come through on the gin. I can handle them. This cotton will take time. But it'll ruin you. You can't pay it. You've got tuition for Amara, taxes —and God, they're rising—all this improvement in the Valley. You can't do it on just a grocery business."

Willy's eyes began to sharpen. "But I must try," she said.

Lon's face reddened. "But that's not the half," he said. "This war is getting serious. Anything can happen!"

"But the raiding's stopped almost altogether!"

"Yes, but that's not the question. I mean the war in Europe."

"Do you think we'll have to fight?"

"For certain! Things can't go on as they are.

They've told us they'll submarine our boats if we ship to France and England. What can we expect?"

"But here on the border?"

"That's the danger! We may have to leave the Valley. This little bandit raiding is B-B fighting to what we're in for. Too many Germans across the river and their start's too good down there."

"You mean they might attack through Mexico if we go to war?"

"They can land in Vera Cruz and charge this border from Brownsville to El Paso without trouble."

"But Carranza's elected President of Mexico. He's declared them neutral."

"But there'll be trouble, Pancho Villa's on the loose and it's their business to make trouble."

"They say Villa's dead. That's why the raiding stopped here on the border."

"It's not that simple. It's stopped to get ready for a bigger deal."

"What do you mean, Lon?"

"The world, Mrs. Westall, is in an awful mess. Russia collapses. We're all huddled up together. We can't let France and England down. But the other side's just as sharp as we are. They use Mexico against us."

"How serious is it, really?"

"Well, they're using our own lines to talk down to Mexico to make a deal."

"What kind of deal?"

"That's what all this Zimmerman Note stir is about. As courtesy we lent them our lines. The English got wind and intercepted. Found out they're offering Texas back to Mexico if she will fight us, and a big slice of something to Japan!"

"Why, the double-crossing scoundrels! That can't happen!"

"That's what I'm telling you, Mrs. Westall. We'll probably have to leave the country. The Valley'll be a no-man's land, like France. That's why I've come to you so soon. I want to get your business straightened out so you can pick up in a hurry."

"Well, what must I do?"

"Get your business in order and that right quickly. Maybe the bankrupt law would do it best!"

Willy's face flared red. "No Westall skips his debts, Lon! When we burned, Pat wouldn't take the bankrupt law, remember?"

Lon got up and began to pace across the floor.

"Of course, Mrs Westall, I understand. That's why I'm here. That cotton crowd're tryin' to skin you because you're honest."

He turned quickly, faced her squarely. "Let me help you!" he said flatly.

"Of course, I know you will."

He came close and leaned over. His thick hair struggled on his forehead. His eyes bulged a little. "I mean really help you! You've got Amara. Then there's Don. Bill's money won't last long. I know what you'll do—just like Bill. You've slaved and worked too long. I came just to offer so you won't worry when these creditors begin to batter and the war begins—" He began to splutter. "But we must educate these children. I've never had a child myself and you must stop this work and rest!"

He leaned over closer. Willy kept on looking but recoiled a little.

"I never knew why I came to Mission. Now I do. When my wife died I left Chicago and came down for the climate, as I thought. Now I know better. I just want to offer, for I know the pressure you're going to get."

Willy looked straight at him.

"I'm grateful," she said firmly. "Deeply grateful. I'll need to borrow some money maybe; that is all."

Lon stepped back.

"I understand," he said. "Really understand," he repeated. "I had to offer quickly. Just know I'm here in case of trouble."

Willy put out her hand. He shook it and turned and left the store.

She sat down in her chair and opened the third letter on the stack. She did it quickly to keep from thinking.

She noted it was perfumed, and the monogram was engraved. The postmark was New York. When she unfolded the heavy paper, a bill fell out, fifty dollars, U. S. money.

She began to read. Written in a bold broad hand it said:

Dear Mrs. Westall,

News just reached me of Judge Westall's death. I wish I could say something that might help. I understand is all I know to say. You know I understand, for you saw me watch Phil Allen die. God help you. It's not easy by yourself.

P.S. The money is for flowers to decorate the grave.

Willy leaned back in her chair again. She was thinking backward through the years, across and forward.

"I'll put the money toward the tombstone," she finally said. "I'll buy a tombstone first before I count up the cotton debts. I'll pay for it as best I can. There has to be a Westall tombstone. Pat wouldn't like to be left unnoticed in the chaparral. War or no war—it must be there for Pat and S'rita."

Her eyes filled up with tears.

"I want a gray tombstone—granite—no dates—just Westall across the top." She picked up a pencil and drew a small design.

"No, maybe it ought to read: 'The Lower Rio Grande Valley.' It'll stand there for us all—Pat, S'rita, Pablo, Ted Tolliver, Mr. Dubose, Phil Allen, Fuego, Chiquita, Bill—and all the others of us when we die; the folks who came first and made the country. If soldiers march through, they can see it as they pass our Valley."

She thought a minute. "No, not in granite. That Valley monument is dirt soaked up in blood, the people who started out from scratch in a delta desert waiting for the hand of man to bless it with a drink. Some got here first to start it. Others came and went. Some made contributions. Others stole what they could get. But it takes them all to make it, good and in-between, I guess."

"Cómo no?" the parrot chirped.

Willy looked at the clock. "Thanks for the interruption. I've got to pay some bills."

She wrote a check for her insurance. That was the place to start. She always wrote that check before she peeped at her balance. It had to come, no matter what.

"Now the tombstone. I'd like to write to Mr. Dubose."

She bit her lip a moment. She touched the lawyer's letter from Corpus Christi, then pulled back, fearful almost.

"Amara can wear the ring," she said.

She looked at her left hand, rough, calloused, tanned. She saw soft white fingers; she thought of her wide gold wedding ring.

"Mr. Dubose was my friend," she said.

She reached over for the next bill but didn't take it. The stack was very high. She owed a lot besides the cotton complication at the bank—coffin, funeral, undertaking, general groceries of the month, taxes. Tuition for Amara was coming due. Even Bill's account for Don was getting short. Business was good but, as Lon said, she ran a little grocery. She couldn't hope for much—and if war came!

The parrot crawled down the perch and squawked. Willy got up and handed him a cracker from the box. Mutt yawned, stretched, and came out from underneath the counter.

"It's not time to go home yet. I've got some things to do," she said.

She sat down and began to figure. Somehow she must pay. Pat's business was his dream in focus—satin wrappers, education for the children, plumes and furbelows. It was a thing she had to do as surely as buy the coffin in the graveyard. You don't let strangers touch your dead—like that night she sat alone with him and figured out their lives together. The children's needs were real. She'd meet them. Youth comes first. Youth has to live. Somehow she'd wriggle through it all and get the money. She'd always got money and she always could!

Yes, money! It had been money here and money there. Money always in a scramble. And money'd come and money'd gone but it had served its purpose as it went. She never could quite get ahead.

Ahead of money?

"It's like herding up the twos and fives," she said, "afraid they'll disappear. I've felt the pinch and needed more and cussed a lot, I guess, but I always made it through."

She looked up at the clock. Her eyes widened. She shut them tight; then looked again. She stood up to be sure she wasn't in a dream. For in the clock's face she saw a vision. It was Bill.

He swung from his saddle out in front. Willy was afraid to turn her head lest he disappear. A horse nickered.

"It's Chiquita!" Then she remembered the little mare was dead. "Am I crazy? Maybe sick?"

Mutt barked wildly and wagged his tail.

Willy turned and looked. She made herself do it, for she was scared. Yes, it was Bill. He was tying a palomino—no, he was unloosing a morral.

She got to the door and stood there, looking at the man before her. Bill was Bill from foot to head—muscled, weathered, aged perhaps, but clean and shining. He wore chaps embossed in silver, new boots, and a Stetson, white and spotless. His shirt was silk. A red bandanna fluttered in the wind.

The palomino glistened in the sun, a dead second for Chiquita and for Pearl. The saddle was from Mexico, flat-horned and sprawling, studded with silver and bright stones.

Mutt kept on barking.

Bill turned quickly. He saw Willy in the doorway. His eyes melted; so did hers. Neither spoke; they just shook hands.

At last a buggy rattling down the street brought them back to earth.

"My God, it's Miz Weisschmidt," Bill said. "I wanted to see you by myself." His voice was shaking, broken.

"Go on into the store," Willy said. "I'll speak to her

out here. She's got her new baby with her. Oughtn't to be getting in and out."

As Mrs. Weisschmidt stopped the buggy, Bill walked into the store. Willy heard the parrot squawking, Mutt barking, and Bill talking.

She kissed her German friend and Guillermita. Little Hans she looked at, as he rested in his mother's arms.

"Such a lovely baby," she said. "And so big!"

"Ya, he tore me awful ven he vas coming."

Willy shook her head. "Childbirth isn't easy. And to have a twelve-pound boy is a feat. Fanny didn't tell me it was hard. Negro women take it all for granted."

She hoped her face looked sympathetic. Her heart certainly was sincere. She had thought a great deal about this woman and the birth, but at the moment she didn't want to listen to her talking.

She heard Bill's voice inside the store. She hadn't decided yet that he was real. It had been so long since she had seen him! She had missed him! Maybe she was dreaming. She wanted to make sure.

"Ve chust drove up to see you," Mrs. Weisschmidt was saying. "Ve von't get out today. Anuder veek it vill be better. For our first outing ve come to you."

The next thing Willy was sure of was the sound of the buggy wheeling down the street. She rushed inside the store.

Bill was sitting in the chair beside her desk. The parrot was on his shoulder, nibbling at his ear. Mutt was jumping up for bites of peloncilla. Bill fed him from his hand.

"Had a time thinkin' up things to bring you all." He looked up smiling.

Willy slipped into her chair. She sat there gazing. She hoped never to rise again. The scene before her was too precious.

"I put your presents by the cash drawer. Couldn't think of nothin' different. That's for you and 'Mara both—and Don."

He hesitated.

"Swell new register you've got."

"Yes, Mr. Dubose sent it."

Bill's eyes glistened. "Saw Lon Stone. Rode by the bank. He looked awful down and out."

"Then Lon told you?"

The smile faded. Bill's face shadowed. The deep-set wrinkles told their story.

"No, Chico brought word to Seralgo right after S'rita went. I was hitched in so close I couldn't come. As soon as I got loose I started. Didn't know about the Judge. Jim Nelson told me in Laredo."

His voice thickened. He dropped his head. Mutt jumped up on his lap.

Willy reached and took the parrot off Bill's shoulder and set him on the perch.

Bill said, "Judge was my friend."

"Yes, and you were his. He talked of you. It was one of the last things he said. He even mentioned Pepe."

Bill looked up. In that instant he seemed to Willy no older than Don.

"Now did he? I won't forget it!—Never! I oughta been here."

"He knew that you were coming. He said so. He never lost his faith."

"Judge was my friend. If I only coulda been as good a friend to him."

"You were, Bill. You did all the things for him on two legs that he couldn't do on one. You made it pos-possible for us to live in the Valley. You fought and whipped and shot and—"

He interrupted. "Yeah, but you don't know, Miz Westall."

Willy saw she had to change the subject.

She started off on Fanny, then all the soldiers in the Valley. She told about Dutch and Duke, Miss Lizzie, Jesse Parnell, and Ted Tolliver's hanging across the river.

Bill looked up quickly. "Some things just have to be," he said.

A car honked on the street. They both looked out. It was Lon Stone passing by.

"Tell me about the war," Willy said.

"The war's over." Bill smiled faintly.

"Over? Why, it's just about to start."

"Yeah, I know; but I mean our war down here on the Rio Grande with Pancho Villa pitchin' ball."

Willy leaned on her elbows.

"Lon says it's serious, Bill. Is it so?"

"Might be in Europe. I don't know. But our war's over except for a little straightenin' out."

"Is Pancho Villa dead?"

"Not unless he died since I left Mexico. I saw him in Seralgo four days ago."

"Does he recognize Carranza? Is he through with his revolution?"

"Well, not exactly; but it won't be long. Him and Obregon can get along."

"But Carranza is the President. He hates Carranza, surely."

"Well, yeah; but things're goin' to change and the border raidin' is over for good."

Willy leaned over closer. "Bill, how did you do it? It stopped all of a sudden. We expect a raid somewhere every day, but none comes any more. Tell me all about it. I've been so worried. You walked out that night. I never heard a word, not even from Thirty-six —except today. She'd heard that Pat was dead."

"Yeah, I know." Bill looked past Willy to a spot somewhere across the store.

"I knew you'd done it. I knew you would. But how did you do it? You saved the Valley. We were headed straight for ruin."

" 'Twas easy once I seen Pancho, as I knowed it would be. Caught him down at El Ranchito where he spent the night. He was off his schedule. His horse got a limp. He couldn't get back to headquarters. I was followin' close behind. Fixed the horse so he would have to limp. Once we got together without the Germans hangin' 'round he was glad to see me. Had a little somethin' he wanted me to do right then and I done it for him. We had a good long talk just before daylight.

"I started on Weisschmidt and his crowd. I showed him what a fool they'd made of him. For example, kept me away from him. That made him mad as hell.

Then I went on to the border raidin'. I asked him why he done it.

" 'I fight for freedom with Madero and you recognize Carranza,' he said back to me.

" 'Yeah,' I said, 'but you can't win freedom for your people by fightin' gringos. Use your ammunition on Carranza. Join up with some other fellows and fight in a little sort of way. Start out in one state, like Morelos, then grow big from state to state. This time when you take the capital, keep it. Then when you win your freedom, the gringos will help you keep it. They'll protect you from foreign people like Juarez done with France. They'd even send an army down to get rid of coyotes like Weisschmidt and his bunch.'

"Then I went on and told him some things to do with some other fellows down there against Carranza and his crowd."

"But Carranza's the President. That's another revolution," Willy said.

"Sure, had to get him off of border fightin'. Anyway, he's got to win the freedom for his people."

"But what about the German influence and this European war? Won't they use him as a dupe against us if we fight? Lon says they'll invade us from the south."

"Of course I can't say for certain, but I think they've shot their wad. Pancho gave me a lot of stuff to use on Weisschmidt and I sent it in."

"You did that, really?"

" 'Twas dead easy once I got hold of Pancho."

He hesitated a long time before he added, "War's a god-damned shame, Miz Westall."

Willy saw Bill thinking. Guillermita was his trouble. He couldn't forget the little German girl.

She asked quickly, "And Pepe. Did you ask Pancho Villa?"

"Yeah, I asked Pancho and he told me."

He was silent for a moment. So was Willy.

"Pepe went to Pancho as he always done about the guns for me and Judge. He wanted to borry five hundred pesos to buy somethin' he said for a little girl;

somethin' he seen pretty in a store, that went with yellow hair." Bill's voice grew heavy.

"Pancho was mad as hell that day. He'd got some news about peace plans with Carranza; a newspaper fellow told him. So he give Pepe the money to do a little job for him and Pepe done it. It happened to be Ojo de Agua."

Willy caught her breath. "Then Pepe gave his life to decorate S'rita's hair?"

"Not double-crossin', that's the point," Bill added. "Pepe tried to warn me."

"Yeah, of course he would. It's all my fault to begin with. He took the money, but he never would have done the job for Pancho if I'd been sober. He'd 'a asked me. I'd 'a made him took it back. I've charged the whole thing up to me—another debt I owe to liquor. Pancho would 'ave understood."

Willy strove for neutral ground. "But news came through that he was killed. I thought maybe you were with him."

Bill smiled slightly.

"Now that's where you was right. Me an' Pancho have been in on a minin' deal together, gittin' gold out of a mountain. He needs lots of gold for all his fightin'."

"Gold?"

"Yeah, plenty of it. All you have to do is get it. That's what I've been doin' for him."

"And I've been thinking of you both in prison or lying dead."

"Well, you ain't altogether wrong. I got in jail once on the deal."

"Got in jail?"

"Yeah, but I got out."

"Yes, I know; but how?"

"It ain't gettin' out that I remember. It's the gettin' in. Them jail doors squeak shut yet when I'm a-sleepin'."

He gazed down at the floor.

"Bill, locked up you would be like an eagle—like S'rita in that boarding school. What did you think of?"

"Nothin' much, I reckon."

He reddened. Willy saw the flush beneath his weathered tan.

"One thing worried me a lot. I had to get out; so I did."

He drawled, hesitated, then leaned over, looked at her squarely.

"Miz Westall, I've got your weddin' ring. I found it on Pepe when he was dead. It was strung right on the string around his neck with his church saint. An' I took it off to give back to you. I meant to. I really meant to, but somehow I never could!"

Then he put his hand into his pocket and pulled out the wide gold band and held it to her on his palm.

Willy stared. The flash of gold brought back a trail of memories: that night in Sugarland—the Baptist church in Franklin—Oklahoma City—the ranch—the long hot miles of coming to the Valley—Mission—Pepe—Bill!

"My wedding ring!" she said.

She looked and saw the ring lying in Bill's hand. She looked up at his face before she tried to speak. Then she didn't speak at all. She couldn't.

She reached out and took the hand that held the ring and looked at it again, not at the gold, but at the hand that had done so much for her. That hand had made a country by its many cruel tasks. It had shot and killed and whipped and fought for everybody else. It asked nothing for itself.

A fine, strong hand; a fine face above it. She glanced up and saw the face as it had looked down at her from a horse that day on the ranch. Bill came to help her with the longhorns. He helped her settle in the Valley. He helped her through the bandits. He helped her with her husband, her children, and her horse. And dearer he had grown with the years for every deep-set wrinkle marked out in callouses and blood. And she knew that she had no notion of all he had done. Bill himself was as shy as a javelina of civilization, yet he furthered it by his every action.

"Here's your ring, Miz Westall," she heard him saying. "I meant to give it back but I couldn't. It was a part of you I had."

She looked up at him.

They stood there, staring.

At last she closed his fingers on the ring. "You keep it, Bill," she said.

Bill slipped the ring back in his pocket. His left hand reached out and got his hat.

"I'm goin' now," he said.

Willy gasped. "Going? I thought you'd come to stay!"

"No, just to see you, Miz Westall. I've got a lot to do. No time to lose, for things're poppin' pretty hot."

"You're going back to Mexico?"

"Got to," he said.

"But Bill, this is your country. We need you. Can't the Mexicans manage by themselves?"

Bill smiled sadly. "Yeah, but I need them!" he said.

"In God's name, what for?"

Bill didn't look at Willy; he gazed down at his feet. "I know my kind and breed," he said. "I served my purpose here in the Valley. It's time to move on now. Too many people! Too much progress! Pancho Villa is my kind. We're sendero cutters; concrete-layin's not our line."

"That's just the trouble. You do the building. Others rush in and get the cash. Look at your business here in Mission. Lon told me."

Bill looked up quickly.

"Had to be, Miz Westall. There was reasons."

"Of course, Bill," Willy said. "It's just that I'm concerned about you. Why go back and join a revolution for the Mexican people? Let Pancho Villa do it now that he's started. He can settle up with Carranza for whatever it is he wants. You've saved the Valley for us. Come back and take up your scraping business! Put in a citrus orchard. Reap the benefits of all your labors. Why take all the chances?"

Bill looked at Willy very sharply. "That's what I'm wonderin' about you, Miz Westall! With this war comin' up you ought to leave the Valley. You've done enough already. With Pat and S'rita gone you and 'Mara could take it easy. Move up to Belton, or to Dallas. That's what Judge used to plan. He'd like it.

There's no need now for all the struggle. You've done your part. Move on!"

Willy's eyes turned from brown into black.

"Bill," she said, "I came to the Valley to make a home for me and others. I've got to make it. You can't quit in the middle of a job!"

"Unless they shoot you!"

"That's just it. Why go back and take a chance?"

"I've got to, but you haven't. I'd like to see you move on to higher ground!"

"Then you won't be back?" she asked flatly.

He didn't answer for a moment.

"I know where I oughta be," he said.

He walked toward the door. Willy followed.

"Are you certain?" she asked.

"Very certain," he replied.

Then they were out in front. What could she say to make him listen?

"Where did you get your horse?" she asked. "She's a dead second for Chiquita."

"Yeah! Got this little filly in Monterrey. Named her Guillermita after you." He stared down at his boots.

"Guillermita?"

One hand picked up the bridle reins; the other patted the horse's head, then stroked her mane.

"You're really leaving?" Willy said.

"I've got to. I knowed it when I come." He looked at her very squarely. His jaw set hard. His face grew rigid.

"But Don and 'Mara! They'll want to see you. So much has happened! They'll never understand."

"Yeah, I know. But I can't risk it. If I saw 'em I'd never have the nerve to leave."

He clutched her hand. He peered up La Lomita and then down. There was not a soul in sight.

"But why?" she said.

He didn't answer.

Willy caught his eyes again. It was the blue that lured her, bright and shining blue, deep and honest, cold and cutting, hard and solid—like God's heaven when He gives it for our varied moods.

If she could keep his eyes to look at! If she could

keep his eyes to hold to! If she could keep his eyes
to lean on!

They grew larger, deeper, sadder as she looked.

The strong hand gripped hers a second. A pain
struck her in the heart.

When she saw clearly, Bill was sitting on his horse.
He said something, raised his hand.

"Adiós!" she heard.

Guillermita's hoofbeats clattered down the street.

Bill was riding south.

42

When Willy looked up from the curb she saw nobody.
She was sitting with her back against the lamppost.
Mutt licked her hand. She heard the parrot squawking
in the store. Her head was very clear. "Another page,"
she said. "Maybe it's the last one in the book."

Mr. McIntire turned round the corner.

"Whatta you doin' settin' on the curb?" he asked.

"Just cooling off," she answered. "It's awfully hot
inside."

"Why don'tcha knock off for supper? It's straight up
six."

She got up and walked back into the store.

The parrot squawked and paced across his perch.
Willy reached and got him and set him on her shoulder. She found it hard to think. When Emelio came,
she'd hurry on to supper. Once the crowd started back
to town there would be an awful rush. With a dance
and the fiesta in Mexiquita they'd work late. She decided to count the cash and have that done. She had
to hurry. Emelio would be there any minute.

And Don and 'Mara would be riding home to eat.
She couldn't trust the children to measure out the corn.
Prince was such a glutton. He always pawed for more.
'Mara couldn't withstand him; she always added some.

Don always quarreled; sometimes Amara cried. So Willy tried to meet them at the lot.

"Supper for the horses—then human folks can eat if they have time." That was Willy's slogan every day at six.

She looked at the clock. The long hand pointed twelve; the short one hung straight down.

"I've got to hurry!" Willy said to Mutt.

She was glad to hurry. It helped to still her heart. She went to the cash register and rang the "No Sale" button to open up the drawer.

"I won't take time to count the change. I'll just push it back."

Her eyes caught sight of a bundle on the counter. Dirty, ragged, yellow paper seemed to cover up a sack. She pushed shut the drawer.

"It's our present! I forgot!" she said. "I thought it must be a pistol, but it's not!"

She reached out to get it, but it refused to budge.

"What in the world!"

She took her other hand, and together her two hands pulled the bundle forward to her reach. She undid the string and started to unwrap. One strong jerk brought a clatter to the floor.

Mutt began to bark.

"In God's name," Willy breathed. She brushed away a curl that dropped down in her eyes; then she saw her feet! Her heavy shoes were covered up in gold—big round flat money pieces, little pieces, each one shining out bright and hot. They kept pouring from the sack.

"In God's name!" she breathed. "I'm bogged right up in gold!"

She stooped down low to look. The parrot squawked in terror and flew down to the floor. The gold kept on pouring and hit him on the head. He kept on squawking, pigeon-toeing back and forth.

Willy spread her apron and began to scoop. At last the money pieces on the counter balanced on the edge. She picked up the last golden circle and staggered to her feet. She opened up her apron on the counter and emptied out the sack.

"This means Bill's not ever coming back," she said.

The parrot gained her shoulder with one flutter of his wings.

Willy turned her head to him to talk. "Bill brought his gift in gold—as always," she said, to clear her thought.

She picked up a handful, let it slip between her fingers, heard it jingle on the stack. The gold glistened, shone bright yellow, shimmered softly. Willy thought she saw a strand of S'rita's hair.

She heard Bill saying, "Leave the Valley; you've done your share already."

"White tablecloths—plenty of servants—no damn cactus!" she was hearing. Then she felt her hands were wet. "It's Bill's way of doing," she said sadly. "He has his reasons. I'll never understand."

She saw the register before her. She punched the "No sale" button. The drawer flew open. She piled in gold. She did it slowly, for she was thinking. The money pieces turned to red, then purple. One handful was bright green, like lettuce, the next one grayish green, like cabbage. One almost smelled like onions. Then one turned back to orange gold.

"It's just my blood," she said. "I don't know how to take it when it comes—but I didn't come to the Valley for money. It was for water mostly, and for green things growing—and people close enough to touch."

Suddenly she was thirsty. She felt Bill's hand in hers. It was hard and rough. She looked down at the money she was scooping into the drawer. She saw only hands before her, soft dimpled hands clutching at the gold. They writhed and twisted. Somebody screamed. She looked around. All she saw was the parrot and the dog.

She had to hurry. She kept on putting money into the drawer. All at once two other hands reached out to help her; brown weathered hands they were. The gold pieces turned to corns and blisters right there before her eyes. She squinted, looked very closely. She saw a wide gold wedding ring. It rested on a calloused palm. She reached to touch it; then it was gone.

She leaned against the counter. She pressed her face into her hands. She closed her eyes and thought.

When she looked up, Emelio was running in the door.

"Madama," he gasped, "they tell us at the rodeo war ees come. Señor Jones spoke very loud. He stood up on a box just wheen Cheeco Rodriquez was to bulldog!" He slumped down on a crate.

Willy ran to the telephone and called Miss Lizzie.

"Yes, news just came in! Wilson delivered his war message to Congress a little while ago. Now we're in a regular fight," she said.

Willy hung up and rushed out on the street. The crowd was coming from the rodeo. An army truck whizzed by.

"On our way to France, Mrs. Westall!" Shorty Morehead hollered out.

"Stop and get Sergeant Turney's groceries for your mess," Willy shouted back.

The Stewarts' car chugged down La Lomita. The old Colonel looked straight ahead. Mrs. Stewart cried. Willy looked away to avoid a greeting. This meant Dutch and Duke would go across the ocean to kill Germans. She turned sick.

Mrs. Randolph bumped her. She was running.

"Excuse me," she exclaimed in passing.

"What's wrong?" Willy asked.

"I'm going home to pack. Can't stay in this Valley. Germans will cross the river any minute. They're all ganged up down there just ready for the hat to drop."

"Don't be foolish!" Willy called.

"I'm not. You'll be foolish if you stay," she called back.

The Gonzales Mexicans trotted by. They took off their hats and bowed.

Mrs. Allen's Ford came around the corner. All six children were in the car. The baby waved her chubby hand. All the children shouted, "Howdy!" Mrs. Allen smiled.

Mr. Conlay walked across the street. He and Willy stood there watching. The crowd hurried by. They seemed so frightened. Soldiers jammed the picture show. Civilians made for the saloon.

"You'd think the battle was at Ojo de Agua. What a bustle! So many people!" Mr. Conlay said.

"Yes, we've grown!" Willy answered.

"Well, you have, anyway, Mrs. Westall. I've watched you. You're like the Rio Grande. You just keep on about your business, let things happen as they will. I tell all the folks about you back in Iowa. I had to leave this country, but you stayed."

"Well, I came to stay, Mr. Conlay. I sold the horses. You remember?"

"How well I remember. You are Mission, really, Mrs. Westall—and you gave your life to the country! I've watched it all!"

"I'd like to thank you for the chance," she said. "You came first and paved the way."

"Left it pretty rough, but you got over and this war's another bump to cross."

"We'll make it," Willy said.

"Yes, you will," he answered. "I wish I were here to help you. I feel wicked now to leave you, but I have another proposition in the North."

"There's nothing wicked about your leaving. You made your contribution. You gave the Valley irrigation!"

"Well, now you have palm-lined highways, orange and grapefuit trees, poinsettias in giant proportions, figs and limes and aquacates, ponderosas and papaya thickets—all set into the mesquite!"

"Yes, once your desert, now a garden," Willy said.

"With a lot of blood spilled in!"

"That doesn't matter, Mr. Conlay. It's what we've got to do to finish up your job—if we can do it with this war!"

"There'll be a lot of setbacks, but you'll do it. Wars and bandits and money troubles are just inconsequentials. Such things're but a moment's notice in the whole big plan of life. It's the learning how to take them that is hard. The day will come, remember, when the Rio Grande will water our delta Valley of its own accord. There'll be gravity irrigation to make it blossom and bring forth. 'Mara and Don will live to see it, but you'll have to pave the way between."

"Well, I've had the best of living because I've seen it grow."

"Yes, but that's not easy."

"Oh, really, yes it is! The hard part's coming yet when we have to stand back and look at what's been done. I'm glad S'rita missed that, and so did Pat. They liked action fast and quick like bandits. They hated dullness. They're like Bill."

Captain Taylor and his troop came trotting by to camp. Cars, buckboards, and horsemen made way for them to pass. The thudding hoofs beat down all other sounds. White dust boiled up and filled the air.

Willy and Mr. Conlay stood there and watched the sun. It burst in crimson radiance, a ball of living fire; then it edged over the horizon until just an arc was left.

"Slicing itself up! Life does our hearts like that," Mr. Conlay said to Willy when the soldiers had passed.

43

When the newspaper boys shouted "Extra!" in San Antonio, Ray Renfro was not in town. He was on his way to Fort Smith to join the army.

Houston Street was thronged with people. They grabbed papers, stopped and read them. UNITED STATES DECLARES WAR!

Strangers nodded to each other. Mexicans shrugged their shoulders. A group of soldiers at the Gunter started singing "Tipperary." A drunken man hollered, "Hang the Kaiser!" A newsboy shouted, "Read all about the Huns!"

Dr. Farr turned the corner. He bought a paper. He read the headlines. "I'll be damned!" he said, and kept on pushing through the crowd until he reached his office. His face was burning when he took off his hat. Late for his appointment, he jerked on his jacket and rushed in to meet his patient. She was a woman, very pale and wan. She looked soft and rich and white. She wore three diamonds on one hand.

The doctor hurried with the examination. He felt he had to rush; the world had just caught fire. People surged along the street. Shouting came up through the window. He heard guns firing. Maybe they were at Fort Sam Houston; yet they might have come from France.

He said to the woman, "There's nothing really wrong."

"But I'm sick," she said.

Then he shot questions fast and thick. She had a baby, dead. She grieved. She had nothing else to do.

"Then get a purpose and come back later. There's no way that I can help you!"

The woman frowned. "That's not enough, Dr. Farr!" she said. "I'll find another doctor who can diagnose my case." She picked up her purse and left.

Dr. Farr looked out the window. Then he called his secretary and told her he was leaving town.

That night he caught the Valley train.

George Farr hated mystery in human bodies or in human action. He always sought the cause, then worked toward relief. Now he had to find the reason in himself.

Since S'rita Westall died he'd found little peace or rest. Her disease was one he didn't understand. It was a cold but not pneumonia; yet she died—just blinked out in a minute and was gone. He had to find the cause for that. It should not have happened. He knew the human cost of children. He was a doctor. S'rita was a child he could not forget. He knew her first back in Austin when she bulged out her mother's little body. That was when he first began to practice. Much had happened in between, but he never lost the thread that held him to her. Their lives had twisted up together in his heart.

He depended on the preacher. He never knew he

did, but he did. When Renfro came back from the Valley, he was broken, shattered to pieces. He wouldn't even talk. He left San Antonio and gave no address. Then George Farr knew he himself had to act. He was glad the war gave him a reason.

Through the night the train was very bumpy; so were George Farr's thinking and his heart. Next morning he woke up alarmed. Before the train arrived in Mission, he wished he hadn't come.

When he got off he looked around and wondered where he was. All he saw was soldiers, army trucks, and cars. He couldn't see the buildings for the people everywhere. As he walked down La Lomita he looked down at his feet.

"I'll spot that booted gent," he said.

But he couldn't. There were boots a-plenty, but they were russet tan shining through the dust. No run-over, high-heeled cowboy feet walked along the street. He heard a clatter and looked up. Three Stetsoned men were trotting by.

He saw a Mexican lolling by a post. He asked him who they were.

"The sheriff and two Rangers." The boy answered without accent.

The doctor walked on. He saw a crowd ahead. They ganged around a door. He circled out into the street. He heard loud talking.

"I'll shoot your guts out!" a gruff voice shouted.

"Try it!" another answered. "I say again he's just a double-crossing bastard. He's left the country. Now we need him. They'll invade us! Wait and see. Bill'll help 'em do it, like Ted Tolliver, and end up on a limb."

A boy's voice screamed, "You're lying! Bill's a different kind of fellow!"

Somebody answered, but the doctor lost the meaning. He walked on into the Westall store. It was jammed with people: Mexicans, ranchers, and soldiers. He saw one Negro woman. She seemed to be giving orders to two boys.

Willy stood behind the counter. She wore her Stetson, and a pencil was in her hair. Black curls straggled all around her face. Her eyes were flashing. They seemed deeper brown than ever. The doctor watched her. She didn't see him in the crowd. She was very busy taking money, reaching here and there, handing things across the counter. She frowned once when she rang up some money, then she smiled and rippled off into a laugh. She looked older surely, but not aging. The face was different from the one he saw in Austin. It was weathered, deepened, strengthened. She looked across the counter unafraid.

The doctor walked out onto the street. He'd come back later. He'd go get himself a room, then sprawl out somewhere in the sun. He'd rest and think. He'd get things straight.

He looked up and saw a palomino and a pinto passing. Amara and a boy were riding by. The boy must be Don—tall and blond and muscled. A scowl was on his face. Amara's black braids hung down her back. Her square chin stuck out slightly. She was talking very fast. They rode very close to where the doctor stood. He caught a scrap of conversation. Their voices rang out in the air.

"But you needn't fight for Bill. Mama wouldn't like it right out in front of the saloon," she said.

"I don't give a damn," he shouted. "We're goin' back to school tomorrow and they'll keep on talkin' behind Bill's back."

The doctor walked on to a place a soldier told him was the Mission hotel, and got a room. He lay down on his bed. He felt very tired and useless. He went to sleep. He didn't mean to, but he did.

When he woke up, it was night. He heard music. He got up and looked out the window. The moon was very bright. A military band was playing in the park. A row of tall palms etched the skyline. He smelled flowers. Straight down beneath the window he saw white blossoms shining—a ponderosa lemon tree. He counted big yellow lemons, smaller green ones, and many flowers. He kept staring.

"That's completeness in all cycles," he kept saying.

He looked at his watch, but it had stopped.

He picked up his hat, then put it down. He took off

his coat and undid his collar at the neck. It was something about the lemon tree that made him do it.

When he walked outside, he breathed so deeply his toes began to tingle. The air was light and cool, caressing to the skin.

A Mexican boy walked by with tamales.

The doctor bought some and ate them standing there. He felt like another person. He ambled on toward the Westall store. The streets were still full of people going here and coming there. He wanted to feel such a nervous undercurrent as he felt in San Antonio, but he couldn't. These people seemed to know what they were about.

Now the store was not crowded, but it was full of people. The doctor looked in, then sat down on the curb. Willy was talking to a big German woman. She held a baby in her arms. Willy's eyes were soft and warm. He turned his head and watched the soldiers trotting by.

He sat there until very late. All the crowd was off the street. He watched the store until even the Mexican clerks had gone.

Willy was counting up the cash.

He walked in and spoke. She looked up and smiled, then rushed around the counter and grabbed his hand.

"When did you get here, Dr. Farr?" she said.

He felt the roughness of her palm in his. He gripped it and kept on holding.

"I had to come!" he said.

"And I'm so glad," she answered.

He swallowed hard. "Got in on the train at two. I've been waiting. Had to see you by yourself!"

She drew away her hand. He kept on talking.

"It's this war, Mrs. Westall. Anything can happen. There's a lot of talk about the Valley. There's already inroad. Carranza says he's neutral, but Pancho Villa's loose. I don't think it's safe. They could make a deal. They might invade us, land in Vera Cruz and Tampico, and march north across the Rio Grande."

"But we'd never let them! We've got too many soldiers!"

"Yes, but there would be a fight. Right here in the Valley would be a fighting spot. From Brownsville to El Paso they could cross the river anywhere!"

"Do you want to scare me?"

"No, I just came down to talk. Ray left San Antonio in a hurry. All he told me was about your husband's death."

Willy looked down at the floor a minute. "Pat loved Brother Renfro very much," she said.

The doctor stepped up closer. "Now you're alone," he said.

"No, I have my daughter and, in a way, a son."

"But you keep them off at school!"

"Yes, they go back tomorrow. They've stayed away too long, but it's been good to have them here at home."

"That is just the point, Mrs. Westall. Why do you do it? It's been so long and hard. Come on up to San Antonio. You deserve a rest."

Willy laughed. "A vacation, Dr. Farr, would kill me. I thrive on work, it seems."

The doctor reached and took her hand. His eyes were piercing. His voice was low and poised. "I mean forever," he replied. "This is war. There's no time for ceremony. But this isn't sudden. It's been growing since you came into my office there in Austin. It's just that the time has come to act. You've got to leave this country. I need a home that I can live in. I need a woman I can love."

Willy drew away her hand. She looked very straight at Dr. Farr and said, "I couldn't, but I thank you."

"Give me a reason," he exclaimed.

"Well, I just can't do it; besides, I have my business and the Valley."

The doctor looked around the store.

"But it's mine!" She spoke the words in pride. "Not much surely, but it's what I had to give—not sacks and crates and cans and counters; it's much more than that besides."

The doctor stopped her. "Yes, I know," he said. "There's no hurry; it's just the danger and the worry.

You see, I know all about it. Ray Renfro told me. I want to lift the burden."

"But there is no burden."

"My God!" he gasped.

"And I couldn't leave my country in a pinch. If soldiers march across the river, they won't stomp down all the greenness. They'll love the orange trees and palms. We've too much room for crowding even for an army. And somebody has to stay right here and watch."

The doctor looked at her sadly. "That's too big a job for one woman! But keep on trying. It's your Valley and your life," he said kindly. "You'll need money. Let me help you! War means hardships and expense."

Willy's eyes began to swim. "No," she said, "I have money—now; plenty of money."

"But I mean at once, before you get the life insurance."

"This came at once. I have it now. I guess it was insurance of a kind; but it didn't come with death; it came with life!" Her voice began to choke. She stopped speaking.

The doctor took her hand in his and held it very tight. "Life's like the ponderosa lemon tree," he said. Then he left the store.

Willy stood there and watched him go down the street. She wiped her eyes and blew her nose and finished counting up the cash.

When she was through, she found Amara asleep and woke her up. Mutt stretched and yawned. She took the parrot off the perch.

"Mama, I dreamed a lot," Amara said, as Willy locked the door. "I saw you at a party in a yellow-satin dress. It was like Miss Crawford wears at school when we have night receptions and all of us dress up!"

"I like yellow," Willy said. The parrot squawked and nestled close in to her neck. "Lupe's head is yellow and so was S'rita's hair!" She said no more. 'Mara took her hand and they walked along together.

'Mara felt warm and full. Mama's hand was all she ever needed. Nothing mattered except to hold that hand and keep on walking. She wished they could walk on forever like tonight. The moon was shining. They were alone with all the world asleep. Tomorrow she would go back to school. She hated that but she had to do it. That was for Mama too. She'd study and make Mama very proud. She must do something. Mama worked so hard!

Mr. McIntire came around the corner. "Pretty late," he said.

"Yes, a big day," Willy said. "Lots of soldier trade."

Willy and 'Mara walked by the corral to look in on Pearl and Prince; then they went to bed.

Willy got up very early the next morning. She had to. The National Guard were moving out and regular soldiers were coming in. They would be in for groceries. She wanted to clean up the store and be ready for the trade.

Just as she finished dressing, Don ran through the gate. He was shouting, " 'Mara, let's go ride before the sun gets up so hot!"

'Mara ran out to meet him. They rushed to the corral and started saddling.

Willy walked on toward the store.

When she turned the corner, she saw a cloud of dust on La Lomita just at the railroad track. It came forward.

She said, "That patrol is pretty early coming in."

She hurried on. The dust hit her nose. She began to cough. She choked a little and sneezed twice.

When she looked up, she saw a flash of red bandanna, then a palomino glint. She blinked her eyes and stared into the whirl of white. A Stetson hat was out in front. Some big sombreros were coming back behind. The horses' hoofs clattered louder as they came. She coughed again and sneezed. When she caught her breath, Bill was on the ground beside her; his hat was in his hand. She grabbed the hitching post and held onto it. Bill stuck out his hand and shook.

"A little early," he was saying, "but we're in an awful hurry. Camped at Madero but didn't take the river road. Wanted to come by and see how you was gettin' on. You oughta know these hombres, Miz West-all."

Willy saw three Mexicans standing there before her. They held their big hats in their hands. All were smiling. For an instant she thought one was Pepe, then she looked at Bill.

"This here is Benito Torres' cousin. Didn't he ever come by the ranch?"

The Mexican bowed and smiled.

"These two hombres are from the Rancho Seco, two of Gonzales' best vaqueros."

They looked a little sheepish when Willy smiled at them.

"Run into 'em all in Seralgo not long back. They've been workin' in my mine."

"Bill," Willy interrupted, "all that money that you gave us!"

He paid no attention to what she said. He kept on talking. "We got word about this German war and hit the trail. Guillermita, here, threw a shoe. We couldn't hurry!"

He stroked the palomino's mane.

"It's not been long! I'm so glad you're back!" she said. "Will there be trouble?"

"Plenty of trouble. That's why we're fightin'."

"But in Mexico, I mean."

"Yes, lots of trouble. Carranza and Pancho'll never make terms."

"What'll happen?"

"I don't know," he said.

"You don't know? Then you've come back to help us, Bill?"

She grabbed his hand and held it tight. They looked at each other very straight.

"Well, this is different, Miz Westall. I've got a man to get. That's what I told the hombres here. They smelled trouble and ducked across the river to get out. If they had to fight, they wanted to fight Mexkins, they told me. Well, that's all right up to a certain point. But Pancho'll get Carranza. Maybe him and Obregon'll make a deal. But I got Weisschmidt to even up and that whole crowd of his. They're the

ones that mixed poor old Pancho up and caused all
this border trouble. Now I've got a chance to do my
fightin' in a war."

"You mean to enlist?"

"Well, there's lots of ways that we can help. We're
ridin' up to Fort Brown now to see what we can do.
That's what I told the boys. They was borned on this
side of the river. You can't leave your country in a
pinch."

"No!" Willy said.

They stood there looking at each other; neither
spoke.

"You're stayin'?" he said.

"Of course I'm staying, Bill."

"Yeah," he said. "I remember! You come to this
Valley, Miz Westall. I knowed it somehow when you
come."

He turned to the Mexicans. "Vámanos, amigos!" he
said.

They mounted their horses.

Bill still held Willy's hand. He looked down at it.
She watched his face. He set his jaw. His forehead
wrinkled. He grasped his pocket, held it tight a second,
then said quickly, "Thanks, Miz Westall!"

"And you?" Willy said. "If I can help you?"

He made a swing into his saddle. "I might send
Guillermita back," he answered.

The horses whirled. Dust fogged up.

"The corral is always waiting," Willy called.

They galloped off. Willy shut her eyes. When she
looked, they had turned the corner at the bank. She
leaned against the post and looked up at the sun. It
was rising. A burst of yellow flooded all the sky, then
it deepened into gold.

"Like S'rita's hair," she said.

"Yes, Madama," came an answer. It was Emelio at
her side. He held some flowers in his hand: jasmines,
crepe myrtle, and ponderosa lemon blossoms.

He handed them to her and smiled. She held them,
reveling in their fragrance. Emelio thought he saw
some tears.

Fanny came around the corner.

"What's the hurry?" she exclaimed. "I told 'Mara for you all to come for breakfast. I've made biscuits and here I find you at the store."

"Its a big day," Willy said. "National Guard are moving out; regular soldiers're moving in. I came down to get an early start. Don and 'Mara went to ride."

"Well, I'll be damned," Fanny said. "And here my biscuits're gettin' cold."

There came a clatter down the street. They looked up and saw a whirl of dust against the brightness, a gleam of red bandanna, then a palomino flash. Pearl was leading; Prince galloped just behind. 'Mara's hair was flying in the wind. Don whipped off his hat and waved.

"There are the children!" Willy said.

"Then let's get started, Miz Westall, for we've got an awful lot to do and the day is just beginning now."

"Yes, Fanny; we've got an awful lot to do!" Willy said.

She stood up straight. She felt very tall. She smelled the flowers in her hand, looked up at the sun, and walked back in the store.

"The day is just beginning, as you said!"

NEW FROM BALLANTINE!

FALCONER, John Cheever · 27300 $2.25

The unforgettable story of a substantial, middle-class man and the passions that propel him into murder, prison, and an undreamed-of liberation. "CHEEVER'S TRIUMPH . . . A GREAT AMERICAN NOVEL."—*Newsweek*

GOODBYE, W. H. Manville / 27118 $2.25

What happens when a woman turns a sexual fantasy into a fatal reality? The erotic thriller of the year! "Powerful."—*Village Voice.* "Hypnotic."—*Cosmopolitan.*

THE CAMERA NEVER BLINKS, Dan Rather with Mickey Herskowitz 27423 $2.25

In this candid book, the co-editor of "60 Minutes" sketches vivid portraits of numerous personalities including JFK, LBJ and Nixon, and discusses his famous colleagues.

THE DRAGONS OF EDEN, Carl Sagan 26031 $2.25

An exciting and witty exploration of mankind's intelligence from pre-recorded time to the fantasy of a future race, by America's most appealing scientific spokesman.

VALENTINA, Fern Michaels 26011 $1.95

Sold into slavery in the Third Crusade, Valentina becomes a queen, only to find herself a slave to love.

THE BLACK DEATH, Gwyneth Cravens and John S. Marr 27155 $2.50

A totally plausible novel of the panic that strikes when the bubonic plague devastates New York.

THE FLOWER OF THE STORM, Beatrice Coogan 27368 $2.50

Love, pride and high drama set against the turbulent background of 19th century Ireland as a beautiful young woman fights for her inheritance and the man she loves.

THE JUDGMENT OF DEKE HUNTER, George V. Higgins 25862 $1.95

Tough, dirty, shrewd, telling! "The best novel Higgins has written. Deke Hunter should have as many friends as Eddie Coyle."—*Kirkus Reviews*